THE PHANTOM IN THE FOOTLIGHTS

Cedar Creek Mysteries, Volume 3

VIOLET HOWE

www.violethowe.com

Cover Design: Robin Ludwig

Published by Charbar Productions, LLC
(p-v1)

Books by Violet Howe

Tales Behind the Veils

Diary of a Single Wedding Planner

Diary of a Wedding Planner in Love

Diary of an Engaged Wedding Planner

Maggie

The Cedar Creek Collection

Cedar Creek Mysteries:

The Ghost in the Curve

The Glow in the Woods

The Phantom in the Footlights

Cedar Creek Families:

Building Fences

Crossing Paths

Cedar Creek Suspense:

Whiskey Flight

Bounty Flight

Fallen Bloodlines

Vampire Born

Angel Reborn (2024)

(Continued on next page)

Soul Sisters at Cedar Mountain Lodge

Christmas Sisters

Christmas Hope

Christmas Peace

Christmas Secret

Christmas Promise

Sail Away Series

Welcome Aboard

Moonlight on the Lido Deck

Visit www.violethowe.com to subscribe to Violet's monthly newsletter for news on upcoming releases, events, sales, and other tidbits.

For Jan and Dan

My adventure partners in food, margaritas, wine, theater, and movies.
Thank you for your unwavering support, friendship, and love.
Oh, and thanks for believing I could sing.
On stage. In French. As a burlesque star.

Chapter 1

The first time I encountered a ghost, I was more worried about losing my mind than being scared. But then again, Chelsea wasn't scary. She appeared as the teenager she was—cracking jokes, being a wise ass, and pleading for my help. Sure, it freaked me out to realize she was no longer among the living, but my curiosity outweighed my fears.

This ghost was different, right from the start.

For one thing, I'd been able to hear Chelsea's voice loud and clear from the moment we met, and although she was translucent, she was easy for me to see, as long as the night was dark and the moon was bright.

This ghost didn't seem to be able to talk, and he didn't become visible until quite a while after I first realized he was there. He did, however, possess a skill Chelsea hadn't been able to master—the ability to move objects from beyond the grave, and it was those clever attempts to grab attention that announced his presence.

That's not all that was different, though.

Chelsea had always come across as innocent, friendly, and for the most part, polite and non-threatening in her requests.

The same couldn't be said of this new phantom. He was angry, demanding, and relentless in his pursuit of being acknowledged.

When I finally saw him, if I had been alone in the dark like I was with Chelsea, I think his antics would have struck terror in my heart.

But I wasn't alone, and therein lies another difference. I wasn't the only one who knew he was there.

Chapter 2

I don't know what it was about the flyer on the bulletin board at the Handy Sack that caught my eye. Perhaps it was the fluorescent lime green paper, or it might have been the words '*ACTORS WANTED*' in bold caps that made me take a second look.

Someone had decided that Cedar Creek needed a community theater.

In addition to seeking actors for parts in a play, it invited sound and lighting technicians, set decorators, and anyone with experience in costuming or advertising to call the number listed.

It had been years since I'd done theater. A lifetime, it seemed.

Among my mother's closest circle of friends, and thereby my surrogate family, were Luca and Simon, the founding members of a successful acting company based in San Francisco. On their stage, the seed had been planted for my acting aspirations at quite a young age.

Long before my mother's boyfriend picked me to star in his movie about a teenage girl who slayed ghosts, I fell in love with the idea of pretending to be someone else amid the greasepaint, the footlights, and the thunder of applause during curtain calls.

Had Glenn's little movie not become a global sensation, I might have set my career sights on a different kind of opening night. I loved the instant gratification that only a live audience could give, but beyond that, I relished the camaraderie of the theater. I've made friends on movie sets throughout the years, but nothing compared to the tight-knit bonds of the theater community. I suppose with my nomadic upbringing, the time I spent in the theater was the closest I ever came to being part of a family.

Of course, once *Spectral Slayer* exploded and my film career took off, I'd left any thoughts of theater behind. There was no time for it in my nonstop, rigorous whirlwind of filming and promotion.

And yet, here I was. Between projects and able to do with my schedule what I chose, to some extent.

A twinkle of yearning tickled my insides, and I bit down on my lip as I stared at the flyer.

Theater. In Cedar Creek.

Talk about being off Broadway. It was about as far from Broadway as you could get.

But still. Theater was theater.

Perhaps this would be a way I could plug in with the people of Cedar Creek. I didn't really know anyone outside of Tristan's family, and Rachel, who'd become a good friend even though she'd started out as a client. My only other close friend in town was sixteen. And a ghost.

I needed to get out more. To expand my community. I needed to meet people in Cedar Creek and let them see I wasn't the villain I'd been made out to be since the paparazzi had descended on the town.

With the success of my latest film and the media's fascination with my new hometown, there'd been an invasion of photographers and reporters, and the local townsfolk didn't take kindly to being jostled off sidewalks or crowded out of the diner and the coffee shop to make way for a bunch of outsiders. Rather than blame the vultures who were out for a payday photo or a juicy piece of gossip, Cedar Creek residents had turned on me. Their good-natured smiles and friendly greetings had been replaced by hostile glares and under-their-breath mumblings about Hollywood types being full of themselves.

As a local deputy, Tristan heard more of the chatter than I did, and though my first instinct had been to hole up inside our house and never go back to town, he'd insisted that would only make things worse.

"They need to see that you're part of the community, babe," he'd said. "From their view, you brought in all this disruption and then left them to deal with it when you retreated."

"I was trying to help. I thought if I stayed out of town, the paparazzi would go away, and they have, for the most part. But then everyone was mad that they lost out on the extra business they'd been getting and blamed me for that."

"I know. But you've dealt with this sort of thing pretty much your whole life. You knew what to expect. They didn't. Cut them some slack, okay? I just think if you start coming back to town more and they get to know you better, they'll come around. It would probably be a good idea to shop local. I know you prefer the stores in Lumberton and Orlando, but if you shop in town whenever you can, I think that will go a long way to help them see you as a member of the community instead of an outsider."

I had reluctantly agreed, which is how I ended up at the Handy Sack despite their limited organic selection and their refusal to carry tofu.

As I stared at the flyer, I thought perhaps my fame and the media following me might be a good thing for a startup theater. Surely, they'd need some publicity.

Of course, I was going on the assumption that they'd want me. I hadn't been on a stage in ages, and my acting experience was largely limited to green screens and heavy post-production. Did I even have the chops to pull off a live performance without an off-camera crew member feeding me lines followed by a healthy dose of editing to clean me up and make me look good?

There was only one way to find out. I tore off one of the little slips at the bottom of the page with the phone number for interested parties to call, and then I made my way to my car, which thankfully had no one standing around it.

I dialed the number, and it went straight to voicemail.

"Hi, you've reached Dani. If you're calling about the Cedar Creek Community Theater, I definitely want to talk to you. Unfortunately, I have no signal whatsoever when I'm inside the building working, and that's pretty much where I am all the time these days. So, leave me a message and I'll call you back, or better yet, just stop by the theater building and say hi. I'd love to show you around!"

The message continued with the building's address and a brief apology to her friends and family for having to listen to the whole spiel every time they called.

The beep came, and I ended the call, not comfortable enough to leave my name and number with a total stranger. I briefly considered doing as her message had suggested and stopping by the theater but then decided it would have to wait for another day. I had groceries in the car, I had a script to read that afternoon and a promise to my agent that I'd finish it by the end of the day, and I had planned to make a new recipe for dinner that night.

Tristan and I both were still amazed at my newfound love for cooking. I'd never pursued it before I met him, always preferring to go out to eat or have something delivered in.

But with time on my hands, a limited number of restaurants within driving distance, and a kitchen fully-stocked with every pot, pan, utensil, and device imaginable thanks to Tristan's late grandmother, I'd begun to experiment and found a passion I'd never known I had.

Between his grandmother's cookbooks and the internet recipe blogs I discovered, there was no shortage of new dishes to try, and thankfully, Tristan and his brother were both willing guinea pigs. So far, I'd had more misses than hits, and more often than not, I screwed up something with the recipe along the way. Holden was brutally honest when it was bad, and neither of them ever missed an opportunity to tease me about my budding abilities, but I always knew I'd done well when they both had hearty seconds.

"Something smells delicious," Tristan said as he came through the laundry room and hung his hat on the rack by the door. "Which means one of two things has happened."

"What do you mean?" I closed the oven door and removed the mitt from my hand as he walked toward me with a grin.

He leaned down to plant a kiss on my lips, and then he slid his arms around my waist.

"One might be that my beautiful fiancée has hired someone to come and cook dinner for us tonight."

My mouth fell open in mock outrage. "Excuse me? I've been slaving over this stove for the past hour, and you think someone else did all this? There is *actual* sweat on my brow."

He chuckled as he pulled back to look down at me. "There is. I see at least three beads of sweat. I guess it must be the second option, then."

"Which is?" I draped my arms around his shoulders and smiled up at him.

"That I'm the luckiest man on earth. I got the funniest, smartest, bravest, sexiest girl to be mine, and it turns out she knows how to cook, too. Man, I hit the jackpot!"

"You most certainly did, and don't you forget it." I pushed onto my tiptoes to kiss him, pressing my body against his and mentally cursing the rigid bulletproof vest for the barrier between us.

"I'm still holding out hope that I'll come home and find you doing housework or weeding the flower beds," he teased, his gray eyes sparkling with humor.

"There's not a chance in hell of that happening, but I do have other skills that might distract you from your disappointment." I teased my tongue across his lips, darting it in and out of his mouth as I pressed my knee between his legs to rub myself against his muscular thigh. With my lips pressed to his, I whispered, "How's the distraction working so far?"

"Mmm. I'd rather not answer until I see what else you're willing to do."

Our kiss deepened, and the pasta water hissed as it boiled over with a rush of steam.

I broke free of his embrace and reached to turn the heat down, and he walked to the table and set about his routine of removing his holster and his shirt so he could take off the heavy vest.

"How was your day?" I asked as I stirred the spaghetti and lifted the lid to check the sauce.

"Uneventful. The defense didn't have much of anything to add, so I think my testimony combined with the evidence we'd collected convinced the jury, but we'll see. We should hear the verdict tomorrow. You need me to do anything to help with dinner?"

I shook my head and opened the oven to put the bread inside. "I think I've got it. I might even have everything ready at the same time, if you can believe that. Of course, it's just pasta and sauce with bread, so there wasn't much to screw up. I opted not to add any sides into the mix, and I made the salad earlier."

"Smart of you." He poured himself a glass of iced tea and took a long drink of it, and then he stood staring at me. His smile had faded.

"What? What's wrong? Why are you looking at me like that?"

"I'm deciding whether or not to say anything."

"About what? Say anything about what?"

He gave a little shake of his head and took another swig of tea.

"Whoa, whoa, whoa," I said, waving the ladle I held. "You can't do that. You can't look at me like you have the worst news to share and then tell me you're deciding whether or not to share it and decide not to. You know my mind. It will go all sorts of dark places, and what you actually have to tell me probably won't be nearly as bad. Spill it."

He frowned and looked down at his boots. "I don't want you to get upset."

"Then you shouldn't have brought it up at all, because now I'll be upset if you don't tell me."

He sighed and set his glass on the counter as he turned to face me.

"I stopped to fill up with gas on the way home, and Mr. Cooper did a U-turn so he could pull into the station and tell me that he'd seen you on the side of the road with Gordie giving you that speeding ticket last week. He wanted me to know it was long overdue and well-deserved. He says you fly past his house on a regular basis, and he worries someone is going to find you wrapped around an oak tree someday."

"Oh, good grief! The man actually stopped to tell you that? It sounds to me like he needs to get a life and stop worrying about mine."

"He also said you came flying past his house today just as fast as ever and that the ticket must not have slowed you down."

"What? That's ridiculous. I've been incredibly careful since Gordie wrote me that ticket. How can Mr. Cooper gauge how fast I was going when I passed his house anyway? Does he have a radar?"

"No. I think he just sees the red blur and knows you're going over the speed limit."

I rolled my eyes as the timer buzzed, and I opened the oven to pull out the garlic bread, which was more brown around the edges than I would have liked.

"Dang. I burned the bread."

"Don't change the subject."

I tossed the oven mitt back on the counter as I turned off the timer and the oven. "I'm not. I don't think I was speeding when I passed his house. What am I supposed to do? Set the cruise control so I don't go over fifty?"

Tristan shrugged. "If that's what it takes. That was the third time you've been pulled over since you got the Ferrari. If the first two hadn't let you off with warnings, you'd be on your third ticket right now. You could lose—"

"I know, I know. You've told me. I could lose my license. I could go to jail. I could get into an accident and kill someone."

"Or yourself." He leaned against the counter and crossed his arms.

"Tristan, we've been through this before. It's not like I don't know or that I don't care. I don't *mean* to be speeding. I'm just driving along, minding my own business, and the next thing I know, the car is flying, and someone is behind me with blue lights."

"So, it's the car's fault?"

"No. I mean, yes, in a way, it is. I know I'm responsible, but I

9

never once got a speeding ticket in a rental car or in your grand-mother's Cadillac." I sighed, and it turned into a groan. "It's just so damned fun to drive that Ferrari."

He stepped forward and cupped my cheek with his hand, his eyes serious as he stared into mine. "I know it is, but you're going to lose it or your ability to drive it if you don't slow down."

"Maybe I should just get rid of it."

He sighed and hugged me to him, and I lay my cheek against his chest and breathed him in.

"I don't think you need to get rid of it, babe. I know you love that car. You just gotta figure out how to drive it without speeding, that's all."

"Easier said than done."

Chapter 3

Tristan kissed the top of my head and then released me before he picked up the spoon and stirred the sauce. "This smells incredible, and I'm starving."

"Don't get too excited. It's just spaghetti Bolognese. It's your mom's recipe, so hopefully, I did it right."

He looked up, mouth open and eyes wide beneath raised eyebrows, and then he broke into a wide grin.

"You called my mom and asked for her recipe?"

I nodded as I pulled a knife from the block on the counter and used it to cut the bread. "Yeah. I think she was as shocked as you are."

He came to stand behind me, his arms around my waist and his chin nestled on my shoulder. "If the smell is any indication, I'm sure it's amazing, but the fact that you went to all this trouble and actually called my mom makes it wonderful no matter how it tastes."

"No matter how it tastes?" I elbowed him in the ribs and gave him a gentle push backwards. "Gee. Thanks for the vote of confidence."

His laughter filled the kitchen.

"That's not what I meant," he said.

"Yeah, well, I've made it this far in life without cooking, so you just say the word, and I'm more than happy to go back to watching you cook or dining out."

"I'm sure it will be wonderful." He turned me to face him and tucked his finger under my chin. "You know you don't have to cook, right? I didn't mind doing the cooking. You told me right from the start that cooking and housework weren't your thing. I'm okay with that."

I stretched up to kiss him and then lay my hand on his cheek, caressing his early evening stubble with my thumb. "I know, and I appreciate that you are willing to accept me for who I am. But oddly enough, I'm enjoying this cooking thing. It's almost...soothing, somehow. The process of gathering everything and putting it all together and seeing how it turns out."

A twinkle of mischief sparked in his eyes, and his lips curled into a grin. "Or not gathering everything and seeing how it turns out with something missing. That's fun, too."

I shoved against him, but he held me fast and bent his head to cover my mouth with his.

"I love you, Sloane," he whispered against my lips before pulling back to grin at me. "I'll even prove it by continuing to eat whatever you cook."

We'd just begun eating when the doorbell rang about twenty times in quick succession. Our eyes met as we said in unison, "Holden!"

When I'd first started living with Tristan, Holden was accustomed to walking into the house without warning whenever he pleased. It had been his grandmother's house before it was his brother's, and he'd always treated it like a second home. It had only taken a couple of close calls with me in a state of undress, or Tristan and I in an act of passion, before we all agreed it would be best for him to ring the bell and wait for someone to invite him in.

Tristan went to the door and brought back his brother, who immediately started sniffing the air and rubbing his belly.

"What's for dinner? Please don't say lentil meatloaf again."

"Nooo," Tristan said. "Thank God."

"Oh, c'mon!" I glared at both of them. "You guys are never gonna let me live that down. I told you, I read the recipe wrong. If I had added the right amount of red wine, it wouldn't have been so dry."

"It still would have been lentils instead of meat," Holden said. "*Meat*loaf is supposed to be *meat*, Sloane. It's right there in the name."

Tristan pointed to his plate and grinned as he sat back down. "She made Mom's Bolognese sauce, and she knocked it outta the park. Make yourself a plate."

Holden's mouth dropped open as he leaned to brace himself on the back of the chair. "Whoa! Sloane cooked something edible? Blink twice if you're lying, bro. Don't make me suffer the same fate as you unnecessarily."

"Very funny." I stuck out my tongue at him as he laughed. "You don't have to eat it, you know."

"I can't let my brother fall on the blade alone."

"It's actually very good," Tristan said as he tore off another piece of bread from the basket. "I think she's been holding out on us. We may have a bonafide chef in our midst."

Holden piled a plate high with pasta and sauce and then sat across the table from me. He shoveled a big forkful into his mouth and chewed slowly before doing a dramatic clutch of his throat as though he'd been poisoned.

"Whatever!" I tossed a piece of bread at his head, and he caught it in his prosthetic hand, his reflexes lightning-quick.

"No, seriously, you did good." He took another bite and smiled as he savored it. "Don't either of you tell Mom I said this, but it's every bit as good as hers."

"Wow!" Tristan said. "There's some blackmail material for ya."

I smiled, the compliment warming me throughout as my chest swelled and my confidence soared.

"Thanks, guys. I appreciate the positive feedback for once, but don't expect this to become a regular occurrence, okay?"

"That's a bummer. It would be nice to actually enjoy the free meals I mooch when I'm here," Holden said between bites. "So, anything happening on the career front, Sloane? Any big announcements? Maybe a blockbuster movie where you'll need a handsome, muscular bodyguard to go walk the red carpet with you and meet all those hot actresses and models?"

"No. Definitely not. Besides, if I need a handsome bodyguard, I've already got one right here." I reached over to stroke my hand up and down Tristan's arm and he winked at me in reply.

"Oh, I heard you got a ticket," Holden said as he took a bite of bread.

I gasped. "Does *everyone* know about this? Who told you?"

I looked to Tristan, but he shook his head and held up his hands in protest.

"Not me. I haven't said a word."

"I heard it at the post office," Holden said. "Two ladies were standing there discussing it, but they got all hush-hush once they saw it was me."

"Does this town have nothing better to discuss?" I pushed my plate back and tossed my napkin on the table. "I swear. These people really need to get something more exciting in their lives."

Holden shrugged. "I saw a flyer in the post office that a community theater is opening up in the old auto shop. Maybe that'll provide some new drama in town, and they'll forget about you."

"Funny you should mention that. I saw that same flyer at the grocery store. I was thinking maybe I'd audition."

I don't know who looked more surprised—Holden or Tristan.

"Really?" Tristan asked.

I'd been wavering back and forth all afternoon, consumed by self-doubt and trepidation over putting myself out there in such a public way in town. Now, having said it out loud, I waffled again and told myself it was a bad idea.

"I don't know. Maybe? Probably not."

"But you're a real actress," Holden said. "A movie star. Isn't community theater, like, people with full-time jobs who pretend to be actors on the weekend?"

"Um, no," I said as I wiped my hands on my napkin. "I mean,

sure, some of the people have full-time jobs, but they're not *pretending* to be actors. What does that even mean, anyway?"

"I don't know." Holden shrugged. "I guess I just think of community theater being amateurs. You know, volunteers. You're a professional. Why would you want to work with them?"

"How are you defining professional? Because if it's just based on pay, many community theaters do offer paid positions. As far as their talent, there are tons of extremely talented people who should be acting but didn't have the opportunity to do that for a living. The love of acting and the ability to do it well isn't limited to the people who are fortunate enough to make it a career, Holden. You can be a fine actor and also have another job."

He put his hand over his heart and bowed his head. "I stand corrected. I am your eager pupil, ready to learn."

"I just thought it might be a way for me to meet other people in town and get involved in something positive for once. You know, give the community something to talk about regarding me that isn't negative."

Tristan reached to take my hand. "I think that's a great idea."

Holden nodded as he twisted spaghetti around his fork. "Yeah, I guess it is when you put it that way. Just don't suck. Then they'll definitely talk about you."

"Really?" Tristan glared at him. "You can't think of anything else to say?"

Holden's words had laid bare the fears that were already eating at me.

"He's right, though. It could backfire on me. I already have a PR crisis in this town. I shouldn't do anything that could make it worse."

"I wasn't saying not to do it," Holden said. "I just said don't suck at it. Which you wouldn't, of course. I've seen all your films. You're good at what you do."

"That's just it, though." I frowned as I pushed my chair back and stood. "I do movies. That's entirely different from doing theater. I have multiple takes. I have multiple camera angles. An entire team of people who go in after I'm done and clean it up. I have no idea how I'd do in front of a live audience. I may completely suck."

As I gathered my dishes and turned to take them to the sink, out of the corner of my eye I saw Tristan punch Holden in his good arm.

"What? I wasn't saying not to do it, Sloane," Holden called after me. "I think you'd be great. They'd be lucky to have you. But you do know that building's haunted, right?

I turned to face Holden. "What?"

"C'mon, bro," Tristan said. "You're not usually one to spread rumors."

"I'm just telling her what I've heard," Holden said to his brother. "They say old man Letchworth's ghost haunts that place. I know you've heard it, too." He looked up at me and grinned. "It shouldn't matter to you with your ghost connections, though. Hell, you're the *Spectral Slayer*."

I looked back and forth between Holden and Tristan, who seemed annoyed by his brother's revelation.

"Who's old man Letchworth?" I asked.

Tristan sighed as he scraped a fork across his plate to gather the final remnants of his meal. "Hyram Letchworth. He owned an auto repair shop in that building for years. I remember going there with our grandparents when we were kids." He looked to Holden. "Hey, do you remember that gumball machine they had in the corner, and no matter what color gum it spit out, they all tasted like Pepto-Bismol?"

"Yeah," Holden said with a grin. "No telling how many quarters we put in that thing, and we always ended up spitting the gum in the trash."

I walked back to the table and stood behind my chair. "Why do people say it's haunted?"

"Supposedly, all sorts of strange things have happened there," Holden said. "Hyram was a grumpy old man, and I don't think he likes people being in his building."

Tristan stood and stretched. "Babe, don't pay any attention to him."

16

"What?" Holden laughed. "I would think she'd appreciate a heads-up about this sort of thing in case she runs into Hyram while she's on stage."

Tristan frowned as he picked up his plate and carried it to the sink, and I followed him, turning on the water to rinse his plate. He placed his hand over mine on the faucet and turned it off before pulling me into his arms.

"Ignore my brother and his ramblings. If you're excited about doing this, then I'm excited for you."

"I don't know. It's probably a bad idea. I just thought maybe acting would be something I could bring to the town that wouldn't piss people off. Then again, I'd need to run it past Priscilla and Douglas. I'm not sure Cedar Creek Community Theater fits into the plan my publicist and my agent have for me."

He tucked his thumb under my chin and lifted my face so that our eyes met.

"It's your life, Sloane. You do what makes you happy. Priscilla and Douglas work for you, not the other way around. They don't control your life, and neither does anyone in Cedar Creek. If this is something you want, I say go for it."

"Me too! You got my vote," Holden said. "I'll be sitting in the front row cheering you on. Heck, the whole family will."

I tried to force a smile, but the thought of the entire Rogers clan looking up at me from the front row was reason enough not to audition.

Later, as Tristan lay on his back in bed with me curled up next to him on my side, he pulled me closer and kissed the top of my head.

"I think this theater thing is a good idea. I know you get bored sometimes when you're here between jobs and I'm working all the time. I think having something of your own to do will be good, and like you said, it's a good way to meet people. Maybe make some friends."

"We'll see," I said. "I figure I'll go by there and meet the girl and see the building. If she seems to know her stuff and I like her, then maybe I'll audition. But if not, I can always say I was simply curious, right?"

"Right." He leaned his head back to look down at me, nudging my chin so I would look up to face him. "I want you to be happy here, Sloane. I know small town life is a lot different than what you're used to, and I don't ever want you to feel like you're stuck here because of me. So, if this is something you can do that might make things better for you here, I'm all for it."

I propped up onto my elbow and bent to kiss him.

"You make me happy, Deputy. Being here with you makes me happy. There is no place on earth I'd rather be."

"Not even the Four Seasons? Because even I gotta admit, that was a kick-ass suite you got us."

"Okay," I said with a grin. "Yeah, the Four Seasons is pretty great. I guess I should clarify to say that as long as you're with me, I'm happy. Wherever we are!"

Chapter 4

I'd never ventured off Main Street while in the city limits of Cedar Creek. I'd never had a need to. The Handy Sack, the post office, the diner, the hardware store—which housed the FedEx desk—and the sheriff's office were all on Main Street, and those were the only places I went.

The theater building was located a couple of blocks off Main, on a narrow side street with a lawn mower repair shop, a thrift store, a VFW, and a couple of houses that looked old enough to have been built before the town.

None of the buildings on the street were new or particularly well-kept, but the building with the bright blue sign out front announcing the new Cedar Creek Community Theater stood out like an eyesore. It appeared to have been abandoned for quite some time, and it was easy to see how it might get a haunted reputation. Weeds had overtaken any remnants of landscaping at the front entrance, and though the exterior appeared to have been yellow at one point, the passage of time and exposure to the elements had faded the peeling paint and made it chalky. There were only two windows on the building, and they were high up near the roof and blacked-out as though they'd been painted from the inside.

It certainly wasn't what I'd expected, and I almost chickened out and kept driving.

A truck with a construction logo on the door and a rack of ladders on top was parked next to the entrance, and on its left sat a shiny silver BMW with an open trunk.

I eased my car into the parking space on the other side of the truck and took a deep breath to muster courage. What could it hurt to go inside and introduce myself? It wouldn't require any commitment on my part. I could still walk away if it didn't seem like a legit opportunity or if I changed my mind about auditioning. I was just there to get information, nothing more.

I'd just shut the car door when a tall woman with dark brown hair exited the front of the building and walked toward the BMW. She wore a pair of paint-splattered jeans and a red T-shirt and kept her focus on the ground as she walked. After retrieving several plastic shopping bags from the trunk, she struggled for a moment to close it but couldn't lift her heavily laden arms high enough. I moved to go around the back of the truck to help her, but she'd already muttered a curse word and headed back inside before I got close.

I walked to the entrance door, pulling it open just as she reached to push it on her way back out.

She'd been looking down at a receipt in her hand, and she swore with a gasp when she looked up and saw me, stepping back with one hand clutched to her chest. "Christ!"

"I'm sorry. I didn't mean to startle you," I said. "I wanted to get more information about the theater."

"Oh, it's fine. My mind was elsewhere, and I didn't see you until you were *right there.*" Her eyes widened as she took a closer look at me. "Wait! You're Sloane Reid!"

"Yes. Hi." I extended my hand in greeting, and she grasped it with an impressive firm shake.

"Danielle Ward. Dani. It's nice to meet you. Did you say you wanted more information about the theater?"

"Yeah. I saw your flyer at the Handy Sack yesterday, and when I called the number listed, it said to stop by the theater. If it's not a good time, I can come back."

"Now's as good a time as any. I'd be thrilled to answer whatever questions you have. Here, let me close my trunk, and we'll step inside."

I waited by the door, and she smiled as she returned.

"My sister told me you were living here now. Wow. How did you end up in Cedar Creek?"

"Oh, my aunt has a cabin on Cedar Lake, and I came to get away from the hustle and bustle of L.A. for a weekend." I smiled at the thought of Tristan. "But then I fell in love with a guy and stayed."

Dani made a noise that might have been a scoff and might have been a laugh. "The things we do for men. You're dating Tristan Rogers, right? The deputy?"

"Yes. Do you know him?"

"No. I've lived in Chicago for the last thirteen years, so I'm out of touch with who's who in Cedar Creek. I only knew his name because my sister told me. I moved back to this area recently to be closer to my family."

"Oh, so you're originally from here?" I asked.

She nodded her head as she held the door open for me to enter the theater.

The smell of paint co-mingled with bleach and lemon-scented cleansers filled my nostrils as we entered the theater, and I flinched at the sound of loud hammering from somewhere deeper inside.

"Cedar Creek born and raised," Dani said, stepping past me. "My parents are still here, and I have several family members in the area. My uncle William has a large horse farm outside of town, and my aunt Patricia and her family live here as well, along with a few other cousins. My sister Amy and her husband have a house right down the road from my parents. They're expecting their first baby, and I wanted to be nearby for that."

"Congratulations! Did you own a theater in Chicago?"

"No," she said with a laugh. "I was in broadcast journalism. I was a producer for one of the local Chicago stations, and I lived and breathed the news. Some would say I was obsessed with my job." She took a deep breath and a shadow passed over her green eyes, dimming their sparkle. "I like to think of this theater as my reboot. My second chance. For reasons that would require a couple of strong drinks to even get into, I found myself needing a change of scenery."

"I'd say you accomplished that. From Chicago to Cedar Creek is a dramatic change of scenery."

She nodded, and the sadness lingered in her eyes. "Yes, it is. I loved Chicago. I miss it. I thrived on pretty much every aspect of big city life. I never would have believed I'd give it up to live in this tiny little town. But here I am. Life has a strange sense of humor sometimes, doesn't it?"

"Definitely."

She seemed to shake off whatever had gripped her as she looked up with a wide smile.

"Enough about me. You wanted to know about the theater. This is it." She spread her arms wide. "Or at least, it will be. You should have seen this place the first time the realtor brought me inside. It was filthy. Layers upon layers of dust, huge cobwebs, and more spiders than you could count. The floor was littered with rat poop, though thankfully, I haven't seen any of the rats who left it. Not yet, anyway. I've worked my butt off getting it presentable enough for the crews to come in and do renovations."

A broom and dustpan leaned against the counter on the far wall where Dani had piled the shopping bags from her trunk, and a box fan sat on the floor blowing air into an open bathroom that gleamed with a fresh coat of white paint.

"This front room will be the reception area," Dani said as she walked toward the counter and straightened the contents of a bag that had fallen over. "I plan to build an old-timey ticket booth on the front of the building, and we'll use this counter for concessions. Maybe build a bar along that wall if I can get the liquor license squared away."

She gestured toward the bathroom as she walked back to the center of the room.

"There's only one restroom up here in the front, but I plan to add another, and then there's two in the back that will be incorporated into the green room if I can ever get rid of all the oil and grease in the men's room. This place was an auto repair shop for years, and that back bathroom must have been the one the mechanics used."

As she turned to face me, I noticed a large smudge of white paint at her temple and extending into her hairline.

"You've got paint, um, right there," I said, pointing to the spot.

She reached up and touched the smudge, rubbing at it as she walked inside the bathroom and looked in the mirror.

"It's a wonder I'm not wearing more of it," she said with a grin. "I'm not a painter, by any stretch of the word. This little front bathroom was dark and dingy, though, and I figured if I was going to use it every day, I might as well paint it. That experience taught me that I definitely need to leave the rest of the painting to the professionals." She laughed as she moved back past me to a set of double doors and swung them open wide.

We entered a large, cavernous room that had been gutted and now stood empty. A newly constructed wall ran parallel to the back of the theater, and the loud hammering I'd heard since entering the building appeared to come from the other side of the wall where men's voices carried on a muted conversation.

Large round lights hung from the open rafters, and the two high windows I'd noticed outside had been boarded over from the inside. On the left wall were three doors—two closed and one open, revealing the nasty restroom she'd mentioned—and on the right wall was a large metal roll-up door.

Dani walked into the center of the room and smiled back at me.

"Here it is! Welcome to the Cedar Creek Community Theater." She gave a soft laugh as she spread her arms wide and spun in a slow circle. "I know it's not much to look at now, but I have big plans. They're constructing the green room now, and then they'll build out the stage in front of it." She walked backwards, surveying the area and pointing here and there as she conveyed her vision. "There's one storage room. Ideally, I'd like to expand with another one added onto the back of the building, but I may have to hold off on that."

Walking toward the back of the room, Dani looked down at a strip of tape on the floor and then looked left to right. "The stage will come out to here, elevated to about this high." She held her hand up a few feet from the floor. "I want footlights. Real, traditional, old-timey footlights. Or ones that look like that, anyway. I'm going for a vintage vibe with the whole place. Red velvet curtains, black and white decor—a Vaudeville theme."

Her eyes sparkled as she described what her mind could see, and it was hard not to be swayed by her enthusiasm, despite the stark barrenness of the room before us.

"Oh! You won't believe what happened with the seating." Her face lit up even more as her grin widened. "The community college is in the midst of a major renovation, and they're updating their main auditorium with a new color scheme. They have rows and rows of theater seating in a deep red. All I have to do is go and get them. They were going to trash them. I mean, a few do have stains and maybe a rip here and there, so we may have to go through and toss some, but there should be plenty to fill this theater. Zero cost. Can you believe that? The universe shined down on me with that one, for sure."

Before I could respond, the lights blinked twice in succession and then went off, plunging us into total darkness except for the shaft of light pouring through the open lobby door.

"Dammit," Dani exclaimed. "That keeps happening, and it's so frustrating. I don't know if it's a short or a surge or what, but these lights go off and come back on all the time. Sometimes, they're off a few seconds, and sometimes it's several minutes. I went and bought a flashlight so I don't get trapped in the dark again, but wouldn't you know that I left it on the counter?"

She walked through the open door into the lobby, and I hurried to follow her, not wanting to be left behind in the darkness. In my rush, I tripped and nearly fell face-first onto the concrete floor.

Chapter 5

"**A**re you okay?" Dani asked, coming to my side with the flashlight in her hand.

"Yeah, I stumbled on something."

She shone the light's beam on the floor, where a large rectangular area of concrete was raised slightly above the rest of the floor.

"Oh, that. The realtor said that was the pit where the mechanics went to stand beneath the cars and work on them. Whoever filled it in did a crappy job of smoothing it out. I'll have to find someone who can even it up before the seats get put in."

A lantern lit up the room behind us as one of the construction workers walked toward us with it.

"Y'all all right?"

"Yeah, Steve," Dani said. "You guys okay?"

"We're fine, but you gotta get somebody to figure out what the hell is going on with these lights. That's the fourth time today."

"I know. I've got another electrician coming tomorrow, and the power company said they'd send someone back out by the end of the week."

"Well, we'll knock off for an early lunch break and hopefully they'll be back on soon," Steve said.

"Hopefully so. Thanks, Steve," Dani said, and then she turned to lead me into the bright light of the lobby, where sunlight poured through the double glass doors.

"I really don't need this headache with the lights." She groaned as she set the flashlight on the counter next to the shopping bags. "It seems to be happening more often. It's the strangest thing. At first, I thought the power was going in and out, but it's only the lights in the auditorium. The air conditioner doesn't cut off, and neither do the outlets or any of the lights out here. Then I thought maybe it was a fuse or a breaker, but nothing's blown or thrown."

I blinked as my eyes adjusted to the bright light. "Maybe something with the wiring?"

"You would think, but I've had two different electricians come out to inspect, and the power company has been here twice. They've checked fuses, switches, wiring—you name it. No one can find a cause. Of course, the lights stay on with no problem when someone is here inspecting the place. I think they were convinced I was nuts, but then it happened a few times with Steve and his crew here, so at least I have witnesses now. I told Steve I was going to make him call the landlord and tell him I'm not some crazy lady."

"The landlord? You're renting this place? Why should it be on you to figure out a wiring issue? Shouldn't the owner take care of that?"

"I told him what's going on, but he lives in Tennessee, and he's pretty hands-off with everything here. He said he'd had no complaints from the previous tenant, but he did tell me if I got something from a licensed electrician saying there's an issue, he'd reimburse me for any necessary repairs."

"As he should," I said as I glanced back at the dark room with a shudder. "It's freaky dark in there when the lights go out."

"Oh, you don't have to tell me!" She laughed with a wave of her hand. "The first time it happened I was working here alone at night. Talk about pitch black! I couldn't see my own hand in front of my face. I've pretty much kept my projects to daytime hours since then, and I went right out and bought that camping lantern and that flashlight along with a ton of batteries. If it's getting close to sundown, or if it's cloudy and overcast during the day, I have that lantern on."

"I hope it's nothing too serious."

"You and me both." Dani shrugged with a sigh. "I already knew I'd need to upgrade the building's wiring to accommodate the lighting and dimmers for the stage, but I didn't factor in a problem with the existing wiring. I keep hoping maybe it will all work out in my favor and the owner might have to cover some of my upgrade costs in the process of fixing whatever's wrong. Wouldn't that be lovely?"

"Upgrading the wiring sounds like a big endeavor. When do you expect the theater to open?"

Her smile faded. "Good question. I'm waiting on some funding to come through from a couple of different avenues, and until I have that squared away, I'm in a holding pattern for most of the renovations. I should have an answer from the county and the city sometime this week on grants I applied for, but with the runaround I've gotten so far, I'm not getting my hopes up."

"The city is giving you a runaround?"

"Yeah. It's one of the few vacant buildings inside the city limits, so some of the city council members feel a different type of business would serve the population better. Let's just say a theater is not at the top of their wish list. Now, mind you, the realtor said the building's been standing empty for a couple of years now, so it's not like there's another tenant waiting in the wings. In fact, the landlord was willing to reduce the lease because it had been a while since he'd had a prospective tenant." She leaned back against the counter and braced her weight on her elbows as she grinned. "The short answer to your question is I don't know when we're opening. I just know that one way or another, I'll get it open. What else would you like to know?"

"I guess I'd like to know what shows you might be doing and what your audition process would look like."

"For you? It would look like you telling me what part you

27

wanted and me saying okay." She laughed, and the sparkle I'd seen earlier returned to her eyes. "No, seriously, no matter what the play is, I'm sure there'd be a part for you. I have to admit, I'm intrigued by your interest. I never in a million years thought you'd be willing to do something like this."

"Why?"

"Because, you're a, well, you're a movie star. This is community theater. In Cedar Creek, no less. It's not exactly the caliber of production you're accustomed to, I'm sure. I'm surprised you'd be interested." Her brow furrowed for a moment, and she tilted her head to the side. "If you don't mind my asking, why *are* you interested?"

"I may be known for films now, but my love of acting started in the theater as a teenager. The lights, the make-up, the costumes. I loved being able to hear the audience react in real time to whatever we did on stage."

"Yes!" Dani nodded in agreement, her eyes bright. "Isn't a live audience the best? You can pull so much energy from them and feed off it. It's like a high, isn't it?"

I grinned, thrilled to talk to someone who understood. "Exactly! To hear them laugh or when they gasp in the right spot, you know you're nailing it. You don't get that kind of immediate feedback with a film. You don't even get reviews on a film until after it releases, and that can be months or even years after you did the scenes."

"I love when the audience goes completely silent. If you can hear a pin drop in the theater, you know you've got them in the palm of your hand." She bit down on her lip and then smiled. "God, I've missed that. I was a die-hard theater rat in high school and college, and I would have pursued it as a career if my parents hadn't been so certain that it was folly. I suppose it's part of the reason I chose television production—lights, camera, action, all that —but I've missed theater. I always swore I'd get back to it someday."

My grin widened at the common bond we shared. "Same here. I got away from theater once I started doing movies, but when I saw your flyer, it reminded me how much I enjoyed it. I'd love to have that experience again. That, and the feeling of belonging you get with the theater community. I don't really know many people in Cedar Creek other than Tristan and his family. I'd like to make some new connections."

"Well, I'm all for making new connections. I'd be honored to have you, and not just because having Sloane Reid on stage as a headliner will be great publicity."

"Yeah, about that." I frowned and twisted a section of my hair between my fingers, pulling it across my chin. "I have to warn you that it might not be as good as you hope. My, um, fame, or status, or whatever, isn't always well-received here in Cedar Creek."

"Trust me," Dani said as she laid her hand on my arm. "Your name would be a big draw for a theater. I guarantee people will come just to see you up close, even if they aren't interested in the show. It would pull in people from outside the town, which I need to do if I'm going to survive. I mean, not that I'm looking at you purely as a moneymaker, of course. I'd love to work with you in whatever capacity you'd want, but I have no doubt that your name attached to a play would definitely bring people in."

The lights came on, steady and bright, and Dani looked up with a grin.

"Well, would you look at that? Let there be light!"

One of the glass entry doors swung open, and Cedar Creek's mayor walked in.

"Good afternoon, ladies," he said as he shook hands with each of us. "Nice to see you both. I left a message for you earlier, Ms. Ward, but when I didn't hear back, I remembered what you said about having no signal in the building and decided to stop by."

"I'm sorry," Dani said, her brows furrowed as she frowned. "I never know if someone calls while I'm here. The phone doesn't ring or notify me of a missed call or message. Please tell me you have good news."

"That remains to be seen. I was trying to let you know the city council is meeting with the folks from the county today to discuss the theater's grants. Cross your fingers, and we'll see how that goes."

Dani's eyes took on a panicked look as her hand went to her hair. "Do I need to be there?"

"No, no. That's not necessary. We'll hash out the details and then give you a call with a summary of the discussion." He turned to me with the fake smile of a politician and gave a slight bow. "I must say, I'm intrigued to see you here, Ms. Reid. It's always a delight to have you in town patronizing our local businesses. Could this little meeting mean that Ms. Ward is bringing you onboard with the theater?"

"We're discussing it," I said.

He clasped his hands together and smiled as he turned to Dani. "Splendid! You didn't mention when we talked before that you might have our resident celebrity attached to the project." He looked back and forth between us with one eyebrow arched.

"Would it make a difference if she was?" Dani asked.

"Yes. I imagine it would. Credentials like hers would certainly elevate the theater's profile. You know you have my full support already, but I think with this news you might be able to sway a couple of the other council members who were straddling the fence." He looked to me with a dramatic bow. "Let me just say on behalf of the city council, if such a valued member of the community as yourself were to get involved with bringing the arts to Cedar Creek, we'd be most grateful."

I wondered if his local constituents would agree with his assessment of my value as I gave an awkward nod and forced a smile, unsure of what I was expected to say.

"I'd be happy to help in any way I can."

He nodded with a grin. "Glad to hear it. Now, I'll let the two of you return to your conversation and be on my way. Have a nice day, ladies."

"I'll walk you out," Dani said to the mayor. "I have the modified business plan in the car if you'd like a copy to take to the meeting with you."

"Of course. Good day, Ms. Reid."

"Good day."

"I'll be right back," Dani said to me as she followed him out.

"No problem. Take your time." I walked over to the open doors that led into the main auditorium and stepped inside, careful not to stray too far from the lobby doors in case the lights went out again.

Steve and his crew were still out for lunch, and my footsteps echoed in the emptiness. I couldn't imagine what it must have been like for Dani to be working alone at night when the place went dark. Even with the lights on, the building held a spooky air of abandonment, and I wished Holden hadn't told me the rumors about its former owner still roaming the place. I wrapped my arms around my waist and glanced up at the lights, willing them to stay on.

Suddenly, my skin crawled with the oddest sensation of being watched, and I turned to look up at the wall behind me, driven by an instinct honed over years of life in the public eye. There was a window high on the wall with dark glass, and its position made it apparent that it fronted a room and not the world outside.

The overhead lights flickered once, and I rushed toward the door without hesitation, not wanting to be stranded in the darkness.

Just as I entered the lobby, the shopping bags Dani had piled on the counter suddenly slid to the ground, scattering their contents across the floor. Bright blue liquid oozed onto the concrete in a vivid puddle from a busted bottle of cleaner, and I rushed to pick it up and hurry it to the sink in the bathroom as Dani came back inside.

"Oh, my goodness," she gasped. "What happened?"

"I don't know," I said, washing the cleaner from my hands. "I walked away for a minute, and when I came back in the lobby, everything fell."

Dani bent to pick up more stuff from the floor as I returned with a roll of paper towels I'd found sitting on the back of the toilet.

She groaned as she pulled a broken plastic soap dispenser from a bag. "I tossed them all on the counter and ran back outside to close the trunk, but I didn't think I left them close to the edge. How strange."

She reached to take the paper towels from me and wiped up the cleaner as I gathered the items from the other bags and set them upright.

"Hey, what's that window on the back wall in there?"

"Oh, it's an office. I guess the guy who ran the auto shop liked to be able to see what was happening on the floor. A way to keep his eyes on his workers, I suppose. I thought maybe I could use it for an audio-visual booth, but I'm not sure if that will work now. It depends on how expensive it would be to wire all the audio system and lighting controls through there. Having the elevated view would be great though, and then I wouldn't lose any seating space to an A/V booth on the floor."

"Is there anyone up there now?"

Her forehead wrinkled in confusion. "No. Why? Do you want to see it?"

"Um, no, that's okay."

"You sure?" She stood and threw the soiled paper towels in the trash can and then washed her hands in the bathroom sink.

I hesitated. I didn't want to make a big deal out of it, but part of me did want reassurance that I had imagined being watched.

"C'mon. I'll show you," Dani said as she wiped her hands. She opened the door to what I'd assumed was a closet off the lobby, and behind it was a narrow staircase.

"Wait," she said. "Hand me that flashlight. At this point, I think I should just carry it around in my back pocket."

My heart pounded as we made our way up the staircase, and I held my breath as Dani opened the door into the little office, not convinced that it was empty until I saw it with my own eyes.

The window offered an excellent vantage point of the whole room below, and I could see the value in using the room as a control booth. As Dani explained her plans for it, I stood and looked down at the spot where I was standing moments before, unable to shake the uneasy feeling that had come over me.

I told myself it was Holden's fault I was jumpy. He'd planted the seed about the place being haunted, and my imagination had fed into it.

Undoubtedly, if Dani had seen anything out of the ordinary, she wouldn't feel comfortable working in the building after hours alone.

Would she?

Chapter 6

"I'm so happy you stopped by," Dani said with a warm smile as we came back downstairs into the lobby. "I was joking earlier about the publicity, but I must say, you're bringing them in already. That's the first friendly conversation I've had with the mayor regarding this theater, and it's definitely the first time he's mentioned that I have his full support. I'll need it if I'm going to get anything from the city. So, if that's the effect you have on him and there's a chance you might have that effect on anyone else on the council, then I definitely want you involved."

Her enthusiasm was contagious, and I returned her broad smile easily.

"I don't feel like I really did anything, but if so, then I'm glad to be of assistance. It's a cool thing that you're doing here. I hope the city gets behind you with the funding."

"Me too. I'll take whatever help I can get," Dani said with a sigh.

"I'm curious why you chose Cedar Creek. I mean, you mentioned your family being here and your sister having a baby, but why not start the theater in a bigger city and have your home here? Ocala and Orlando are both within driving distance and have a larger potential audience, not to mention city governments that might be more inclined to work with you."

"True, but bigger city means heftier leases and more competition from theaters that are already well-established. Right now, I'm self-financing to get things going while I wait to hear back on the local grants and a couple of other national grants I applied for. I don't know that I could afford to do that in a more expensive location. Hell, I can't afford to do it much longer here."

She held the door open for me, and as we walked outside, her smile returned.

"The sooner I get open, the sooner I can start taking in some money to let the place finance itself. My goal is to eventually be able to take a salary from the theater and even pay performers and crew, but I know that's gonna be a while down the road. I feel like I'm better off here where I can manage the lease, even if it means stringing out the renovations and doing a little at a time."

Dani paused and shoved her hands in the back pockets of her jeans as she looked across the parking lot. "Besides, I moved back to be close to my family. To reconnect with them after being away for so long. My life has been an out-of-control roller coaster the past few years, and right now, I need that security blanket that only family can provide, you know?" She looked back to me with a grin. "I'm sure you understand that, being a celebrity. You need people you can trust. People you can rely on. There's nothing like family to ground you when you feel like it's spinning out of control."

I smiled and gave a slight nod as though in agreement, but I had no family to speak of. My mother and I hadn't talked in a couple of years—not due to any rift or falling out, but because she was too busy to be bothered, and I'd given up long ago on trying to matter to her. Aunt Virginia and I kept in touch, but our relationship was superficial at best.

My inner circle—those I chose to rely on and trust—consisted of my agent, my publicist, my accountant, and Tristan, of course. I could stretch that to include Holden and Rachel, I suppose. Well, and Chelsea, but her being a ghost limited our relationship in many ways.

"It was nice meeting you, Dani, and I appreciate the tour. I have to fly out to L.A. for re-shoots next Tuesday. I'm not sure how long I'll be gone, but I'm hoping not more than three or four weeks. I'll stop by when I return and see how far you've gotten and if you've decided on a play by then."

"That would be awesome. Here, let me give you my card in case you need to get in touch with me." She went to her car and came back with a business card. "I have no idea why you'd need to get in touch with me, but hey, I got these printed up, so I might as well hand them out, right?"

I smiled as I took the card from her.

She let out a low whistle as we neared my car. "I can't believe I didn't see a Ferrari convertible in the parking lot when I got the bags out of my trunk. That goes to show how preoccupied I was at the time."

"Yeah, it's usually pretty noticeable. I definitely didn't consider how much attention it would get before I bought it."

From the moment I drove it off the lot, the car was like a flashing beacon that drew people toward it. They didn't even need to know who was behind the wheel to be fascinated. In fact, seeing someone famous step out was almost like an afterthought. Icing on the cake, really.

"Wow! I love the way that red paint sparkles in the sunlight," Dani said as she bent and gave it a closer look. "It's a gorgeous car, that's for sure."

"Thank you." I smiled as a warm blush crept into my cheeks; I was always uncomfortable with the amount of attention the car commanded.

It *was* gorgeous, and I loved driving it, even though it had been a bad choice.

I'd never purchased a car before, and I had picked a vehicle that would allow me in some way to hold on to Lucy Landry—her daring, her flash, and the status she had helped me achieve for my life. It was the kind of car I could see Lucy driving, but in hindsight, a fiery red Ferrari Portofino convertible wasn't a wise decision for Sloane Reid if I wanted to in any way blend in or avoid attention.

The car had served as the final nail in the coffin for my short-lived private eye aspirations and ruined any chance I might have had at anonymity in my local surroundings even if the paparazzi hadn't descended in full force. My low-key, virtually unnoticed trips into Cedar Creek, Jensen, and Lumberton became a thing of the past when my car screamed my arrival every time I parked it.

In hindsight, I would have been better off with a regular four-door sedan in a common color. Maybe silver or white. And not even a BMW or a Mercedes. More like a Honda or a Toyota.

It would have cost me much less, and not just because of the sticker price or the fact that I'd been pulled over three times since I'd gotten it.

"Well, good luck with the city council," I said as I opened the car door. "Oh, and with the lights. I hope you figure out what's causing that."

"One way or another, I will. I have to."

Dani and I said our goodbyes, and I left, energized with the prospect of working with her and being part of the new theater.

I picked up my phone to call Tristan and tell him how excited I was about meeting Dani, but I decided to wait until I could see his response in person. It was always more fun to share things with him when I could watch him react. I loved the way his gray eyes lit up when he was happy.

He'd likely pick me up and spin me around in a huge bear hug, his gravelly laugh tumbling out as he said something like, "Babe, I'm so excited for you!"

And I knew he would be. He welcomed any opportunity for me to be happy, but the theater was doubly good, because me pursuing a new endeavor locally meant more time at home. It also further solidified my commitment to establishing a life in Cedar Creek.

It was a gorgeous day, and I had the afternoon free, so I decided I'd drive into Orlando to my favorite organic supermarket. I hoped they'd have some porcini mushrooms for a risotto recipe I'd been wanting to try, and I planned to bring home a loaf of their fresh-baked bread along with a bottle of Tristan's favorite wine.

I was in the mood to celebrate, and since Holden was in Tallahassee meeting with legislators for his non-profit organization, Tristan and I might actually be able to have an uninterrupted romantic evening.

As I made my way out of Cedar Creek and onto the winding back roads that led to Orlando, I was reminded of all the things I loved about the Portofino. It drove like a dream, and it hugged the twists and curves of Lake County's rural roads like it had been custom-made to drive them. I finally understood what Julia Roberts meant in *Pretty Woman* when she said, "Man, this baby must corner like it's on rails!"

In between the curves, there were often long straightaways that were impossible to resist. Every time I had gotten pulled over, it had been on those back roads where the car's abilities had proven more of a detriment than an asset.

The Portofino didn't need a heavy foot or a lot of room to fly. It could go from zero to sixty in three seconds, and I'd often glance down to find myself going upwards of seventy or eighty miles per hour yet feel like I was barely moving.

I'd only had the car a few weeks the first time I'd seen blue lights in the rearview mirror and heard the wail of the siren closing in on me. I'd never even had so much as a parking ticket, and I went into a state of panic. I didn't know what to do or how to react. Luckily, the officer was Kyle Hightower, one of Tristan's fellow deputies who knew me. He let me off with a warning and cautioned me on the dangers of driving too fast.

The second time was up near Ocala and out of Tristan's immediate circle, but that cop happened to be a *Spectral Slayer* fan. He'd been so thrilled to get an autograph and a selfie with *the* Lucy Landry that I think he forgot why he'd stopped me in the first place.

The third time, however, was not a charm. Deputy Gordie McDonough knew Tristan and had met me several times, and if anything, that only added to the downright glee he exhibited in writing me my very first speeding ticket. It had taken my best acting skills to paste on a polite smile and not curse at him or take the ticket and tear it up into little pieces in front of him.

After Gordie's ticket, I'd been diligent at keeping an eye on the speedometer, but as I sang along to the radio on the way to Orlando with the car's top down, the wind in my hair, and the sun on my face, my guard slipped.

I took the curves tight, easing over the line here and there as the tires gripped the pavement.

When the road opened up into the last straightaway before the county line, there wasn't another car in sight either behind me or in front of me, and with no intersection or turn-off coming up for a couple of miles, I figured it was a safe spot to unleash the car and let it flex its muscles.

The horses under the hood needed very little encouragement to get up and go when I gunned the gas, and I giggled at the rush of adrenaline that coursed through me as the engine roared and the trees became a blur.

At the first sight of the distant blue lights in my rearview mirror, I released the accelerator and a stream of expletives simultaneously. I looked at the speedometer, shocked to see its needle falling past one hundred on its way back down.

The patrol car closed the distance between us in no time to ride my bumper with the siren blaring, and I prayed it would be a friendly face as I searched the narrow shoulder of the road for a place to pull over.

As I looked in the mirror to see the deputy step out of his car, I groaned. It was a very familiar face, but nothing about it looked friendly in that moment.

Chapter 7

"Have you lost your damned mind? Are you trying to kill yourself?" Tristan asked, whipping off his sunglasses as he approached my car door.

I moved to open it, but he barked immediately.

"Stay in the car!"

"Hi, honey," I managed to get out, forcing my voice to sound much more cheerful than I felt. "Where'd you come from? I didn't see you."

"I can't imagine that you would have." He spat the words out, and the tight set of his jaw and the pulsing muscle in his cheek conveyed that he was in no mood to joke around. "Do you have any idea how fast you were going?"

"Not really, but I think it's safe to guess that it was over the speed limit."

He pushed his hat back and squinted down at me in the bright sunlight.

"You *think*? You flew past me like a red flash of lightning. I didn't even get a chance to clock you."

"Oh, well, that's a good thing, right? I mean, if you didn't clock me, then—"

"No, Sloane. It's not a good thing." He frowned and swore under his breath as he took off his hat and ran his hand through his hair. "You had to be going over a hundred miles an hour. At least twice the posted limit!"

"I'm sorry. It was such a gorgeous day, and there wasn't anyone in this straightaway. Well, at least I thought there wasn't. Where were you?"

"I had pulled off the road into a shady spot, hoping to eat my sandwich with a few minutes' peace. Next thing I know, you blow by like a bat out of hell." He slammed his hat back on his head. "Didn't we just talk about the dangers of driving too fast on these little two-lane roads? Do you want to get yourself killed? Or kill someone else in the process?"

I knew his points were valid, but my response to being chastised still leaned toward defensive.

"There wasn't anyone else around. I would have slowed back down before I got closer to the curve, and I wouldn't have gone that fast except this is the longest straightaway I've found."

"Whether or not anyone else is around is not the point, Sloane. It's dangerous. Not to mention that you're breaking the law. You literally just got a speeding ticket that could have been a reckless driving charge if Gordie had wanted to push it. Do you understand that you could lose your license? You could lose the ability to drive *anything*?"

I pushed the door open despite his protests, uncomfortable with having to look up at him as he talked down to me.

"Please get back in the car," he said again as he looked left and right. "It's not safe for you to be standing on the side of the road."

I did my own sweep in both directions and put my hands on my hips as I glared at him. "There's no one coming. And you're standing on the side of the road, aren't you?"

"It's my job. Now, would you please get back in the car while I go and write your ticket?"

My mouth fell open, and my eyes nearly bulged out of my head. *"You're going to write me a ticket?"*

"I sure as hell am. Something has to get through that thick skull of yours, so you'll slow down and drive the speed limit."

He'd drawn himself to his full height as he stared down at me, and his intimidating stance only served to make me angrier and more defensive.

I moved closer so that we stood toe-to-toe. "The speed limit on this road is fifty miles per hour. That's ridiculous! Do you have any idea how hard it is to drive a Ferrari that slowly? I might as well keep one foot on the brake the whole time to hold it back."

"Then get something else that you're able to drive without breaking the law or endangering yourself and others."

I leaned back against my door and crossed my arms. "Oh, so now you *do* want me to get rid of my car?"

"No, I want you to drive the speed limit and use some caution on the road. Do you have any idea what it's like to work an accident scene, Sloane? Do you know the things I've seen? What has to be done to pull mangled bodies from twisted wreckage? When I think about what would happen if I came up on you—" His voice broke and he looked away from me, then he opened my car door and motioned for me to get inside. "Someone's coming. Get back in the car."

I turned to see a truck approaching in the lane nearest us, and despite my defiant nature, I didn't dare taunt fate or risk Tristan's ire by refusing to get out of the way. I returned to the driver's seat and glared straight ahead, pissed that my happy day had been ruined.

The driver honked and waved, and Tristan waved in response.

"Give me your license and registration," he said once the truck has passed.

I looked back up at him in disbelief. "You've got to be kidding me. You're actually going to write me a ticket. Your own fiancée."

"I'm going to do my job, Sloane. You were traveling well in excess of the posted speed limit, and I have to give you a citation and hold you accountable for breaking the law."

"Oh, stop being a hard ass! All right, I admit I shouldn't have been speeding. Okay? Is that what you wanted to hear? I was wrong. Are you happy now?"

He extended his hand, palm up, as he looked down the road toward the cars approaching from the opposite direction. "License and registration, please."

"Come on, okay? I get it. I screwed up. I won't do it again. I'll drive five miles under the speed limit no matter where I am. Just let me go with a warning."

"You've already had two warnings from other officers, and you obviously didn't heed them. License and registration."

"I already got a ticket, too. Evidently, I didn't heed that, so what good is it going to do to give me another one? I'm telling you I'll slow down, okay? I won't speed again."

He continued to look up and down the road in silence, his hand still extended.

"Dammit, Tristan! You are really determined to do this, aren't you? What if I refuse to give it to you?"

He looked back to me, and the tender gaze I was accustomed to in those gray eyes had been replaced by a hard steeliness. He wasn't going to budge.

"If you refuse to give it to me, I'll put you in handcuffs. Again."

I narrowed my eyes at his reference to the first night we'd met, and then I slapped my palm against the steering wheel as another car drove past. "C'mon. You don't have to do this. You've made your point. I know I was wrong. You can let me go, and I swear you will never catch me speeding again. Just let me go. Please?"

A brief hint of tenderness sparked in his eyes, but the hard set of his jaw was unrelenting.

"No, I can't. I don't think you realize how many people complain about your speeding and how they think you get preferential treatment because of our relationship."

"But no one knows I was speeding except you, so they won't know if you let me go."

"What about the people who have passed by?"

"Maybe we were just having a chat or a lovers' quarrel. They don't know."

He pulled his hat down lower on his forehead and sighed. "Sloane, hand me your license and registration."

"Fine. You know what? I don't care." I retrieved the items and flung them into his outstretched hand. "Write me a ticket. Handcuff me. Whatever you need to do to feel good about yourself, Deputy."

He turned to walk to his car, unable to see the middle finger I flipped him as I began to go through a mental list of everything about him that had ever pissed me off. Tears of anger stung my eyes as I realized how few items were on the list, and I closed my lids against the tears.

He was right, of course. I had been speeding. I had been warned. I had gotten off easily twice before.

None of which made it feel better that my own fiancé was delivering my second speeding ticket less than two weeks after the first one. Damn Tristan's stupid code of honor and his strict adherence to right over wrong.

"I tried to cut you as much slack as I could," he said when he returned, citation in hand. "Technically, I didn't have an official speed clocked, so I wrote it up as ten over the limit."

I snatched the ticket from him along with my driver's license and registration, and he leaned forward, bracing his hands on the car.

"Babe, it's not like I want to write you a ticket. I'm not trying to be a hard ass or whatever you called me. I'm trying—"

"Am I free to go, or am I still being detained?"

He stood upright and crossed his arms, and I turned the key in the ignition.

"Where are you headed, anyway?"

"To Orlando. Why? Are you gonna call your cop buddies there and have them pull me over too?" The angry resentment in my voice tasted bitter, and I didn't even care.

He frowned, and I looked straight ahead with my hand on the shifter, tempted to drop it into gear and peel away but not willing to chance him chasing me down and arresting me.

"Am I free to go or not, Deputy?"

When he didn't answer, I glared back at up at him.

He looked so dejected for a moment that I almost felt sorry for him, but then he stepped back and spread his arms to indicate I could go, and I didn't stick around any longer.

Chapter 8

After getting the ticket, I wasn't much in the mood for mushroom shopping, so I opted for retail therapy at the mall instead. I returned home with Prada sunglasses, a Louis Vuitton bag, and a pair of Jimmy Choos—none of which made me feel any better.

I'd tried to stay mad at Tristan, but the little voice inside my head wouldn't stop reminding me that I was the one in the wrong. I'd been caught speeding and deserved the ticket, and I knew he'd only been doing his job in giving it to me.

But if two other deputies had let me go, obviously Tristan could have too. It was his *choice* to ticket me, and every time I thought about that, I got mad all over again.

By the time I'd gotten home and put my purchases away, the seesaw of anger and guilt had taken its toll, and I sank into a bubble bath to drown away the day.

It had started on such a high note with Dani and the prospect of the theater, and I wanted to recapture that excitement. I longed to be able to tell Tristan about my morning and have him share my happiness without any barrier of anger or frustration between us. I needed to find a way to have the romantic evening I'd envisioned before the need for speed had got the best of me.

Perhaps I could distract him with a well-planned seduction. Surely, he'd be willing to set aside our roadside encounter for the evening if I greeted him at the door wearing nothing but my new Jimmy Choo heels with a glass of his favorite wine and our special playlist providing background music.

I couldn't help but smile as I stepped from the tub and dried off, anticipating his touch as I smoothed perfumed lotion across my skin and dusted my shoulders and breasts with a bit of shimmery powder.

Just the thought of his likely reaction was enough to ramp up my own desire, and by the time I'd finished drying my hair, I couldn't tell if my skin was flushed from the heat of the blow dryer or the risqué images in my own mind.

His laughter rang out from the kitchen as I unplugged the dryer, and I frowned. I hadn't expected him to be home for another half hour at least, and he hadn't called to let me know he was on his way as he usually did.

At first, my disappointment at the seduction plans being dashed kept me from questioning why he was laughing, but it soon became clear that there was another muffled voice in the kitchen in conversation with him.

I slipped my arms inside my robe and tied it around my waist as I opened the bathroom door and went to put my ear against the bedroom door.

It was a female voice, and my first thought was that perhaps my friend Rachel had stopped by, but then I recognized Rita's laughter and frowned again.

Why was Tristan's mother in our kitchen? She lived almost an hour away. Had he told me she was stopping by? Had I forgotten about plans or failed to check the magnetic calendar on the fridge?

I pondered hanging out in the bedroom to see if she would leave soon, but then curiosity got the best of me and I decided to make an appearance.

I pulled on a cotton sundress and then misted my hair with a setting spritz before pulling it up into a ponytail.

The two of them stood talking in the kitchen when I came down the hallway, and Rita rushed forward as soon as she saw me.

"There you are!" She wore a huge smile, her face radiant as she greeted me with a hug.

I met Tristan's eyes over her shoulder, hoping he would smile to let me know all was well between us, but instead he looked away.

I wanted to go to him, to put my arms around him and breathe him in, but Rita held me tight, taking my hands in hers as she released me from her hug but not her grasp.

"I apologize for barging in unannounced, but I was so excited that I simply had to come by and talk to you in person."

"To me?"

"Yes, you! A little bird shared your news with me this afternoon. I must say, I was quite surprised, but I think it's a wonderful development."

She looked overjoyed and expectant, though I had no clue of what or why.

"What little bird?" I looked toward Tristan with the question, but he shook his head with a shrug.

"Wasn't me. I have no idea what she's talking about."

I turned back to Rita in confusion, not sure who she would have talked to with any information about me.

Tristan's brain worked faster than mine.

"Was it someone at the Arts Alliance meeting?" he asked, and a light bulb went off in my head.

I'd forgotten that Rita was chair of the county's Arts Alliance, which means she would have been in the meeting with the mayor to discuss Dani's grants. But how did that involve me? Had the mayor mentioned that I might be in a play? And if so, why would Rita be so excited about that?

Rita nodded to Tristan as I tried to put the pieces together.

"Are you talking about the theater?" I asked.

"Yes," she exclaimed as she squeezed my hands. "The mayor said he'd come from meeting with you and Dani and that you were

46

officially onboard. I was so surprised! I had no idea you'd be interested."

I tried to smile and return her exuberance, but I was still confused. She hadn't been nearly this enthusiastic over my latest movie premiere. Why would an as-of-yet-unnamed play make her so ecstatic?

"Theater has always been an interest of mine," I said, trying to explain and understand at the same time. "I just haven't had the time to pursue it."

"Well, that makes sense. Wow!" She released my hands as she turned to Tristan. "Can you believe our dear sweet girl here is a key investor in the new Cedar Creek Community Theater?"

A key investor? What the hell did that mean and where did she get that idea?

Tristan raised his eyebrows and blinked with wide eyes.

"A what?" His face held a bewildered expression that mirrored my own feelings. "You're investing in the theater?"

Rita didn't give me a chance to answer as she looked back at me in a panic. "Uh-oh. Was this supposed to be a surprise? Did I ruin the surprise?"

I gave a little shake of my head as I opened my mouth to protest and ask why she thought I was investing, but Rita kept right on talking, her attention focused back on Tristan.

"I assumed you already knew. Isn't this a wonderful surprise?"

"It is," Tristan said without a hint of a smile. "A wonderful surprise, indeed."

"It was actually Sloane who sealed the deal for the theater," Rita said, still beaming. "The Arts Alliance has had an uphill struggle getting the city council to see this as a benefit to the community, but when the mayor assured them it has Sloane's backing and she's willing to be an investing partner, it gave them the incentive they needed to open up the purse strings."

"Wait," I said as I processed her words. "Are you saying that Dani wouldn't have gotten the money if I wasn't involved?"

"That's right." Rita wrapped me in an inescapable mama bear hug. "I am so proud of you, Sloane." She pulled back from the hug and squeezed my arms. "I know what a struggle it's been for you to fit in here. I can't imagine what an adjustment it would be to move to such a small town from a place like L.A., and Ray and I have worried ourselves sick about how on earth the two of you would be able to make it with such different backgrounds."

What? What did she mean by that? Had she and Ray been thinking this whole time that Tristan and I wouldn't stay together?

"But now look at you," Rita continued. "You've found your place. You're making your mark on this town in a positive way, and I can't tell you how happy I am to see it."

She smiled at me with a maternal tenderness I'd never experienced from my own mother. In fact, I don't think anyone had ever looked at me with such pride and approval before. It made it damned near impossible to speak up and tell her she had it all wrong.

She released me to turn and face Tristan, who stood staring at me with a clouded expression I couldn't decipher.

"I don't know why I didn't think of it when I first heard that Danielle wanted to open a theater in Cedar Creek. Why, of course, that's the perfect fit for Sloane with her acting!" She grinned as she looked back at me. "I never dreamed you'd be open to investing in a local business, though. After everything Tristan had told me about your issues with, well…" Her face contorted into a momentary frown and then immediately returned to her joyful smile. "I'm sure I speak for our entire family when I say we're thrilled that you've decided to put down more permanent roots here and get involved with bringing arts to the community."

Her eyes welled with tears, which threw me even farther off-guard as my mind raced to catch up with everything she'd revealed.

Why did the mayor think I was investing? Where did he get that idea? And if that was the reason they'd approved Dani's grants, would she lose their approval if I wasn't investing?

Would I lose Rita's?

I still didn't understand why me committing to give money to a theater meant so much to her or why it gave her reassurance I hadn't known she'd needed about mine and Tristan's future.

If she considered our relationship that fragile, why would a financial contribution make her think we were on solid ground?

Had Tristan known his mother and father were sick with worry about us? Was it something they'd discussed? Did he feel that way, too?

What had Tristan told his mother about me having issues? I mean, obviously I had them, but did that topic really qualify to be a family discussion behind my back?

I had thought he was happy, but perhaps I was wrong.

As my thoughts became more panicked, Rita moved to loop her arm through Tristan's and wink up at him. "Now, we just need to get a wedding date set."

"Mom, don't start."

"I know, I know. I'm not supposed to say anything about that, but you can't blame a mother for trying. I can't wait to tell the world our family's news, Oh, speaking of which, did I tell you your cousin Austin got engaged? The new doctor has had quite a year. He's only just graduated and opened his own chiropractic office, and now he's getting a wife."

The two of them continued to discuss the upcoming nuptials as a nauseous dizziness came over me.

Everything felt out of control and too entangled for my liking.

"Will you excuse me for a moment?"

I moved toward the hallway with a forced smile, avoiding eye contact with them both.

"Oh, wait, Sloane honey, I'm gonna run," Rita said. "We're supposed to meet the Hyders for dinner tonight, and Ray will be wondering where I am if I don't get myself on the road. I just had to take a minute to stop by and congratulate you."

I nodded at her and mumbled something that sounded like, "Thanks." Time was running out to speak up and correct the situation once and for all, but as she rushed to give me another quick hug, I couldn't find the words.

"All right, I'll see you both soon," she said. "Maybe y'all can come up for dinner next weekend and we'll celebrate."

"I'm headed to California next week," I said, thankful for the escape.

"Okay, when you're back then."

"I'll walk Mom out," Tristan said as the two of them headed for the door, and I nodded.

I knew I had questions to answer once he came back inside, and I needed a few answers myself.

For the second time that day, my plans for a romantic evening had gone horribly awry.

Chapter 9

Hurt lingered in Tristan's eyes when he came back inside.

"So, I take it you did stop by the theater today, huh? This Danielle lady must have one helluva sales spiel." He held up one hand and cocked his head to the side. "Don't get me wrong. I think it's great. I'm thrilled for you if this is something you're excited to sink your teeth into. I just feel a little, I don't know, blindsided, maybe, to find out from my mother that you met with the mayor today and agreed to be someone's business partner. When were you going to tell me?"

"I didn't *meet* with the mayor. He happened to stop by while I was meeting with Dani, and I didn't agree to be her business partner."

"Okay, well, whatever you're calling it—help me understand how this went down. You drove into town today, met some woman, and decided to be a key investor in her business on the spot?"

"No, it's not like that at all. I'm not investing in the theater. At least, I don't think I am."

Tristan's eyebrows scrunched so close together they almost touched. "What? You don't *think* you are? What does that mean?"

"It means I don't know what I'm doing."

I walked to the sofa and plopped down on it. I'd been so excited to tell him about the theater earlier, but now it looked to be a much different conversation.

"I did stop by the theater this morning, and I met Dani, the woman who is opening it. I think we kind of hit it off—"

"I'd say so if she talked you into giving her money the first time she met you," he said as he came and sat in the chair next to the sofa.

"It's not like that. Dani never asked me for money—"

"So, you just volunteered to invest in her business all on your own? Wow."

I crossed my arms and glared at him. "Are you going to let me tell you what happened, or are you going to continue to interrupt me with your own assumptions? How do you ever get information from a suspect in an interrogation if you do all the talking without taking the time to listen?"

He sat back in the chair and rested his elbow on the armrest, cradling his head in his hand. "Proceed."

I let out an exasperated sigh. "Dani gave me a tour of the theater and told me her plans for renovations. While I was there, the mayor came by and told her about the meeting with the county regarding her grants. He asked if my being there meant that I was coming onboard with the theater, and Dani and I answered that we were discussing it—which, we were, but in a capacity of me being on stage in a play. Nothing at all was said about me investing in the theater."

His eyes narrowed with confusion.

"So, why did the mayor tell my mother you were?"

I shrugged one shoulder. "He must have misunderstood."

"How did you and Dani leave the conversation?"

"She thanked me for stopping by, and I told her I was headed to California next week but would check in on her progress when I got back."

"I don't understand. Where did investing come in? Did Dani misunderstand?"

"No, I don't think so. We never discussed money. I mean, we discussed that she needed funding, but she never asked me about it."

He rubbed the stubble on his chin with his thumb as he considered my words. "Do you think she might have called the mayor after you left and told him you were investing? You know, trying to sweeten the deal and get the grants she wanted?"

I frowned as I considered the idea. "I don't think so. I don't think Dani would do that."

"How do you know what she might do? She sees you come in, and she probably thought she'd hit the jackpot. Or she might have at the very least thought she could name-drop to her advantage to get the city and county to give her the grants."

"I really don't think she would do that. You have a skewed view of people from working with so many criminals. Dani's not like that."

"You were around her, what, a half hour? An hour? How much do you really know about her, babe?"

"I don't know anything about her, but I usually have a good instinct about people using me or trying to capitalize on their association with me. I didn't get that vibe from her at all."

His eyes fixated on a spot next to me on the couch, and I could tell his mental wheels were turning.

"But if you're telling me that you never discussed investing with this woman and it was all a big misunderstanding with the mayor, then why didn't you explain that to Mom?" He looked up and frowned. "You never corrected her or told her it wasn't true."

I didn't have an answer for that. I was still working on understanding it myself, so I figured my best option was to deflect.

"Speaking of your mom, what *issues* of mine have you been discussing with her?"

His frown deepened as he sat back in the chair.

"I haven't been—"

"She said from everything you'd told her about my *issues*. Now, I'm the first to admit I have some, but what was so unbearable that you needed to go behind my back and discuss it with your mother?"

"It's not like that," he said, leaning forward again. "I can assure you I didn't go to Mom complaining about you or telling her you had issues."

"Then why would she say that?"

"Because she sees it! I mean, not that you have…well, what I mean is, um…oh, hell. Look, babe, it's no secret that you've been reluctant to embrace being engaged and that you've had…some qualms, shall we say, about moving to Cedar Creek permanently. It's obvious that it's been a big adjustment for you, and she's a pretty intuitive lady, okay?" As he talked, he stood and walked toward the French doors to look out over the lake. "When Mom heard we were engaged, she wanted to start planning right away. That's her. That's what she does. She was confused as to why you didn't want anyone to know and why you never want to discuss a wedding. She didn't understand why you said they couldn't tell anyone."

I flung my hands out in frustration. "Because I didn't care to have my personal life become a media circus!"

He turned back to look at me. "I know that. I understand that. But I think Mom is used to brides being excited about being engaged, you know? Most people want to shout it from the rooftops. You remember how upset she was in the beginning when you didn't seem to want to do things with the family, and I had to explain to her how you were brought up differently. How commitment's harder for you because of your background. But I didn't say you had *issues.*" He ran his hand through his hair and sighed. "I said you had a different way of looking at life based on your experiences."

I tucked my feet beneath me as he walked back to the couch and sat next to me.

"She's my mom, Sloane. She worries that I'm going to get hurt, and I think she saw your reluctance as some kind of red flag or a sign of trouble in the relationship."

"Does it bother you that we don't tell people we're engaged?"

"No. It doesn't." He laid his hand on my thigh and gave a gentle squeeze. "I get it. And if it did bother me, I would tell *you*, not my mother. Just like I told you when it upset me that you wouldn't commit to living here and making it your home. We talked through it, we worked through it, and that's how I want it to be between us.

Open communication. Which is why I was hurt when I thought you'd decided to make a major investment in this theater without even telling me."

"I fully intended to tell you about meeting Dani and touring the theater. I started to call you when I left there, but I decided I'd rather tell you in person. However, the next time I saw you was when you pulled me over and wrote me a ticket."

He groaned and moved his hand from my thigh as I sat up and turned to face him.

"As you can imagine, I didn't feel much like chatting with you after that, but I still planned to tell you. In fact, I'd planned a romantic evening for the two of us, but then when I got out of the shower, your mom was here and all hell broke loose with this news from the mayor."

He scrunched his eyebrows together again. "I still don't understand why you didn't just tell Mom that it was a misunderstanding."

I stood and walked toward the French doors with a loud exhale. "Because she was so damned excited. She's never looked at me like that before. Hell, my own mother has never looked at me like that before. She seemed so proud and so happy that I didn't want to let her down." I turned to face him, fighting against the lump in my throat. "Look, I'm not stupid. I know things haven't always been rosy between me and your parents, and I'm sure there are plenty of other prospects they'd rather have for a daughter-in-law." An image of picture-perfect-pixie Becky flashed in my head, and I closed my eyes at the thought of Tristan's ex-wife and his parents' affection for her. "For a brief moment in time, I got to see what it felt like to bask in the approval of Rita Rogers. It did something to me, and I couldn't speak up and tell her she was mistaken."

Tristan stood and came to wrap his arms around my waist. "Sloane, my parents love you, but even if they didn't, it doesn't matter. You don't need my parents' approval. I love you, and I choose you. It has nothing to do with them."

"That's sweet of you to say, but it's not realistic. Your family is a close one. What they think does matter to you, and that makes it matter to me. I don't want to spend the rest of our lives together feeling like I don't measure up to what they'd want for their son. I just didn't know investing in a freaking theater was what it would take to get in your mother's good graces."

He held me tighter, stroking my back with his hands as he kissed the top of my head. "I appreciate that you care what they think, but you don't have to jump through any hoops for them. And you definitely don't have to invest in anything. Why didn't you just say something?"

"I don't know. And then when I didn't speak up at first, it became too awkward to say *'Hey, by the way, about that theater…you got it all wrong.'* I would have looked like an idiot." I pushed away from his embrace and walked back to the sofa. "Now I don't know what to do."

"Start with telling Mom the truth. She's going to find out one way or another, especially if this alliance board she's on is giving the theater grants."

"That's the thing, though. If they gave Dani the grants based on me being involved, then if I correct the misunderstanding, Dani might lose the money."

"I'd say that's not your problem." He came to sit next to me on the couch and took my hand in his. "She's the one who opted to start a theater here. She must have known what it would take. If you hadn't walked in today and if the mayor hadn't stopped by while you were there, you wouldn't be involved in her finances at all. You only intended to inquire about auditioning for a play, right?"

"Yeah, I guess."

"You guess?"

"I don't know. After hearing her vision for the place, I kind of would like to be a part of making it happen. You're always telling me that I need to be more involved with the community. If it makes your mother and the mayor this happy, then who knows? Maybe it might make other people happy, too."

"Sloane, you can't invest in a business with some woman you just met to impress my mother and the people in town."

"I'm not doing it to impress anyone. Not really. I believe in the magic of the theater and what it can do for a community. I've told you before how much I loved my theater experience as a teen."

"Just because you love the theater doesn't mean you have to sink your money into one. I'd say it's a risky investment, given that Cedar Creek isn't exactly the culture center of Central Florida. Are there enough people in this town to sustain a theater? How many would actually attend a show?"

"Even if it didn't make any money, a theater would still be beneficial for the town. It provides a place for young people to get connected and involved. It gives a creative outlet to professionals and artistic people trapped in non-artistic jobs. And yes, it gives the residents a chance to experience culture."

"Okay, but even if the idea of a community theater is something you support, you know nothing about this Dani person. You have no idea what kind of businesswoman she is or what her background is. You can't just jump in and invest in something with another person without doing your research. How much are we talking, anyway?"

"I have no idea. Like I said, we didn't discuss money. I know she has some pretty extensive renovations planned, but I have no clue how much she needs or how it would work. I need to talk to my accountant. I'm sure Marc will be able to advise me on how best to go about this."

Tristan stared at me for a moment.

"So, you're really considering doing this? You honestly *want* to invest in this theater?"

I stared out the window toward the lake in the distance as I considered all the changes in my life since I'd met Tristan and moved to Cedar Creek. This was my home. The first home I'd ever really had. I wanted this to be my community. I wanted to fit in, and I wanted the other residents to look at me with something other than contempt. If I was going to live here and make my life here, I wanted it to be the best community it could be. And I'd been sincere when I explained all the reasons I believed a theater would be beneficial.

I drew in a deep breath and turned back to Tristan. "Yes, I do."

He leaned back against the sofa and stared at the ceiling. "I think you need to just bite the bullet and call my mom. Tell her there was some confusion and misunderstanding, and that you're going to be involved with the theater in an acting capacity."

"But what about Dani and the grants? What about the renovations?"

He turned his head to look at me. "I still say that's her problem. It's her responsibility to get this funded. Not yours."

"Even if I'm only going to be a member of the cast there, I want the theater to do well. I want Dani to have what she needs to bring her vision to life and give the theater a chance to win over the people of this community. If I can help her do that, I think I should." I looked down at my watch and stood. "I need to call Marc and see what he says. Then, I want to talk to Dani before the mayor does, if he hasn't already. I don't want her to tell him he misunderstood if I can make this happen."

Chapter 10

I t took a bit of convincing to get Marc on board. Having been my accountant for most of my career, he knew better than anyone my shortcomings in making sound financial decisions, and he shared Tristan's concerns about the viability of a theater venture in Cedar Creek.

Once he'd realized my mind was made up and I was determined to get involved despite his misgivings, he'd reluctantly agreed to handle the matter, but not without muttering under his breath that I was going to drive him into early retirement with a full head of gray hair.

I called Dani right away, excited to offer my assistance and eager to reach her before the mayor did. It went straight to voicemail, and I wondered as I peered through the window into the dark, if perhaps, she was still at the theater working.

"Did you get in touch with Dani?" Tristan asked as I came back into the living room.

"I left her a message to call me back."

He extended his arm in an invitation for me to join him on the sofa, and I wasted no time in accepting, curling up against him as he wrapped his arm around me and hugged me to him with a kiss to the top of my head.

"I know I might have seemed less than enthusiastic before about the theater, but if this is something you want to do, I'll support you every step of the way. I just want you to be sure and do your research before you commit to this, ya know? Check things out before you dive in. I know I'm not telling you anything you don't already know, but people will try to take advantage of you—your status, your money, your fame. You've got a big heart. Don't let that get in the way of common sense, okay?"

I nodded as I nestled in closer.

"I hear ya. I'll have Marc go through everything with a fine-tooth comb. He's a stickler, and I trust him. But I also trust Dani. I get good vibes from her."

"What's Dani's last name? Is she new to town?"

"Ward. She just moved back to this area from Chicago, but she said she has family here. In fact, she said her uncle has a horse farm in Cedar Creek. Doesn't your friend Levi work for Ward Farms?"

He reached up to rub his knuckles across his chin. "Yeah. Well, if she's one of the Wards that makes me feel better. They're a respectable family. Does she have any experience running a theater? Is that what she did in Chicago?"

"No, she was in journalism. TV news, I think."

"Why did she leave Chicago to live in Cedar Creek?"

"She said she moved back because her sister is having a baby."

"Ah. I wonder who her sister is. I'll have to ask Levi and put the puzzle pieces together in my head."

I leaned back away from him and grinned. "Are you gonna open an active investigation into her? Run a background check? What's with all the questions, Deputy?"

"Just trying to do my job. Protecting you."

He pulled me back in closer, and I bit down on my lip and resigned myself to saying what needed to be said.

"Speaking of your job, I'm sorry I was such an ass on the side of the road today. I know I shouldn't have been speeding, and you had every right to pull me over and give me a freaking ticket."

His arm tightened around me as I lifted my face to look up at him. He pressed his lips to my forehead, and then he looked down at me, his gray eyes soft and tender as he stroked my cheek with his thumb.

"I don't want anything to happen to you, babe. I couldn't bear it."

I sighed as I lay my head on his chest. "I'll go the speed limit from now on; I promise. Hell, I have no choice. If I get another ticket, I'm definitely going to jail, and orange is not my color."

"I wasn't sure you'd be here when I got home. You were so pissed I half expected to pull up to a dark house. I was relieved when I saw your car in the garage."

"You didn't act like it. You wouldn't even look at me when I came into the kitchen."

"Just because I was relieved you were here doesn't mean I wasn't still angry with you. I was mad that you put yourself in danger and that you put me in that position of choosing between my feelings for you and what I knew was the right thing to do."

"I'm sorry," I said as I squeezed my arms around his ribs. "I know the law is very important to you."

"So are you," he whispered against my hair.

I sat up and moved to straddle his hips, bending to press my lips against his as he wrapped his arms around me.

The kiss was gentle at first, tender and apologetic. Impatient for more, I licked at his lips with the tip of my tongue, and he accepted the invitation wholeheartedly, burying his hands in my hair to cup the back of my head and pull me in closer.

We melded our mouths together, twisting and turning to go deeper as the passion took over. His lips left mine to nibble and suckle at my neck, and then I rushed to help him as he lifted the hem of my dress to pull it up and over my head. With one swift flick of his thumb, my bra clasp released, and he lifted the lacy garment away from my skin and tossed it aside as my nipples hardened with the sudden exposure.

The gray of his eyes darkened as he cupped my breasts in his hands and dipped to tease them with his tongue.

I closed my eyes with a moan and grabbed his head in my hands, pressing him to me as I lifted my chest, eager for his touch. He kissed his way back up my neck to claim my mouth once more, and then I slid his shirt over his head and leaned forward, reveling in the feel of his bare skin warm against mine.

We made up for the tension of the day with skin-on-skin apologies that had no need for words. Our lovemaking burned frantic and eager in the beginning, but by the time we moved to our bedroom down the hall for the second round, it had slowed to a more tender and poignant pace. Any earlier conflict was forgiven and forgotten as we lay twisted and tangled in the sheets of our bed, breathless and spent in the aftermath of passionate exertion.

Once our hearts had slowed and our breathing had returned to normal, Tristan shifted to his side and nestled his face into my hair. I was on my back, enjoying the weight of his arm across my stomach and the sound of his breathing steady in my ear.

I had begun to doze when I heard his voice, barely above a whisper.

"I tore up the ticket."

"What?" I asked, suddenly alert.

"It wouldn't have stood up in court without a clocked speed."

"You think I would take you to court?"

"I had no idea what you were going to do. Or rather, what you might have your Hollywood lawyers do. You were pretty mad at the time."

"So, you tore it up to keep from losing in court?"

"No," he whispered after a long pause, his voice thick with the need for sleep. "That's not why I tore it up."

I waited for him to explain, but he said no more. He just pulled me closer against him, and then his breathing deepened in slumber.

No longer drowsy, I lay awake in his arms and thought about all the changes in my life since I'd met him.

If anyone had told me before I came to Cedar Creek that I would commit to marrying someone and settling down in a small town, I would have said they didn't know me very well. If they'd told me I'd consider investing in a local business in that same small town, I would have said they were downright crazy.

Yet here I was, engaged to be married and ready to forge ahead with a new business venture in town.

I hoped I wasn't making the financial mistake Marc and Tristan feared, but losing money wasn't what I was most worried about. After all, if the theater failed and I took a hit on my investment, I had future projects lined up that would replace what I lost.

But what if the theater wasn't what failed? What if it was me?

My stomach flipped at the thought of the headlines a performance flop would generate.

Sloane Reid Tanks on Small Stage

Scream Queen's Film Career Exits Stage Right

Sloane Reid Misses Mark in Small Town Production

If I got panned in theater reviews, would that affect my offers in film?

The flip side of that worry was equally as distressing. What if the performance went well and my name being attached drew the publicity that Dani seemed to think it would? Would it bring more unwanted attention for the town, and would they blame me again?

I wanted my involvement to be a positive thing for the community and for Dani, and I had no way of knowing as I waited for sleep to come that my concerns were about to be the least of our problems at the theater.

Chapter 11

When I didn't hear back from Dani in the morning, I assumed it was due to her phone issues and drove into town to talk to her at the theater.

Her car was there, as I expected, and it only took her a moment to come to the door when I knocked.

I smiled and waved as she approached, but her wave back was weak, and her smile seemed half a frown. I thought perhaps she was tired from a late night working, but as she held the door open for me to step inside, the dark circles and puffy bags beneath her red-rimmed eyes made it obvious there was more to her sour expression.

"Hi, Sloane. I got your message, and I'm sorry I haven't called you back."

"It's all right. Are you okay?"

She shrugged as she walked back toward the main auditorium. "It depends on your definition of okay."

I followed her inside the large room, and she pointed to the floor as I entered.

"Watch your step."

A gallon paint can lay on the floor, severely dented and open. An explosion of white paint surrounded it with tentacles seeping out in all directions from the central puddle. Dani knelt and picked up a paint-soaked cloth and scrubbed at a smeared area that she seemed to have been working on before I arrived.

I let my gaze follow the trail of paint to the wall, which was splattered in white beneath a gaping hole.

"What happened?"

She let out a deep sigh as she moved the cloth back and forth across the floor.

"It seems someone chucked this can of paint at the wall hard enough to dent it open."

"Who? Who would do such a thing?"

"Beats me," she said with another sigh.

Another knock came from the front door, and she plopped the cloth back into the bucket and rubbed her wet hands on her jeans. She stepped into the lobby and stopped as she stared at the door, swearing under her breath.

"You've got to be kidding me," she muttered as she moved forward to open the door and let in the deputy on the other side.

It was Seth Donovan, one of Tristan's fellow deputies and good friends.

"I told them it wasn't necessary to send anyone," Dani said as she opened the door.

"Any time someone calls with a possible breaking and entering, we'd prefer to check it out."

"Yeah, well, as I mentioned to the dispatcher, nothing was stolen and there doesn't appear to be any sign of forced entry, so I think it's a non-issue. I shouldn't have called. I was just in a panic when I opened the door and found the paint on the floor, and once I calmed down, I realized it doesn't matter."

"Okay, well, since I'm here, would you mind if I take a look around?"

"Sure. Knock yourself out."

She seemed incredibly tense, her body rigid, and her voice tight with emotion. I thought at first it was due to the vandalism, but as I watched the two of them interact, I realized Seth seemed more tense than I'd ever seen him as well.

His usual easygoing personality and quick wit had disappeared, and he seemed nervous, and ill at ease. Was this his professional persona? Had I only seen him in moments when he was off-duty or in a non-official capacity?

"Where is the spilled paint?"

"In here," she said, leading him into the main auditorium.

He nodded towards me with a polite smile as he walked past.

"Hi, Sloane."

So clipped. So businesslike. So unusual for him.

"Hi, Seth." I stepped back, not wanting to interfere or be in the way.

"Here it is," Dani said, sweeping her hand toward the hole in the wall and the paint on the floor.

Seth knelt beside the paint can and then turned to look up at Dani.

"You told dispatch all the doors were locked when you arrived?"

"Yep."

He stood and looked around before pointing toward the boarded windows.

"Those are the only exterior windows?"

"Yes," Dani said, shoving her hands in the back pocket of her jeans. "Well, except for the bathroom windows, but they're both intact and locked from the inside."

Seth nodded as he peered up at the windows. "The boards were still in place on those windows when you arrived? No sign of entry there?"

"Not that I can tell from down here," Dani said with a cocked eyebrow. "I didn't get a ladder and climb up there to check."

The anger in her voice surprised me, and I hoped Seth would realize it was just the stress of the situation, although I was certain he was accustomed to dealing with people under stress.

"What about the roll-up door?" he asked as he walked toward it.

"The roll-up door has a padlock that's locked. Look, I'm thinking it had to be someone with a key. I called and left a message with the realtor this morning to ask if the locks were changed between leases. If not, it could be anyone."

Seth's brow furrowed as he walked into the center of the room and looked around.

"Even so, why would someone with a key let themselves in to throw a can of paint against a wall?"

Dani shrugged. "I don't know. Kids, maybe?"

"You said nothing else is damaged. If it were kids, I'd expect broken mirrors or some kind of mess made. Spray paint. Even this paint would be smeared or used to write something obscene. Not likely that kids would have access to a key and then let themselves in to do this one thing and leave."

She crossed her arms and shifted her weight in her stance. "Okay, so what's your theory?"

"I don't know, Dani. Have you given a key to any contractors?"

"Steve Abbott has a key, but it's not likely he'd come in during the night and bust a can of paint against the wall."

Seth tapped his fingers against his thigh as he stared at the spilled paint.

"Have you pissed anyone off since you've been back in town?"

"Excuse me?"

He looked up at her and held up a hand in apology. "What I meant was, do you know of anyone who might want to sabotage what you're doing here?"

"I don't think I've made any friends at the power company with my demands for answers on why the lights keep going out, but I don't think you have any suspects there."

Her mention of the lights made Seth and I both look up toward the overhead lamps.

"You're having issues with the lights?" he asked.

Dani groaned. "You know what? This is unnecessary. Whoever did this obviously had a key, and I intend to ask the owner today if I can change the locks, so it's a moot issue. Thank you for your time and diligence, but there's nothing to see here."

She pressed her palm to her forehead and drew in a deep breath, and I worried that she was about to come unglued.

What had her so upset? She seemed to want to brush off the

incident and not want the deputy to investigate, but she also seemed unnerved by it.

Their eyes locked eyes in silence, and the tension in the room became almost unbearable. I had the strangest sensation that I didn't belong, that I was somehow an outsider in a moment that should have been private. The feeling was so strong that I almost turned to go back to the lobby, but then Seth exhaled with a loud huff and gave a nod in Dani's direction.

"Then I'll be on my way. Give us a call if anything else happens or if you find anything out of the ordinary."

She nodded and rubbed her hands together, like she was eager for him to be gone.

He walked toward her and stopped a few inches away, his eyes still locked with hers and his voice quiet and low when he spoke. Almost tender.

"I heard you were back in town."

"I heard you became a deputy."

The air felt so charged I feared it would crackle with electricity and send sparks shooting across the room. It was obvious these two knew each other on a deeper level, and I wondered how much of the tension I'd sensed had nothing to do with spilled paint.

Seth smiled then, a tentative half-smile that didn't reach his eyes.

"I hope it goes well with the theater. I've never wanted anything other than happiness for you."

With a tip of his hat toward her and another tip toward me with a smile, he left.

Dani stood rooted in place, her eyes closed as two large tears rolled down her cheeks.

I didn't know what to say or what to do. My presence felt intrusive, but it felt wrong to leave her.

"Can you make sure he's gone?" she whispered.

"Yeah, sure."

I went to the front door and watched his car leave the parking lot, and then I came back inside to find Dani wiping at her eyes with the hem of her shirt.

"He's gone."

"Aargh. Of all the people they could have sent."

"Are you okay?"

She looked at me with tear-filled eyes and shook her head as she walked into the lobby and retrieved a tissue from the bathroom.

"No, but I will be."

"I take it you guys knew each other from when you lived here before?"

"Yeah." She dabbed at her eyes and groaned. "I knew I'd run into him eventually. Cedar Creek's not that big, so it was inevitable. Just my luck that the first time I see him I'm covered in paint with no make-up and swollen eyes from crying all night. That's not how I pictured it happening. If you're gonna run into an ex-boyfriend, you want to look like a million bucks, right?"

"You don't look bad," I said, smiling when she glared at me. "Okay, woman-to-woman, you can tell you've been crying, but you don't look...*horrible*. Besides, you have every right to look upset. Someone broke into your building."

"That's not why I'm upset. I mean, obviously, I'm not thrilled about it, and I do wish I could know for sure who it was, but in the grand scheme of things, it doesn't even matter." She took in a ragged breath and folded the tissue into a neat square. "I'm not going to be able to open the theater, Sloane. My funding fell through, and I don't have a path forward."

Her voice broke as she unfolded the tissue and dabbed at her eyes again.

"Wait. Dani, did you talk to the mayor?"

"No," she said as she walked past me and hoisted herself up to sit on the concession counter. "He left me a voicemail yesterday afternoon, but I didn't get the message until I'd left the theater, and his office was closed when I called back. It doesn't matter anyway. I can't afford to open."

I hesitated. It wasn't my place to let her know they'd voted to approve her grants, but I hated to see her so upset.

"I probably shouldn't tell you this, but you got approved. They're gonna give you the grants."

Dani looked at me with a smile that wasn't nearly as enthusiastic as I'd expected. "How do you know?"

I twisted my lips together, reluctant to reveal my source but seeing no way around it.

"Tristan's mom is chair of the Arts Alliance. She stopped by last night and said that they had approved you." I forged ahead, needing to tell her the rest since I'd already spilled the beans. "There is one thing, though. Somehow, the mayor got the idea from seeing the two of us together that I would be investing in the theater."

"What?" Dani asked, her forehead wrinkled in confusion.

"Yeah, not sure how that transpired, but listen. I admire what you're trying to accomplish here, and I very much want to help you get this venture off the ground and on its way. So, if you'd be willing to have me as an investor, I'm in."

She smiled as she looked down at her hands, and when she looked back up at me, the tears had returned to her eyes.

"That's truly kind of you, and I appreciate the offer. If you had told me this yesterday, I would have been overjoyed and welcomed you with open arms. Unfortunately, I got some bad news last night, and this project is not happening. I intended to call the mayor and let him know this morning, but then I came in to the paint issue and got sidetracked."

"What do you mean it's not happening? You've got the grants, and I'm willing to help fund it."

She drew in a deep breath and looked up at the ceiling, blinking back her tears before looking back to me.

"I had intended to finance this endeavor with the proceeds from selling my house in Chicago and what I had left in savings after the move. I found out last night that those funds will not be available. I'm shutting everything down. I left a message for Steve on my way in this morning so he didn't waste time with his crew coming, and when I talk to the realtor today, I'm going to ask how to break the lease."

I stared at her, stunned.

Until that moment, I hadn't realized how excited I was about the theater and my potential involvement. I felt crushed and disappointed, but what I felt was nothing compared to the pain in Dani's eyes.

"Undoubtedly, we can work this out," I said, walking toward her. "If the sale on your house fell through, I'm sure it's only a matter of time until you get another offer. How much are we talking to get the renovations done? I can talk to my accountant."

Dani shook her head as she slid off the counter. "I don't want to involve anyone else in my mess. Thank you, Sloane. I appreciate it; I really do. I thought I could escape. I thought I could come back home and find myself." Her tears flowed, and she let them. "I can't believe I did this to my life."

It was obvious her turmoil ran deeper than money issues and vandals who spilled paint. I wished that we knew each other better so I would know if I should hug her, press her to talk, or excuse myself and leave her alone. I'd never been comfortable watching other people in pain, and I felt helpless not knowing what was going on or what she needed.

"Dani?" I hesitated, trying to find the right words when I had no idea what to say. "I know we don't know each other very well, but I feel like we made a connection yesterday. I don't know what all you're trying to escape, but I do know what it's like to want to get away from your life so you can find yourself. That's how I ended up in Cedar Creek. I'm here if you need to talk, and I can go if you need to be alone."

"I wish I could talk. I really do. My parents and my sister are the only ones who know anything that's going on, and even they don't know about last night yet. I have to be careful what I say."

Now my curiosity threatened to overtake my concern. What on earth was she trying to escape that she couldn't talk about?

"Are you okay, Dani? Are you in danger?"

She shrugged with a small shake of her head. "I don't think so. I don't know. I shouldn't say any more."

I went to her and laid my hand on her arm and squeezed. "Dani, Tristan can help you. We can go to him and tell him whatever you're dealing with, and I'm sure he can think of something to do."

She let out a laugh tinged with more hopelessness than humor. "There's nothing that Tristan can do that the FBI can't."

"The FBI?"

She looked at me for a moment, her eyes darting back and forth as they searched mine, and then she pressed her lips together and said, "Screw it. This is all going to be in the papers anyway. It's not like I could keep it a secret if anyone really wanted to know. I need some coffee, though. Can we get outta here?"

Chapter 12

Dani lived only a couple of blocks from the theater on another side street of Cedar Creek I'd never visited. It was a small clapboard house, painted bright yellow with white trim and a white spindled porch spanning the front. Flower boxes hung off the porch railing with petunias in vivid colors of fuchsia, purple, and pink.

"This is so charming," I said as I followed her up the porch steps. "It's like something out of a movie set in a different time."

"It was my grandmother's house," Dani said as she unlocked the door and held it open for me to step inside. "My cousin had been living here since Gran passed, but he moved to Orlando to be closer to his job pretty soon after I came back home. It's small, but it's plenty big for just me."

She led me through the house to the kitchen in the back where light poured in from large windows and shone onto bright yellow walls. She pulled out a chair at the round wooden table and indicated that I should sit as she went to the counter to make the coffee.

"I don't know if I have any cream," she said as she opened the fridge and peered inside. "Ah, yes, there's a little container here. Cross your fingers that it's not expired."

She read the date on the carton and frowned, and then she opened it and took a sniff.

"It smells fine. You wanna smell it?"

The thought of smelling questionable creamer turned my stomach, and I frowned. "It's okay. I can drink it black."

"I still can't believe that's how I saw Seth. It shouldn't matter, should it? That was so many years ago. Back then, everyone was certain we'd get married. Even us." She shook her head as she chuckled. "The problem was I envisioned us getting hitched and leaving Cedar Creek behind to conquer the world. We'd talked about that all through high school and even most of the way through college. As it got closer to reality, Seth began to waver, though. The more I itched to go, the more he wanted to stay."

She stared at the coffee streaming into the pot, her arms crossed as she leaned against the counter.

"I knew it scared him to leave his parents behind, to leave everything behind. I guess I thought that if I went, he'd follow. I was certain he loved me. I never considered that he'd actually choose Cedar Creek over me. So, I took off to Chicago, and he stayed here." She rubbed her temples and then pulled the elastic band from her hair, shaking it free from its ponytail. "I was devastated, but it made me more determined than ever to make it away from here."

"So, is today the first time you've seen him since you left?"

She nodded and then pulled her hair back up and twisted the band back in place. "Yep. Once I left, I stayed gone. I didn't come back for holidays. I didn't come back for birthdays. I flew in the day before my grandma's funeral and flew out the day after. I turned my back on my family and my hometown in order to prove that I could. To prove that my life existed elsewhere, not here."

The coffeemaker chimed, and she pulled two mugs from the cabinet and poured the steaming liquid into them.

"I put everything into my career, and it paid off. I went up through the ranks at the station in record time, and I loved my life. I loved my job, my city, my local restaurants, and even my social life, as limited as it was to my work colleagues and people I met at yoga.

I told myself I didn't have time to date, which was true, but it was more than that. I knew that when you love someone, you're more likely to compromise your own goals for them, and I wasn't willing to do that."

She set a coffee mug in front of me and took a seat at the table.

"But then I met Victor." She rolled her eyes with a slight shake of her head. "I'd never been swept off my feet before. Even with Seth, my first love, we grew up together. We'd known each other since kindergarten, and somewhere along the way a friendship with a strong attraction developed into more as we became teens and hormones hit. We were just always together and that seemed natural and safe. With Victor, it was like I'd been picked up by a tornado and carried away. My heart, my emotions, my body—I was all in from the first time I laid eyes on him. Has that ever happened to you?"

I shrugged as I sipped my coffee. "Not really. I mean, I've definitely never felt what I have with Tristan before. I was attracted to him from the start, but he tried to arrest me the first time we met, so I didn't really have love on my mind at the time."

Dani grinned. "That's just it, though. I didn't have love anywhere in my plan when I met Victor. I had just bought an older house in a newly reimagined neighborhood, and it needed extensive renovations. I called a contractor based on a friend's recommendation, and Victor showed up. I literally opened my front door, saw him standing there, and immediately felt something like a lightning bolt. I don't know how to describe it. We locked eyes, and I thought to myself that I was going to spend the rest of my life in his arms. It sounds like some stupid movie cliché, I know. It was unlike anything I'd ever experienced. It was cosmic, chemical, an other-worldly thing."

"So, what happened?" I asked, eager to hear the rest of the story even though her present circumstances made it obvious there wasn't a happy ending.

A quiet stillness hung over us as she stared unfocused toward the window, and I wondered if perhaps she didn't want to say more.

But then she looked back at me, and I winced at the pain in her eyes.

"What happened? Insanity happened. We sat on my back deck and talked until four in the morning that first night. The next night, he slept over, and he never left. It was the first time I'd ever dreaded going into work and counted down the hours until I could go home. We spent every minute we could together, and it was never enough. We always wanted more. Two weeks to the day after we met, we went to the courthouse and got married."

My eyes widened in surprise, and I used drinking my coffee as a shield to mask my shock.

"I know," Dani said with a weak smile. "I realize how crazy that sounds. How crazy it was. But at the time, it seemed right. I don't know how to explain it, Sloane. I don't even understand it myself. I just knew in my heart that it was right." She looked down and frowned. "At least, I thought it was."

It was hard for me to conceive making that kind of decision so hastily. Tristan and I had been together a year before we got engaged, and in the year that had followed, I still wasn't ready to discuss taking the next step and making it official. I loved him, and I wanted to spend my life with him, but getting married and being legally bound still felt suffocating to me at times, and I didn't know if I'd ever feel at ease with it.

"My parents went ballistic," Dani said as she traced the rim of her mug with her index finger. "I'd already kind of solidified my title as the black sheep of the family for moving away and never coming home for visits. But this—" she raised her eyebrows and blew out a whistle "—this put my mother over the edge. The idea of me meeting someone and getting married without even telling them was more than she could handle. The fact that I'd only known him two weeks and they'd never met him only added insult to injury. If only it could have all worked out, then perhaps at some point they could have forgiven me, you know? If it had been the love for the ages that I thought it was, then maybe eventually they would have accepted my choice."

She took a deep swig of her coffee, and when she put the cup back down, the tears had returned to her eyes.

"We'd been married two months when they arrested him. It was a Saturday morning, and he was scrambling eggs to make me breakfast in bed. The eggs burned on the stove while they shoved him face down on the new carpet in the living room and handcuffed him. I was standing in the snow on the front lawn in nothing but thin robe as they put him in the back of the squad car and drove him away. He kept saying that he loved me over and over again as they led him out my house."

"What did they arrest him for?"

She looked away and swiped at the tears with the back of her hand. "It turns out that my funny, kind, sensitive, romantic, well-spoken, well-traveled, highly-educated, teddy bear of a husband was a part of the Chicago Outfit, one of the largest and most powerful crime syndicates in American history."

I gasped and my mouth dropped open. "What?"

"Yeah, as you can imagine, it came as quite a shock to me, too. I'd been a reporter, for Christ's sake. I lived and breathed the news in Chicago, and yet I saw nothing. I knew nothing. I didn't even have a suspicion. The past two years since he was arrested have been hell. Getting myself untangled has been damned near impossible. The divorce was delayed as he moved through the court system and my association with him was put under a magnifying glass. I had to prove as best I could with no way to do so that I didn't know anything and that I wasn't involved in any way. As it continued to play out, my upper management at the station suggested it might be best that we do a severance rather than me produce daily segments about my own husband as his case went to trial."

"Holy shit."

She smiled, a genuine smile though it held pain. "I know, right? It's a lot to take in. In a matter of months, I went from single and successful, to blissfully married, to divorced and under suspicion, and then unemployed. As soon as I was cleared to leave the area, I came home with my tail between my legs, my heart and my pride shattered. Thank God my family welcomed me back. For the first month, month and a half, I stayed cocooned in my sister's guest bedroom like it was a tomb, and there were days that I honestly think I would have rather died than face reality. But eventually, I emerged, and I decided to find my next chapter."

"With the theater."

"Yep," she said with a nod. "It was something I always wanted to do, and if I was going to reinvent myself, I needed to let go of everything I'd built in Chicago and start anew. Luckily, the neighborhood where I lived there had thrived, and with the renovations, the house appraised at far above what I had paid for it. I put it on the market, figuring that with what I made with the sale and what I had in savings combined with the severance, I had enough to get the theater started and self-finance it for at least the first season, maybe more."

Her voice had grown shaky, and I reached to put my hand over hers, trying to offer whatever comfort and support I could.

"It's a seller's market right now," she said as she turned her hand to hold mine. "I got a contract on the house within days of listing it. I should have waited until the sale was final, but I was just so eager to get started. I wanted something to look forward to, something I could get out of bed for and throw myself into. So, I went ahead and used savings to secure the lease and pay Steve. I applied for every grant I could find, and I figured when the house closed and that money came through, I'd be golden to finish the theater renovations and get the season started."

"But then something happened last night?"

She nodded. "When Victor was first arrested, they combed through my bank statements and looked at everything to determine where our assets were linked. There was some confusion and uncertainty regarding the house. I had purchased it prior to our marriage, but Victor had completed some of the renovations through his uncle's contracting company, which was, of course, under scrutiny. It was finally determined that it was mine, free and clear, and I was able to sell it outright." She drew in a deep breath, and her hand trembled in mine. "But those were state charges. Now, new charges have been filed against Victor. Federal charges. My attorney said they're trying to put more pressure on Victor. They want him to talk, to turn. They've upped the ante, and in the process, they've frozen all my assets and the sale of the house."

"Can they do that?"

"Temporarily, yes. The federal charges are linked to some kind of mob statute; I think it's called RICO, or something like that. My attorney says it gives the feds more leeway, but he assures me that it will all be cleared again once they've completed their investigations. That house was mine. Our banking and our finances were never combined. But evidently, the federal powers are pretty broad in what they can freeze in these types of organized crime cases, and my attorney says that with the current backlog in federal courts, I could be looking at a lengthy delay. I'll probably have to return to Chicago to meet with federal prosecutors. I feel like Pacino in that last Godfather film. Just when I thought I was out, they're pulling me back in."

"Dani, I'm so sorry. I don't know what to say."

She pulled her hand from mine and wiped away her tears. "There's nothing to say. I was a foolish woman. I let my heart run wild, and I threw caution to the wind. I unknowingly invited a murderer in my home and in my bed. I'm lucky to be alive. I'm lucky that no one in my family has been harmed."

"Do you ever worry that…well, that you might still be in danger?"

She bit down on her lip and looked away from me toward the windows.

"When it all first happened, I was terrified. I couldn't sleep. I constantly looked over my shoulder, and I jumped every time someone came into a room. I was certain for a while I was being followed, and I didn't know if it was the mafia or the feds or who it might be. It's gotten better since I came here. I haven't noticed anyone strange watching me or seen any unfamiliar car lurking."

I knew enough from my own experience with being pursued and watched how uncomfortable that could be, and people were only after me for a photo or a tidbit of gossip. Even with the rare encounters I'd had with overzealous fans, I couldn't imagine the fear

Dani must feel from the very real possibility that someone might aim to do her harm or even kill her.

"How can you stand to stay in this house alone? Or be at the theater alone? You mentioned you've been up there at night before."

She shrugged and looked down at her hands. "After a while, I relaxed. I let down my guard, I guess. Cedar Creek seems worlds away from everything that happened in Chicago. I figured everyone involved decided I'm a non-issue. I just wish I—" With an almost imperceptible shake of her head, she looked up at me with a smile. "Do you want more coffee?"

"No, thanks," I said as she took my mug and placed it in the sink with hers. I wondered what she had started to say and why she changed her mind. "Have you talked to Victor? You know, since—"

"No. Not at all. My attorney advised against it." She stood at the sink staring out the window above it. "It was like someone died and I wasn't even allowed to grieve. The person I loved, the man I married, was there one moment and gone forever the next. I don't know that he ever really existed. I don't even know who Victor is. There's no way to know how much of what he told me, what he presented himself as, was even true. It was suggested that he might have been trying to get close to me to have access to our news sources. To sniff out a mole. I don't know."

She took a deep breath and blew it out as she crossed her arms.

"I thought I had put this all behind me. I felt like I was finally able to breathe again. This theater was my lifeline. I was throwing everything I had into it, and it was my light at the end of the tunnel, my second chance. It was also a way for me to give back and somehow redeem myself. I don't know what I'll do now that it's gone."

I stood and went to her.

"It doesn't have to be gone. Let me help you. You've got the county grants and the city grants, and I can fund whatever is needed until you get everything sorted."

"Thank you, Sloane, but I have no idea how long that might be. It could even be years from what my attorney says. Federal cases move slowly."

"It doesn't matter. It's not like I need the money back in a certain time frame. How much money are we talking? One hundred grand? Two hundred grand? I don't say this to brag, but I make ridiculously good money, and I have several projects lined up that will pay very well. My living expenses have been dramatically reduced since I moved here where there's nothing to do. I can afford to help you. Please let me."

"I don't want to involve anyone else in this chaos I brought on myself."

"You're not. You're allowing me to be part of bringing the arts to Cedar Creek. It would mean a lot to me. Besides, my life has always been chaos. It's kind of the norm for me."

Dani bit down on her lip as she turned to face me, and I could tell that she was considering my offer.

"I don't know how that would work legally," she said. "I don't know if I'm able to accept a loan like this."

"Well, that's what we have attorneys for. They can figure all that out."

She started to smile, and then it faltered.

"Are you sure you want to do this? You want to go into business with me and get involved financially, knowing that I have the poorest judgment of anyone on the planet?"

I smiled at her and cocked my head to the side. "Yeah, I would. Making rash and reckless financial decisions is nothing new for me, but I am normally a surprisingly good judge of character. I think you're okay, Dani, and I'd love to bring this theater to Cedar Creek with you."

Chapter 13

W e left it to the attorneys and accountants to work out all the details, and by the time I returned from a month of reshoots, interviews, and photo calls in L.A., the abandoned building had been transformed.

The exterior had been painted a gleaming white, and the landscape beds had been weeded, replanted, and filled with mulch.

The ticket booth's frame had been built on the front of the building, the interior walls of the reception area had been freshly painted, and the concession counter had a new glass case in its center.

"Wow!" I exclaimed as Dani led me into the main room, which now looked more like a theater *house*. The stage had been built with wings on either side leading back to the newly-constructed green room, and three men were installing the stage's wood flooring. "It's really coming along. I can't believe how much you've gotten done since I left."

"We've had a couple of bumps and hiccups, but we're actually a bit ahead of schedule. When does that ever happen with construction? It's amazing what you can get done with proper funding. I can't thank you enough for your help."

"I'm happy to do it."

"The electrician will be here this afternoon to finish running the new wiring, and soon they'll finish installing the lighting. The walls in here will be painted black. Oh, and the ceiling," she said, pointing upward. "I met with a guy yesterday to determine what we need to insulate the ceiling and help with acoustics."

I looked up at the ceiling and gave a wary glance at the overhead lights.

"Did you figure out what was causing the lights to blink?"

Dani frowned and shook her head. "No, but they've been on for two weeks steady without so much as a flicker, so here's hoping they'll stay on. The power company never could find anything, and we've had three different electricians inspect the building. They're all stumped."

"If they can't find a cause, then we don't know that it won't happen again, maybe with a full house."

"You're right, but there's nothing I can do if the professionals are telling me everything checks out. Right now, they're on, and all I can do is hope they stay on."

I pointed toward the back wall of the stage, which was painted in a forest scene with varying shades of deep greens and blacks. "Who painted the back mural?"

"I did that," she said with a blush. "I get bored standing around watching all these guys work, so I decided I'd try my hand at doing a backdrop."

"Wow." I leaned back with a dramatic nod and an appreciative smile. "I'm impressed."

"Yeah, well, if you get closer, you can see all my mistakes, but I think from here it will be fine once the lights are dimmed."

"So, does this mean you've decided on a play if you're already creating the set?"

Dani's eyes widened, and her smile filled her face. "Did I not tell you? I thought I did. I'd been going back and forth, but I decided I'm just gonna be all nostalgic and go with my favorite."

"Which is?"

"*A Midsummer Night's Dream.*" Her tone and incredulous expression indicated she found it ridiculous that I didn't already know.

I bit down on my lip, wondering how to tell her I hated Shakespeare. That revelation never went over well with other stage actors.

"You look disappointed," she said, her smile fading. "Do you have something against *Midsummer Night's?*"

"No. I've never seen it actually."

"What?" Now her eyes and her mouth were both open wide with disbelief. "Shut up! You're kidding me. You've never—You've got to be kidding me. It's like Shakespeare's greatest play."

"Yeah, well, I hate to admit this, but I've never been a huge fan of the Bard."

She stepped back and put her hand on her chest in dramatic shock. "What is this blasphemy? You must be joking."

I shrugged with a grin. "I've just never gotten into his works."

"We must rectify this," Dani said, her voice and her eyes solemn. "We must correct this travesty. If you've never seen Midsummer Night's, then I'm guessing you never read it either?"

"Definitely not."

"Trust me," Dani said with a wink. "I will teach you to love Shakespeare. I will consider it my personal mission in life."

The spark flashed in her eyes as her grin widened, and I couldn't help but smile in response.

Suddenly, a loud crash clattered behind the green room wall, and I followed Dani as she headed toward the sound.

The construction foreman who had been there the day I met Dani was standing in the green room with his hands on his hips, staring down at a toolbox upturned on the floor with its contents scattered across the cement.

"It happened again," he said. "No one was anywhere near it, and after the last time, I made sure it was in the center of the table and closed. No way in hell that thing just fell over and opened up on its own. This is getting out of hand. We can't work under these conditions."

"C'mon, Steve," Dani groaned. "Not you, too. You're buying into this stuff now?"

Steve removed his cap and scratched his head. "I'm not inclined to, but damned if I can explain this. Can you?"

She bent and picked up a hammer, turning it over in her hand before laying it on the table. "Just because I can't think of a reasonable explanation doesn't mean there's not one. There has to be one."

Steve plopped the hat back onto his head. "I might have agreed with you at first, but you have to admit, something's going on here. My guys are getting antsy, Ms. Ward. I've had a couple who already refuse to come back inside the building, and the rest of them are on the verge of walking. I understand why you don't want to consider the possibility that this is all supernatural, but I think it's time to accept you have a ghost."

"A ghost?" I asked, immediately recalling Holden's warnings. I'd pretty much pushed that conversation from my mind in my excitement to get involved with the theater and with Dani. But had Holden been right? Was the building haunted? I gave a wary glance around the room, not too keen to find out first-hand what the answer might be.

Dani frowned as Steve's eyes widened in recognition.

"Hey, aren't you—"

"Sloane Reid," Dani said, her voice clipped with frustration. "Yes. She is." She waved her hand from one of us to the other in introduction. "Sloane Reid, Steve Abbott. Sloane is my business partner, or at least she was, before you made her think we have a ghost."

Steve ignored her admonishment and thrust his hand out to shake mine. "I thought that was you the first day you were here. The lights went out before I could get a good look then, but now that I see you close up, there's no doubt. Well, I guess if you have a ghost, there's no one better to have around than a ghost slayer."

"Um, I'm not actually a ghost slayer," I said, unable to tell if he was kidding. "I just played one on film. Why do you think we have a ghost?"

Dani groaned. "We don't have a ghost. I don't believe in ghosts. There has to be a logical explanation for all this."

I tried to ignore Steve's grinning stare and focused my attention on Dani. "All what? What's going on?"

"Nothing." She ran her hands through her hair with another sigh. "Nothing's going on. Just imaginations running wild."

"Excuse me?" Steve asked with his arms spread wide. "I didn't imagine my tools being scattered all over the floor, and my crew hasn't imagined everything else that's flown off counters and tables. They also haven't imagined that toilet back there flushing with no one near it, or the lights going off and on for no damned reason at all. And maybe a guy misplaces a tool every now and then, but when things are constantly going missing and found in other places that make no sense, it's damned unsettling. You can't say this is all our imagination."

"I'm sorry, Steve. I didn't mean anything against you or your crew. They've been amazing, and I know there have been difficult circumstances, but to say that it's something supernatural is a leap I'm not prepared to make."

Steve crossed his arms over his chest and raised an eyebrow. "What about the can of paint thrown against the wall in a building that was locked up tight? What about the whiskey?"

Dani pressed her hand to her forehead and closed her eyes. "Someone must have drunk it."

"Yeah," Steve said with a wry grin. "The ghost."

"Wait, what happened with the whiskey?" I asked, still trying to wrap my head around the other incidents Steve had mentioned.

Dani shot a stern look at Steve and then looked back at me. "I left a nearly-full bottle of whiskey here one night, and when I came back the next morning, it was empty. Not a drop left."

"She thought perhaps someone from my crew got into it, but none of my guys have access to this building after we leave for the day, and it was locked, same as when the paint spilled."

"Someone had to open it," Dani said, her chin lifted with defiance. "There was no sign of it being spilled, and it was exactly where I left it. Someone drank that whiskey."

Steve's grin disappeared. "I asked every one of my guys, and they said it wasn't them. I believe them."

"Well, that doesn't mean no one else was in here. I still say it's possible someone else has a key. The realtor assured me the locks were changed before my lease began, but the fact remains that someone has gotten in here twice that we know of."

Steve chuckled. "Right. And this person with a key comes in after we all leave and doesn't steal anything of value like tools or lighting equipment. They just move stuff, hide stuff, throw around paint, and drink your whiskey? Not likely."

"Much more likely than a ghost," Dani said. "It's probably teenagers."

"Look, Ms. Ward, some of these men I've known all my life. Strong men. Tough men. These aren't folks who spook easily, okay? When they tell me they feel like they're not alone or they feel like they're being watched, I gotta think they're telling me the truth."

The hairs on the back of my neck stood up as I recalled experiencing that sensation while standing beneath the office window.

Dani sighed and squared her shoulders as she crossed her arms. "I'm not saying they're not telling the truth. Maybe they think they feel something; I don't know. All I know is I've been here working by myself at all hours of the day and night, and I haven't once felt anything unusual. There are no such things as ghosts. There has to be a reasonable explanation for everything that has happened."

"Yeah, you keep telling yourself that," Steve said as he bent to pick up his tools. "And when you can't find a crew to work in this place, see how that works out for ya. Or better yet, wait until you have the seats all filled with paying guests and something comes flying off the stage at their heads. See how that goes over!"

"This is ludicrous." Dani spun on her heel and left the room, and I nodded to Steve and followed her. She turned to face me once we were in the reception area.

"Can you believe this? Grown-ass men not wanting to work because they think there's a ghost watching them. Have you ever heard anything so ridiculous?"

I bit down on my lip, wondering if it would help anything for me to speak up. She wouldn't give any credence to local rumors; of that I was sure. I was wary of admitting I'd had my own encounter of sorts in the building, though, and I wasn't about to tell her I had a close relationship with a teenage ghost.

I understood her mindset. Until I'd met Chelsea, I'd never believed in ghosts, and I'd been skeptical of anyone who did. I needed to get Dani to accept the possibility of supernatural activity. But how?

"Okay," I said, trying to figure out a tactic. "You said there was a reasonable explanation for everything that's happened, right?"

She nodded. "There has to be. Ghosts don't exist."

"So, then we just need to prove that to Steve and his crew. Let's show them the explanations. Now, the lights, you said you haven't been able to find a reason that they're flickering."

"But they've stopped."

"Right. But what about the toilet? Steve said it's flushing?"

She pushed herself up to sit on the counter and exhaled a sigh. "Yes. The men's room in the back flushes randomly on its own. I had a plumber come out and take a look at it, but he couldn't figure out why." She looked up at me and arched an eyebrow. "That doesn't mean there's not an explanation, though. It didn't happen while he was here, so he wasn't able to replicate it and determine a cause."

"And what about the stuff flying off tables and counters? I remember those bags falling the first time I was here. I wasn't anywhere near them."

"I had put them on the counter haphazardly, though." Her tone was defensive, and defiance flashed in her eyes. "I just piled them up there. They probably shifted."

"Okay, that's reasonable. What about Steve's toolbox and the other things he mentioned falling or disappearing? He said he put the toolbox in the center of the table and made sure it was secure."

Dani's eyes narrowed, and she tilted her head to one side.

"Whose side are you on here?"

"I'm not on any side. I'm just trying to reason through things with you to determine if maybe the answer could be supernatural."

Her mouth dropped open, and her eyes widened. "Please don't tell me you believe in ghosts."

I hesitated, still uncertain of how much I wanted to reveal about my own experiences.

"I, um, well, I believe there is a supernatural world. I didn't for most of my life, but then something happened that changed my perspective."

Her frown was a mixture of incredulity, doubt, and disappointment.

"What? You saw a ghost?"

I chose not to answer the question directly.

"Let's just say what I experienced made me believe."

"Well, I've certainly never had an experience like that, and I've been in this building more than anyone on Steve's crew. Hell, I've even been in here alone at night when the lights went out, and I didn't see any ghosts."

"Dani, I know it sounds crazy, but have you considered that maybe you can't sense the ghost, but others can?"

"Oh, so now there's a discriminating ghost who picks and chooses who he haunts?" She rolled her eyes.

I sighed as I searched for words. "I think some people are more sensitive to a supernatural presence than others, and sometimes, for reasons I have no idea how to explain, a spirit may be able to communicate with one person or make themselves known to someone even when other people in the same room have no idea they're there."

She held up both hands with a quick shake of her head, as though she was rejecting even the mention of the idea. "You're telling me you think there's a ghost here?"

I shrugged and tried to smile. "It would explain a lot of things."

"Yeah, and it would leave a lot of other things in need of explanation. Like how it's possible, for instance. There are no such things as ghosts. I don't for one moment believe that there's a ghost in this building, or anywhere else, for that matter. There has to be a reasonable explanation. There has to be!"

Behind me, the door to the main room slammed shut, and I let out a little scream at the shock of the unexpected sound.

"What about that?" I asked, spinning to point toward the door. "How is there a reasonable explanation for that?"

"Easy. Steve or one of the crew probably opened a door in the back of the building, causing a draft, which pulled the door closed."

It was no use. Dani wasn't going to budge unless she had an encounter with a ghost that left no room for doubt. Luckily, I knew a ghost who might be willing to help. I just wasn't sure I wanted anyone else to know about her.

Chapter 14

"How's the theater coming along since you left?" Tristan asked that night when he got home with dinner.

"Great. Dani's ahead of schedule with the renovations, she's chosen an opening show, and she has a ghost she doesn't believe in who's about to run off her construction crew. But hey, other than that, great."

He set his take-out container on the counter and pulled a plate from the cabinet. "What do you mean she has a ghost?"

"Evidently, Holden was right about the place being haunted. Remember I told you about the lights going off? Well, that stopped, but toolboxes are being dumped on the floor and the construction guys keep having stuff knocked off tables or moved while they're trying to work. Oh, and evidently, he has a taste for whiskey."

Tristan lifted an eyebrow. "Who? The ghost? The ghost drinks whiskey?"

I sighed as I pulled my salad container from the restaurant bag. "I don't think so. I mean, how the hell would he? But Dani left a full bottle of whiskey at the theater, and the next morning it was gone. The whiskey, not the bottle."

"Sounds like one of the workers has a taste for alcohol."

"Steve, the guy running the crew, swore it wasn't any of his people. He's threatening not to come back unless Dani gets rid of the ghost, and I don't see how that would be possible even if she did believe there's a ghost. Which, she doesn't."

Tristan carried his plate to the table and pulled out a chair for me. "Have you seen anything while you're there? Shimmers? Lights? Whatever it is you see when Chelsea's around?"

I shook my head as I sat. "No, and I'm okay with that. I don't want to go around seeing other dead people. Chelsea is, well, Chelsea. I don't mind seeing her. But I did feel like I was being watched that first day I was at the theater."

Chill bumps rippled across my skin at the memory.

"Maybe you should ask Chelsea to take a look around," he said. "See if she can tell this ghost to lay off the antics."

"Oh, I wouldn't do that. Don't you remember how freaked out she was when I asked her to go to Rachel's with me to see if Vincent's ghost was real? Besides, I'm not sure what we're dealing with, so I wouldn't want to involve Chelsea."

"You think it's a bad ghost?"

I shrugged. "I don't know. Bad ghost. Good ghost. Who knows? I only know that he's causing Dani problems that she doesn't need."

Tristan wiped the barbecue sauce from his fingers onto the napkin. "I've heard before that the place was haunted, but I figured it was just talk."

"Yeah, well, evidently there's some truth to it. Holden said it was the guy who owned the auto repair shop, right? It's definitely male because he keeps flushing the toilet in the men's bathroom. Never the ladies' room."

"Ah, a urinating spirit who drinks. The worst kind." He grinned at his own joke.

"Very funny."

"What's Dani going to do?"

I dipped my fork into the salad dressing and then stabbed a tomato slice and a piece of cucumber.

"I don't know. She keeps saying there must be a reasonable

explanation for everything that's happening, even though she can't come up with one."

"Maybe you should convince her that ghosts are real," he said before biting into another piece of chicken.

"I was thinking to do just that. Bring her over here and take her out on the deck and have Chelsea do some tricks. Dani is gonna be a tough sell, though. She hasn't been the least bit fazed by anything that's happened at the theater."

"I think I was a tough sell, but the two of you convinced me. Of course, that would mean confessing to someone else that one of your closest friends is a ghost. Right now, that info's pretty well contained. Maybe you should keep it that way."

I popped a cherry tomato in my mouth and mulled over the possible repercussions.

"I think I can trust Dani," I said after some consideration. "She's shared some pretty personal stuff with me about her life, so I don't see her shouting any of my secrets from the rooftops. She doesn't strike me as the type to publicize it if she decides to believe in ghosts, so I don't think she'd out me for it either. It's a chance I have to take though, if I'm going to make any kind of return on my investment. It's in Dani's and my best interest to get this theater open on time and have it do well. A menacing ghost might get in the way of that."

He wiped his mouth with the napkin and pushed the plate aside to find the wet wipe the restaurant had provided. "Are you gonna tell her you're inviting her over to meet a ghost?"

I shook my head. "Definitely not. Can you imagine? *'C'mon over! I'll make pasta, we'll have wine, and my friend from the afterlife can stop by.'* I don't think that would go over well. You said you're pulling a late shift tomorrow night, right?"

"Yeah. We've got a sting operation, so I'm not sure what time I'll be done."

"All right. I'm thinking it will be best if it's just me, Dani, and Chelsea. I don't know how Dani would feel about being put on the spot with a deputy sheriff for an audience."

I waited until he had gone to bed to step out on the deck and broach the subject with Chelsea.

"Hey, Chels? You there?"

No matter how many times I did it, it never ceased to feel awkward to stand outside in the dark and call out to no one expecting someone to appear.

I glanced up at the night sky and frowned at the cloud cover.

"Chelsea? You there?"

"I wonder how long I could stand here without you knowing," she said with a giggle.

Her voice came across the breeze from the corner of the deck nearest the garage, and I whirled to find her but saw nothing.

Damn clouds. I'd been hopeful that the half-moon would cast enough light for me to at least catch a glimmer. It still creeped me out to hear her voice when I couldn't see her at all.

She laughed, and I could tell she was closer, just over my shoulder to the right.

"I'd be great at hide-and-seek, wouldn't I? I hated that game when I was alive, but I'd be the champ at it now."

She was even closer behind me on my left that time, and I spun, but without being able to see her, I could only peer in her general direction. "Would you stop that? Stand still so I know which way to face when I talk to you."

She laughed again, a high-pitched tinkle like the shattering of a thin glass.

"This is fun. How many times can I make you spin?"

I went and sat on a lounge chair and reclined with my eyes closed, refusing to be the fodder for her games.

"Oh, all right." Her voice was right next to me, and I knew she was settling into the deck chair nearest mine. "How was California?"

"It was good. Too long of a trip, though. I was ready to get back home." I kept my eyes closed as I talked, and it almost made it feel like a normal conversation.

"I suppose that having a fuzzy concept of time passing is an advantage in some ways," she said. "It seems like you just left."

"I was gone for a month." I looked toward her voice, still unable to see her. "So happy to hear how much you missed me."

Her laughter rang out, and I tried to follow the sound with my gaze as she moved again.

"Of course, I missed you, silly!"

The clouds parted to reveal her standing on the railing of our deck, pretending to balance as she hovered an inch or two above its surface.

"I need to ask a favor, Chels."

"Is that why you called? Gee, and here I thought maybe *you* missed *me*." She shot a playful glare at me over her shoulder and then did a perfect pirouette above the beam.

"I always miss you when you're not around, but I also need to ask a favor."

She hopped off the railing and put her hands on her hips. "Does this involve running around in the woods chasing insane killers? Because the last couple of times you needed a favor, things got intense."

"No, nothing like that at all. I just want you to meet someone."

"What? Why?" Even in the dim light of the partially covered moon, I could see disdain for the idea written all over her translucent face.

"Remember I told you about the theater in town? Well, it appears that the building has a ghost."

Her eyes widened, and she waved her hand in a shimmering wisp. "Oh, no! No way. I already told you I don't want to meet any other ghosts. I'm scared of ghosts. You know that."

I sat up and leaned forward as I sought to reassure her. "I know. I'm not asking you to meet the ghost. I'm asking you to meet Dani, the lady who owns the theater. She doesn't believe in ghosts, and I need to convince her that they're real—that *you're* real—so she'll take this seriously."

Chelsea came back to sit cross-legged in the deck chair next to me just as a passing cloud made her flicker in and out of view.

"Ugh. I don't want to meet anybody. Especially not someone who doesn't even believe I exist."

"C'mon, Chels. This is really important to me."

She groaned and laid her head back with an eyeroll.

"What would I have to do?"

From the whiny tone of her voice, you would have thought I was giving her household chores. I gritted my teeth and reminded myself that I was dealing with a teenage girl who was stuck at sixteen and therefore, trapped in the often moody and put-upon stage of life for all perpetuity.

"I just need you to do the same thing you did with Tristan and Holden. I'll explain to her that you're here, and you let her feel your presence."

"So, basically, blast her with frigid cold air and scare the crap out of her?"

I tried to ignore how much her mood had perked up at the thought.

"I wouldn't say *blast* her. We're not trying to convince her you're a mutant from the X-Men. Maybe just a gentle cold breeze would be nice. I need her to feel you—to know you are there and that you exist. I need her to understand that I can communicate with you, even though she can't."

"Fine," she said with a groan as she got up and twirled around the deck. "When is this meeting happening and where?"

"I'll invite her over here for dinner, and we can introduce the two of you out here on the deck. I'm hoping she's available tomorrow night so we can go ahead and get this over with."

"I'll have to check my calendar and get back to you," she said as she faded away under a passing cloud. "Just kidding. I'm available. It's not like I have any other plans, ya know?"

Chapter 15

I told Dani the next morning I wanted to discuss the Shakespeare play over dinner, and we arranged for her to come over that evening when Tristan was out. I was relieved when I saw that the forecast called for clear skies. Even though Dani wasn't likely to be able to see Chelsea, I knew I'd feel more comfortable if I could easily see her.

All day, I wavered back and forth on whether or not it was a good decision. I knew that once I confessed to Dani that I had a relationship with a ghost, I couldn't come back from that. It felt vulnerable and risky to expose myself, even if Dani did walk away a believer.

I hoped Chelsea would be in a better mood and more cooperative than she had been the night before. I was nervous enough without dealing with teenager attitude.

"Thanks again for having me over," Dani said as we settled in on the deck after dinner. "I still feel like I'm on eggshells around my parents, and I think I've just about worn out my welcome at my sister's. I hate cooking for one."

"I hate cooking, period." I refilled both our wine glasses and set the bottle on the table. "I usually don't even bother when Tristan's working a late shift. I wish we had a sushi place in town. I could pick up a tuna roll and be perfectly content."

"Oh, God, I miss sushi. That's one thing about small town life. Our food choices are extremely limited. I could get anything I wanted to eat in Chicago. I know L.A. was the same for you."

"Yep. Maybe we should open a sushi bar in the front of the theater."

She laughed at the idea. "Can you imagine? That would certainly set us apart."

I wondered how to bring up the subject without it being awkward, but as the hour grew later, I knew I was running out of time and had to just do it.

"So, Dani, you know how we were talking the other night about whether or not I believe in ghosts?"

"Ye…e…s," she said, drawing out the word with some mixture of hesitation and curiosity.

"Well, I thought perhaps it might help if you understood *why* I believe. I told you that something happened that changed my perspective." I drew in a deep breath and rushed the words out before I lost my nerve. "You asked if I'd seen a ghost, and the answer is yes. When I first came to Cedar Creek, I encountered a young girl named Chelsea. Chelsea lost her life in a car accident near here when she was only sixteen years old."

Dani took a gulp of her wine, and though her face was filled with doubt, she didn't protest and continued to listen.

"For reasons I can't explain, I seem to be the only one who can see Chelsea, and I can only see her when the light of the moon reveals her."

She glanced at the moon overhead and back to me. "Can you see her right now?"

Before I could answer, she laughed and tossed her head back.

"I'm sorry," she said between laughs as she held her hand to her belly. "I can't! I was trying to be respectful of what you're telling me, but surely, you realize how this sounds. Is this a plot for one of your movies? You're pulling my leg, right?"

I sensed that I had a limited amount of time to persuade her before she stood and left, convinced that I was crazy.

"Chelsea, can you come and meet my friend, Dani?"

On some level, Dani must have believed, because her smile faded and she froze in place, motionless except for her eyes darting left and right as they searched the deck.

I was searching the deck too, but there was no sign of Chelsea. With the moon high in a clear sky, she should have been visible, but there was no sign of her.

"Chels? Are you here?"

Not a word of acknowledgment or the slightest shimmer of light in response.

I swallowed hard, aware that Dani was staring at me. "Chelsea? Are you playing around again? We're not doing hide and seek, okay?"

Nothing.

"Chels, c'mon. You're making me look like an idiot here."

Dani chuckled as she stood and placed her wine glass on the table, and I stood with her.

"Look, Sloane, I appreciate what you're trying to do. Really, I do. And I'm sure you believe that you saw something or met something, er, someone. But I'm telling you, there's no such thing as ghosts. You're not going to convince me otherwise. But thanks for trying. I should probably go."

"Chelsea!" My voice was loud and my tone demanding, and it worked. She shimmered into view with her hand over her mouth as she laughed.

"Oh my gosh, you should see the look on your face! It's priceless," Chelsea said as she hovered on the other side of the table.

I walked toward her, wishing I could throttle her. "What took you so long? I told you this was important to me."

"I know. I was just teasing you. I wouldn't have let her leave without showing up."

"Well, you almost did." I spun back to face Dani. "Chelsea's here."

Dani's face had gone pale, and her eyes were open so wide that the whites appeared to glow.

She swallowed hard and gave a quick nod. "And you can see… *her*…right now?"

She looked as though she believed I was insane much more than she believed I was conversing with a ghost. Any fear or worry on her part was for my well-being, not any real consideration that someone had joined us from the afterlife.

"Boo," Chelsea yelled as she appeared right in front of Dani before bursting out laughing again.

I admonished her, even though Dani was completely unaware of what she'd done.

"Stop that. Don't be rude."

Chelsea flung her arms to the side and dropped her mouth open. "I thought you wanted me to convince her I was real."

"I do, but that's not how I want you to go about it. You know that won't do any good."

Dani cocked her head to one side and stared at me, her expression growing more wary by the minute. I could only imagine her thought process, and I hoped she wasn't going to bolt from the deck and call someone to take me away to a padded room.

"Dani, I know this sounds crazy, but if you'll give me a chance, I think I can prove to you that Chelsea's real. Hold out your hand, and I'm going to ask Chelsea to touch you. You'll feel cold air. It won't hurt, and it's not uncomfortable, just chilly."

Dani took a step back as her eyes scanned the deck.

"Please," I said. "Just trust me. Hold out your hand."

"I've never felt so ridiculous," she said as she lifted her arm slowly. "I'm only doing this because I owe you."

When her arm was extended, I nodded toward Chelsea, and she traced her fingers along Dani's forearm.

Dani recoiled and clutched her arm to her chest. "Holy shit! What was that?"

Chelsea laughed and twirled in a circle, brushing against Dani as she did so. Dani shivered and hugged herself as she looked to me, her eyes even wider and her mouth open.

"Okay, how are you doing that?"

"I'm not," I said with my hands spread wide. "Chelsea is."

Dani spun around as Chelsea blew against her hair.

"All right," Dani said. "It's not a breeze. Too pinpointed for that. Can't be a fan for the same reason." She looked up. "Unless it's a drone. You could accomplish it with a drone."

"But you'd see it or hear it if it was that close, wouldn't you?" I grinned as I watched her process what was happening and grasp at explanations. "Take out your phone and open up a random picture. Don't let me see it, and Chelsea will tell me what's in the photo."

She hesitated for a moment, and then pulled her phone from her pocket, only to return it as she shook her head. "No. A drone could see a photo."

"But how would it tell me what was in the picture?" I pulled my hair back so she could see my ears. "I'm not wearing an earpiece or headphones. You can take a closer look if you want."

She bit down on her lip and pulled the phone back out. She slid her fingers across the screen a couple of times and then nodded.

"Okay."

"It's a picture of her eating a chocolate ice cream cone," Chelsea said as she peered over Dani's shoulder. "It looks yummy, too."

Dani watched me as I nodded and thanked Chelsea, and then her eyes widened and her mouth dropped when I told her it was a chocolate ice cream cone.

She looked up and around, as though she was determined to find a drone.

"All right," she said, her lips tight with determination. "Let's try this."

She leaned over to place the phone under the table, bending to peer at it as she swiped her fingers across the screen.

"Okay," she said with a single, strong nod. "No way a drone can see that."

"Of course not. She has it right up against the bottom of the table," Chelsea groaned. "I can't see it either unless I bend into an unnatural position."

"Unnatural? C'mon, Chelsea," I said with a grin. "Do you really want me to state the obvious?"

"No, I suppose not." She crouched beneath the table and craned to see the phone, laying her hand on Dani's arm as though she could pull it down to see better.

"Oh, God!" Dani exclaimed as she jerked her arm out from under the table and stood up. "That cold is just freaky."

"It's a picture of a little dog in someone's sink," Chelsea said as she flitted around the deck, quite pleased with herself. "The dog is wet and covered in soap suds."

"Chelsea says the picture on the screen is a dog taking a bath."

Dani looked down and then back up at me. "Well, I'll be damned."

She collapsed backwards into the chair and grabbed the wine glass, draining it of its contents before holding it up toward me. "Do you have anything stronger?"

Chapter 16

"Let me see what we've got in the bar cabinet," I said, glancing over my shoulder at Chelsea as I headed inside the house.

She stood staring at the wind chimes with such focus that I knew she was still trying to move them, despite the many times she'd decreed that she was done trying to get physical objects to do her bidding.

After seeing the havoc the theater ghost had wreaked, I breathed a sigh of relief that Chelsea couldn't move things. I could only imagine how much mischief she'd cause if she mastered that beyond-the-grave talent.

When I returned to the deck with a half-empty bottle of vodka, Dani stood at the rail, gazing out toward the lake.

"We've got some vodka," I said from the doorway. "I could mix it with orange juice if you'd like."

She turned to face me and crossed her arms. "Have you always been able to see ghosts? Is that why you chose to be the *Spectral Slayer?*"

"No." I shook my head. "Chelsea was my first encounter."

"First? Have there been others since her?"

I set the vodka on the deck table and joined her at the railing. "Not that I can see or hear. Chelsea was able to see the late husband of a close friend and deliver a message from him while I was there to translate, but I never interacted with him directly."

"What about the theater? Have you seen or heard anything there? Do you think it's haunted?"

I twisted my lips to the side and gave a little shrug. "I do. I agree with Steve that there are too many things happening without a reasonable explanation."

She opened her mouth as though she was going to protest, and I held up my hand.

"I know, Dani, I know. There *could* be an explanation for the lights and the toilet flushing, but no one has been able to find one, and you've had several people looking. I also believe Steve's crew when they say they feel like someone is watching them. I had that same sensation the first day I was in the building." Chill bumps rose on my skin with the memory, and I shivered and moved to sit in the nearest chair, pulling my feet up as I hugged my knees to my chest. "I felt like someone was in that upstairs office watching me, but when you came back in, we went up and no one was there."

Dani's skepticism seemed to have been replaced by curiosity, and she raised her eyebrows as she considered that piece of information. "Really? Why didn't you say anything?"

"At the time, I shrugged it off as an overactive imagination in a dark building with faulty lights."

She came to sit in the chair across the table from me and began to rub her temples with her fingers.

"Okay. So, I've got a ghost. Now what?"

"You've got to get rid of him somehow. At the very least, he could delay our opening if Steve and his crew walk out. Steve made a good point about the audience, too, though. These issues might be inconvenient to deal with now, but what about when the theater opens? You can't have things flying across the stage or tumbling to the floor in the middle of a performance. Not to mention that the patrons probably wouldn't take too kindly if their own personal belongings were affected."

She sat back in the chair and stared at me with a lopsided grin.

"I suppose I should be happy about this." She picked up the wine bottle from the table and filled her glass halfway. "Perhaps it makes us more legit. Isn't every theater supposed to have a ghost? Maybe I should ask the electricians to install a ghost light on the stage and go ahead and reserve two seats like the Palace Theater in London. Would that make the ghost happy so he would quit his pranks?"

"Those are superstitions, not solutions," I said. "The ghost light is actually a safety standard so no one trips or falls with a dark stage. And the Palace? They used the bolted seats reserved for ghosts as publicity all those years. When *Harry Potter and the Cursed Child* sold out and they needed more seats, they sold the bolted ones without any qualms."

She stared at me over the rim of her glass. "Honestly, if I thought it would drum up good publicity, I'd consider it." She took a sip of the wine, and then her frown deepened as she set the glass down. "I honestly thought my luck was changing, that things were looking up. I have to get this place open, Sloane. For you and for me."

I frowned at the desperation in her voice. For me, it was a business investment and a passion project. While I'd sunk a significant chunk of money into the venture and had pledged to invest more, I would still have my job and my income if it failed. Dani's stakes were much higher. The theater was all she had.

She leaned forward, bracing her elbows on the table's edge as she clasped her hands together.

"Well, *Spectral Slayer*, this is your area of expertise, is it not? What do you suggest I do?"

"Oh, I don't know. Like I told Steve, that's all fiction. In my extremely limited real-life experience, a ghost is usually hanging around because they have something to say or something they need to accomplish. Tristan's brother said the rumors around town are that the building is haunted by the original owner."

"Hyram Letchworth? That's who owned it when I was growing up."

"I guess. Holden seems to think it's because the man doesn't like other people being in his building."

"Great. So, what am I supposed to do about that?"

I shrugged. "I don't know, but we have to figure out a way to appease him if we're going to keep him from wreaking havoc."

"Right." Dani's cheeks puffed out as she let out a loud exhale and sat back against the chair again. "Add that to my to-do-list. Speaking of supernatural"—she looked around her and dropped the volume of her voice as she looked back at me—"is that ghost friend of yours still hanging around?"

I smiled toward Chelsea, who was busying herself with cartwheels down on the lawn. "Yep. She's still here."

"Do you think you could ask her to do that thing on my arm again? That was mind-blowing. I had no idea what was happening the first time, and it's kind of a blur. I'd like to experience it when I'm prepared so I can pay attention to the sensation."

"You can ask her yourself if you'd like."

"She can hear me?"

I grinned as I nodded, and then I called out to Chelsea.

"Chels, can you come here a minute?"

"Is she standing near me?" Dani asked as she scanned the deck.

"She is now. Just ask her."

"Um, Chelsea?" Dani called out before looking at me with an eyeroll. "Talk about feeling ridiculous…I am literally speaking to the air." She chuckled and cleared her throat as she lifted her arm and held her palm up. "Can you touch my palm, so I know you're here?"

"Sure," Chelsea said, even though she knew Dani couldn't hear her. She pointed her finger toward Dani's open hand and traced a *C* in the center of it.

Dani shivered and closed her hand into a fist as she pulled her arm back. "Oh my God! That's wild. That's freaking amazing! We should try to communicate like this with the ghost in the theater."

"I don't know if it's a good idea for us to strike up a conversation with some random spirit on our own."

"He's not random if we know who he is. We should try to

reason with Hyram and ask him to move along. In fact, we should go now so that when Steve and his crew arrive in the morning, we can tell him it's all clear."

I shuddered at the thought of confronting an unknown spiritual being in the dark of night.

"Dani, don't you think maybe we should bring in some kind of professional? You know, someone with more experience dealing with this sort of thing?"

"You have experience."

"With one ghost," I said. "A friendly teenage ghost who wouldn't harm a fly. We don't know what kind of spirit we're dealing with at the theater."

Her expression changed as she processed my words. "Oh. Do you think Hyram's spirit is bad or evil or something like that? He's only flashed the lights and knocked over tools. Nothing menacing. I mean, even if it was him who drank my whiskey and bashed my paint can, he's been more annoying than anything. What could it hurt just to ask him to leave?"

"I'm not sure if this works the same way with all ghosts. Chelsea is the only one I've ever interacted with, which is fine with me. I don't want to go around seeing dead people all the time."

"Right, but hear me out. I can't see or hear Chelsea, but she can obviously see and hear me. So, it stands to reason—reason being a relative term in this situation—that Hyram's ghost would be the same. We should just go in there and talk to him. You know, reason with him." She put her hand on her forehead and exhaled. "This is surreal. I can't believe I'm seriously discussing having a conversation with a ghost. Wait—how many people know about this? About you and Chelsea?"

"Not very many," I replied. "Tristan knows, of course, and a few others. I'd like to keep it that way. I'm sure you could imagine what a media fiasco this would be for my career."

"Really? I would think it might actually give you more cred as a ghost slayer."

"Yeah, maybe, but I'm not doing those movies now, and I'd like to move away from that image, not conform to it more."

"Ah, I understand," she said with a nod. "Well, thank you for trusting me with your secret."

"You trusted me with yours."

"Yes, I did."

We both smiled, and then she sat up with wide eyes.

"Hey, I've got an idea. Why don't we get Chelsea to talk to Hyram? Have a little ghost-to-ghost chat?"

Chelsea looked up from the corner of the deck where she'd been pretending to balance and twirl on one foot.

"No," Chelsea said, coming to my side. "No, no, no, no, no. Tell her I'm not talking to anyone. I'm outta here!"

Her apparition disappeared before I could assure her that I wouldn't ask her to.

"I don't think that's a good idea, Dani. We really don't know what we're messing with here, especially if this guy's angry about us being there. I'd feel more comfortable if we got someone who knows what they're doing to talk to him."

"What? Like we go to Craig's List and post a want ad for a ghost interpreter? Or search some crackpot's website where they ask for an exorbitant fee to tell me it's my great-aunt Audrey checking on me from beyond the grave? You've already said you want to keep this on the down low, and I don't necessarily want to confirm the rumor that my new business venture is haunted. I'd rather this stay between the two of us"—she glanced around the deck—"or, um, three of us, and not involve anyone else."

I hesitated, and she leaned forward, more eager.

"C'mon, Sloane. What do we have to lose by asking him to behave? Let's just calmly and politely ask Hyram to knock off his antics and let us get on with what we need to do. If he doesn't seem amenable to that, then we can call in bigger guns."

I noticed that Chelsea had returned and was listening in on our conversation from the hammock in the corner. She and I made eye contact, and then she vanished again.

Dani stood and rapped her knuckles on the table. "Think about it, sleep on it, and let's touch base in the morning."

"Where are you going?" I asked, standing with her. "You're not going to theater alone, are you?"

"What, and have you miss all the fun? No. I'm gonna head home and do some research. I can't be the only logical, practical person to discover that ghosts are real. I want to see if I can find anything remotely scientific about hauntings and what it takes to get rid of one."

"Okay. Sounds like a good plan," I said, relieved that I didn't need to talk her out of going to the theater or be put in a position where I felt obligated to go with her.

"Thanks again for dinner, and for…well, let me just say again, this has been…surreal. It's a lot to process." She paused and looked around the deck as though she was searching for someone. "Um, Chelsea, if you're still around, nice, um, er, *meeting* you. This is so weird," she said with a glance back at me. "So, this is what it's like to hang out with Hollywood types, huh? Geez!"

Chapter 17

Dani texted at eight o'clock the next morning and asked me to join her at the theater as soon as possible.

I knocked on the locked door, and she came to answer it with bright eyes and a big smile.

"Come in, come in."

As soon as I stepped inside, the overpowering scent of something burning filled my nostrils.

"What the hell is that smell?"

"I was trying to burn sage, and I accidentally set some paper on fire in the process," Dani said as she locked the door behind me. "Most of the scientific info I found online dealt with discrediting ghosts or detecting them. Since we've moved past both of those and are focused on removal, we're gonna have to rely on the less scientific methods I found. It seems sage is supposed to be effective. Garlic, too." She pointed above the door frame, where several heads of garlic were tied up along a string.

"Garlic? I thought that was for vampires. What if the ghost doesn't use the front door?" I asked, covering my nose and mouth with my hand in an effort to breathe through the combined smell of garlic, sage, and burnt paper.

"Oh, I've got garlic all over this place. I bought out the Handy Sack's garlic supply as soon as they opened this morning."

"That would explain the smell. You really think this is going to help?"

"It can't hurt. You'll also be thrilled to know my research revealed that quite often, it really is as simple as asking the ghost to leave. So, our original idea might do the trick, but I thought I'd hedge our bets with the sage and garlic for good measure."

"I don't know that I would use the word *thrilled.*"

She put her hands on her hips and grinned. "You look terrified. Why? Here you are, the *Spectral Slayer*, and you look like you're ready to turn and run. If anyone's lacing up their running shoes, it should be me."

"How many times do I have to remind you that those movies were all CGI and special effects, nothing more?"

"Yeah, but you also talk to ghosts in real life. You're experienced at this. I'm the amateur here."

"One ghost. I've talked to *one* ghost."

"Well, that's more experience than I have. I thought you said there was a message from a friend's husband?"

"Yeah, but he talked to Chelsea, and Chelsea talked to me. Still only one ghost."

"All right, so why can't we ask Chelsea to come talk to our ghost?"

"Uh, no. That's not happening. Chelsea is terrified of ghosts."

Dani scrunched her eyebrows in confusion. "But wait—Chelsea *is* a—"

"I know. Believe me, I know." I waved my hand in dismissal of the topic. "She feels strongly about this. She won't do it."

"All right, then it's up to us. Now, according to what I read, sometimes it's a matter of the spirit being confused. We simply have to explain that he no longer belongs here. We tell him my name is on the lease and that he needs to go. Are you ready?"

She reached to grab the knob of the door leading into the main room, and I took a step backwards.

"No, I'm not ready. Are you insane?"

Dani sighed. "This from the person who asked me over for dinner last night so I could meet her ghost friend?"

"That's different. I know Chelsea. I don't know this guy, and from all we do know, he's not going to take too kindly to being asked to leave his place of business. Are you not weirded out by this *at all?* Yesterday, you didn't even believe in ghosts, and today, you're all gung-ho and enthusiastic to talk to one. Does this not spook you or make you at least a little bit scared?"

"No, I wouldn't say I'm *scared.* My adrenaline levels are elevated, for sure, but I think that's to be expected, don't you? If anything, I'd say it's exhilarating. It's a rush. C'mon, you ready?"

I wasn't sure what being ready meant in that situation or what it would take to get me there.

"I don't know about this," I said, but Dani just grinned and pulled the door open to enter the main room.

"Go ahead," she whispered once we'd walked inside. "Tell him."

"Why are you whispering?" Despite my question, I realized I had done the same in response. "You realize if there's a spirit here, he can hear us whether we whisper or not."

"Right. So, tell him."

"You tell him. It's your building."

"Yeah, but you're the one who talks to ghosts."

"Not all ghosts...just one."

Dani looked up toward the dark office window above us. "You said you sensed a presence up there, right?"

I nodded, unwilling to look up at the window for fear that I'd sense it again.

"Excuse me," she said loudly toward the window. "My name is Dani, and this is my friend, Sloane."

"You're doing introductions?" I scoffed. "Seriously?"

She turned to me and spoke in a much quieter voice. "The article I read said to introduce yourself and explain your purpose for being in the building and why you have a right to be there."

"All right. As long as he doesn't talk back or tell us why we *don't* have a right to be."

She looked back up at the window. "I understand that this may be confusing for you, but you are a ghost. You are in the spirit world, and we"—she pointed her finger back and forth between us —"are in the living world. I know you may think you still own this building, but I've signed a lease. I have a legal right to be here."

She spoke slowly and pronounced each word with care. It was like she was explaining a complicated matter to a child. For some reason, it struck me as funny, though it could have been my nerves giving me a case of the giggles at the sheer lunacy of what we were doing. I covered my mouth to keep from laughing out loud.

Dani cast me a frowning glance and whispered, "Don't laugh. We need him to take us seriously."

I bit down on my lip and tried to compose myself as she continued.

"I need you to stop messing around with the tools and anything left lying on a table. I need you to stop flushing the toilet. Oh, and the lights! If that was you, you can't do that anymore. I need the lights to stay on. We're going to have a lot of people in here soon, and you can't be causing all this trouble. In fact, I think it would be best if you would just leave the building altogether."

I braced for a reaction, but none came.

Dani looked at me and shrugged. "Do you think that did it? Do you think he's gone?"

I shrugged back. "I don't know."

"Well, when you talk to Chelsea, how do you know if she hears you?"

"She answers me."

"Right. We need some kind of acknowledgment. We should ask him if he heard us."

I put my hand on her arm. "Wait. Are you sure you want to do that? It's one thing to make a statement to the ghost. It's something completely different to engage him and ask him to communicate back."

"How else will I know if he heard me?"

"Either the shenanigans will stop, or they won't."

She sighed and ran her fingers through her hair. "I can't wait around to find out, and I can't risk Steve and his crew quitting. I need to know this ghost got the message loud and clear and that he's going to leave us alone." She turned toward the dark window and put her hands on her hips. "Hey! I need to know that you heard me. If you're still here, can you send some kind of sign?"

Nothing.

"Maybe that means he's gone," I offered, finally venturing a glance up toward the window.

"Maybe so. See, that's all it took." She rubbed her hands together motioning like she was casting off dirt, and then she held her palms up with a triumphant smile. "A polite explanation with a request. Well, and some burning sage and more garlic than an Italian grandmother's kitchen."

Suddenly, the door to the reception area slammed shut as the lights went out, plunging us into total darkness as we both screamed.

I don't think I've ever moved as fast in my life as I did making my way through the dark toward where I knew the door should be. We both reached it at the same time, crashing into each other as we grappled for the door handle.

I got my fingers wrapped around it first, and though I feared it would be locked, it turned easily in my hand. I flung it open, and the two of us rushed across the reception area to the front door. Dani wasted no time flipping the deadbolt, and neither of us stopped running until we were midway across the parking lot.

Dani bent over, gasping for breath, and I stared back at the building, my chest heaving and my heart pounding so loudly I was sure she could hear it.

"Well," Dani said with a grin after she'd caught her breath. "I think we definitely still have a ghost."

"Oh yeah. Definitely." I looked up at the sky and tried to slow my breathing. "One thing's for sure, though; I'd say he heard your message loud and clear."

"Do you think that was him saying *'Sure thing! Let me pack my bags, and I'll be out of your way.'* or *'Screw you!'*?"

I arched an eyebrow with a sideways glance. "What do you think?"

Chapter 18

We stood side-by-side watching the building, and then Dani twisted her hair up on her head and held it as she fanned the back of her neck. With a sigh, she turned to face me.

"If you want out, I completely understand. No one knows you're involved yet, well, other than the mayor, the city council, the Arts Alliance…Steve…Tristan…your accountant…oh, and our attorneys. So, several people, I guess, but hey, we haven't made any official announcements. You could just go back to whatever other projects you have in the works, and there will be no hard feelings." She grimaced and released her hair as she scrunched her nose with a frown. "I'll admit that it will be tough if you pull your funding at this point, and God only knows when I can pay back what you've already invested, but I'll figure out a way. We can work that out if we need to." She took a deep breath and exhaled it before continuing. "As for me, I have to make this work. I've got nowhere else to go. This was my life plan B. I don't have a plan C. So, one way or another, I gotta get rid of this ghost and get this theater open."

She smiled at me, but her eyes held a silent plea that made it hard to look away.

There was no part of me that wanted to go back inside that building and confront whatever angry spirit we were dealing with, but I also understood what a solitary battle this would be if Dani had to go it alone.

I'd carried a ghostly secret before and tried to keep it under wraps, and it was damned hard not being able to discuss what you were going through with anyone.

It didn't feel right to abandon her, or to abandon my intentions for the theater and the town of Cedar Creek.

None of that changed the fact that we were in over our heads, however.

"We're going to need to do more research about this Hyram guy," I said as I looked back toward the building. "We need to figure out what he wants and what it would take for him to leave on his own."

"Okay." Her eyes brightened, and her smile ceased to look forced.

I tried to smile back, but I couldn't muster it. "You said you knew him when you were growing up?"

She shook her head. "I didn't *know* him. I knew who he was, and I knew he owned the auto repair shop. I think my dad might have brought our cars here once or twice."

"Could you ask your dad about him? See what he may know about Hyram?"

"I'm not sure I want to involve my parents," she said with a frown. "My relationship with them is still strained from everything that happened in Chicago, and telling them I think I have a ghost may not be helpful."

"I can ask Tristan. He's only lived in Cedar Creek for a few years, but his grandparents lived here most of his life, and he spent a lot of time with them growing up. Maybe he knows someone we can talk to if nothing else."

We both turned back to face the building and stood in silence.

"Okay," Dani said after a couple of minutes. "You go talk to Tristan, and I'll go home and change my underpants." She laughed at my startled expression. "I'm kidding, of course, but man, that was wild. Intense! However, the last thing I want to do is have this jerk think he won and I'm giving him the building. I need to get back in there and get back to work to show him that I'm not going anywhere."

I shuddered at the thought of going back in. "Are you sure that's a good idea? What if he's angry?"

"What if he is? From everything I read, they can't physically harm you. They're in the spirit world, not the physical world."

"Uh, yeah. I've read that, too, but he's found a way to move physical objects, so I'm not sure anyone explained the rules to him."

"He hasn't hurt anyone, though. Nothing he's done has been harmful. Just annoying."

She had a point, but I shook my head and dismissed it as quickly as I'd conceded it.

"Still, that was all before you basically told him he's being evicted. What if he's pissed now?"

She looked toward the building and then back to me.

"You said you sensed a presence before, that you sensed someone watching you. Did you get the feeling it was evil? Did you feel like you were in danger?"

I thought back to the sensation. It was the same feeling I often got when I realized a photographer's camera lens was focused on me or a fan was staring at me. I didn't recall it being in any way sinister.

"No, I suppose I didn't, but I wouldn't use that as your justification for going back in."

She chewed on her cheek for a moment. "All right. How about this? While you're talking to Tristan, I'll go home and do some research online for ways to get rid of a ghost who doesn't want to leave. When you finish with him, why don't you stop by the house and we can recap what we each found out?"

"Sounds like a plan," I said, and we began to walk back toward the building.

I pulled my keys from my pocket as we neared my car.

"My purse is inside along with my keys," she said with a frown.

"You want me to take you to your house?"

"No." She shook her head. "I really don't believe he can do me any harm. Or that he means to."

"Yeah, well, yesterday you didn't believe he existed."

"True. I think I have to show him I'm not scared, though."

"But aren't you? Even a little bit?"

She grinned and stuck her hands in the back pockets of her jeans.

"I'd be lying if I said I wasn't uneasy. I've never been scared of ghosts because I didn't believe in them, but now, yeah, I guess you could say I'm a bit spooked." She looked down at the dirt and kicked at a rock with the toe of her sneaker. "But to be honest, after Chicago, I still think the living are much more frightening."

"That's understandable."

Her smile returned as she stepped back from my car.

"See what you can find out from Tristan and I'll see what I find online, and then we'll touch base, okay?"

I nodded, trying to ignore the nagging feeling that I should offer to go in with her to get her purse. It wasn't anything I wanted to do, but it was what I would want a friend to do for me.

She turned to walk toward the door, and I wrinkled up my nose in disbelief that I was about to volunteer.

"Wait up," I called out as I followed her. "I'll go in with you to get your stuff."

She stopped and looked back at me with a grin. "You sure? You don't have to. I'm fine. I promise."

"I don't mind," I lied. "But please tell me your purse is in the reception area. I don't want to go back in that auditorium just yet."

She laughed as she pulled the front door open and peered inside. "It's on the concession counter. Here, you can stand in the doorway and hold it open, and I'll walk across and get it."

I leaned against the glass entry door and pushed it all the way open as I straddled the threshold.

The lights were back on and there was no sign of any damage or paranormal activity, but I still felt skittish.

Dani crossed to the concession counter and grabbed her purse, and I motioned for her to hurry as she turned to come back toward me. She paused by the door into the auditorium and glanced back at me.

"What are you doing?" I asked as I pushed my back even harder against the glass door to ensure it didn't close an inch. "C'mon."

"I want to turn the lights off."

"Are you kidding me? You can leave the lights on for a couple of hours. It will be fine. I'll pay the power bill if I need to."

She hesitated as she stared into the room, and then she looked back at me. "I kind of want to tell him that I'll be back. I want him to know that I'm not leaving because of him, and that he still needs to go."

"You just did. I'm sure he heard every word. Now, c'mon!"

She stepped out of sight into the main room, and I called her name just as she began to talk louder.

"Listen up. I have some errands to run, but I'll be back. I'm not giving up my theater; do you hear me? My name is on the lease, not yours. You might have startled me, but I'm not scared of you. You have no place here."

She came back into view and walked toward me a faster pace than I'd ever seen her walk before.

"How was that?" she asked as she turned the key in the deadbolt to lock the door once we were both outside.

"Great. I'm sure he's shaking in his ghost boots now."

"Well, he should be," Dani said with a laugh. "He's dealing with the *Spectral Slayer* and...and...dang! We need a name for me. You already have a cool ghost-fighting name, and I need one too. And before you tell me it was just a film, remember that they say an actor carries a little piece of every character inside them. So, part of you is Lucy Landry, and right now, we need her."

Chapter 19

When I left the theater, I stopped by the sheriff's station to chat with Tristan and see what he could tell me about Hyram.

"I went there a few times with my grandfather when I was a boy," he said as he rubbed his knuckles across his chin. "I don't know whether or not Hyram built that shop, but it was his for as long as I can remember. His family was big into citrus—one of those old money Florida families—but he ran that auto shop, and his brother took over the family groves."

"Do you know how Hyram died?" I asked as I perched on the edge of Tristan's desk.

Tristan sat back in his chair and shook his head. "I don't recall. It must have been some time while I was in Afghanistan, because when I came back, his shop had been turned into a motorcycle repair place. If memory serves me correctly, that was run by someone in Hyram's family. It closed not too long after I started working here. It was a florist after that, and for the longest time, there was a sign up saying it was going to become a dry cleaner, but that never came to pass."

A knock sounded on Tristan's door, and I stood and smoothed my skirt as he called out, "Enter."

The sheriff opened the door and stepped inside the doorway, smiling when he saw me.

"Ms. Reid, always lovely to see you. How are you today?"

"I'm good, Sheriff; thanks, and how are you?"

"Good, good. I need to steal him away for a minute." He turned his gaze to Tristan. "Speak with you in the conference room?"

"Be right there," Tristan replied, leaning over to forward his phone before standing. He planted a kiss on my lips and smiled once the sheriff was gone. "Sorry. Duty calls."

"Hey, how would I find out how Hyram died? Or maybe more about who he was? You know, what kind of person he was."

He paused for a moment and then grinned. "Well, the quickest way to find out anything in this town is to go talk to Mrs. Myrtle McGillicuddy at the beauty salon two blocks down." He looked down at his watch and frowned. "She'll probably have a customer in her chair, but she might let you wait around until she breaks for lunch. Tell her I sent you."

"And say what? That Hyram Letchworth is haunting the theater building and I need to know what might make him leave?"

He chuckled as he put his arms around my waist.

"Tell her you're investing in the theater, and you'd like to know the building's history. She'll be happy to talk, trust me."

"All right, thanks."

He bent his head to kiss me and then took my hand to lead me toward the door of the station.

"Oh, by the way," he said as we stepped outside into the sunlight. "About Mrs. Myrtle, be prepared to answer more questions than you get answered, and don't be surprised if you end up telling her something you didn't mean to."

"Babe, if there's anything I've mastered being in the film industry since I was sixteen, it's the art of the tight-lipped interview."

He squinted into the sun and adjusted his hat on his head with a smirk. "I guarantee you've never been interviewed by anyone like Mrs. Myrtle. The sheriff jokes that he's gonna hire her to be our chief interrogator. She gets people to tell her stuff in that beauty salon that they never planned to confess. That's just how it goes with Mrs. Myrtle."

"Great. Well, she won't get anything out of me."

He smiled and reached to brush my hair back behind my ear before kissing me again.

"Gotta go. See you later. Love you," he said, leaning forward to open my car door for me.

"Love you, too. Now, you go catch the bad guys."

He tipped his hat as he took a step backwards. "And you go catch the ghost."

I dialed Dani's number as soon as I was in the car. "I talked to Tristan, and he couldn't tell me much about Hyram, but he seems to think there's a lady at the salon in town who might be able to tell me more. You wanna meet me there?"

"He means Mrs. Myrtle, and no, thank you," Dani said. "You go right ahead, but for God's sake, leave my name out of the conversation if you can."

"Oh." I frowned at the unexpected response. "Is there bad blood between you and Mrs. Myrtle?"

"That woman has had her nose in everyone's business since Moses was a baby. The newspaper in this town calls her to verify their stories before they print them. I've been off her radar for quite a while now, and even though I'm certain she's aware that I'm back, I'd rather lay low. No need to subject myself to her line of questioning."

"Yeah, Tristan did warn me about that."

"Good luck," Dani said with a laugh. "You'll need it."

The lady seemed innocent enough when I approached her.

She stood behind the reception desk in the small salon, and I knew it was her because the black smock she wore had *Mrs. Myrtle* embroidered on it in hot pink cursive letters. Her hair, which was pulled back tight into a stern bun high on her head, was a shade of jet black, much too dark for her pale skin and much too uniform to have been natural. She wore bright pink lipstick and a heavy-handed eyebrow pencil in a shade almost as dark as her hair.

Judging by her appearance alone, I would have been terrified to have my hair or make-up done at the salon, but the place bustled with activity. The swivel chair stations lining either side of the shop were all filled save one, and as the beauticians and their clients chatted away over the drone of hair dryers and the smell of peroxide and dye, a couple more clients sat waiting on a pink velvet sofa beneath the window as they thumbed through hairstyle magazines.

"Thank you much, Corrie Lyn," Myrtle said in a thick Southern drawl with a singsong quality that ran the two names together into one. She took a handful of cash from the customer and placed it in the register. "You be sure and tell your mama that we missed her today. Hope she's up and out of the house soon. Just have her call me when she's ready for a cut."

"I will, Mrs. Myrtle. Thank you."

The customer departed, and Myrtle turned toward me.

"Hello there! How can we help you? Do you have an appointment with us today?"

Her smile was wide and her voice warm, but her eyes scanned me from head to toe in a brief but thorough inspection that made me reach to tug my skirt down a bit lower on my legs.

"My name is Sloane, and Deputy Tristan Rogers sent me to you. He said you might be able to help me?"

Her smile spread to her eyes at the mention of Tristan, and she came around the desk for a more personal greeting.

"Why, butter my biscuits! Would you look at you! I'm tickled pink we finally get to meet. I've heard so much about you, and I told that boy the last time I saw him he needed to bring you in to see me. What can we do for you today?" She reached over the desk to grab the appointment book as she talked, tracing her index finger down the page with a perfectly manicured hot pink nail. "We're all booked up for hair, unfortunately."

My hand went to my hair in a protective gesture as she gave it another scrutinizing glance.

"Oh, um, no," I stammered. "I didn't mean—um, I wanted to know more about the history of Cedar Creek, and Tristan said you'd be the person to talk to."

"Well, he's right about that." She grabbed a pen and scribbled something on the page before setting the book back on the desk. "I was about to take a break to unpack some supplies in the back, but I can squeeze you in for a manicure before my eleven-thirty arrives."

"Oh, um, I didn't plan—"

She took my hand in hers and lowered her black-rimmed cat-eye glasses on the perch of her nose as she turned my hand this way and that to peer at my nails.

They were polish-free and cut short, just the way I liked them when I was off set. Easy to maintain.

"Hmmm. Oh my," Myrtle said as she pulled my hand closer to her face.

"Is something wrong?" I asked, bending my head to take a closer look myself.

"No, no, nothing's wrong," she said as she patted my hand. "Nothing a good paraffin treatment won't fix. Follow me."

"But I didn't intend—"

"It's okay. C'mon."

She turned to go without another glance in my direction, and I hurried to keep up as she led me behind the partition wall to the rear of the salon, seemingly oblivious to the other patrons and hairdressers staring at me as we went.

Chapter 20

Myrtle waved her hand toward the manicure desk to indicate that I should sit, and then she sighed as she took the seat across the desk from me.

"I don't normally take walk-ins, but for Tristan, I'll make an exception. I don't know if he told you, but we're cousins on my mama's side. Distant, of course, but Tristan's mother, Rita, and I came up together, and his grandmother, Nanette, practically raised me. She held such a special place in my heart." Myrtle gazed toward the ceiling and clasped her hands as though in prayer. "God rest her beautiful soul."

She turned and busied herself with setting up supplies on the nail station, and I couldn't help but hear the buzz of whispers as recognition swept through the salon.

Myrtle must have heard it too, because she lifted her chin and gazed at the others with an admonishing glare that reminded me of the ballet teacher I'd only lasted one class with when I was five. The entire salon went silent as she stood and walked over to the seated hair dryers behind me and flipped two of the heavy bonnets down before turning them on. They came to life with a steady roar, and she returned to me with a conspiratorial grin and a wink.

"That should give us a little privacy. You can pick out a color from the selections on the wall there."

"I would prefer not to have a color. Clear, please." If I was going to be strong-armed into a manicure, I thought I could at least have a say-so in the end result.

Myrtle scrunched her nose in distaste and picked up a bottle of a deep burgundy polish.

"A rich color would go so lovely with your skin tone. Of course, to pull it off, you'd want to wear at least a bit of blush and some lipstick. Maybe a touch of foundation. You know, something more than just mascara. You have such natural beauty—a blessing, for sure—and it seems a waste not to enhance it when it would take so little effort."

The crinkling concern of her eyes and the softness of her tone seemed a stark contrast to her criticism about my lack of make-up. It was like an insult delivered sympathetically with my best interests at heart. She was smooth; I'd give her that. I wondered how many people had left her salon with makeovers they'd never intended to have.

I considered explaining that I preferred to keep my cosmetic routine to a bare minimum when I wasn't working because my job required so much heavy makeup and time in a chair getting ready, but I decided against it. I didn't owe Myrtle McGillicuddy an explanation. If letting this woman paint my nails and critique my appearance helped me get the information I needed, I was willing to oblige her. After all, I'd had critics writing up their opinions of my appearance my entire life. There was nothing she could say that hadn't been said already.

"Can't believe this is the first time we're seeing you in here," she said as she began to file my nails. "Why, you and Tristan have been together, what, must be about two years now? I would have thought you might need your hair or nails done at some point while you were here."

"My publicist in L.A. has a stylist she uses, and I think she'd be upset with me if I went elsewhere."

"Your publicist, huh?" She smiled but never looked up from my hands. "I suppose that makes sense that you'd already have your own people you want to go to. Folks around here can't expect that you'd patronize local businesses just because you moved into town. Now, to tell you the truth, some might be offended by that, but I understand that a relationship between a woman and her stylist is sacred." She cast a glance up at my hair and frowned before turning her focus back to my hands. "I'd love to get my hands in that hair of yours, though. It could use a good thinning, but I'm sure your L.A. stylist knows best about that. Lord knows what those fancy salons out there must charge. Whew! I can't even imagine."

I marveled at her ability to make rudeness sound so sweet. Must be the Southern accent that masked the acidity and made it sound like honey. I decided it was best if I took control of the conversation so I could get what I came for.

"Tristan says you know quite a bit about the history of the town. Your family must have lived here for a while."

"Oh, my great-grandparents on my daddy's side were two of the ten that settled this place. Yes, ma'am, they were here at the start of it all. Cedar Creek royalty, if there was such a thing. For many years, everyone who lived here was in some way connected to those first five families—by marriage, business, or birth. But times have changed, haven't they? Why, now there's so many coming in from Orlando and Ocala looking to escape the chaos of the city." She shook her head as she buffed my nails. "Them city folk come out here seeking the peace and quiet of the country, and danged if they don't bring all that congestion and chaos with them. Next thing you know, we'll have a Target and a Home Depot right out there on Main Street."

I didn't dare tell her what a good idea I thought that might be.

"Of course, then we have folks like you," she said as she looked up at me and smiled. "Meet someone from here and fall in love and settle down, looking for their happily ever after. Now, will you and Tristan make Cedar Creek your primary home after you marry, or will you take him off to L.A.? I can't imagine it would be easy to run your type of career from here, but Lord, I can't see that boy out yonder in California separated from his family, either. Such a tight-

127

knit family, they are. Always have been. He was especially close to Hank and Nanette. More like a son than a grandson, but I'm sure he's told you that, hasn't he?"

I was well aware that she had slipped a marriage question in there, but she didn't wait for me to confirm or deny it. She clucked her tongue and continued talking without even taking time for a breath.

"Nearly killed Rita when Ray turned his back on that boy, I declare. Why, here Tristan was, trying to do his part for his country. It wasn't his fault what happened here at home while he was gone, and it wasn't his responsibility to keep his brother safe, either. How could he?"

I glanced over my shoulders at the other clientele, uncomfortable with her discussing personal matters about Tristan's family in such a public setting, but no one seemed to be paying attention.

Myrtle smiled as she grabbed a cuticle stick.

"Don't worry, love. They can't hear us with those dryers going between us and them. This is the most private spot in the shop, and you'd be surprised what all secrets have been shared in that seat you're in." She tapped the long pink fingernail of her index finger against her temple. "This here is a vault. What goes in, stays in. It only leaves my lips to go to the ears of our dear Lord. Because sometimes, when people share their burdens with me, I simply must pray for them."

She sighed with a shake of her head as she squeezed my hand in hers.

"Lord knows I prayed so much for that family that I had calluses on my knees, I tell ya. Between you and me, I think Rita would've finally left that fool for the way he treated Tristan if she hadn't had her hands full with poor Holden."

She released my hand and reached behind her to grab a bowl.

"Oh, Lord have mercy. That broke all our hearts. The injustice of that handsome baby boy coming back in pieces. In *pieces*! Nanette was beside herself. God rest her beautiful soul," she said with a glance heavenward before continuing. "I thought for sure it would kill her, but she soldiered on, as we strong women do. She had to, of course, so she could help Rita. But then eventually, I think Nanette realized it was Tristan who needed her help the most. The boy was in a dark place of pain, and when that marriage ended the way it did, well, we all feared he might not come back from it."

While it still didn't seem right for her to air the Rogers family laundry, part of me was curious to hear what this outside observer might have known or what insight she could give me.

She didn't stay on that topic, though. She changed gears and brought it back to me as she began to rub an exfoliating scrub on my hands and arms.

"I tell you, I couldn't be happier for you and Tristan, though. Now, I know Rita will want to be involved with your wedding plans no matter where you have it, but what about your mom? That I know of, she hasn't visited here since you moved to town. Has she met Tristan yet?"

I bristled at the uncomfortable line of questioning, but if Myrtle noticed, she didn't let on. Nor did she wait for a response.

"Let's step over here where we can rinse you off." She stood and walked toward the sink on the back wall, and I followed her, a bit shell-shocked.

Chapter 21

S
he turned on the water and began to spray the exfoliating cream off my skin, and I rushed to ask a question before she started talking again.

"I'd love to hear more about the building where the new theater is going in. I love the idea of bringing the arts to Cedar Creek, and I was wondering if there's ever been a theater here before. I think someone said that building was an auto shop? Is that right?"

"Yes, it was an auto shop, for years and years. Your aunt Virginia probably remembers it being one, in fact. I don't know if you knew, but she was a regular of mine whenever she was in town."

"You know Aunt Virginia?"

I suppose I should have realized that was a possibility given the amount of time my aunt had spent in Cedar Creek, but it was a shock, and I'm sure it showed on my face.

Myrtle smiled as she took down a towel and began to dry my hands and arms.

"Sweetest woman you'd ever want to meet. She doesn't come down so much since your uncle passed, and I've sure missed her. She was right proud of you, I tell ya. She had fretted so over you and your mother, but it seems like you survived all that and turned out just fine. Now, step right over here, and we're gonna dip your hands in this wax."

I blinked, stunned at the revelation that Aunt Virginia had discussed me and my mother with Myrtle. I couldn't help feeling like Myrtle was alerting me that she knew more about me than she had let on, and I weighed my options for response as I followed her to the small vat of melted wax.

My first instinct was to tell her that my mother and my wedding plans and my fiancé's family trauma were none of her business. But I'd learned long ago that the bigger the protest you make over something, the more attention it draws.

Besides, if I alienated the town's main source of information, I risked not only missing the opportunity to get what I needed but also making an enemy of someone very well-connected whose favor would be preferable to her wrath.

"Spread your fingers and dip in slowly," she said as she guided my hands into the wax, which was almost too hot but yet oddly comforting to sink into. "Okay, pull them out, and we're going to dip again. You only need to go a little above the wrist, not far at all. Do that a few more times. That's it. Now, hold them up like this."

She nodded as I correctly mimicked her action, and then she covered each hand with a plastic bag. Next, she wrapped a small towel around each hand and led me back toward the nail station.

"Does your mother still travel a lot?"

"Her job keeps her quite busy. So, about the theater—"

"I imagine it would. Virginia said your mother had always been a bit of a wild one; a nonconformist, she'd say. She worried that all that traveling and the lack of stability had affected you, but I suppose, given your career choice, it was excellent preparation, don't you think?"

"About the theater," I said, forcing a smile and forcing the conversation back on my terms. "Tristan says a man named Hyram Letchworth owned the auto shop when he was a boy. Did you know Hyram?"

"Oh, of course. Everyone knew Hyram. Everyone knew everyone in those days."

"How did he die?"

Myrtle dipped her chin to peer at me over her glasses.

"You didn't hear this from me, but I guarantee it was cirrhosis. Now, the family liked to tell people it was natural causes, and that's not necessarily a lie. The man was eighty-seven, and he'd been drinking like a fish and smoking like a chimney pipe his whole life. But all the signs were there."

"Did he happen to die in the building?"

She leveled her stare at me, and it was the first time she'd been silent for more than a breath since I'd arrived. She cocked her head to one side and smiled. "How well do you know Danielle Ward?"

The abrupt topic change caught me off guard, and I stammered.

"Um, I, uh, not that well at all. I've only recently met her."

I saw no reason to tell Myrtle that Dani and I had transcended from casual acquaintances to business associates, confidants—and dare I say, friends? —in that short time. Especially since Dani had requested that she be left out of the conversation.

Myrtle cocked her head to one side as she tapped the bottle of dark burgundy polish against the palm of her hand.

"Do you know that some say Hyram cursed that building?"

A chill ran over me, and I felt I was finally getting somewhere. "Cursed? What do you mean?"

"Folks say it's doomed. I don't know about that, but he was certainly the only one who could seem to find success inside its walls."

"What can you tell me about Hyram? What kind of man was he?"

She shrugged and lifted part of the towel to check the wax.

"He was a stubborn old coot, hard on his workers, rude to his customers, and not quick to make friends. He knew his business—there's no denying that. Folks would come from all over to have him work on stuff for them, but the man had no people skills at all. He never married, and he had no offspring that anyone knew of, so when Hyram passed, everything went to his brother, Claude." She pulled a plastic bin into her lap and began to remove the wax from my hands. "Claude had taken over their father's groves when the old man died, and folks say there was bad blood between him and Hyram over how the inheritance was divided. They didn't speak for years, and Claude didn't have much interest in running the auto shop once Hyram was gone, so he put one of Hyram's foremen in charge. That fool ran it in the ground within two years, and they had to shut it down."

I wondered if perhaps that could be the reason Hyram was so upset in his afterlife. If he was already bitter about what his brother got from their father, and then his brother inherited his life's work and destroyed it, that might be enough to keep him from finding peace beyond the grave.

"How long ago was this?" I asked as Myrtle applied a clear base coat.

"Hmmm," Myrtle closed her eyes for a moment. "Let me see if I can remember. Pauline passed of the stomach cancer. I expect that's been at least eight years ago, and Claude went not too long after her. Died of a broken heart if you ask me. So, I'd say it probably closed seven years ago? Somewhere between Pauline's death and Claude's."

"And nothing has stayed open long since then, right? Is that why people say it's cursed?"

She moved my hands under the dryer and opened the bottle of color.

"There's more to it than that. Let's just say that building has a history since Hyram died, and it ain't a good one. Some say it's not only cursed, but haunted. I don't know what you think about that, you making all those ghost movies and such, but I tell you what. I'm not one to put much stock in ghost stories—or curses, for that matter—but I've heard many a person I know and respect talk about the strange happenings in that there building."

She looked up, and our eyes locked.

"I can see by your reaction that you know exactly what I'm talking about. I figure that's why you're here asking questions, but let me give you a word of warning. Before you get all worked up over curses or ghosts, you might ought to look a little deeper into your new business partner who you say you don't know much about."

"Dani?" I asked as she pulled my hands from the dryer and began to apply the polish.

"I happen to know that you're bankrolling this little venture of hers." Myrtle sat up straight and scowled. "Now, what you do with your money is your business, and I've never been one to give financial advice. But that girl's bad news, and you'd do best to keep your distance. If she'd stayed around here, she'd know why that building was empty."

I'd given Dani my word that she wouldn't be a topic of conversation, and I moved to change the subject as Myrtle focused on my nails.

"So, these strange happenings, do you know if anyone has investigated? You know, looked into it further to see what the cause may be?"

Myrtle looked at me as though I was daft.

"Investigate? Honey, have you not listened to a word I've said? We know the cause. Hyram Letchworth cursed the building and haunts it. What is there to investigate?" She sighed as she placed my hands beneath the fan to dry, and then she wasted no time in bringing the conversation back around to me. "I guess you're relieved that all those reporters and photographers have left town. Lord knows, we all are. I couldn't find a parking space for my own Cadillac, much less be able to have any available for my customers. Now, what on earth will y'all do to prevent that kind of madness at a wedding? I guess that's when it might be best to elope, huh?"

The time had come to shut it down. She had taken my silence as confirmation, and I didn't want to be reading about my supposed wedding plans in the papers or tabloid rags any time soon.

"You've mentioned us marrying a couple of times now, but Tristan and I are not in any hurry to take that kind of step. We're just enjoying each other's company for now."

She smiled a knowing smile and winked at me as she leaned across the table and lowered her voice.

"I understand. Best to keep the details under wraps. That's hard to do, though I would expect you already realize that. Why, I've had it from several reliable sources—one in our own family—that an official engagement has been enacted even if not yet announced." She glanced around the salon and leaned in closer, her hand on her chest. "You didn't hear this from me, but I've heard tell that a certain deputy has referred to you as his fiancée on occasion, and word on the street is that you introduced yourself as such when he was in the hospital with that gunshot wound. But don't worry, dear." She made a zipping motion across her mouth. "My lips are sealed. If you hear anywhere that a source has been quoted, you can rest assured it wasn't me. I owe that much to Nanette—God rest her beautiful soul."

I had no idea what to say to that, but as was her general manner, Myrtle didn't seem to need a response.

"A theater, huh?" She chuckled and set about applying the topcoat. "Well, we'll see. I'm not sure how anyone could expect to make a living around here doing that, but I suppose you have plenty of money to allow Danielle to pursue her folly. All I can say is my sister's boy dodged a bullet there."

"Your sister's boy?" I asked before reminding myself not to encourage or engage her.

"Oh, I guess you wouldn't know not being from around here. Danielle used to date my nephew, Seth. That boy was right smitten with her. He would've married her, but she thought she was too good for Cedar Creek. Seth would have lassoed the moon and put it on a silver platter if he had thought it would keep her here, but she had dollar signs in her eyes. She took off to Chicago without even giving him so much as a forwarding address. He never heard from her again. Ain't that something? She practically abandoned her family. Only came home for funerals, and I think that was inheritance digging on her part." She shook her head. "Seth's done just fine without her, though. Got himself a good job with the sheriff serving this community. Maybe you know him since he works with Tristan?"

"I do. I didn't realize Seth was your nephew."

She beamed with pride as her smile filled her face.

"Yes, he most certainly is. Will you do me a favor? When you see Danielle Ward, you tell her Seth is better off without her." She clamped her mouth shut and then waved her hand with a frown. "On second thought, don't you tell her any such thing. I don't want her to know I wasted any time or energy discussing her, nor do I want her getting any thoughts about sinking her claws into him again." She reached to turn the dryer off and motioned for me to pull my hands out from under the fan. "Now, there. You're done. Don't your hands look so much better?"

I spanned my fingers wide to survey the results. They did look pretty, but the value of my visit had come in the information, not the manicure.

"Beautiful! Thank you," I said as I stood. "I appreciate you sharing what you knew about the theater building as well."

"Oh, sure. I enjoyed talking with you and getting to know you a little. My granny Daisy used to say all the time that I get too familiar with folks. It's just my curious nature, you see. I'm a people person at heart, and I just love finding out about people's stories. That's probably why I got into hair, to tell the truth." She held up her hands and grinned. "Don't get me wrong, now. I love a good makeover, but it's the connection with the people that make it worth the effort." She came to stand beside me and laid her hand on my arm. "I'm sorry if I brought up any sore subjects. I suppose since I was so close with Nanette, well, you know, us all being family and everything, I forget you and I don't know each other so good yet. Forgive me, please."

She grabbed my shoulders and leaned in as though she was going to hug me, but she kept several inches between us as she craned her neck to the side in some sort of awkward air hug.

"Mustn't mess the hair or makeup," she cautioned.

I paid her for the manicure and stepped outside into the bright sun to take a deep breath of fresh air.

I had been duly warned by both Tristan and Dani, but nothing could have prepared me for Mrs. Myrtle McGillicuddy.

Chapter 22

After leaving Myrtle's salon, I went straight to Dani's house to discuss my findings.

"You look excited," she said as she held the door open for me to enter. "Please tell me you have good news."

"I might have, and I might have bad news, too, depending on what your beliefs are."

"As you well know, I have found in the past twenty-four hours that my beliefs are more flexible than I thought they were." Dani grinned and motioned for me to sit on the sofa. "Nice nails, by the way."

"Thanks," I said, holding my hand up with my fingers wide-spread as I sat back against the fluffy sofa cushions. "I didn't have much of a choice in the matter, but at least I do like the color she picked."

Dani chuckled as she plopped down into the overstuffed chair in the corner with one leg tucked beneath her. "Mrs. Myrtle's a piece of work, isn't she?"

"I've heard about ladies who could use the Southern accent as a weapon, but she is a bona fide ninja. I feel dizzy from trying to keep up with her. It was like a minefield—a compliment here, a veiled

insult there, an invasive personal question followed by a helpful revelation, and all of it padded with a bit of gossip. It was definitely the
most interesting manicure I've ever had."

"I don't even want to know what she said about me." She leaned
forward, her elbows braced on her knees and her hands clasped.
"Skip straight to the good news and the helpful revelations."

"Well, I think I know why Hyram is so pissed."

"Do tell."

"Myrtle said there was bad blood between Hyram and his
brother going back to their father's death. Hyram didn't have any
heirs, so his brother got the auto shop when Hyram died, but
evidently, Claude mismanaged the shop so badly it ended up
closing."

"Ah, that's kind of what we thought, huh? He's resentful that his
business was ruined, and now he doesn't want anyone else in the
space. So, the question is, how do we give him peace? What is he
looking for?"

I shrugged. "I don't know. It's not like we can fix what happened
between him and his brother. They're both dead."

"True, but maybe if we acknowledge his disappointment or his
anger and explain that we understand where he's coming from, he'd
be willing to leave."

"Based on what Myrtle told me about his personality, I don't
think that's likely."

Dani sat back and chewed on the inside of her cheek.

"Okay," she said, staring at the ceiling. Her eyes widened and
she looked at me with a grin. "Hey, what if we invite him to stay?"

"What?"

"If he views it as his building and he doesn't want to leave, then
let's tell him he's welcome, but with ground rules. He can't disrupt
things or cause problems."

"You're going to create boundaries for a ghost? And what are
you going to do if he ignores them? Ground him? Take away his
phone privileges? If there's anything I've learned dealing with
Chelsea, it's that I have no control over what she does."

"It's worth a try." She looked at her watch and stood. "C'mon.

I'm meeting my cousins Piper and Lauryn in a little while to help plan my sister's baby shower, but we should have enough time to go to the theater and have a conversation with Hyram before then."

I shuddered. "Are you sure we want to do that?"

"What other option do we have? If we can't get rid of him, then we need to get him to calm the hell down. The sooner, the better."

"Aren't you even the least bit curious about the bad news portion of my time with Myrtle?"

"No," Dani said as she slid her feet into a pair of sneakers. "I figure it was something she said about me, and I stopped caring what Mrs. Myrtle McGillicuddy thinks a long time ago."

"Uh, no. Myrtle said that the building is not only haunted but cursed."

"What? Give me a break. Don't tell me you believe in that crap, too."

"I'm not saying I do or I don't," I said, holding up my hands. "I just thought you should know. She said no business has been successful in that building since Hyram was alive."

Dani rolled her eyes as she stood and walked to retrieve her purse from the dining table.

"Yeah, well, maybe the building and I have both had a streak of bad luck, and now, it's time for our luck to change."

I followed her out of the house with a churning in my stomach that could have been excitement, adrenaline, fear, or anxiety—quite likely, a nauseating combination of all four.

Chapter 23

My heart pounded as Dani turned the key in the deadbolt of the theater door.

"Okay," she said, turning back to face me with her hand still on the door handle. "Whatever happens, we can't run this time. He has to know he can't make us leave, and that we're gonna stand our ground. Let's go in there and tell Hyram we know who he is and we know why he's upset, and then we're gonna give him two options—stay politely or go."

"Right," I said, wiggling my fingers at my sides to release tension. "What if he doesn't want to do either?"

"We'll cross that bridge when we come to it. Now, look, it didn't go so well when I talked to him. Maybe you should try. Work some of the ol' *Spectral Slayer* magic on him. I know, I know—it's only fiction, but maybe you could try to say it like you're the *Slayer* and it would lend your voice some authority or something."

I had often summoned the presence of my character for courage, but it had been a while since I'd needed her. I hoped Lucy Landry was still inside me somewhere as we stepped inside the theater.

Everything appeared to be exactly as we'd left it that morning.

There was no sign of paranormal activity or vandalism as we proceeded into the main auditorium.

Dani flipped on the lights as I rubbed my hands across the back of my denim skirt, hoping to wipe away the damp perspiration of anxiety.

"I'm ready when you are," she said in a low voice as we both scanned the room and hoped not to see anything.

I closed my eyes, trying to picture myself as Lucy Landry. It would have been easier if I'd been in her signature black clothes and had her heavy sword in my hand. At the very least, I wished I'd had time to braid my hair to help me get in character.

"Any time now," Dani whispered with a nudge at my elbow.

I jumped, startled at the contact, and she put her hand over her mouth to suppress a laugh.

"Sorry," she said once she'd regained her composure. "Go ahead."

Gazing up at the dark office window, I cleared my throat and then squared my shoulders, assuming Lucy's stance.

"Hello there," I called out. "We've done a little research, and I think we know why you're resistant to leaving. It has to be hard to see a business you worked so hard for replaced."

I glanced over my shoulder at Dani, and she nodded in encouragement as she put her hands on her hips. I looked around for any sign of reaction before continuing.

"We are going to open this theater, one way or another, but here's what we're willing to do. You can remain here in your building; you don't have to leave. But if you want to stay, we need you to stop the shenanigans. If you're not willing to do that, then we'll be forced to bring in professional help to evict you."

No visible response occurred, and Dani stepped closer and leaned in to whisper, "Do you think maybe he's gone?"

"I don't know," I said, though the tingling sensation creeping across my skin told me it was highly doubtful.

Dani looked down at her watch and frowned. "I have to meet my cousins soon. We gotta wrap this up."

Our eyes met, and then I turned my attention back to the

window. "All right. What's it gonna be? Are you gonna stay and work with us? Or are you going to leave? What do you choose, Hyram?"

The window exploded, and shards of glass rained down onto the concrete floor as Dani and I ran for the back of the room with our arms covering our heads.

"You okay?" she asked as we stood in the green room, wide-eyed and panting for the second time that day. "Did any glass get you?"

"No," I said, shaking my head. "I don't think so."

She walked back to the doorway leading into the auditorium and stood with her hands on her hips as she stared at the glittering sea of glass scattered across the floor.

"Now what?" I whispered as I moved to stand beside her.

Suddenly, the back door opened behind us, and we both jumped with loud shrieks.

"What the hell?" Steve asked, startled at our reaction. "What's wrong? Are y'all okay?"

"Yeah," Dani said, still breathless. "We're fine. What are you doing here on a Saturday?"

"We have a fire alarm beeping at home with a low battery, and the ladder I need to reach it is here."

He looked up at the string of garlic cloves hanging from the door frame above our heads, and then he arched one eyebrow with a wry grin.

"What's with the garlic?"

"It's a long story," Dani replied. "One I don't have time to get into right now."

"Oh, great. Do we have vampires now, too? Like a ghost isn't nuts enough." He walked past us into the auditorium to retrieve his ladder but stopped short and let out a low whistle when he saw all the glass. "That's a mess. What happened there? Or do I even want to know?"

"It's another long story," Dani said with a resigned sigh. "I'll get the broom."

Steve folded his ladder as Dani retrieved the broom and dustpan to begin sweeping. He looked up at the hole where the window should have been, then he looked back down at the glass, and then to Dani.

"Let me guess. Neither of you broke the window?"

Dani frowned as we made eye contact, but Steve didn't need us to confirm it. He already knew. He rubbed his hand across the back of his neck and sighed.

"Maybe we should just shut the project down until you get this squared away and figure out what's going on."

Dani turned to face him, her voice and eyes both pleading. "No, Steve, I can't. Look, you were right. Obviously, it's something supernatural, okay? Now that I realize that, I'm doing everything I can to fix it, but I don't know how long that might take. Can you tell your guys I believe them, and ask them to be patient a little longer? I can't shut it all down. I need to get this place open. I gotta hold auditions and get rehearsals going. I need to get tickets sold. I can't delay the renovations."

Steve hesitated, and I sensed his next words wouldn't be good news.

"What if we paid a premium?" I asked, trying to head him off. "Would it make it worth it to put up with a ghost if your guys got paid more?"

He didn't answer right away, but the slight tilt head of his head and the rise in his eyebrow indicated the offer might be considered.

"We could do a bonus," I said, making up the plan as I went along. "For every day worked under these conditions, they earn an extra amount. Once we have the problem taken care of, they go back to regular wages."

"I can think of a few who might go for that," Steve said with a shrug.

"Believe me, I get that these are unusual circumstances," Dani said. "I'm scrambling to find a solution, and if need be, I'll call in professional help. I just need more time."

He stared back and forth between the two of us and then gave a quick nod.

"Let me talk to my guys."

Dani smiled at the possibility. "Thanks, Steve. I appreciate it. We both do. Oh, and please remind the guys to keep this on the down low. I know folks around town already think the building's haunted, but I don't want to confirm the rumor."

"They've been told not to run their mouths." He hoisted the ladder onto his shoulder. "Now, let me get back home before my wife blows her top over this damned beeping."

He went back out the way he came, and Dani let out a loud exhale.

"Thank you, Sloane. That bonus was a brilliant idea. I hope they go for it."

"It still doesn't solve our biggest problem, though." I glanced toward the office window's gaping hole and lowered my voice, though I knew it didn't matter what volume it was. "We can't have rehearsals or open the doors to paying customers unless we reach some kind of agreement with our resident troublemaker."

She had begun to sweep again, but she turned to look up at the window with a frown.

"We have to figure out a way to appease him," she said.

I grabbed the dustpan and held it for her. The tinkling sound of the glass shards smashing into each other as she swept them into the pan reminded me of Chelsea's high-pitched laughter.

"It would be helpful if he could just tell us what he wants instead of breaking stuff," I said with a sigh as I moved the dustpan to keep up with Dani and the broom. "Thank God Chelsea could talk so I knew what she needed from me."

"Yeah, why can't he just talk? Not that I'm sure I'd want to be able to hear ghosts, but it would make it easier. What might soothe him? Does he want the building named after him to preserve his legacy? Does he want it to be an auto repair shop again? I mean, his options are rather limited, don't you think? He's dead, someone else owns the building now, and there's not much we can do for him."

"It sounds to me like he needs to make peace with a family member who's also dead, and I have no clue how we're supposed to help him with that."

An alarm reminder pinged on her watch, and she raised her wrist and tapped the screen.

"Shoot! I gotta go. I'm gonna be late."

We hurried to finish cleaning up the glass and then walked outside together.

"You know," I said as we reached her car, "we may not be the only ones who have had these encounters. If we could talk with some of the previous tenants, and it turned out they had similar issues, you might be able to appeal to the landlord to break the lease."

She lifted her hand to shield her eyes from the sun as she looked at me.

"I don't want to break the lease. This is the only building available in the city limits that's suitable for a theater." She paused. "I feel like I keep hitting roadblocks, and I don't know whether the universe is testing my resolve and my will to succeed, or whether it's trying to tell me that this is not the right path."

"My aunt Virginia has always said that whenever I'm faced with a decision, I need to make sure my head, my heart, and my gut are all in agreement. If not, then I need to wait and figure out why before I move forward."

She considered my words for a moment before responding.

"I really think this is where I'm supposed to be and what I'm supposed to be doing. I've already put in blood, sweat, and tears to get it this far. I'm not ready to give up yet." She took in a deep breath and let it out in a loud rush of air as she stared at the building. "Is that ridiculous of me?"

"No, I get it. We'll figure out a way to make Hyram happy, and we'll get this place open."

Chapter 24

That night after dinner, once I'd given Tristan a play-by-play of my encounter with Myrtle, our conversation turned back to the theater building and its ghostly inhabitant.

"I have no idea what we're supposed to do to get this guy to leave," I said as we loaded the dishwasher together.

"Have you talked to the owner? I'd think this is more his problem than yours or Dani's."

"Dani doesn't want to involve him if we don't have to. She's a little hesitant to tell people she thinks there's a ghost, which I understand, believe me."

"Understandable, for sure, but she's probably not the first tenant to lodge this complaint." He closed the dishwasher door and started the wash cycle. "The owner may be able to give some insight from what others have experienced."

"Yeah, well, ever since the issue with the lights turned out to be nothing, he's been a little terse with her in his emails and texts. She suspects he thought she was trying to get money out of him or that she wanted to get out of paying for the electrical upgrades. He's been kind of a jerk about it, so I agree with her that he probably wouldn't be open to talking about such a divisive issue."

"You could go directly to his previous tenants and ask if they experienced anything," Tristan said, leaning against the counter with crossed arms as I wiped down the table.

"How would I know who they were?"

He shrugged. "That should be easy to find out. If they filed an occupational business license, that's public record. Let me make a call in the morning, and I could probably get someone to run a report for you. The contact information may not be current, but you'd at least have names to go on."

"Thanks," I said as I tossed the cloth in the laundry room and then came to stand in front of him. "You're not working tomorrow, are you? I thought you were supposed to have the day off."

"I do, but I promised Holden I'd go out to the construction site for the animal clinic and help him with a few things in the morning. You wouldn't believe what all they have going on out there. They're tearing down buildings, putting up buildings. It's crazy." He brushed my hair back off my shoulders and rested his hands there, his thumbs stroking each side of my neck. "You know, it's supposed to be a gorgeous day tomorrow. I'm thinking I should be done with Holden by lunchtime or early afternoon. Let's pack some sandwiches, some fruit, and take the boat out. We can get away from everything. No criminals, no ghosts. Just you and me, babe. Maybe even stay out late enough to watch the sun set."

"That sounds wonderful," I said as I wrapped my arms around his waist. "We haven't had a day on the boat in a long while."

Our boat escapes were one of my favorite things to do when Tristan was off. We could leave the world behind as the shoreline receded, and the boat would become our own little floating island, a refuge from reality.

I went to bed excited about the prospect of a relaxing day with just the two of us, and when I woke late the next morning, the weather proved as gorgeous as he'd promised, and then some. The sky was a brilliant deep azure, dotted with the fluffiest white clouds that made the blue even more vivid by contrast. Though the sun was hot, the constant breeze kept the air energized and moving so it never felt stagnant or stifling.

It had taken a bit longer at Holden's than Tristan expected, and by the time he got home, I'd already packed our cooler with yummy snacks, reusable bottles of water, and plenty of ice.

"Anything else going down to the boat?" he asked as he lifted the cooler to carry it outside.

"I have a tote bag with some towels and a swimsuit cover-up, but I'll bring that down when I come. I just need to braid my hair and I'll be ready."

"All right. I'll see ya down there. I think there's some sunscreen on the boat, but you might want to bring an extra, just in case."

"It's already in the bag."

"Of course. I should have known you'd be prepared," he said with a grin as he walked out the door.

Once I'd braided my hair, I grabbed the bag I'd packed and tossed in a baseball cap from the closet, and then I headed down to the dock.

Tristan stood with his back to me as I approached, and the sight of him shirtless in nothing but a pair of board shorts took my breath away, as it always had since the very beginning.

The taper from his broad shoulders down his back to his narrow waist was perfection, as was the way the board shorts clung to his slim hips and hugged the curves of his muscular back side as he bent to pick up a rope. He stood and began to untwist the rope, and the large eagle tattoo that spanned his upper back fluttered its wings with the flex and release of his muscles as he moved his arms.

He turned at the sound of my footsteps on the dock, and my heart fluttered at his grin. Would I ever tire of looking at this man? Would I ever stop wanting him with a desire so strong that it made it hard to focus on anything else when he was around? Would there ever be a time that his touch didn't make my pulse race and my insides quiver?

God, I hoped not.

He dropped the rope and greeted me with a kiss as he took the bag from me and loaded it on the boat.

"All set? House locked?"

"All set and locked, Deputy. The key's right here," I said, patting the front pocket of the denim shorts I wore over my bikini bottoms.

He extended his hand to help me onto the boat, and I wrapped my arm around his neck and clung to him as I stepped off the dock.

His skin was warm to the touch, and the brilliance of the sun made his gray eyes even lighter than usual. I breathed him in, and the combination of sunscreen, cologne, and perspiration on his skin smelled like summer in the best kind of way.

I sat on the bench seat in the back of the boat and applied more sunscreen as Tristan continued the departure preparations, and then I settled back and stretched my legs out in front of me with my feet propped on the cooler. I grabbed his hat from my bag and plopped it on my head, pulling it low over my eyes just as he stepped onto the boat.

"Damn, you look sexy," he said as he bent to kiss me. "Maybe we should say screw the sunset and head back up to the house."

"Can we make at least one loop around the lake first? I already applied all this sunscreen, and I'm wearing a new swimsuit."

He laughed as he took his place behind the wheel.

"Hey," I said, leaning forward to catch him before he turned on the motor. "I meant to ask you earlier, but did you remember to ask about the previous tenants?"

"I made a call this morning, and I should have an email with those answers by the time we get back."

"Awesome. Thanks, Deputy. You make a good assistant." I sat back and propped my feet up again to watch Tristan pilot the boat, appreciating the view of his body just as much as the lake and the sky above.

He navigated away from the dock and then opened up the throttle once we were out of the shallow water near the shore. I lay my head back and closed my eyes, soaking up the rays of the sun and enjoying a moment of bliss with the wind on my face, the crash of the waves against the sides of the boat, and Tim McGraw belting out songs over the stereo system.

The afternoon was as perfect as the weather.

We enjoyed the exhilaration of speed and then the relaxation of bobbing in a secluded cove. We ate, we laughed, and we talked. We sang along with the stereo, and we slow-danced. We lounged on our backs in the sun and caressed with sweaty skin, deciphering shapes in the clouds.

Despite being a sunny weekend day, the lake didn't seem crowded, and though we'd occasionally see another boat passing by, we were still pretty much alone and away from prying eyes in our own little world.

"I want to go away with you," Tristan whispered against my ear as we sat shielded from the late afternoon sun under the boat's canopy, bobbing with the waves. I reclined against his chest with his arms wrapped around me, mine entwined with his.

"What do you mean?" I asked, leaning my head back to look up at him.

"I want us to take a trip together. Somewhere tropical."

"Mmm," I moaned as I nuzzled my nose against the scruff of his chin. "That sounds heavenly."

"But not like a Ritz or a Four Seasons. I want some hole-in-the-wall, off-the-beaten-path place where no one cares who we are—or, I guess I should say, where no one cares who you are—and we don't have to pack anything other than swim trunks."

"Trunks, eh? So, I'm going topless this entire trip?"

He chuckled and squeezed me tighter. "You know what I meant. But hey, I wouldn't complain if you wanted to go topless."

I sat up and leaned forward, reaching behind me to untie my bikini top as Tristan burst out laughing.

"What are you doing? Oh my God, Sloane. What the hell? I didn't mean now."

I flung the bikini top to the floor of the boat and resumed my spot nestled against his chest.

He wrapped his arms around me to cover me. "What if someone comes by?"

"Look around," I said, sitting up and scanning the horizon left to right. "Do you see any boats close by? The nearest one is that tiny speck way over there, and they're not close enough to see anything."

I turned in his arms so I could see him, and he grinned.

"You're crazy," he said, his voice barely more than a deep rumble, and then he kissed me. He ran his hands up my back and into my hair, our lips never parting as he adjusted his position to lay flat on the bench seat and pull me down on top of him. As our kiss intensified, we forgot the world around us again.

At some point, the whine of a boat motor growing closer brought us back, and Tristan held me against his chest as he reached for my bikini top and handed it to me.

"You might want to put this back on."

"Such a prude, Deputy."

"Yeah, well, I'm just trying to uphold the law and at the same time, protect my girl from the prying eyes that always want a peek at her."

I laughed as I sat up and tied the straps around my neck, and as I did so, he pulled the others around the middle of my back to tie them. I flipped my braid forward out of his way, and once he'd finished, I stood and adjusted the top to ensure that I was covered in all the right places.

Tristan stood behind me and wrapped his arms around my waist. He spanned his hands across my stomach, sending little tremors of sensation all over my skin as his thumbs teased beneath my bikini top.

I leaned back against his chest as he pressed kisses along the side of my neck, and then I lifted my arms to reach behind my head and thread my fingers through his hair.

He nibbled at my earlobe, chuckling as I shivered, and then he whispered, "Whaddya say we head back to the house and explore which articles of clothing are optional in the privacy of our own bedroom?"

"Fine with me," I said with a grin, "but I thought you wanted to see the sunset."

He turned me to face him and closed his mouth over mine as he let his grip drift down to cup my rear and pull me against him. "I did, but having you in bed beneath me seems much more enticing."

I stood on my tiptoes to press my lips to his, using my tongue to express my enthusiasm for his new plan. It was all we could do to make our way home without throwing caution to the wind and taking each other right there on the floor of the boat. It's a wonder we didn't take out the entire dock bringing the boat in, but luckily, Tristan navigates well even when distracted.

We didn't bother to unload anything from the boat. We headed straight for the house, touching, kissing, and teasing the entire way.

With only his swim trunks and my bikini and shorts to shed, we were completely skin on skin the moment the door closed, and he lifted me to wrap my legs around his hips as he walked us to the bed and dropped me there.

I stared up at his sun-kissed, chiseled torso and allowed my gaze to linger over his rounded pecs and well-defined abs leading the way to the deep Adonis V-lines. Pangs of desire coursed through me, and I reached for him with both hands.

He nudged my legs apart with one knee as he joined me on the bed, and all the build-up and anticipation of an afternoon filled with foreplay exploded into passionate fury as our bodies finally came together and found the release we'd been seeking.

For a few moments afterward, neither of us moved or spoke. He lay still upon me, his weight partially braced on his elbows and his head nestled against mine on the pillow.

I pressed my lips against the salty skin of his shoulder, and he moved to shift his weight, but I tightened my legs and arms around him, holding him close.

"Don't go yet," I whispered.

He relaxed, and I lifted my hand to run my fingers through his hair, damp with perspiration.

"I gotta move," he said with a chuckle. "You're like a damned furnace, putting off heat."

He kissed me and rolled to his side, bending his elbow to prop his head in his hand and gaze down at me.

"I was serious about us going away. We've never had a real vacation together. I should be able to take some time off once we wrap up this case. A few days anyway…long enough to get away to some little beach hut on an island somewhere."

I rolled to my side to face him, and he reached to lay his hand across my hip.

"One of the makeup artists from my *Slayer* days was from a small island in the South Caribbean. It's not one that well-known, and he always said they had the most beautiful beaches but without the tourist traffic of some of the bigger islands."

"Sounds like the perfect place to me."

"I'll reach out to him and see what I can find out."

He rolled to the side of the bed and stood to retrieve a pair of gym shorts from the chair in the corner.

"I'm gonna head down to the dock and get everything out of the boat," he said as he pulled the shorts on.

"You want me to come help you?" I asked as I sat up.

"Nah," he said, bending to kiss me and brush back the hair that had escaped my braid. "Why don't you run a bubble bath, and I'll join you when I'm done?"

"Oh, that's a wonderful idea!" I groaned, arching as I reached over my head to stretch my arms and legs.

He let out a low whistle as his gaze roamed over me from head to toe.

"Damn, you make it hard it walk away."

I arched my back and then rolled to my side, jutting my hip toward him in what I knew would be a seductive visual.

"The sooner you go, the sooner you can come back for a second round."

"God, woman, you're going to be the death of me, but what a helluva way to go."

He bent to give me one more lingering kiss, and then he swore under his breath and went to take care of the boat.

Chapter 25

I filled the tub and sank into it with a deep sigh of contentment, closing my eyes as I lay my head back.

My thoughts drifted all over the place, jumping from Hyram to Dani to Tristan to the wedding with all sorts of side tangents in between.

I couldn't imagine being betrayed to the level that Dani had been. I felt confident that I knew who Tristan was, but how would I feel if suddenly one day I found that was all a lie? I shuddered at the thought of him being ripped away and me never being able to talk with him again. No more kisses. No more touch. No more laughter. No more love.

Dani was fortunate that she had a home to come back to and a family who welcomed her. If something like that happened to me, where would I go? Would I settle back in L.A.? Who would I turn to?

There were only a handful of people in my life who even knew I was dating someone, even fewer who knew we were engaged. I pondered how much of my need for secrecy was to protect our relationship and how much was to protect me in case it didn't work out.

While we hadn't had the whirlwind intensity of Dani and Victor, I could relate to what she'd described about it being different.

I'd never loved anyone the way I loved Tristan. I was certain I wanted to spend the rest of my life with him. Every day, every night. In fact, I couldn't imagine my life without him.

And yet, the thought of announcing a wedding made my entire body tense. It seemed so final. So confining. The public proclamation. The invitation for the world to weigh in.

How often had I seen my fellow celebrities blast their lavish ceremonies and receptions all over the news and across the pages of every magazine only to split within a year or two?

It almost felt like a jinx to me. Like setting ourselves up to fail.

As though my thoughts had summoned him, Tristan walked into the bathroom and sat on the edge of the tub.

I smiled and sat up to greet him, relieved that his presence had rescued me from the downward spiral of my anxious thoughts, but the contented, happy smile he'd worn when he left me in bed had gone.

His jaw was tight, his mouth a rigid frown, and his eyes seemed clouded, though I couldn't decipher whether it was anger or hurt that narrowed them as he looked down at me.

"What's wrong?" I asked, reaching to lay my suds-covered hand on his thigh.

He stared down at it and then looked back to me.

"I got the info you requested for the people who have operated businesses in the theater building since Hyram died."

His voice held a bitter edge, and I couldn't grasp the reason why.

"Okay," I said, my forehead scrunched as I stared at him. "What's happened? Are you all right?"

"Why does the county have you listed as the owner of the theater company?"

Ah. Realization dawned. I hadn't considered when Tristan offered to have someone do the research on past business occupants that they would include the current one as well. I sat back against the tub and let the swirl of bubbles hide me as much as possible.

"Oh. That. Well, um, Dani ran into some difficulties with her funding. I'm basically covering her costs and standing in as owner until she gets that squared away, and then I'll turn everything back over to her. It's a formality, really. We changed all the county paperwork once everything was moved into my name. The attorneys thought it would be best if we made everything official."

"The attorneys? What attorneys?"

"You know, my attorneys and Dani's."

He crossed his arms, and his eyes narrowed even more. "What did I miss? The last conversation you and I had, you were going to offer to pump some money into this venture to help get it started, but it was an investment. How did that go to you being the owner and having attorneys involved? And why is this the first I'm hearing of this? That paperwork was filed over a month ago."

"Right, well, here's the thing. Dani unexpectedly lost her funding, and I felt bad for her, so I offered to be the owner temporarily until she gets her problems worked out. It was kind of a last-minute, I guess you'd say, impulse decision on my part."

"Impulse? You decided to own a business on impulse? You know what? Never mind. I'm actually not surprised that you'd make that kind of decision impulsively. But why wouldn't you tell me, Sloane? Why wouldn't you discuss that with me?"

As usual, my go-to reaction to being put on the defensive was anger.

"Are you saying I need your permission to make decisions on what to do with my own money?"

He scoffed and ran his hands through his hair as he stood and paced the bathroom.

"No. Of course, you don't need my permission." He stopped and stared at me with his hands on his hips. "But I would think that we would discuss a major decision like this, or at the very least, that you'd tell me about it."

"I couldn't."

"What? Why?"

"Dani didn't want me to say anything to anyone." I bit down on my lip and considered my words. Dani hadn't technically said that I couldn't tell Tristan, but she had mentioned that she didn't want other people to know.

He crossed his arms again, widening his stance. "So, let me get this straight. This person whom you barely knew had some major issue with her funding, major enough that she needed someone else to own her venture, and she wanted you to take on the financial responsibility for her but asked you not to tell anyone? This has red flags all over it."

"I know, which is why I involved the attorneys. I wanted to make sure I had professional opinions on the best way to handle everything."

He widened his eyes. "So, you knew there were red flags, and you thought it was important to discuss it with attorneys—which is good—but you never thought to discuss it with me? You never thought to include me in your decision-making process?"

Part of me knew he was right, and I hated feeling like I was wrong. I also hated feeling like I was at a disadvantage with me sitting and him standing, so I stood and grabbed a towel to wrap around me, ignoring the water and suds that sloshed onto the floor as I stepped out of the tub soaking wet.

"The decision didn't involve you or your money, so again, I didn't think I needed your permission."

He shook his head as he stared up at the ceiling and then looked back to me. "It's not about permission, Sloane. It's not even about the money. It might have been an impulse, but it was still a big decision. You chose to put your name on a business in the legal sense and be financially responsible for it. Why would you not even think to mention that to me? You say Dani had some issues she wished to keep private, and I can respect you not wanting to betray her trust. But why hide that you did this? Why keep it a secret?"

"It wasn't a secret," I said as I dried my legs and arms with the towel and tossed it across the rack. "I wasn't trying to hide it. I just didn't know how to tell you."

"Why?" He followed me from the bathroom and stood in the

doorway of the closet as I grabbed a pair of shorts from a shelf. "Why not just tell me exactly what you've told me now? That Dani needed help for reasons you can't disclose, and you made a decision to help her but consulted attorneys to protect yourself."

"I think you still would have been mad," I said as I pulled a tank top over my head.

He stepped aside for me to leave the closet, and then he followed me back into the bathroom.

"I'm not mad, Sloane. I'm hurt. If we're gonna walk through this life together as partners, we have to communicate. I thought we'd both kind of agreed on that."

"So, that means I have to tell you every little thing?" I bent to open the cabinet and pull out my conditioner.

"This isn't a little thing. You decided to own a business with someone you don't even know. Someone who must have pretty questionable credit if she needed a bailout like this. And who starts a business and is already underway with renovations before she realizes she doesn't have the money?"

I paused in rubbing leave-in conditioner through my hair and glared at him.

"I told you, she lost her funding unexpectedly. She was counting on something to come through, and it didn't."

"Then she shouldn't have moved forward until she knew for sure." He leaned against the doorway as I flipped my head over to continue working the conditioner in. "Why are you taking a risk like this for someone you don't even know?"

I stood upright and flicked the strands of wet hair off my face. "You know what? This is why I didn't tell you. This right here. Because I knew you'd pick it apart and ask a ton of questions and tell me all the reasons I shouldn't do it."

"And that's a bad thing? It's wrong of me to be concerned about what you're getting into? To want to look out for you, to protect you?"

"Yeah, well, I don't need you to protect me, okay?" I pulled open the drawer in the vanity and took out my moisturizer and began to apply it. "I've been making my own financial decisions my whole life, and I think I've done just fine."

"Really? You wanna go there?" He cocked one eyebrow with a smirk. "You've made millions from your films, and you basically have nothing to show for it other than a closet full of labels."

My eyes met his in the mirror with a glare. "That's not true. I have an investment portfolio that's worth quite a bit, thank you."

"Only because your accountant and I both insisted you needed to do that after the sale of your house and the success of your last film. I'm willing to bet you have no idea what's in it, though. You don't even know how much you have in the bank unless your accountant tells you. You blow money like it's always going to keep coming in, but you don't plan for a future when it might not."

Fury and embarrassment flooded my cheeks with heat.

"So, that's what this is about? You don't approve of the way I spend money? You don't think I'm responsible with it? Well, you know what? That's none of your concern, Deputy."

"Isn't it, though? When two people get married, the financial decisions they make affect each other."

"Yeah, well, we're not married, are we?"

He opened his mouth to say something, but I didn't let him.

"I promise you I will never need one red cent from you, okay?" I stepped closer to him. "In fact, maybe we should sign a pre-nup and keep our finances completely separate so you don't have worry about what I have and what I spend. I bet Dani sure wishes she had signed a pre-nup right about now. She damned sure wouldn't be worried about some guy taking her money if she had."

Tristan took a step back, almost like he'd been struck.

"That's what you think of me? You think I'm after your money? Wow."

He turned to walk away, and I stared at my reflection in the mirror for a moment before going after him.

"Tristan, wait."

He stopped in the hallway but didn't turn around.

"I'm sorry," I said as I walked to him. "I shouldn't have said that, and no, that's not what I think."

"But you did say it." He turned to face me. "On some level you must have thought it."

"Yeah, well, you said I'm financially irresponsible, and I blow money."

He lifted one eyebrow, and I shrugged.

"Okay, so maybe there's some truth to that, but I hate feeling like I have to get permission from you to make decisions or like you're checking in on me. I've never had to get permission from anyone to do anything since I was a teenager."

"I'm not saying you need my permission, Sloane. But people in a relationship do discuss their decisions with each other. I get that you've always been on your own, but I have to wonder if you're ever going to stop thinking of it as *you and me* and start thinking of it as *us*. Like, seeing *us* as in this together."

"I want that. I do. I just hate thinking there will be something I want to do and you'll tell me no, or you'll tell me you don't think it's a good idea and then be upset with me if I do it anyway."

"First of all, I'm not suggesting a situation where I have the ability to tell you no. I'm simply saying I want us to communicate. To talk things through. And yeah, there may be times when we don't agree, but I respect that you are your own person and have your own decisions to make. I'm only asking that you have enough respect for me to include me in the decision-making process."

I walked to the foot of the bed and sat down, and he came and sat beside me.

"It's not that I don't respect you, Tristan. I do, and usually what you say makes good sense. I know that I make crazy impulse decisions and that I don't always think things through, and you provide that voice of reason. I don't always appreciate that in the moment, but I realize you have my best interests at heart." I turned to face him, drawing my leg up underneath me. "This thing with Dani...I think I didn't tell you because I knew what you'd say, and I knew you'd be right, but I wanted to help her anyway."

"That's one thing I love about you. You have a huge heart for helping others." He smiled and then sighed. "I just wish you'd protect yourself better when you do it."

"I don't think I'm unprotected here. I told you that I had the lawyers look over everything, and worst-case scenario, Dani's funding doesn't get released and I end up owning the theater company permanently."

"Is that something you want to do, though? Or are you just doing it to help Dani?"

I bit down on my lip and looked away from him.

"It certainly wasn't something I had planned to do, but since when do I ever make financial plans?" I looked back at him with a smile. "I think this is good. It makes me feel more like I'm part of the community. Besides, Dani's doing all the hard work. Other than putting up the money, I really don't have to do anything. Well, except help her get rid of a ghost."

He reached to take both my hands in his, and his expression grew more somber, his gaze intense as his eyes darted back and forth looking into mine.

"If you want me to sign a pre-nup, I absolutely will do that. Without hesitation. I don't ever want you to feel like—"

"Stop! Just stop. I know you, Tristan. And maybe what happened to Dani has me all weirded out and it's raised my anxiety levels, but in my heart of hearts, I know who you are. I know you're not after money. Hell, you were right…I blow it all, so there wouldn't be any for you to get anyway."

"Just think about it, okay? Talk it over with your attorney or your accountant or whoever you need to discuss it with. If it makes you feel more comfortable, I'm down for it."

I frowned as I stared into his eyes.

"Doesn't a pre-nup feel a little like we're going into the marriage expecting it not to last?"

"No, it feels like being prepared and protecting interests." He lifted his hand to cup my cheek, stroking my skin with his thumb. "I love you, Sloane, and I intend to spend the rest of my life by your side. Whether you're penniless or a millionaire really doesn't matter to me, but I want you to feel comfortable with the decision to join our lives together."

I reached to put my hand over his on my cheek. "I have no

doubts about spending my life with you. I just doubt that I'm cut out to play the role of someone's wife."

"Well, you don't have to be *someone*'s wife. You can be mine, and you and I get to decide what that role looks like. We also get to decide when, and it doesn't have to happen until you're sure that you're ready. I'm not going anywhere."

Chapter 26

We went for a second round, and then afterwards, Tristan made us dinner while I called Dani and gave her the info about the previous tenants.

"Great," she said. "Thanks for getting these names. I'll do some research and see what kind of contact information I can turn up."

She called back in an hour with a much more frustrated tone.

"That ended up being a dead end. Literally, in two cases. Looks like the guy who owned the motorcycle repair shop died a few years back, and so did the dry cleaner."

"Still think it's malarkey that the building is cursed?"

"Yes. Their obituaries said nothing about their cause of death, but I would think if it had been mysterious circumstances at the building, my searches would have turned up newspaper articles or something of the sort. In better news, I think I found the florist, or at least the same owner name and same business name, but in Miami. I left a message on the voicemail for the shop, and we'll see if anyone calls me back."

"All right. Maybe we could try and find family members of the two who died."

"Funny you should mention that. In the obit for the motorcycle guy, his father is listed as Ronald Fisher. That's my landlord."

"Oh wow. Okay. Well, at least you know how to reach him," I said as I grabbed two plates from the cabinet and set them on the table.

"Yeah, but I'm not so sure I want to ask a bunch of questions about his son's death. Which means other than the possibility with the florist, it looks like we may be back at square one."

"Right. Okay. Any other ideas?"

She paused. "I have one, but I don't like it, and I don't think you will either."

"Uh-oh. This doesn't sound good."

"Why don't you go talk to Mrs. Myrtle?"

"What? No. No way."

Tristan turned to look at me, his eyes wide with concern, but I shook my head to let him know he didn't need to worry.

"C'mon, Sloane," Dani pleaded. "You have to admit you got some good info from her the last time, and you know as well as I do that she can probably give us the dirt on every single person on our list. I'd go myself if she didn't hate me so much."

"I don't know. I feel bad going back to the salon just to get intel."

"It's called gossip in a hair salon, and it's a service they offer when you book an appointment for something else."

"Appointment? No way. I am not about to let that woman touch my hair."

"Then chip a nail and tell her you need her to fix your manicure. Desperate times, desperate measures. We've got to figure out a way to get rid of Hyram. We can't delay opening. As it is, the city keeps hounding me for an opening date to put on their events calendar, and I keep giving them vague excuses. I've also got people calling me about auditions, which I can't do in the theater if Hyram is still wreaking havoc."

"Well, that's a good thing that people are calling," I said as I refilled my glass of ice water. "It's great to know we have community interest."

"Yeah, I've been pleased with the number of calls I've gotten, not only for actors but also for lighting, sound, and backstage crew. I've kept a running list of names and numbers, and I've basically told everyone I'll call them with dates once I have them. Who knows whether or not any of them have any actual talent; we'll see. One in particular I'm excited about is my uncle William's granddaughter, Eva. He had told me she was talented, so I went to her school play while you were in California, and he was right. She's a natural."

"Awesome!" I looked down at my nails, still in perfect condition from the morning's manicure, and sighed in resignation. "Okay. I'll figure out a way to talk to Myrtle. You keep trying to reach the florist."

When our call had ended, I explained the situation to Tristan, and he grinned at my discomfort while I frowned at his glee.

"I am not about to let her cut my hair, or thin it, or whatever it is she seems to think is necessary."

"I don't blame you," Tristan said as he laid on the couch and picked up the remote. "Why don't you just call her? I'm sure I can find her number somewhere."

I looked up in surprise at the simple genius of his suggestion. "Now, why didn't I think of that?"

A phone call was a brilliant idea. I could get the information we needed without sacrificing myself to Myrtle's beauty services. I also figured it might be easier to control the conversation and prevent her bulldozer questioning if we weren't sitting face to face.

I think Myrtle knew that as well, which is probably why she insisted that I come over when I called.

"Oh, I don't want to intrude," I insisted, mortified at the very thought of dropping by Myrtle's house for a visit.

"Nonsense! It's no intrusion at all. Lloyd and I just finished up dinner, and I was about to cut into a pound cake. We'd love for you to stop by and have a piece. You and Tristan both, if he's not busy. We're only about a mile down the road from you as the crow flies."

"Oh, I, um," I stammered as I tried to think of a good reason to decline the invitation.

"Do you want vanilla ice cream or chocolate with your cake? It gets so hard in the freezer, and I'll have Lloyd take some out so it'll be soft enough to scoop by the time you get here."

"Oh, I don't want any ice cream, thanks." I glared at Tristan who was covering his mouth with his hand as he laughed. "But I'm sure Tristan would love some chocolate with his cake."

He stopped laughing and stared at me as he shook his head.

"No," he mouthed, and I suppressed a giggle.

"Wonderful!" Myrtle said. "I'll have Lloyd take both flavors out in case you change your mind. We'll see you soon."

We said goodbye, and I groaned as I tossed my phone on the counter. "That didn't exactly go as planned."

"Why'd you have to invite me?" Tristan asked.

"I didn't. Myrtle invited you, and it's only fair that you come since you got me into this."

I was happy for him to accompany me. I figured his presence would be a buffer for Myrtle's questions and keep her from venturing too far into his personal history.

However, that hope dissipated soon after we arrived. Once pleasantries had been exchanged and the cake and ice cream had been served, Myrtle dismissed the men to the den and announced that the ladies had talking to do in the kitchen.

"If you want to know more about Hyram's building, then I'll take that to mean you don't intend to heed my caution about going into business with Danielle Ward," she said once Lloyd and Tristan had left the room. "Suit yourself, but don't say I didn't warn you. Now, what did you want to ask me?"

"As I said on the phone, your mention of the building being cursed, and um, haunted, piqued my interest earlier. You said you'd heard about strange happenings there, and I'd love to hear more. I also wanted to see what you knew about the former tenants. I thought I might be able to track some of them down and hear first-hand what they experienced."

She tilted her head and lifted a finger to slide her glasses down her nose as she stared at me.

"Were you out in the sun since we saw each other? Your skin looks awful pink. The rosiness looks good on you, but it might be best to protect yourself from the sun while you're still relatively young."

My hand went to my cheek as it turned even rosier with an embarrassed blush.

"I do. I always apply sunscreen before going outside. We spent this afternoon on the boat." Why did I feel the need to defend myself to her?

"That must have been a nice way to spend the day" She pushed the glasses back into place and then stuck her fork into the cake on her plate. "This pale skin of mine hasn't always been *en vogue*, as they say, but I've got far fewer wrinkles than some of my customers who baked in baby oil and iodine back in the heyday of tanning. Now, some of that is genetics, of course. Your aunt Virginia has a right nice complexion. How's your mother's skin?"

"Fine, I guess," I said, eager to get back to the subject I came for. "Tristan mentioned that there was a motorcycle repair shop in the building when he moved here. Did you know the man who owned that?"

"It was Claude Letchworth's grandson, so Hyram's great-nephew. What was that boy's name?" She tapped her fingernail against her lip as she gazed up toward the ceiling. "Alex, I believe. I don't recall that I ever met him, but in a town as small as ours, everyone knows everybody to some extent. Yes, I'm certain now it was Alex. He was Claude's only heir, born to Claude and Pauline's only daughter, Claudette, who died in a car accident when the boy was just nine. Claude and Pauline raised Alex and doted on him. Why he wanted to fool with those motorcycles, I'll never know. They used to be deafening, running up and down the town, in and out of that shop. So loud."

She took a bite of cake and moaned a little as she savored it.

"Mmm. That is good if I do say so myself. You've barely touched yours. Eat up!"

"I was busy listening," I said, which made her smile as she continued.

"The boy inherited everything Claude and Pauline had and became wealthy beyond measure in his early twenties. I hear tell he'd always been popular with the girls—he was a looker like his mama—but once he got that money, they were all over him like flies flocking to honey. I'm afraid you won't be able to track him down, though."

I decided not to let Myrtle know what little knowledge I had about the building from Dani's research, figuring she might reveal more if I let her tell me herself.

"Why's that?"

"He's dead," she said with a frown. "I declare, that family's had more tragedy than the Kennedys."

I tried to feign some sort of shock to the news of his death.

"Oh, no! How did he die so young?"

"He'd been diabetic since childhood, and everybody said he never did do well with keeping his insulin straight. From what I heard, he drank a lot, and they said he'd sometimes forget to eat until his sugar dropped. I reckon that carelessness caught up with him. They found him in a coma, too far gone to save."

"That's so sad."

She nodded as she scraped the last crumbs of cake from her plate with her fork and then sighed. "That was when folks started talking about the curse, and it only got worse from there. A sweet family from South Florida moved in next. They were florists, a young couple with two kids who had the softest, most unruly curls you'd ever want to see. They were precious young'uns, but Lord, what a messy head of hair to cut. Soft and fine—just like cotton candy."

Lloyd called out from the living room asking for another serving of cake, and Myrtle beamed with joy as she leaned across the table to whisper to me, "He loves my pound cake."

She asked Tristan and me both if we'd like another slice, and then she cut Lloyd a piece and delivered it to him.

"Now, where was I?" she asked when she returned.

"You were telling me about the florist family."

"Ah, yes," she said with a smile and then got serious again. "Now, her parents lived with them, but the old man got sick and needed heavy tending, so they moved back to South Florida to be closer to their extended family. You could probably find them if you looked hard enough. After that, a couple from Boston came in with plans to make it a dry-cleaning place, but they didn't make it far with their plans at all. He was on a ladder one day, painting inside the building, and wouldn't you know it? He had a heart attack and fell off that ladder and died."

My eyes widened in surprise, and Myrtle seemed pleased that she'd shocked me.

"Did he die in the building?" I asked, and she shook her head as she swallowed her last bite of cake.

"No, hon. His wife called an ambulance, and he died on the way to the hospital. She has family from these parts. I might could get her number if you'd be interested in talking to her."

"Yes. That would be great. Thanks."

She gathered our plates and carried them to the sink as she continued. "I don't know of anyone who actually died inside that building, but spirits don't have to expire some place to attach themselves to it. Why, that shop was Hyram's life and his reason for living! He didn't have to die there to decide he wasn't going to leave, and he's outlasted anyone that tried to take over. That's the reason it's been sitting empty so long. No one from around here wanted to move in it, that's for sure."

Sensing where she might be headed, I rushed to ask another question before Myrtle could attack Dani again.

"What can you tell me about the guy who owns the building now? When did he buy it?"

She scoffed as she returned to her seat at the table.

"Ronald? That worthless, good-for-nothing, lowlife didn't buy anything. He was Alex's daddy, though he skipped out on Claudette at the first mention of her being pregnant and didn't turn back up until that boy was nearly twenty." She clucked her tongue against her teeth and shook her head in disapproval. "He inherited that shop when the boy died, along with everything else that had been in Claude's family for a century. It's a miracle they don't have fresh soil turned over every day down at the cemetery, because I can assure you all those Letchworths are spinning in their graves to know that no-count snake oil salesman got it all."

"There was no other family member on their side to claim it?"

"The boy had papers drawn before he died leaving it all to Ronald, who, of course, up and sold every acre, every tool, every vehicle—everything he could get a dollar for—within just a few months of his son being buried. The only thing Ronald kept was that building. He even had it up for sale, too, but then he moved to Tennessee before it sold, so I guess he decided to lease it instead."

"I wonder why he kept it."

"Hmmph. Probably so he could keep milking the boy's inheritance for all he could get out of it. As far as I'm concerned, Ronald Fisher is rotten to the core. If we were standing outside, I'd spit on the ground for having had his name in my mouth, and I'm not a spitting lady." She exhaled as she stood and reached for my cup. "Would you like some more coffee?"

Myrtle looked tired, and I felt bad for coming into her home in search of information.

"No, thank you. We should probably go." I stood and pushed my chair back under the table. "Tristan has to work tomorrow, and I'm sure you probably do as well."

"Oh, yes," she said as she placed our cups in the sink. "A full appointment book tomorrow and all hands on deck."

"Thanks for the delicious cake, and thanks, too, for the history lesson. I'm just fascinated by all this."

She came and stood in front of me with a smile and then bent toward me to do her awkward air hug. "Y'all are welcome to stop by any time. We'd love to have you over for dinner some night. It would do my soul good to feel like I was looking out for Nanette's favorite boy and his bride."

I stiffened, wary of the conversation turning to wedding talk again, but she moved past me to the door leading into the living room.

"Lloyd, turn off that TV, and let's see these young folks out."

Her husband did as he was told, and we left with little fanfare.

"Did you get what you needed?" Tristan asked as we turned out of their driveway and headed for home.

"Yeah, I think so."

"You don't seem too happy about it."

I bit down on my lip, considering my words carefully. "Well, I think I might know a way to for us to appease Hyram."

"Isn't that a good thing?"

"I don't know. I think I may need to buy the building."

Chapter 27

I called Dani as soon as we arrived back home and relayed my conversation with Myrtle.

"To say Myrtle doesn't think highly of your landlord would be an understatement," I said once I'd finished.

"My interaction with him has been limited, but he definitely gives off an asshat vibe." Dani sighed. "So, where does this leave us? How are we supposed to get Hyram at peace when someone he loathed owns his building?"

I hesitated a moment, not sure I was ready to throw the offer out there. There didn't seem to be any other option.

"What if I bought the building?"

"What? What good would that do?"

I exhaled a nervous breath and prepared to support a case I wasn't certain I believed in.

"It might not do anything, but I'm thinking if we explained to Hyram that we understand why he's so pissed and then tell him I'm willing to buy the building to try and right history somewhat, that might go a long way with him."

"How does that right history? You're not a family member."

"No, I'm not, but I'm also not someone who has screwed their family over. Our other alternative would be to try and track down a family member and see if they're interested in buying the place."

"I would think if Hyram had a cousin with the means and the desire to do that, they would have already tried to do it. We don't even know that Ronald would sell."

I pulled my feet underneath me on the couch and hugged a throw pillow against my chest.

"True. Myrtle said he sold everything else, though, and he did have it up for sale at one time. So, that leads me to believe that if the price was right, he'd be willing."

"Sloane, do you seriously want to buy this building? I feel like you're getting in deeper and deeper, and I worry that wasn't your intention. You were looking for a way to get back on stage, not to own one."

I tossed the pillow onto the sofa beside me and sighed. "Obviously, I didn't set out to own a building in downtown Cedar Creek, but I'm open to it. My accountant has been on me for years to invest in real estate."

"Um, okay," Dani said with a chuckle. "Good advice under normal circumstances, but I don't know that a run-down building in Cedar Creek, Florida, with a reputation for being cursed and haunted is what your accountant had in mind. It doesn't exactly scream *good investment opportunity*, and I say that as someone who would benefit greatly from you making this purchase. I would much rather have you for a landlord than Ronald Fisher."

"I suppose it depends on what the building might be worth and what it would take to get him to sell." I smiled and took the glass of wine Tristan offered me on his way out to the deck. "I don't have a clue what something like that would go for."

"We could talk to my realtor, Cheryl. I'm sure she could give us a good idea of what it's worth. I'll text her when we're done talking."

"Okay, sounds good. Then, once we have a ballpark figure, I'll talk to Marc and have him run the numbers, and we can go from there. Like you said, Ronald may not be willing to sell, so it might be a moot point, but we can at least figure out if it's feasible to make an offer."

"All right. I guess for now, that's all we've got. I'll try the florist again tomorrow. Did Mrs. Myrtle say when she might have a phone number for the dry-cleaning lady?"

"No. I'm not even sure she'll be able to get it, or if we should use it if she does." I cringed at the thought. "Do we really want to call this poor woman and ask her questions about how her husband died? That seems pretty insensitive."

"I wasn't going to ask specifically about that. I was going more for whether or not they saw anything suspicious during their time there."

"Still, I think that might be awkward," I said as I took a sip of wine.

"You forget that I started my career as a reporter. Awkward questions are standard operating procedure."

"Oh, right. I guess I view things from the other side. You know, the receiving end of said awkward questions."

"Don't worry," Dani said. "I'll be compassionate and considerate. Believe it or not, I was a damned good reporter. I made people feel comfortable talking to me, but I also had a knack for detecting bullshit. Well, you know, if you set aside my inability to detect that my husband was a murderer for the mob."

"Maybe that says more about his ability to lie than your ability to detect a lie."

"Maybe. Thanks for talking to Mrs. Myrtle, Sloane. I know I've said it before, but I really appreciate all you're doing to help me. Now, go spend time with that deputy of yours, and we'll talk in the morning."

"Hold on, Dani. Before you go, there's something I need to ask you."

"Sure. What's up?"

I stood and walked to the French door to peek out at the deck and make sure Tristan was out of earshot. He was in the hammock on the other end, but I turned and moved toward the kitchen just to be safe.

"Would you be okay with me telling Tristan why you needed me to take over the finances?"

"Of course! I kind of assumed you had told him already, to be honest."

"Oh, well, you seemed concerned about who knew, so I didn't want to betray your trust."

"I appreciate that, and yeah, I definitely would prefer that everyone not know. I'm not telling anyone outside my closest immediate family. Well, and you, of course. Like I said before, it's public knowledge if someone looks for it, but the longer I can keep my name out of Cedar Creek's grapevine, the better. As far as Tristan, you trust him, right?"

"Definitely. I've never in my life met anyone with more honor than Tristan. That's part of the problem, I suppose. Not that I'm *not* honorable or that I have anything to hide. It's just that he wants us to be honest and forthcoming about *everything*, which is good, I guess, but I've always been on my own. This whole concept of telling someone what I'm doing or asking their opinion about it feels very foreign to me."

"I get where you're coming from," she said with a sigh. "I've always been a loner, too, and I was never one to poll my friends or call my family and have them weigh in on my decisions before I did something. A large part of the reason I avoided relationships was so I didn't have to answer to anyone or consider someone else's opinion. But after going through this madness with Victor's shadow life, I look at things differently. If I was ever in a relationship again—and I don't think I ever will be nor do I want to be—but if I was, I'd want someone who could open up to me. Someone who could let me know what was going on in their world and in their mind. I'd want someone who would share what they were thinking and value my input enough to ask for it."

I leaned back against the counter as I considered her words. It wasn't the same situation, of course. Neither Tristan nor I was involved in criminal activity kept hidden from the other.

But it wasn't altogether different either.

Tristan wanted what Dani would want. A deeper intimacy. A

deeper commitment. A willingness to be open and vulnerable with each other.

It sounded like something I should want. And I suppose on some level, I did. But it also terrified me. Not because I felt anything other than safe with Tristan, though. I meant what I'd told Dani. I trusted him.

So where was the disconnect? Perhaps I didn't trust myself?

"Are you still there?" Dani asked.

"Yeah."

"Did I say the wrong thing? Because I was just thinking about the flip side. If Victor had told me the truth, I would have left him, without a doubt. You know, the only thing saving me right now with both the federal prosecutors and the mob is that I truly didn't know anything. I can't help or hurt either side. He protected me by keeping me in the dark." She paused. "Not that I'm advocating that or saying it's a good idea. God, I need to just shut up. I'm not making any sense."

"Yes, you are," I said as I pushed off the counter and walked to look out at Tristan again, who appeared to be sound asleep in the hammock. "Your points are valid, Dani, and I appreciate the insight."

"Tell Tristan the truth, okay? But can you please ask him not to say anything? Especially to Seth. I know it's probably stupid, but I don't want Seth to know what happened in Chicago, to know how bad I screwed up. Okay?"

"He won't say anything, I promise."

I continued to weigh the decision as I walked outside onto the deck after ending the call, and my mind wavered back and forth on whether to tell him the truth as I approached his sleeping form in the hammock.

He looked so peaceful, so serene. I bent to press my lips to his, and he stirred, reaching for me without ever opening his eyes.

"Climb in with me, and let's sleep out here tonight," he whispered.

"No way," I said with a laugh. "The last time we did that, the gnats nearly ate us alive in our sleep, and I woke up looking like I had the measles. Come on, Deputy. Let's go to bed."

He tumbled out of the hammock, and I took him by the hand and led him inside. He yawned as he pulled the door closed and locked it.

"Sorry, babe," he said as he rubbed his eyes. "It must have been all the sun and the physical workouts you put me through earlier, topped off with cake and ice cream. I'm exhausted, and I can't hold my eyes open."

The conversation would have to wait. There would be a better time to tell him that I'd financed the theater because Dani had been swept up in Victor's federal organized crime charges.

Tristan had enough trouble sleeping as it was. No need to give him more to worry about when it was likely nothing to worry about at all.

Chapter 28

Determined to have Hyram gone as quickly as possible, Dani became relentless in her pursuit of information and a solution.

She'd invited me to ride with her to the community college to look at the seats for the theater, and by the time I arrived at her house that morning, she'd already left another message for the florist, gotten answers for me from the realtor, and researched the options for paranormal investigators in Central Florida.

"Just in case," she said with a grin. "I figure we should have all the bases covered."

"Right. Makes sense. I'm gonna email Marc your realtor's contact info and just have the two of them talk."

"Sounds good. I also think I may have found a cousin of Hyram's who lives up near Gainesville. Her phone number is unlisted, but I reached out to her on social media and asked her to contact me."

"What are you going to do? Ask her to come and talk to Hyram?"

"Maybe, it depends on how the conversation goes *if* she decides to contact me. More than anything I'd like to feel her out and see if she has any interest in the building. Do you want a cup of coffee before we go?"

"Do we have time?"

"Sure. I told them we'd be there this morning, but I didn't say a specific time."

She poured me a cup of coffee and we sat at her kitchen table.

"Aren't you having any?" I asked.

"I already had two cups earlier, and I don't need any more caffeine. I'm bouncing off the walls with energy as it is. I've got that journalistic buzz going. I always got it when I knew there was a story brewing, and I was in pursuit." She grinned and then she leaned forward, resting her elbows on the table. "I've been thinking that maybe we should revisit your idea to ask Ronald if he's had complaints from other tenants. I'm willing to bet he has, and if so, pointing that out might make him more willing to accept when you offer to buy."

"It's possible. Do you think we should wait and hear from the other tenants first, though? That way we'll know for sure if he's aware there's a problem. We also might want to wait until I hear back from Marc about whether I can even make an offer."

"I don't know that I could trust someone else with my finances that way. You have a lot of faith in this guy, huh?"

"Yeah, I do. We've been together a long time. I was one of his first clients when he opened his own firm, and I was barely of a legal age to be making my own financial decisions and I'd just fired my mother as my manager. I knew nothing. So, Marc's kind of been part accountant, part money manager, part pseudo-family member who happens to have a lot of financial knowledge."

"Nice."

Her phone rang, and she pulled it from her pocket and grinned when she saw the screen.

"It's the florist."

I sat and sipped my coffee while Dani stood and took the call, and though I could only hear one side of the conversation, it was obvious the woman wasn't comfortable giving Dani information.

"Nothing?" I asked as she flung the phone on the table next to her.

"She said she was sorry she couldn't help me, and she suggested I contact the landlord instead. I think she has to know something. Otherwise, why wouldn't she just say she didn't? The fact that she's sending me back to Ronald tells me something happened." She sighed and stuck her hands in the back pockets of her jeans.

"Well, I guess we're in a holding pattern until we hear back from everyone."

"If you're finished with your coffee, we can get going. I'd like to stop by an antique store on the way back and look for some props."

"Sure. Tristan's working, and I have a script I need to read, but I can do that later."

We talked about her plans for theater decor and the set for the upcoming play on the way to the college, and we'd just left the campus after picking through the chairs when Dani's phone rang.

She glanced down at the number on the dashboard screen. "That's weird. It's a Miami number, but not the same as the florist. It's two digits off."

She answered it through the car's system so we both could hear.

"This is Danielle Ward."

"Hi, um, you called my mom earlier about the place in Cedar Creek?"

The voice was a young male's, so quiet and timid that Dani had to turn up the volume so we could hear him.

"Yes, I did."

"Okay, well, my grandma asked me to call and tell you that you need to stay away from that building."

A shiver ran down my spine as I looked over at Dani, whose eyes were as wide as my own.

"Why's that?" she asked.

An older female voice said something in Spanish in the background.

"My grandma says there's an angry spirit there, and she says the place has bad energy."

The woman spoke again, and the boy rushed to translate.

"She said your business won't do good there because the man is unhappy."

"Can you ask her if she could give us some specifics? Was there something in particular that happened to make her think this?"

The woman's muffled response was short and harsh.

"She says I need to go. My mom can't know that we called you, but my grandma wanted to warn you."

"Okay. Please tell your grandma I said thanks, but could you ask her if she has any idea what the ghost wants?"

"I gotta go."

He ended the call, and Dani glanced over at me.

"I guess we have our confirmation that there's a ghost."

"Did we still need confirmation at this point?" I asked with a chuckle.

"A reporter always tries to find corroborating evidence. I wish I'd thought to ask if they let Ronald know."

"I don't think they intended to provide any additional details."

Dani tapped her fingers on the steering wheel as she drove. "Mrs. Myrtle said they left town because a family member was ill?"

"Yeah. The grandma's husband, I think."

"I wonder if they just said that to get out of the lease. They weren't even in the building a year, and then the dry cleaner never even opened, so they were only there a couple of months. Undoubtedly, Ronald would be willing to sell if he can't get anyone to stay for a full lease. Maybe I should make him think I'm considering breaking the lease, too."

"What if he calls your bluff, though?"

"Then I stay."

My phone rang, and I was surprised to see Priscilla's name on the screen when I pulled it from my purse.

"I'm sorry, but I need to take this. It's my publicist."

"Of course," Dani said.

"Hi, Pris. What's up?"

"You haven't seen them, have you?"

A feeling of dread dropped into my gut like a lead balloon. "Seen what?"

"*Insider Lens* just dropped a photo spread of you and your guy."

"Wait—what? A photo spread? Of me and Tristan? How? We haven't been anywhere."

"You were on a boat, on a dock, on a lawn, on a deck. Pretty amorous shots, babe. Like, va-va-voom."

Memories of our afternoon on the boat flooded my mind, and a hot rush of embarrassment colored me pink from head to toe. "Oh my God, Pris! Am I topless in the pictures?"

Dani's head whipped in my direction, and then she looked back to the road.

"What? No," Priscilla said. "At least none that I've seen. Why? Please tell me you weren't topless with photographers around, Sloane."

"No, I wasn't. At least, I don't think I was. We were on the boat, and there was no one near us. No one close enough for pictures, anyway."

"C'mon, Sloane. You know these guys have massive zoom lenses. Why would you take that chance?"

"I swear, Pris, there's no way. There wasn't another boat anywhere around. Like anywhere within view."

"Well, they were certainly close enough to get these pics, and you may not be topless, but you don't really have to be when you're wearing a bikini and he's only wearing a pair of board shorts. Looks like the two of you were all over each other."

I covered my face with my hand as a hundred mortifying thoughts swirled in my head all at once.

Tristan. Tristan's parents. Tristan's boss. My pending contract for the TV pilot. Two pending contracts for roles in rom coms. The theater. Cedar Creek.

"Oh, God, Pris! What are we going to do? How bad is this?" I flung my hand toward Dani. "Can I borrow your phone? I have to see these pictures for myself, but my phone won't load them while I'm on the call with Priscilla."

Dani grabbed her phone from the pocket of the door and handed it to me.

The pictures popped up with only my first name; I didn't even have to type my last.

I scrolled through images of our foreplay that had been captured and shared.

A passionate, lip-locked embrace as we docked the boat. Tristan carrying me across our dock with my legs wrapped around his hips and his hands beneath my rump, my head tossed back in laughter. Another embrace with a passionate kiss about midway up the lawn, this one with my hand clearly inside the front of his shorts. Three more photos showed us on the back deck in even more compromising positions. There was even a shot through the French doors of our bedroom, though the zoom had been magnified so much it was pixelated and too blurry to decipher that it was us on the other side of the doors.

My stomach roiled with the realization that someone had been watching us in what we thought was our private space. Tristan's back lawn was massive and lined on either side by acres of woods. We had no neighbor within a mile in any direction, and only the lake beyond the lawn to the back.

The photographer had either been in the woods, and therefore on our property, or he'd been on a boat that came close enough to shore to zoom onto our deck and into our bedroom without detection.

Granted, we'd been distracted and not paying attention, but we hadn't thought we needed to. Even at the height of interest about me in Cedar Creek, no one had violated boundaries in such a way. I should have known eventually they would.

"I understand you're upset," Priscilla said, her voice quiet. "These photos are personal, and they're a clear invasion of your privacy. I'm not downplaying that. But hear me out, okay? You're in between projects, and we don't have anything to publicize right now. I say we take control of this story, Sloane. You've never made a public statement confirming your relationship with your deputy. People are obviously curious about it, and these pictures going viral shows that there's an interest. I say it's time to drop the vague denials and redirects. Take the bull by the horns and overshadow these pictures by announcing your engagement."

My mind reeled even further at the thought of a proclamation that would be ripped apart by every gossip mag and would only serve to heighten interest in my relationship with Tristan.

I flipped through the photos again, enraged that such a happy, intimate moment had been marred and shared with the world.

"No," I said, but it came out as a croak. I cleared my throat and tried again, willing my voice to work. "I won't do that to Tristan. I can't. This is ours. It means something. I can't sacrifice that for a headline just to protect myself."

"You need to listen to me, Sloane. It's a slow news week. No one has overdosed, none of the couples with merged names has split, and no one beloved has passed from old age. You've got a moment of bad publicity going viral, but it could be used to generate good publicity. Let me do my job. Let me take control of the news cycle regarding you and give them something more positive to focus on. It won't stop people from sharing the pictures, of course, but we can steer the legitimate outlets toward the engagement story instead."

I closed my eyes and lay my head back against the seat, my cheeks burned by the slow, fat tears as they rolled.

"I have to talk to Tristan. It involves him just as much as it does me. I won't make this decision for him without his input."

"Fine, but time is of the essence. Call me back."

Chapter 29

As someone whose life had been largely private, Tristan had tolerated the publicity aspect of my job with a begrudging but polite acceptance. He never complained if a fan interrupted our dinner while out at a restaurant, and he always stood by with a calm smile if I was stopped on the street to sign an autograph or pose for a selfie.

His patience with the paparazzi had worn thin over time, though.

He'd always disliked their tactics and their aggressive manner, but when they'd invaded Cedar Creek after the success of my last film, he'd hardened toward them. He resented the chaos they'd caused in our small town and the negative blowback on me that resulted from it.

Most of all, he hated their sneakiness in trying to invade my personal space or capture me without my knowledge. If we were out somewhere and he spotted a photographer following us or lingering out of sight to snap a picture, his mood always deteriorated.

For the most part, his training and his general demeanor allowed him to stay calm and not show any outward reaction to them, but I could sense the tension building inside him. Though I'd never seen him hit anything or anyone, I worried it was only a matter of time before Tristan made his own headlines for smashing a camera or someone's nose.

Worried that this latest development might be the final straw, I called him when Dani dropped me off at my car and asked him to meet me in the parking lot outside the station. I figured it was best to prevent any outburst taking place in front of his co-workers.

In hindsight, I probably should have had him meet me somewhere completely out of earshot of other people, because anyone near the parking lot at the moment I showed him the pics got an earful of expletives.

"I want to know who took these," he said, his face beet-red with anger and his jaw clenched.

"They won't release the name of—"

"Who published them? What company?"

"Tristan, it does no good to go after—"

"I want to know who's responsible, Sloane. Someone had to be on our property to get these, and that's trespassing."

"They could have been on a boat."

"No. Look at this angle." He scrolled back to a shot of us on the deck and tapped his finger on the phone's screen.

I had to agree with him. There was no way it had been taken from the water.

Tristan handed me back the phone and swore again. "Someone was in our woods. They were at our damned house. If I find out who this was…" He paced back and forth beside my car; his hands balled into tight fists by his sides.

"They're not going to tell us who, Tristan, and we can't get all worked up about it. Look, I know this sucks, but—"

"Sucks?" He stopped and looked at me, his mouth tight with anger. "This more than sucks, Sloane. They were on our property. They were lying in wait, watching for you. Basically, stalking you! If I could get my hands on whoever did this—"

"Okay, okay, okay." I stepped in front of him and put my hands on his chest, steering him away from the gawking couple that had just exited the station. "Why don't we get in the car? Let's take a ride."

"I want to take a ride to wherever this photographer is, and I want to—"

"Listen to me," I said in as quiet and calm of a tone as I could muster. "You gotta calm down. People are staring."

"Let 'em stare," he roared, turning back to glower at the couple, which sent them scurrying toward their car. "Hell, the whole world might as well stare. They won't see as much as they did with those pictures."

"I'm sorry."

"What? What are you sorry for? This isn't on you. It's on those damned leeching scum."

"I know, but it comes with my job, and I hate that I brought this crap into your life."

"No. That's bullshit. Your career choice doesn't give anyone the right to come onto private property and take pictures of you without your permission."

I sighed, trying to control my own frustration and anger, entangled as it was with embarrassment and regret.

I'd let my guard down. I knew better. I'd spent my whole life getting caught in one lens or another, and I should have known that eventually they'd cross a line to get their shot.

When the bulk of the photographers left Cedar Creek, I'd relaxed and become complacent. We were so far removed from L.A. and the celebrity scene. I still scanned my surroundings when I was out and about at a store or a restaurant, but I'd been naive to think they wouldn't come for me at home.

After all, I'd basically laid out a gauntlet and challenged them to prove me a liar.

Whenever I'd been asked directly about Tristan in interviews, I'd always denied the seriousness of the relationship in an attempt to protect it. I'd routinely downplayed it as two people enjoying each other's company with a 'we'll see what happens' attitude. If they pushed, I laughed it off and said time and time again that my affinity for Cedar Creek was simply a desire for a slower pace and a small-town community, nothing more.

Now, the truth was out, and I had hard choices to make to manage the fallout.

"I know this probably isn't the best time to mention this," I said as Tristan continued to pace, "but Pris would like to announce our engagement in hopes that it would overshadow this."

He stopped and turned to stare at me.

"What?"

"Um, Priscilla thinks that if we announce our engagement, that could bump the pictures out of the news cycle. I mean, they're already out there, so obviously people will see them and share them. The cat can't be put back in the bag. But she thinks we could take the publicity and give it a positive spin."

"Are you willing to do that? Do you even want to do that?" He came and stood in front of me. "You've said all along you didn't want to tell people we were engaged. That you didn't want the scrutiny and the publicity that would bring."

"I didn't, but now, we've got that scrutiny and publicity whether we wanted it or not. We might as well take control of the situation and put out the narrative we'd rather have them talking about."

He turned his head to the side, and I could see his pulse pumping through the vein at his temple.

"So, this is strictly PR, then? You'd announce that we're getting married as a power move?"

"No." I groaned with a loud exhale. "I mean, yes. Partially. We were going to announce it at some point, anyway, so, why not now when it could be advantageous, right?"

His eyes narrowed. "You're asking me? I haven't been the hold-up. I would have told the entire world the moment you agreed to spend the rest of your life with me. You're the one who wanted this all private, and I respected that. Which is why I'm having a hard time understanding the change in perspective. You want to renege on all that just because some jackass posted pictures of us basically making love with our clothes on?"

I had no idea how to answer him. I didn't understand it myself.

My mind had been in panic mode since Priscilla first called, and I suppose I hadn't taken the time to process what she was asking of me or whether or not I genuinely wanted to do it.

"I don't know, okay? Part of me wants to do it just to shove a middle finger at these pictures. To say, you know what? You've got nothing on me, and you're not revealing anything I didn't already want you to know. But yeah, of course, I still want to protect us. To keep this private. I would have preferred that we put this news out there in our own time, on our own terms. But...maybe now's the time."

He stepped toward me and wrapped his arms around my waist. "This is your decision. I won't push you either direction. You decide, and I'll follow your lead."

I laid my head on his chest and wrapped my arms around him, and his embrace tightened as he bent to kiss the top of my head.

"I'm sorry I didn't protect you," he whispered.

I leaned back to look up at him with a frown. "No, don't even think that. There's no way you could have known, and there's nothing you could have done. Trust me, I've been dealing with this type of stuff for years. They always find a way to get their shot."

"Yeah, well, they won't find it so easy the next time. I'm gonna tell the sheriff I need to take the rest of the day off, and then I'm calling the security company to come and upgrade our system. I want cameras looking at every angle from every corner of that house. The dock, too. Hell, I want cameras on random trees in the woods. If some SOB steps foot on our property again, I will know it, and he won't get away without answering to me."

I shuddered at the cold resolve in his eyes, and then he stepped away from me toward the station.

"I need a few minutes to tie things up inside," he said. "You want to come in with me?"

"No, I'll head back to the house."

"Let me call Holden and see if he can meet you there."

"Holden? Why?"

"I don't feel comfortable with you being there alone."

"Oh, babe, C'mon. It's fine. It's not like someone's going to be there again today. Besides, even if they were, once I pull the car in the garage and shut the door behind me, I'm inside and out of view."

He hesitated and then let out a loud sigh. "All right. I'll be there as soon as I can."

"Take your time. I'm fine. Really."

By the time he arrived home, he had calmed down somewhat, which I was grateful for. I'd never seen him that angry, and I think if he could have discovered who the photographer was, my deputy very likely would have been arrested for assault.

Frustrated with the lack of options for retaliation, he focused instead on ensuring that our privacy couldn't be invaded to that extent again.

Within a couple of hours, he had walked the house inside and out with the security company regarding the system upgrade and then met with a fence company to walk and measure the perimeter of the property, which extended far into the woods on either side of the sloping lawn.

In between those, he called a window-tinting company and made an appointment to have someone come out and give us an estimate for covering all the window exteriors with a privacy film.

"Did you talk to Priscilla?" he asked once the fence guy had gone.

"Yeah."

"And?"

"She wants to shop around exclusive rights to an interview. Then, when she has that lined up, she'll call a few outlets and give them an off-the-record statement. They'll publish it and say it was from 'a source close to the couple' or something like that. Then, they'll run her official statement confirming the news on my behalf, and the interview will follow within a couple of days."

His forehead wrinkled, and his brows scrunched together. "Why not just have the official statement without the source runaround? And why wait to do the interview? It seems like that would be the best way to announce it."

I shrugged. "It's the way things work if you want to drive the news cycle. It spreads faster when people think it's a scoop, and then the confirmation legitimizes it and it goes even farther. Then once the public interest is heightened, you follow up with the interview. You have to strike while the iron is hottest, though, before they're bored with the topic or have moved onto someone else's scandal."

"Sounds like a lot of stress."

"Yeah, but if it works the way it's planned, then we essentially take the lemons presented by these pictures and turn them into lemonade. They made my name trend, so now we keep it trending in the positive for the maximum time possible."

"And that's what you want, right?"

"Yeah." I nodded with some trepidation. "It is."

He came and wrapped his arms around my waist with a smile.

"So, if all goes well, by the end of the week, it will be official across the land, huh?"

"Yep," I said as I put my arms around his neck. "No backing out now."

"Wait, so backing out was an option before now?" He rolled his eyes and let his mouth drop open in mock shock. "No one told me. You mean, I could have gotten out of this?"

"Very funny." I stretched onto my tiptoes to kiss him, and he lifted me to make it easier.

Then, he pulled back from our kiss and frowned.

"You sure you're okay with all this? Going public and everything?"

"Yeah," I said as I ran my fingers into his hair. "Oddly enough, I'm actually kind of excited. I thought I'd be freaked out more."

"Gee, thanks."

I gave him a playful thump on the back of the head. "That's not what I mean, and you know it. I thought I'd have anxiety about answering questions and all the commentary by the talking heads on the entertainment shows. But instead, I feel pretty chill about it."

"Maybe you're in shock, and it's going to wear off once you see the headlines splashed across the news."

I pictured those headlines as he grinned, and they made me smile back at him.

Sloane Reid Finally Finds True Love
It's Happily Ever After for Former Spectral Slayer
Small Town Romance with Small Town Hero for Big Screen Star

"Oh, by the way," he said, "I talked to Mom and gave her a heads-up about the pictures."

My smile faded in seconds.

"What did Rita say? Is she mad?"

"No. Not at all. She asked how you were doing, and she said she'd give you a call when she gets home."

I groaned and pulled away from his embrace to retrieve my glass of wine from the counter. "I don't want to talk to your mom about pictures of me with my hand down your pants or pictures of you with your mouth inside my bikini top."

"I don't think she was calling to discuss specifics, babe. I think it was more checking in to see if you're okay."

"Still, that's just awkward."

"Well, look on the bright side. You get to tell her our engagement's going official. She'll be thrilled about that."

"And just like that, my anxiety is back."

Chapter 30

True to her word, Rita called within an hour.

"Oh, Sloane, honey. Are you okay? What a rotten thing to happen."

"Yeah, it's not my favorite thing to deal with, for sure."

"I haven't seen the pictures, and I don't intend to," she offered, even though I hadn't asked.

It was a relief to hear, though.

"I'm sorry, Rita. The last thing I want is to bring any kind of scandal to the family."

"Oh, sweetheart. Don't you worry about that. This family isn't lily-white, you know! Besides, from what Tristan said, it's not that bad. Just some photos of two people in love with a healthy appetite for expressing it. When Ray and I were your age, we couldn't keep our hands off each other. We've slowed down a bit in recent years."

She chuckled, but I cringed at the thought of Tristan's mother and I discussing her sex life or mine.

"Can Tristan hear me?" she asked.

"Um, no. He's outside watering plants."

"Good. I'm gonna share something with you that I don't tell many people, and I'll ask that you keep it between us, okay?"

"Of course." I braced for whatever was coming next, hoping it wasn't some lewd bedroom confession from my future mother-in-law.

"When I was twenty, I came home from college for summer break, and boy, was I full of myself! I'd been on my own while I was away at school sowing my oats in the big city, and I came back to town thinking I was grown and could do whatever I wanted. Back then, just like now, the headsprings of the river were a popular swimming spot. That water was so danged cold you went numb within a couple of minutes, but it was crystal clear, which made it easy to see the shells on the bottom of the river, or the fish, or even a manatee swimming by. Well, that also made it ideal for skinny-dipping."

A mental image of Rita in the water flashed into my mind unbidden, and I slapped my hand against my forehead to dispel it.

"It was a late afternoon mid-week, and a handful of us went down to the springs to cool off, and wouldn't you know it? A park ranger walked up and yelled at us to get out. My friends who were on the opposite bank took off running, and those closest to the bank with the ranger obeyed his order. I was a little farther out, closer to the middle with a male friend I wanted to impress, and I got a little mouthy with the ranger. I started spouting off about my daddy being the sheriff, and after a verbal back-and-forth with the ranger, I refused to get out of the water."

My mouth dropped open at the thought of a nude but head-strong Rita going at a park ranger. As though she could sense my astonishment, she laughed at her own memory before she continued.

"As you might could guess, that didn't work out well, especially once my friend swam to shore and left me treading that freezing water alone. Long story short, I ended up arrested in my birthday suit, although he did let me get dressed before he cuffed me. He took me into my father's station handcuffed and dripping wet, and would you believe my daddy threw me in a cell and locked it when he heard what I'd done and how I'd treated the ranger?"

"Rita! Oh my gosh, how embarrassing!"

"You better believe it. Now, back in those days, the local paper published the arrest dockets in a column on the front page as a deterrent. It being such a small town, you know, folks didn't want to be publicly shamed that way. Well, the newspaper editor and my daddy didn't exactly get along, and that man took an opportunity when he saw it. Not only did my name run in the front-page arrest column, the editor did a full front-page story on the problems caused by young folk skinny-dipping in the springs. They ended up shutting the springs down for a while and not allowing anyone to swim there, and of course, everyone blamed me."

"That's horrible. I can't believe the editor did that to you."

"That's not all. Unfortunately, the young man I was swimming with was not the young man I was going steady with back at school, and when word got back to campus, my steady dumped me, as well he should have. It was not my best summer, to say the least. But listen, all I'm saying is, no one looks good under a magnifying glass, even if they're doing the same thing everyone else is. So, don't you worry about a thing. As long as you're happy and Tristan's happy, it doesn't matter what anyone else thinks. And from the sound of things, you're both happy, am I right?"

I felt a strange kinship with her after she'd shared her story, and I wanted to share something back. I took a deep breath and plunged in before I changed my mind.

"By the way, we're making a public announcement about the engagement this week. As soon as I have the go-ahead from my publicist, I'll let you know, and then you can tell whomever you'd like."

She squealed so loud that I had to hold the phone away from my ear. "This is wonderful news. Congratulations—again! I am so excited. So, wait, I can tell people now? Or I'm waiting to hear from you?"

"I'll let you know when. It should be in the next day or two."

"Okay, my lips will stay sealed until I hear from you. But when you give the word, I am telling everyone I know. Do we have a wedding date yet? Can we start planning?"

A rise of panic welled up within me, and I rushed to close the flood gates. "No. I mean, not yet. I'm not even thinking about that yet. I'd like to let this news settle for a bit."

"Okay, that's fine. I won't push. You just let me know when you're ready, and I'll be ready."

I didn't know that I'd ever be as ready as she was, but I assured her again that I'd call and after at least three more squeals and pronouncements of excitement from Rita, we said our goodbyes.

Chapter 31

"Did you hear anything from Priscilla?" Tristan asked when he came back inside.

"No. Not yet."

He frowned and went to the sink to wash his hands.

"You look disappointed," I said as I handed him a towel.

"Me? Not at all." He shrugged as he dried his hands. "I'm fine. I already know I'm engaged. That's old news."

My phone rang, and we both looked at it and back at each other.

This could be it. This could be the last moment of calm before the storm. That chill feeling I'd had earlier dissipated, and apprehension rolled over me in hot waves.

He picked up the phone from the counter and handed it to me.

"It's Priscilla," I said, but I think we both already knew.

"Okay, love," she said after a quick hello. "We've had a bite on the television exclusive. They want your man to make an appearance on camera, though."

"Oh, I don't know. I don't think he'd be comfortable with that." I looked at Tristan, who raised his eyebrows in question, and I turned away from him.

"Well, tell him it's important," Priscilla said. "Everyone's already met him via these pictures, so to speak, so there's a genuine interest there."

"I'd rather not involve him in that way, Pris. Can't they do it without him?"

She wasn't happy.

"You do realize that you're announcing an engagement, right? That means two of you, love. It's not nearly as enticing if it's just you talking about him, and knowing you, you'd be likely to say you couldn't share any information about him anyway."

Tristan motioned that he was going to shower, and I nodded and went to the sofa to sit.

"Look, Pris, I already feel like I'm exploiting our relationship for publicity here. The least I can do is not put the guy in front of the firing squad personally."

"Oh, for Pete's sake, stop being so dramatic. You're not exploiting anything. It's an engagement, Sloane. Most people are happy to tell everyone they're getting married. It's supposed to be good news, you know? Something you *want* to share. I can't believe you've kept it a secret this long."

"What are our options if we take the television interview off the table?"

"You're killing me here." She groaned and paused for a moment. "I suppose we could look at a print interview. Not the same exposure, but if he's willing to do some photos and maybe contribute a response or two during the interview, it could be effective."

"I'll need to talk to him and get back to you."

"Okay, but again, timing is crucial here, Sloane. I don't want to move forward with any announcement until we have this exclusive sewn up and the details hammered out. Of course, we'll need to discuss what you're going to say and how we'll frame it."

She continued to rattle on, but at some point, I tuned her out.

This was what I'd tried to avoid all along. I didn't want my wedding to be a news cycle. That didn't mean I wasn't happy about it, or that I didn't think it was good news. Was it so terrible that I wanted it to be something personal between Tristan and me without the world's intrusion?

I closed my eyes and willed myself not to cry as I flopped down across the sofa and listened to Pris talk. I didn't move from the spot once the call had ended, and I was still lying there when Tristan came back from his shower.

"How did it go?" He sat on the edge of the sofa next to me, and his smile faded when he saw my tears. "Hey, whoa, what's wrong? You okay?"

I turned my face from him as I blinked the tears back and rubbed away those that had fallen with the back of my hand.

"I thought I could be okay with this, but I'm not. I don't want this to be a circus. I don't want to answer a bazillion questions about what flowers I'm choosing or what favors we'll have or who's designing my dress. I just want to marry you. That's it. I don't want all the hoopla. Once we put this out there, then this wedding belongs to the world, and we can't take it back."

"Sure, we can," he said as he brushed away a tear from my cheek. "No one has any say-so in what we do or how we do it. No one has to know anything we don't want them to. It could just be me and you at the courthouse if we wanted."

I rolled my eyes with a sniffle. "Right. Like your mother would ever allow that."

"It's not up to my mother. Or anybody other than me and you." He leaned across me to brace his shoulder against the back of the couch as he gently brushed his hand across the top of my head. "This is *our* wedding. *Our* engagement. Us. No one else. Even if we tell the world, so what? Nothing has to change other than now they know."

"You don't understand." I pushed his hand away and moved to sit up. "It's not as simple as just telling them. No matter what I give them, they're always going to want more. Everyone will want to weigh in on what we do or don't do. And Pris is out of control with this. I thought she understood that I wanted low-key. Release the statement, do an interview, and be done. She's hyping this up like we're having the wedding of the century or something. She wanted us to do a television interview together."

His eyes widened, and I held up my hand and rushed to reassure him.

"Don't worry. I told her we weren't interested, but now she wants us to do a print interview, and a photo shoot, and she wants us to leak a ring shot between the unofficial statement and the official statement. I told her I don't even have a ring, and she suggested I go buy one just for a picture. This is insane, and it's exactly what I dreaded. We haven't even announced it yet, and it feels like it's spun out of control already."

"So, take control back."

"How?"

"They can't interview you without you agreeing to do it. You set the rules. Let them know how you want to be interviewed, and what you're willing to discuss or not. And don't forget, Pris works for you, not the other way around."

"I know, but to some extent, we have to play the game."

He paused, his eyes somber as he stared into mine.

"Okay. Then figure out how to play it on your terms. What do you need to get out of this? How does this benefit you?"

"Positive publicity."

"All right. And an interview with the two of us together would accomplish that?"

I rubbed my eyes and stared up at the ceiling with a sigh.

"I won't ask you to do that. I don't want to get you involved at all, but Pris is right. They'll be curious about you. They'll want to see you, and right now, all they have are those pictures of us in our swimsuits. The less we give them, the more they'll dig to find. Remember our friend Tank and the lovely story he put out about you and Becky last year?"

How could he forget the pushy paparazzo who had interviewed half of Cedar Creek for a blistering report on Tristan's failed first marriage and the tragic loss of their baby girl?

"Oh, I remember." He sighed and ran his hand through his wet hair. "Look, I'll do whatever you need me to. Obviously, you're much more comfortable with this sort of thing than I am, but I don't care. I've dealt with reporters shoving microphones in my face before at work. Undoubtedly, I could manage an interview with you by my side."

"I have no doubt you could manage it, but you shouldn't have to."

He bent his forehead to mine, his hand on the back of my neck. "We're in this together, remember? Come what may, it's me and you. I knew this publicity crap was part of the package when I signed up for it."

I tried to muster a smile. "I appreciate how understanding you are about all this."

He pressed his lips to my forehead and whispered against my skin, "I just want you to be happy. I wish our engagement could be a good thing for you, something you could enjoy instead of all the stress it brings."

I slid my arms around his shoulders and leaned back to look at him. The sadness in his eyes struck my heart, and suddenly, I felt horrible for making it a negative thing.

"Sorry I'm being a brat."

He frowned. "I didn't say you were."

"I know, but it's ridiculous for me to be this upset. I'm getting married to the most awesome guy on the planet, and of course, people want me to talk about it. Why wouldn't they? It *is* a good thing, and it should be something we can enjoy. It's happy news. I've made you and your family keep it a secret, and that was selfish and unfair of me."

His eyebrows raised, as though he was surprised by my words, but before he could say anything, I reached to kiss him and then lay my hand on his cheek as I looked into his eyes.

"I am honored to be your fiancée, Tristan Heath Rogers. From now on, I will shout that from the rooftops for anyone who will listen."

He smiled. "You don't have to do that for me. I never thought you were being selfish or unfair. I understand why you want to keep it under wraps."

With a deep inhale and a slow exhale, I firmed my resolve.

"Yeah, well, it's not a secret anymore. Let's tell everybody. Let your mom tell anyone she wants. Let's do the interviews; let's do the photo shoot. Let's make it official."

I grinned, and he grinned back.

"You're sure that's what you want?" he asked.

"Yeah. I am. I've let myself get all worked up about this, but the reality is, this is just publicity. Good publicity. Like you said, no one has any say-so in what we do or how we do it. So, if you're willing to be interviewed with me, I say let's go for it."

"I'm willing to do whatever you need me to."

"Thanks. And if I freak out again, because we both know I probably will, then just remind me, okay? No matter what anyone else thinks, we do *our* wedding *our* way for us."

He smiled and gave me a kiss that was gentle and soft, and I responded with a more urgent and fervent passion. I buried my fingers into his wet hair and pulled him closer, breathing in the intoxicating scent of his lavender soap and his woodsy, citrus aftershave.

I shifted my weight on the couch so he would have room to lie next to me, but instead, he pulled back with a mischievous grin.

"I'll be right back." He stood and walked toward the hallway.

"Wait," I said, raising up on my elbow. "Where are you going?"

He turned back with an even wider grin. "Sit tight. Don't move."

I adjusted the pillow behind my head and settled back to stare at the ceiling while I waited for him to return, my body longing for his touch.

It only took a couple of minutes, and he was back, kneeling beside the couch with that silly grin I loved on full display.

"Will you sit up, please?" he asked.

I obliged the request, but not without questioning. "Why? What are you up to?"

He indicated that I needed to swing my legs around to sit facing him, and I laughed as I followed his instruction.

"What are you doing, Deputy?"

He took a deep breath and cleared his throat before he spoke.

"The last time we did this, I was in a hospital bed half out of it on meds, and you'd spent the previous night stuffed in a trunk and chased through the woods by a killer."

My skin tingled all over as I realized his intentions, and my breath caught in my throat as he continued.

"I've always wanted a do-over, but the timing never seemed good," he said. "Now that you're ready to tell everyone, well, I don't want to wait any longer to do things right."

He reached into his shorts pocket, and a huge lump formed in my throat. It was silly, really. We were already engaged. We had been for months. The ring was a formality, and neither it nor the proposal on one knee was something I'd needed him to do.

Yet, now that it was happening, I found myself giddy with emotion. I wasn't the only one, judging by Tristan's charming nervousness and his obvious joy. We both had glassy eyes as he opened the blue velvet box.

I gasped at the sight of the most beautiful ring I'd ever seen. Though I'd never been one to sit around and daydream about what constituted the perfect ring, there it was.

The center stone was an emerald cut diamond, not garishly large but not minuscule either. It was framed by a baguette accent on each side, all on a narrow platinum band.

He cleared his throat again and chuckled.

"I don't know why I'm so nervous," he said, his grin so wide it filled his face. "You've already said yes once, so I'm pretty confident about the answer. Sloane Carol Reid, now that we're doing this official-like and making it public, I'm gonna ask you again...will you marry me?"

I nodded and squeaked out a yes between giggles.

We kissed, and then he took the ring from the box. Both our hands shook as the band slid onto my finger, and then Tristan grasped my hand tightly as his eyes met mine.

"I know this is probably not a Hollywood-worthy ring, but it was Nan's, and she and Hank had the kind of marriage I've always dreamed of. I would be honored if you would wear it as my wife."

I threw my arms around his neck and slid off the couch to kneel knee to knee as I conveyed my enthusiasm and my answer in a passionate kiss I hoped would leave no doubt in his mind.

"Do you like it?" he whispered as he pulled back from our kiss to take my hand in his and look down at it.

"I love it. It's perfect."

He turned my hand this way and that, and the diamonds sparkled as they caught the light and reflected it.

I couldn't believe how natural it looked on my hand. Like it had always belonged there. I spanned my fingers wide and held them up to stare at it, grateful that Myrtle had insisted on a manicure.

"I've wanted to give it to you for so long," Tristan said as he watched me. "I can't tell you how many times I've had it in my pocket, waiting for the right circumstances, the right moment. I wanted it to be special, and this is probably not the most romantic way to do it, but…"

I shook my head. "No. This was perfect. I didn't have a clue what you were doing, and I am so surprised and so happy."

"Really?" His forehead creased and his eyes filled with concern. "Are you sure? I don't want you to feel like you've been forced to announce everything and that you have to take the ring. You don't have to wear it, you know. I'm okay if you—"

"Are you kidding me?" I laid my hand on his chest and stared at the stunning sparkler, unable to stop grinning. "I'm not ever going to take it off. Well, I mean, if I'm required to for a role, then I have to, but otherwise, I will always wear it."

If anyone had told me I'd feel that way, I would have thought they were nuts. I had no idea wearing Tristan's ring—his grand-mother's ring—would affect me so deeply. Though I had no doubt it held great monetary value, the sentiment and history attached to the family heirloom made it priceless to me, and I felt uncharacteristi-cally sentimental about such a tangible connection joining me with Tristan and his family.

My happiness overflowed in giggles and happy tears, and Tristan laughed as he wrapped his arms around me and bent his head to kiss me.

As our kiss deepened with a slow, gentle burn, he eased us down to the floor between the coffee table and the sofa, nudging the table aside with his hip to make more room. We celebrated our newly recommitted and properly ringed engagement with a tender intimacy, each of us pausing at some point between caresses and kisses to look at the new bling on my finger.

We took our time, in no hurry for the moment to end, and when we'd finally collapsed together, spent and satiated, he threaded his fingers through mine and brought the back of my hand to his lips.

"It makes my heart happy to see this on your hand. Thanks for wearing it."

"Thanks for offering it to me." I stretched up to kiss him, and he smiled.

"Nan told me one day while we were sitting out on that deck that she didn't want me to give up on love. She told me to guard my heart but to keep it open, and that one day, I'd find the one I was meant to share it with." He looked down at the ring and rubbed his thumb across it. "She said that when she died, she would leave this ring for me as a reminder that I was worthy of a love like the one she and Hank had."

I squeezed his hand as I pulled it toward my heart.

"She sounds like a smart lady, and she was right, you know."

"I hope so," he said, kissing me once more.

Chapter 32

Dani and I had planned to meet in Jensen the next morning to look at fabrics for the stage curtains, which would need to be custom-made. I opted to drive myself so I could run errands after our meeting, and she pulled into the parking lot a few minutes after I arrived.

She got out of her car and walked toward me with a huge smile. "Good news! I stopped by the theater before coming here, and Steve is there working with a few members of his crew."

"The bonuses did it, eh?"

"Yep," she replied. "He said they're willing to work as long as no one gets hurt and things don't get too crazy. So far, so good. He said it had been a quiet morning. Oh, and I have someone coming tomorrow to replace the office window. The new audio-visual panels will be installed up there Wednesday, so I wanted it back in place before then."

"Do you think that's a good idea? Putting the expensive electrical equipment in before we're rid of Hyram?"

Dani shrugged as we walked toward the entrance of the building. "I don't see how I can wait. They're hanging the rest of the lights and wiring and installing the footlights this week. We've also got a speaker system coming. I need the control boards installed in conjunction with all of that. And I can't push any of that back because then that affects the painting, which in turn pushes back the delivery of the seats. Any delay will be a domino effect. We've just got to hope Hyram doesn't destroy anything or run anyone off before we can get on friendly terms with him."

I reached to pull my sunglasses off as we neared the door, and Dani grabbed my left hand.

"This is new. Is that what I think it is?"

Her eyes were bright with excitement, and I grinned back at her, feeling the same giddiness I had when Tristan slid the ring on my finger.

"I suppose that depends on what you think it is," I said with a nervous laugh, pulling my hand from hers.

"Did you get *engaged* over the weekend?"

Her mouth dropped open as I laughed again, and she took my hand and stared at the ring as she launched into a series of rapid-fire questions she gave me no time to answer.

"When did this happen? How did he do it? Where were you? I want every detail. Well, I mean, unless it was, like, some intimate moment you don't care to reveal. Was it romantic? Did you cry? Why didn't you call me? This ring is gorgeous."

"Thanks. It was his grandmother's." My chest swelled with pride, and I couldn't believe how different it felt to wear a ring. To wear *his* ring.

"So? Spill the beans! C'mon, gimme the goods."

"It's no big deal, really," I said as I put the shades in their case and slid it back in my purse.

"No big deal? You got engaged, chick. That's a big freaking deal."

"Technically, we already were. This is more of a formality than anything." I took a deep breath and sighed. "We've decided to go public with the news. My publicist is going to release a statement either today or tomorrow. She's just waiting to hear back on a few things."

"Oh, crap. You have to release a *statement*? That's insane. I don't think I'd like that. I'm more of a 'my business is my business' kind of girl. I figured when I didn't hear from you that you were busy dealing with the picture scandal situation, but dang, girl. You were busy, all right." She grabbed my hand again, pulling it toward her for a closer inspection. "That is beautiful. When's the wedding?"

That old familiar anxiety panged in my gut, and I looked down at the ring to remind myself it was okay to be happy.

"We haven't gotten that far. We're just enjoying this part for now. By the way, I heard back from Marc. He and your realtor have been corresponding, and she's going to reach out to Ronald today to let him know she has a potential buyer. Feel him out and see if there's any interest."

"Let's hope he's willing to sell," she said as she pulled the door open.

The receptionist greeted us and led us in the back for our appointment. As we oohed and aahed over the bolts of fabric, I couldn't help staring at the ring. It caught my eye pretty much every time I moved my left hand, and I found myself moving it more often just so I could see the ring.

It felt good to be happy about the engagement and to be excited about the ring. I hoped that whatever Priscilla arranged didn't turn into a publicity storm that would rain on our parade.

I hadn't felt compelled to check my phone for messages all morning, knowing that with the time difference from Florida to California, Priscilla wouldn't be in the office yet. But as it got closer to lunchtime, I began to feel antsy and question my decision to go public.

As much as I didn't want the heartache Dani had suffered, I envied her ability to be a 'my business is my business' kind of girl. My business had been the world's business since I was sixteen, and one of the most personal decisions of my life was about to put out there for a very public Q&A.

Once Dani and I parted after the meeting, I stopped by the drugstore to pick up a few toiletries. As I stood perusing the toothpaste selection near the back of the store, a woman at the pharmacy counter lost her temper with the young girl attending to her.

"Are you trying to kill me?" the woman shrieked.

My instinct was to turn and look, as was everyone else's in the vicinity.

The girl shrank back as she stammered an apology. "I'm s-s-sorry, ma'am. I m-m-made a mistake," said the young voice.

"A potentially deadly mistake!"

Over the course of the next few minutes, the irate customer gave the entire store an education about the differences in types of insulin and the particularly deadly consequences of using a regular syringe versus something she called a tuberculin syringe.

Not satisfied with the girl's apologies or the pharmacist's reasonable explanations, the irate woman insisted that she needed to speak with the manager.

"We apologize profusely for the error," the flustered manager said.

"Potentially deadly error! One that never should have happened. She has no business being behind the pharmacy counter if she doesn't know the difference in a U100 insulin syringe and a U500 syringe."

"As we explained, she is part of our college tech program, so this has been a learning experience for her, and I'm sure she won't make the same mistake again. You've now received the proper syringe, and I'm not sure what else we could do to correct the situation, Mrs. Fisher."

My ears perked when I heard her last name, and I moved to the endcap filled with bandages to get a closer look at her. Was this possibly a relative of Ronald's?

"There's nothing you can do," Mrs. Fisher said. "You've lost my business, and I guarantee you that I will not shop here again when I'm in town."

Everyone behind the pharmacy counter looked relieved to hear that news as Mrs. Fisher gathered her belongings and turned to go.

Just as she walked past me, a woman came down the aisle with a huge smile on her face.

"Cecile? I thought that was you. I heard that voice, and I said to myself, 'That sounds like Cecile.' I had no idea you and Ronnie were in town. When did you get in?"

I stared at them openly as they hugged, and I wondered if I had heard correctly. If this was Cecile Fisher, and she was in town with her husband Ronnie, then this could be the landlord's wife. And if he was in town, we might be able to meet with him to discuss the supernatural events at the theater building.

"Hi, Judy. I got back on Saturday," Cecile said. "I'm staying at my brother's for a few days."

I picked up an antibiotic ointment and busied myself reading the back of the box so it wouldn't be so obvious that I was listening.

"Oh, that's nice," Judy replied. "We've missed y'all so much since you moved. Why, it's been years since we had one of our game nights. Maybe you and Ronnie could come over one night while you're here. We could grill some burgers and play some cards, like old times."

"I'm by myself this trip," Cecile said, her tone clipped.

"Oh, well then, maybe you and I can have a girls' night. We could meet at the Mexican restaurant. They have two-for-one margaritas on Wednesdays."

Cecile paused, and I glanced over my shoulder at her just as she smiled. "You know what? I'd like that. I've really missed my friends since I've been in Tennessee."

"Girl, you call me," Judy said. "We'll do it. Wednesday night!"

"Wednesday night," Cecile agreed, and they hugged once more before parting ways.

Cecile walked toward the store's exit, and I hesitated only a moment before following her.

It felt like some kind of weird opposite déjà vu, since I was usually the one being followed and approached by a total stranger.

"Excuse me," I said just before she reached the end of the aisle.

She turned, her eyes wary.

"I couldn't help overhearing that your name is Cecile Fisher. Do you and your husband own the old auto repair shop building in Cedar Creek?"

She bristled. "My husband does. Why? Who are you?"

"My name is Sloane Reid." I extended my hand in greeting as I spoke, and she stared at it a moment before reaching to shake it. "I'm working with Danielle Ward, who's opening a theater in the building. She leases it from your husband. I apologize for bothering you, but I'd love to ask you a few questions about the building."

"I wouldn't know about anything about it. My husband took it over when his son died. Belonged to his son's family before that."

"Right, the Letchworths. What I wanted to know, and I realize this may sound bizarre, but did either you or your husband notice anything strange about the place? Any odd circumstances? Things going missing? Anything like that?"

She arched an eyebrow and crossed her arms. "Pardon me?"

"I've heard folks around Cedar Creek say the building is haunted. I was just wondering if you or your husband might have heard or seen anything unusual."

"I can't say I was in that building more than a handful of times. I certainly never saw or heard anything out of the ordinary."

"Okay. Do you know if your stepson ever mentioned anything? Or perhaps any of the tenants? We're just trying to talk to people who have been in the building to see if we can trace when the stories started. You know, trying to investigate the building's history and the things that have happened there so we can shut down rumors and such."

She tilted her head to the side, and her bright red lips twisted into a tight pucker.

"What did you say your name was again?"

"Sloane Reid. I'm Danielle's business partner."

"Like Sloane Reid, the actress?"

I grinned and spread my arms wide with a mock curtsy. "Um, one and the same."

"And you're doing theater in Cedar Creek?" She smirked. "Fell on hard times, huh?"

"Well, no. I actually live in Cedar Creek now, and I wanted to be a part of bringing the theater to the community and help Danielle with the renovations. It looks like a completely different building inside. You should stop by and see it while you're here."

"Hmm." She looked me up and down, and then she adjusted her purse on her shoulder and smiled. "Like I said, that's my husband's pet project. I'm not involved."

"Maybe you could ask your husband if he's heard any of the stories, or if his son said anything about strange happenings during the time he owned the shop."

"I'm pretty sure if Ronnie had heard anything, he would have told me. Now, if you'll excuse me, I need to go."

"All right, well, could I give you my number? That way if you think of something—"

"I don't think that will be necessary." She smiled and slid on a pair of dark sunglasses that completely hid her eyes. "You have a nice day, now."

Chapter 33

W hen I left Jensen, I called Dani and told her about my dead-end conversation with Cecile, and then I headed over to my friend Rachel's to lend her moral support as they demolished the old farmhouse on her property.

She and Holden had partnered their non-profit foundations, sharing a common interest in animal rescue, training, and rehabilitation. The agreement meant they would share Rachel's property, and in addition to a new house for Rachel, they were busy constructing a training center for Holden's animal therapy efforts and a hospital with a separate rehabilitation building for Rachel's animal sanctuary goals.

It had been over a month since I'd been out to the farm, and Tristan had told me on Saturday to expect big changes when I went. The reality far exceeded my expectations. I literally stopped in Rachel's driveway and stared in awe at the transformation of her property.

Her old barn and storage sheds had been demolished, along with the building that had been her deceased mother-in-law's hair salon. A large section of woods off to the left had been cleared for the new house, and huge mounds of dirt dotted the pasture. The entire place was abuzz with activity as a hard-hat army of tradesmen worked in the individual construction sites.

Rachel walked over to greet me as I parked my car in a roped-off area alongside Holden's truck and the rest of the worker vehicles, safely away from the demolition.

She and I shared a big hug, and then she grinned as we turned to look at the various ongoing projects. "Hard to believe it's the same place, isn't it?"

"I'm blown away," I said as I looked around. "I can't believe how much you guys have gotten done. I'm sorry I haven't been out here sooner. It's been crazy lately, but I was determined to be here for this."

I had worried about the toll it would take on her to see her former home demolished, but she seemed to be taking it in stride.

"You almost didn't make it in time," she said, nodding toward the old house. "They're about to knock it down."

"You're sure about this, huh?" I asked her as we stood and watched the hydraulic excavator move toward the house. "If you're having any doubts, now's your last chance to speak up."

"I'm sure," she said with a nod and a faint smile as she crossed her arms and prepared to watch her former home be demolished. "It's time for new beginnings, and the house would never have felt the same after everything that happened."

"It's coming down," Holden said as he approached us. "Destruction and construction all at the same time."

"It's unbelievable," I said to him. "There's something going on everywhere you look."

I glanced over my shoulder at the heavy equipment hauling dirt across the pasture to where the new house would be built and then turned to watch the crew pouring the foundation of the new rehab facility.

"Speaking of unbelievable," Holden said, "I heard you and my brother are finally going official with the engagement announcement. About damned time!"

I lifted my hand and wiggled my fingers, showing off my new bling.

Holden wrapped me in a bear hug as Rachel reacted to the news with a huge smile.

"Congratulations, officially," she cried. "Let me see that ring."

"It was our grandmother's," Holden explained as he and Rachel both leaned over my hand to peer at it. "I had begun to think my brother never would convince this one to wear it."

"He's never asked me to wear it," I said in my defense.

Holden laughed, and Rachel cast him an admonishing glance.

"Well, you're wearing it now," she said. "That's all that matters."

"Did he do it proper?" Holden asked. "Did he get down on one knee and everything?"

"Of course," I said.

A loud crack pulled my attention back to the farmhouse as a huge section of the second floor collapsed, and Holden and I both looked to Rachel for her reaction. Her face was a mask of calm resolve, and if it bothered her to watch the house she'd fought so hard to keep be leveled to the ground, she didn't show it.

"Did you talk to the foreman about that crack in the driveway pavement?" Rachel asked Holden, turning away from the demolition to face him.

Holden nodded. "Yeah, he said it would be best to wait until all the heavy equipment moves out before putting more asphalt down, but they'll take care of it."

"There's a crack?" I turned and looked back toward the driveway. "I didn't even notice. It's so much better than it was before. I never would have been able to drive my new car down your driveway when it was still dirt."

"That fancy car of yours would have bottomed out in the first hole," Holden said. "It barely makes it up Tristan's gravel drive without scraping the ground."

"Yeah, he's already said we may need to pave it. I can't wait to see this place after the two of you are done with all this construction. There's so much happening all at once that I don't know how you're even keeping up with it."

"It's gone smoother than you might imagine," Rachel said. "We're both using the same builder, and Holden has been great

215

about coordinating both projects. He keeps me in the loop and consults me for any decisions on my part, and he's made himself available to deal with everyone here so I can focus on work at the hospital."

Holden watched her as she talked, and I hoped his warm smile didn't mean what I thought it might. They'd spent quite a bit of time together since committing to sharing the property, but I didn't think Rachel was anywhere near ready to consider a new romantic interest. I didn't want to see Holden get hurt.

My phone vibrated in my pocket, and I swore out loud when I pulled it out and saw who was calling.

"It's Jennifer," I said, shocked to see her name on the screen for the first time in almost two years.

"Uh-oh," Holden said with a grin. "Mommie Dearest."

"You call your mom Jennifer?" Rachel said.

"She thought it made her sound old if people knew she had a daughter, so I was never allowed to call her anything but her name," I explained as I stepped away. I took a deep breath and steeled myself for the conversation.

"Well, hello. What's up?"

"What's up? I'll tell you what's up," she said, and my body tensed at the irritation in her voice. "I received a call just now asking me for a quote about your engagement. What the hell, Sloane?"

I cringed. I wasn't aware that the story had broken, and I wondered why Priscilla hadn't called to tell me. My mind went into a mild panic as I realized our secret was officially out, and we wouldn't be able to keep it to ourselves any longer. Even though I'd known it was only a matter of time, I wasn't ready for the maelstrom yet.

"I'm sorry," I mumbled to my mother. "I should have called and told you. I was trying to keep the news private a while longer."

"You think I'm upset that you didn't tell me? I'm upset that you're even considering the idea. You've obviously lost your mind and disregarded everything I ever taught you about men. You can't be serious. Is this true? Are you really planning to get *married?*"

She said the word with such obvious distaste that I flinched at the sound of it.

"I don't know," I said, stumbling to find words in the barren wasteland of shock. "I mean, yes. I'm engaged. I plan to get…m-m-married."

"This is ludicrous. Who is he? Please tell me it's not this sad sap deputy you've been linked with. For God's sake, Sloane. If you're going to chain yourself to someone, couldn't it be someone wealthy? Not a public servant. Have I taught you nothing?"

I looked back over my shoulder at Holden and Rachel, who both looked away and appeared to busy themselves with the clouds, the grass, and anything but eavesdropping.

"Now's not really a good time to discuss this," I whispered into the phone as I walked farther away. "Can we talk later?"

"So, it's true? You've decided to ruin your life."

"No. I mean, yes, it's true. But I'm actually quite happy about it. Would it be too much to ask for you to be happy, too?"

"Why would I be happy that you're ruining your life? That you're giving up your independence, your career, your future?"

I pressed my hand to my forehead and closed my eyes. If I'd thought the worst part of the news breaking would be the interviews and the paparazzi swarming, I was wrong.

"I can't talk about this right now. I'll call you later."

I ended the call with trembling hands, not bothering to listen to her response. I took a moment to try and compose myself before turning. I didn't want Rachel and Holden to see me upset. I didn't want to cry in front of them.

A rumble louder than thunder filled the air, and I turned just as the remainder of the farmhouse gave way, sending up a huge cloud of dust.

"You okay?" Holden asked, coming to place his hand on my shoulder as he looked into my eyes.

"Is there anything we can do?" Rachel asked, and I tried to smile and act cool and nonchalant, even as my body broke out in a clammy sweat.

The quiet life I'd enjoyed was about to implode in more ways than one, and my mother would be driving the bulldozer.

"I need a stiff drink," I said. "And a one-way ticket out of town."

"What happened?" Holden asked.

"Evidently, the story is out. I don't know why my publicist didn't call and tell me, but someone called my mother and asked her for a quote. I guess I should have let her know before now, huh?"

"Ah," Rachel said. "So, your mom's upset that you didn't tell her?"

"I'm sure that's part of it, but she's more upset that I'm getting married. She's pretty much drilled it in me for my entire life that marriage is a prison sentence."

Someone in the background called Holden's name, and he looked toward them and then back at me, his eyes filled with concern.

"I'm okay," I said. "Really. Go do what you need to do."

"You sure?"

I nodded, and he hugged me again.

"Let me know if I can do anything," he said. "And I'm glad we can tell people now. I swear I've almost screwed up and said something more times than I can count."

I watched him walk away, and then I looked to Rachel.

"I'm sorry, Rachel. I'm supposed to be here offering you support, and just when you need it most, I take a call and have my own drama unfold."

"Nah. You were already there for me when I needed it most." She smiled and looked toward the rubble of the house. "Today was a lot easier than I thought it would be. It helps to say goodbye to the past when I can see the future being built already."

I thought about my future, and I tried to reclaim the happiness and excitement I'd felt earlier. I looked down at the ring, which had given me so much joy, and suddenly it felt tight on my finger. I reached to twist it, and Rachel smiled.

"I know this is hard for you, Sloane, and I'm sure her calling doesn't make it any easier, but you and Tristan are meant to be together. Just because your mom never found someone she wanted to spend her life with doesn't mean you have to suffer the same fate. Marriage can be a wonderful experience."

I frowned at the sadness that passed over her eyes, and I knew she was thinking of her late husband, Vincent. I felt guilty for any hesitance to marry my love when hers was gone forever.

"I have to get going," she said. "I have a night shift, and I need to go back to my apartment and take a shower and get changed."

"You won't be in that apartment much longer. Before you know it, they'll be done with your new house, and you'll be back out here in the sticks. You better enjoy that high-speed internet while you can."

She laughed and nodded. "So true. I can't believe this is finally happening. It seems like forever ago that, you know, I had to leave this house behind."

Our eyes met, and I knew we were both thinking of the crazy circumstances that led to Rachel's house being uninhabitable and her needing an apartment in town.

She took a deep breath and took a step back. "I'll see you soon, I hope?"

"Definitely. I'm in town for a while, so we should get together."

She turned to go, and I walked back toward my car, anxious to call Priscilla and find out what she knew about my mother being asked for a quote.

I hated that Jennifer had found out from someone other than me. I'd been meaning to call her, but I'd put it off, knowing she would be livid about my plans.

I tried not to let the conversation with her squash my joy, but by the time I reached the end of Rachel's driveway, the old familiar anxiety had come creeping back, squeezing my rib cage and making it hard for me to breathe. I stared at the shiny ring on my finger as I turned the car onto the narrow, curving road that led away from Rachel's house, and then with a shaky exhale, I blinked back tears and called Pris.

Chapter 34

I could hear voices that sounded as though they were far away, and yet I could feel the touch of a hand on my wrist.

"She's got a pulse," said the male voice. "She's breathing. Did you call for an ambulance?"

"Yeah, they said they'd be here as soon as possible," said a woman's voice. "Should we try to get her out of the car?"

"No. Best not to move her in case her back or her neck is broken. She hit that tree awful hard."

I struggled to open my eyes, but they were too heavy. I tried to speak, but it was as though I had no mouth and no way to form words.

Was I dead? No. I couldn't be. He'd just said I had a pulse and that I was breathing.

"I bet this car is totaled. Dang. You know it cost a lot of money, too," the woman said.

"She's lucky," the man replied. "The passenger side and the front end took the brunt of the impact."

"There's no telling how fast she was going. She flies up and down these roads like a bat outta hell, so it was only a matter of time."

No! I wasn't speeding.

I could think it, but I couldn't say it, and my mind was too fuzzy to try and figure out why. Then I realized that I had no memory of any of it. Not of hitting a tree, or crashing, or whether I was speeding or not. I just knew that I wasn't. I hadn't at all, not a single time since I'd promised Tristan.

Oh, God. Tristan! He would be so upset. What if he was the responding deputy? *Oh, Lord, please don't let him be the responding deputy.* He didn't need to see me like this.

Wait! Like what? How bad is it?

I tried to focus on my body and do some kind of inventory, but it was so hard to concentrate.

"She's moaning," the man said. "I think she's coming around."

Pain began to seep into my consciousness, and a throbbing sensation in my left shoulder and the left side of my neck became so intense that I couldn't fathom not being able to feel it just seconds before.

Stabbing thrusts of agony pulsed in the left side of my head, and I tried to reach up and touch it, worried that somehow part of it was missing and laid bare.

"Whoa, whoa, whoa," the man said, and I felt his grip on my arm. "Just be still now. Help's on the way."

The distant wail of sirens began to grow louder as hot tears rolled down my cheeks.

Somewhere in my brain, the signals connected again, and I felt my eyelids flutter as light flooded in.

My car. Oh, God! My car.

With one glimpse at the twisted, mangled metal bashed against a large oak tree in a cloud of steam and smoke, my first instinct was to get out.

"Hold on, hold on," the man said as I shoved the door open and rushed out past him. "Take it easy."

"Are you okay?" the woman asked, and I stared back and forth between the two of them and my car, trying to process what I was seeing.

"What happened?" I asked, searching my mind for any recollection and drawing a blank.

"You wrecked," she said as she took a step toward me. "Are you okay?"

"She's probably in shock," the man said.

I lifted my hand to my aching head, relieved to find that it felt whole and didn't seem to be gushing blood. A wave of nausea hit, and I bent with my hands on my knees, and then a terrible thought occurred. Had I hurt someone else?

"Are you all right?" I looked around for any sign of another crumpled vehicle but saw none. "Is everyone all right? Did we crash into each other?"

"No," the man said. "We were driving by and saw you, so we stopped to see if we could help."

"What happened?" I asked again as I walked toward the front of my car.

He shrugged. "We don't know. You had already wrecked when we got here."

I stared at the damage in disbelief. How had this happened? How was I okay?

"They're here," the woman announced as the ambulance arrived, followed by a highway patrol car, both with sirens so deafening that her proclamation was unnecessary.

The questions and the examination were a blur, and the next thing I knew, I was in the back of an ambulance, despite my insistence that I was fine.

"Is there anyone we could call for you, ma'am?" the trooper asked from the rear of the ambulance before we left for the hospital.

I hesitated. I didn't want to call Tristan and scare the crap out of him, but I knew he'd be furious if I didn't have them call him.

"Yes, please call Deputy Tristan Rogers, but make sure you tell him that I'm fine, okay? Tell him I'm all right before you tell him anything else."

"I will."

I'm sure he did, and I'm certain they explained it again to Tristan before he came into the examination room to see me, but knowing I wasn't seriously injured did nothing to ease the fear in his eyes or the stricken expression on his face when he first saw me.

"Are you okay?" he asked as he cupped my face in his hands.

"I'm fine. I have a hellacious headache and a concussion from where my head hit the driver's window, and the beginnings of what will probably be some nasty bruises from the seatbelt, but no broken bones or other injuries."

He turned to the doctor and asked for confirmation of what I'd told him, going through a checklist of X-rays and scans to ensure they'd done everything he felt was necessary.

"Oh, God, Sloane," he said when the doctor had left the room. He wrapped his arms around me, and I winced.

"Easy, Deputy. Gingerly, please."

He waited until they'd released me and we were on our way home before he asked, "What happened?"

"I don't know. Like I told the state trooper, I don't remember anything other than getting in the car and leaving Rachel's. The next thing I knew, people were talking about whether or not I was breathing."

His left hand gripped the steering wheel tighter as he reached to take my hand with his right.

"Did something run out in front of you? Did you just lose control?"

"I told you, I don't remember."

He glanced over at me and then back to the road. "Holden said you'd just gotten off the phone with your mother not too long before this happened. Were you upset? Were you going too fast?"

I groaned at the reminder that she'd called, and then I bristled at his question.

"No. I know I wasn't speeding."

"You said you don't remember."

"I don't, but I can tell you I wasn't speeding. I haven't ever since I promised you I wouldn't."

"You went off the left side of the road in a straightaway. There's no skid marks, and no sign of a tire blowing, and—"

"Can we talk about something else, please?"

He frowned and nodded. "Yeah. I'm sorry. I'm just frightened, and I'm trying to make sense of things."

"Me too, but I can't think straight right now, and you asking me questions is only making it worse."

He brought my hand to his lips and kissed it, and then he remained silent the rest of the way home.

When we turned in the driveway, I was shocked to see Holden's truck, Ray's truck, and Rita's car.

"Why is everyone here?" I asked when Tristan came around to my side of the truck to open my door and help me get out.

He looked at me as though it was the silliest question he'd ever heard.

"Because they're worried about you."

"Didn't you tell them I'm okay?"

"Yes, but I suppose they want to see for themselves."

I already felt crappy, but walking in to be surrounded by the concern committee made things even more awkward.

Rita was the first to greet me, her eyes all red and puffy.

"Oh, Sloane, thank God you're home! You gave us all such a scare."

She put her arms around me in the gentlest of hugs, even as Tristan cautioned against it.

"She's sore, Mom. Go easy on her."

Rita took my hand and squeezed it. "We dropped everything when we got the call and came right away."

"I'm fine," I pulled my hand back, my cheeks hot with embarrassment. "You guys didn't have to come. I'm all right, really."

"Let's give her some space, folks," Tristan said as he led me past them to the couch.

"Can I get you anything?" Rita asked. "You want a glass of tea? Are you hungry?"

"Mom, you're hovering," Tristan said as he stood between his father and his brother.

Rita came to sit next to me on the sofa.

I looked up at the circle of eyes staring at me. "Um, thanks for coming. I appreciate you all being here, even if it does feel a bit overwhelming. I've never had this...*family* thing...before. Of course, I've never been in an accident, either, not even a fender bender. So, this is all a little much to take in."

"You got any word on the car, yet?" Ray said to Tristan. "Is it totaled?"

Rita gave him a stern look. "Raymond, it's not the time for such discussions. If you must, then go outside on the deck to do it."

"You all right, girl?" Holden asked. "Did you forget you're not a stunt driver?"

His mother turned her glare in his direction. "Holden, don't tease."

I stuck out my tongue at Holden, and he laughed.

Rita reached to take my hand, and I looked down and realized my ring was gone.

"My ring! Crap! They made me take it off at the hospital for the CT scan, and they didn't give it back."

"I have it," Tristan said. "They gave me a bag with your purse, your phone, and your jewelry. You want me to get it for you?"

I hesitated, mortified to discover that I was about to cry. The trauma, pain meds, and unexpected family gathering had my emotions all over the place, and I needed an escape.

"Actually, I think I'd like to go lie down, if that's okay."

Ray and Holden chorused together with "Sure" and "Yeah, no problem", but Rita frowned.

"I don't think that's a good idea with a concussion. You're not supposed to go to sleep."

"The doctor said it's fine for her to sleep," Tristan said as he came to my side and helped me stand. "They told me what to watch for, and as long as she doesn't have dilated pupils or trouble walking or carrying on a conversation, she's fine. I'll check in on her often and make sure she's okay."

He walked me down the hallway to our bedroom, and he closed the door behind him.

"I'll get rid of them," he said as I sat down on the bed. "I'm sorry."

"No, it's fine. I appreciate that they care. I'm just wiped out."

He knelt beside the bed and slid the ring back on my finger, kissing my hand as he did so. He lay his head in my lap and wrapped his arms around my hips, and his heart thumped a steady beat against my thighs.

"I am so glad you're all right," he whispered. "I was half out of my mind when I got the call. It was like one of my nightmares come to life. I couldn't get to you fast enough."

I buried my fingers in his hair and bent to kiss his head. "I'm fine. I'm home, and we're together. We're okay."

The tears that had threatened to fall made their way past my defenses, and he sat up as I brushed them away.

He frowned, and then gave me a half-smile.

"Let me go get rid of my family, and I'll be right back, okay?"

I nodded, and he bent to remove my shoes and then helped me get settled in the bed, pulling the covers up to my shoulders. With a gentle kiss to my forehead, he was gone, and within minutes, sleep overtook me.

Chapter 35

I woke to the sound of my own screaming as I sat up in the bed and jerked the covers back.

Tristan burst through the bedroom door within seconds and was by my side as I sat on the side of the bed trying to catch my breath.

"You okay?" he asked, almost as panicked as I was.

"Yeah. Must have been a bad dream."

"Hey, I'm the only one who gets to terrify us both with bad dreams, okay?"

He smiled, and I managed a smile in return.

"How long have I been asleep?"

"Almost two hours," he said, smoothing my hair down as he pushed it away from my face. "I came in earlier when everyone left, but you were sleeping so soundly I didn't want to disturb you. I was gonna come in soon and wake you to check on you and see if you wanted something to eat."

I shook my head, nauseated at even the thought of food.

"Your phone has been lighting up with missed calls from Priscilla. I started to answer and let her know what happened, but I wasn't sure you'd want me to."

Priscilla. I had the vaguest feeling that we had talked. I remembered that I had called her when I was leaving Rachel's place, but I couldn't recall the conversation. I'd wanted to ask her how my mother knew about the engagement and if the story had already broken.

"Have you watched the news?" I asked Tristan. "Have you seen or heard anything about our engagement?"

"No, why? Do you think that's why she's calling? Did she release the announcement?"

"I don't know. I seem to remember us talking, but I don't know what Pris said. When my mother called before, she told me she'd been asked for a quote about our engagement, so someone somewhere knows."

"What did she say? Jennifer, I mean. Holden said you were upset by the call."

I lay back against the pillow and frowned. "Oh, her usual encouraging words. Can you please bring me my phone so I can call Pris?"

He brought me the phone and a glass of water, and then he sat on the edge of the bed as I dialed Priscilla's number.

"Oh, thank God!" Priscilla said instead of hello. "You had me scared half to death. Don't ever wait that long to call me back again, you hear me? I was about ready to call the local authorities there in that podunk town of yours and put out an APB on you."

"I'm sorry. I didn't have my phone with me until just now. I wrecked my car. I'm fine, but I think my car is probably totaled."

"Oh, no! Sloane, that's terrible. Was it because of the jackass in the SUV?"

"What?"

"The person who was terrorizing you on the road. Did they make you crash?"

"What are you talking about?" I asked, and then I put the phone on speaker so Tristan could hear her answer.

"You don't remember?"

"No. I have no memory of our conversation, or of anything that happened leading up to the accident."

"When we were talking before, there was someone who came up on you in a black SUV, and you said they were riding you pretty hard, even though you slowed down for them to pass. Then when they did pull around to pass, they kept inching over and almost ran you off the road. So you slammed on the brakes to let them get around you, but then when they got in front of you, they kept putting on their brakes and speeding up and then slowing down, screwing around with you. You told me you were hanging up to pass them and then you'd call me back. But I didn't hear from you again."

Tristan's eyes narrowed and his face went white as he grabbed his phone from his hip and left the room.

"Thanks, Pris. That's valuable information. As far as we knew, no one else was involved, and I just lost control."

"Well, I can't say for sure that this person had anything to do with it, but they were damned sure messing with you, and it had you rattled. You sure you're okay?"

"Yeah. I've got a concussion and a badge of seatbelt honor in way of a bruise, but it could have been a lot worse." I pulled the covers over my legs and scooted deeper down the bed. "Hey, I'm sure we already talked about this, and I apologize for not remembering, but my mother called and said she'd been asked for a quote. Did something get released?"

"No, like I told you earlier, it didn't come from me. I can't say for sure that someone I talked to wasn't trying to jump the gun and get their own spin ready, though. I did get a call this afternoon about a print interview, and I should hear back by end of day if they're willing to accept our terms. If so, then I'll put the word out, if that's still the plan."

"Yeah, sure," I said with a yawn. "I'm gonna go. I feel like someone stole all my energy."

"Be safe, love, and keep me posted. I'll let you know if I hear anything on this end."

I placed my phone on the nightstand and nestled into the covers, trying to recall anything about the accident. The doctor had said the memory would probably come back, but he cautioned that it might not.

It seemed so bizarre to have a big chunk of my day missing, especially one that had proved so disastrous.

"You're done with Pris?" Tristan said as he walked in, his phone to his ear.

"Yeah." I propped up onto my elbow as he frowned. "What's up?"

"I wanted to ask her about what you told her."

"I can call her back."

He told the person on the other end of the line that he'd get back with them, and then he walked over to sit on the side of the bed as I reached for my phone.

I dialed her and explained that Tristan had questions, and then I lay back down and listened as he asked her for any details I'd provided her to describe the vehicle or its driver.

"What did she say?" I asked when he ended the call. "What did I tell her?"

"You just said it was a black SUV. You didn't give her a make or model."

"What about the driver? Did I tell her anything about who was driving?"

"You said the windows were tinted so dark that you couldn't see the driver and that the windshield had a strip of tinting across the top that blocked the face."

His forehead was creased and his jaw was tight, and I could feel the tension rolling off him.

I frowned at his frustration, irritated with myself that I couldn't provide the answers he needed. "That's not enough, is it?"

He looked back and reached to put his hand on my thigh. "It's fine, babe. Don't worry your pretty little banged-up head. You want me to make you something to eat?"

"The doctor said I might remember."

"I don't want you to worry about it," he said, leaning forward to kiss me as he tucked his thumb beneath my chin. "I've got people on it, and if there is anything to be found, they'll find it. If someone caused you to crash, and they fled the scene without helping you, then I will find them, and they will answer for it."

"But how? We don't know what kind it was, and we don't know anything about the person driving."

"Chances are, someone else on the road saw something. We'll put it out to social media and see what we get. They're going to take a closer look at your car to see if there's any paint transfer, and they'll comb over the crash site to see if there's any debris from another vehicle. They won't be able to hide, babe. I'll find them."

"And what if there was no one else involved? What if I just lost control and I don't remember?"

"Let's just see what the evidence shows, okay? Are you sure I can't get you something to eat? You need to put something in your belly."

I rubbed my hand across my stomach and tried to think of something appetizing. "Maybe a bowl of oatmeal?"

"You got it."

I was asleep before he returned.

Chapter 36

"I asked Holden to come and stay with you today," Tristan said as he got ready for work the next morning.

"You got me a babysitter?"

"I don't feel comfortable leaving you here alone, and I have to go. I don't want you getting dizzy and passing out or something." He came and sat on the bed facing me. "Just humor me, okay? I'll feel better if he's here."

Truth be told, it made me feel better, too. Holden was the perfect nurse for me. He could always make me laugh, and though I had no doubt about his concern, he never took the situation too seriously.

"I like it," he said when he arrived and saw the black eyes I'd developed overnight. "Raccoon is a good look on you."

"Yeah, I'm thinking it could open up a variety of new roles for me."

We settled onto the couch to watch *Buffy* reruns after Tristan left, and before we'd finished the second episode, Dani showed up at my door with coffee and bagels.

"I hope you don't mind me coming by. I needed to see for

myself that you were okay. My aunt Patricia works at the hospital, and she called me last night to tell me what happened. I tried calling you, but it went straight to voicemail. Are you okay?"

"I'm much better now that I have bagels. Where on earth did you get these?" I stared inside the bag in a state of wonder and confusion. "No one in Cedar Creek sells bagels."

"There's a little place in Winter Garden that has them. I was up early, and I needed to kill time so it would be late enough to come check on you, so I drove over there." She offered a cup of coffee to Holden and smiled. "Want some coffee? I brought an extra cup because I thought Tristan would be here. I have cream and sugar, too."

"Do you two know each other?" I asked.

"We do now," Holden said with a grin as he pulled a bagel from the bag. "Anyone who brings bagels and coffee is an automatic friend of mine. I'm Holden Rogers, Tristan's brother and Sloane's keeper for the day."

Dani grinned. "Nice to meet you. I'm Dani Ward. Sloane and I work together at the theater."

"Oh, you're the one hunting ghosts with Sloane, huh?"

Dani looked to me with alarm, and I smiled as I grabbed two knives, one for each container of cream cheese she'd brought. "Holden knows all my secrets. It's fine. He can be annoying as hell, but he doesn't run his mouth."

"My silence can be bought with bagels," he said, and then he went back to the couch and started flipping through channels as Dani and I carried everything to the dining table and sat.

"I wasn't sure what kind you'd like, so I bought an assortment," she said.

"You did great." I pulled a poppy seed bagel from the bag and spread it with the strawberry cream cheese. "I'm sorry I didn't call you. Everything was a blur yesterday, and I forgot to plug my phone in to charge last night, so it was dead this morning."

"Oh, you don't have to apologize. I'm sorry for dropping in like this. I just felt a little frantic and needed to know you were all right.

Aunt Patricia said they released you, so she thought it must not be too serious. Are you okay?"

"Yeah. I have a concussion, hence the lovely black eyes. Holden told me I look like a raccoon. I'm sore all over, and I've got some ugly bruises. My head hurts, but given how bad it could have been, I'm fine."

"What happened?" Dani asked.

"Unfortunately, I don't remember."

"Is your car messed up bad?"

"I haven't seen it since they took me in the ambulance, but yeah, it looked pretty bad."

She nodded, and then she looked away and back at me a couple of times as we ate.

"What?" I finally asked. "I can tell you want to say something. Go ahead."

"I don't know if it's inappropriate, you know. Like, the wrong time."

"Just say it."

"I heard back from Hyram's cousin Dianne last night. I told her that we wanted to buy the building, but we wanted to see if anyone in the family had an interest first. She said she and the other cousins would have liked the opportunity to have some things out of the farmhouse before Ronald sold it—family heirlooms, personal mementos, and such—but the auto repair shop didn't interest any of them."

"Well, that's unfortunate. That could have been a good solution for us and for Hyram. Did she say anything else?"

"She did mention that they were all surprised when Alex left everything to Ronald. She said Alex wasn't initially receptive to his dad's efforts to reconcile, but that after Claude died, Ronald and Alex started spending more time together and had forged a relationship of sorts. She just didn't realize they'd gotten close enough that Alex would draw up paperwork naming Ronald as his heir. She seemed to think about as highly of Ronald as Mrs. Myrtle does. I guess the guy wasn't that popular around Cedar Creek."

"Well, if he's anything like his wife, I can understand why."

Holden came back inside and grabbed another bagel, and the three of us turned to talk of Holden's foundation and the challenges he'd found with trying to pair homeless dogs with wounded veterans and train both to heal each other.

He looked up toward the front window and frowned.

"Do either of you know why Mrs. Myrtle would be coming up the driveway?"

"Oh, no," Dani exclaimed as she stood, her eyes panicked. "I do not want to see that woman. I gotta get out of here."

"Wait 'til she rings the doorbell, and I'll keep her occupied at the front door while you go out the back," Holden said.

"Thanks," Dani said as she gathered her purse and keys and walked toward the French doors leading out to the back deck.

"What's she doing here?" I asked.

Dani scoffed and rolled her eyes. "Probably coming to get a report from you so she can pass along the news to everyone at the salon."

"She's carrying food," Holden said as he watched her out the front window.

"Great," I said to Dani as she stood by the back door, waiting for the signal to go. "He'll let anybody in if they have food."

"Mrs. Myrtle's a good cook," Holden said. "She brings me her leftovers sometimes."

The doorbell rang, and Dani said her goodbyes and went out the back door as Holden went to the foyer to open the front door.

Holden kept Myrtle talking at the door for a couple of minutes, and then he led her inside, his eyes scanning the French doors for any sign of Dani.

"Mrs. Myrtle came by to check on you, Sloane, and she brought a casserole for dinner." He carried the casserole dish to the kitchen while Myrtle walked into the living room and sat on the sofa next to me.

"There you are! I've been frantic with worry since I heard. Sugarpie, are you okay?"

"Yeah, I'm fine," I said, sitting up straighter to pull my feet out from under me and put them on the floor. "How did you know?"

"Good news travels fast, but bad news travels faster. Why, everybody in town is talking about it. You and your pretty red car all smashed up."

Another warm flush of embarrassment washed over me at the thought of the entire town of Cedar Creek gossiping about my accident.

"I wasn't speeding," I said in my defense, even though she hadn't asked.

"Accidents happen, and everyone is just happy you're okay. That's all that matters. I can't stay long. I have a dentist appointment, but I wanted to drop off that casserole for y'all and let you know I cared."

Holden came and leaned over the back of the sofa. "I put the casserole in the fridge, and I'm gonna go out on the deck and make some phone calls. I'll give you ladies some privacy."

I gave him a death stare and tried to communicate telepathically that I didn't want to be left alone with Myrtle, and I swear he was grinning when he walked out the French doors.

"Bless your heart," Myrtle said when he had gone. "You look like you've been in a boxing ring with a kangaroo. I can show you how to cover those shiners with some makeup; don't you worry about that. A little concealer blended well, and you'll be right as rain."

I decided if I had to suffer through an appearance critique from Myrtle, I might as well get something out of it.

"I saw Ronald's wife, Cecile Fisher, in Jensen yesterday. I guess she's in town for a visit. She seems like piece of work."

She leaned back and peered over her glasses at me. "Oh, you have no idea. That one's a viper. I heard she was back in town. Now, tell me what happened. They say you crashed in the straightaway. What caused it?"

"I don't have any memory of it, so I don't know."

"Oh, so you may have been speeding."

"No, I don't think I was."

"But you don't know."

I shifted on the couch and turned to face her. "Why do you say Cecile's a viper?"

"Why do you say she's a piece of work?"

"Someone in the pharmacy made an error, and she made her displeasure well-known for the entire store to hear."

Myrtle's lips pursed together. "Sounds like her. I say she's a viper because she preys on people. She poisons them, and she sucks them dry. She was seeing an older gentleman in our church for a while, Mr. Ollie Harper. We all knew she was looking for a sugar daddy, and I think Mr. Ollie did, too, but he liked her *attention*, if you know what I mean, so he was more than willing to spend the money on her. But before long, his daughters noticed he was answering the phone less, and he always seemed to have some reason it wasn't a good time for them to visit. Next thing they know, Cecile had herself set up with power of attorney and control over his estate. Diabolical."

She shook her head with a disgusted frown and reached her hand up to smooth the back of her updo.

"Were the daughters able to do anything about it?" I asked.

"They hired an attorney and were finally able to sit down with Mr. Ollie. That poor man had no idea what he'd signed, and he had no intention of giving Cecile control over anything. The girls suspected the documents were forged and that their daddy hadn't even signed them, but they couldn't prove it, and Mr. Ollie refused to press charges against Cecile. It wasn't too long afterwards that she took up with Ronald. I think those two were kindred spirits when it came to gold-digging. Two peas in a pod, right there, and both of them worthless."

I nodded, at a loss for words.

She paused a moment, and then asked, "Did she introduce herself as Fisher?"

I thought back to the encounter, which seemed ages ago with everything that had happened since. "She didn't exactly introduce herself to me. The pharmacist called her Mrs. Fisher, though."

"Hmmph. They must have gotten married in Tennessee. No one

I know got invited, so it might have been a courthouse thing. Did she say what she's doing in town?"

I tried to shrug, but the pain in my shoulder was too great. "She said she was visiting her brother for a few days."

Myrtle clucked her tongue against her teeth. "Really? Now, that's surprising. I can't believe he'd have her in his house. He is her only family, though. Have you heard yet if your car will be totaled? That's a right expensive car. I would imagine the insurance company won't be too happy about it."

"We haven't heard their assessment yet. Why are you surprised that Cecile would stay with her brother?"

She leaned in close and lowered her voice, even though we were alone. "You didn't hear this from me, but a few years back, her brother figured out Cecile had forged his and his wife's signature on credit card applications. She ruined their credit, and the wife wanted to press charges and have Cecile arrested. The brother refused. He and the wife ended up divorced over it, and then he and Cecile had a big blow-out about something right around the time she moved to Tennessee. I'd heard they hadn't spoken since. Hmm. I wonder what caused them to make up?"

She patted her hands on her thighs and stood with a big sigh.

"Well, I should go. I put a little note on the casserole dish with baking instructions, and if you need anything at all, don't hesitate to call me."

"Thank you. I appreciate you stopping by."

She looked around the room, and I was shocked to see her eyes fill with tears as she laid her hand on her chest.

"It looks so different here now since Nanette's gone. Lord, I miss her so."

I followed her to the front door, wishing I knew what to say to offer her comfort.

She stopped just as we reached the foyer and turned back to face me, any trace of tears gone.

"I never did get that number for you, did I? The one who wanted to open the dry-cleaning place. What was her name? Krista!"

"Oh, no, you didn't."

Myrtle frowned as she pulled the front door open. "I'll make another call to her aunt today. Of course, if Krista doesn't feel comfortable talking, there's not much I can do."

"I understand. Thank you. I appreciate you trying."

We shared one of her awkward air hugs, and then she patted my cheek and was gone.

Chapter 37

H olden opened the French door from the deck and stuck
his head inside.
"All clear," I said as I sat back down on the sofa.
"She's gone."

"We heard her car, but we wanted to be sure."

"We?" I asked, just as Dani walked inside behind Holden. "I
thought you left."

"I couldn't," she said with a sigh. "Mrs. Myrtle's car was parked
behind mine. I've been sitting on the deck talking to Holden and
hoping she'd leave before I passed out from the humidity. I certainly
never missed that when I lived in Chicago."

"It is a hot one out there today," Holden said. "You want some
water?"

"Yes, please," Dani said, sitting on the sofa next to me. "So,
what did Granny Gossip want?"

"I think you were right. She came to get details about my accident that she could pass along, but she also gave me some more
information on Cecile, so I suppose it was a fair trade."

She thanked Holden for the water and sucked down about half
the glass.

"You gonna be here a few minutes?" Holden asked her. "I need to run over to the construction site and sign off on some paperwork. I won't be gone more than a half hour. Forty-five minutes, tops."

"I'm fine," I interjected. "Go if you need to. I don't need a babysitter, I swear."

"Yeah, I can stick around," Dani said, completely ignoring my protest.

"Where's your phone?" Holden asked me as he looked around for it. "You already got me in trouble because my brother had been trying to call and you didn't answer. He called my phone, and I told him you were inside with Mrs. Myrtle. He wanted you to call him as soon as she left."

"It's on my nightstand. It should be charged by now."

I gave Dani the rundown of my conversation with Myrtle while Holden went to get my phone.

"Thanks," I said when he handed it to me. "Oh, I have a missed call from Marc."

Dani frowned. "Yeah, I think I know what that's about. I got a text from the realtor a few minutes ago. She heard back from Ronald, and he's not interested in selling."

I sighed and reached to adjust the toss pillow behind my head. "Well, that sucks. I had hoped we could pull that off and make Hyram happy."

"Me too."

"I'm heading out," Holden said. "I'll be right back though. I know you and I have been through this drill before, Sloane, but it's worth saying again. Please don't injure yourself while I'm gone, or my brother will kill me."

I held both thumbs up. "I'm fine. Dani will take good care of me."

"And don't forget to call Tristan."

"I will."

Dani finished the glass of water and leaned forward to set it on a coaster on the coffee table. "So, Cecile seems to have a reputation for forgery, huh?"

"Yeah, so it seems."

She took a deep breath and tapped her fingers against her bottom lip as she stared at the ceiling.

"What?" I asked. "What are you thinking?"

With a quick exhale, she shifted her weight on the sofa and turned to face me. "I know this is probably way off base, but hear me out. Dianne said the family was surprised that Alex left everything to Ronald. What if…what if Ronald and Cecile faked the will? Maybe Alex *didn't* leave everything to them. I mean, what twenty-three-year-old has a will, for Christ's sake?"

I lay back against the pillow and considered her theory. "If that's the case, that could be why Hyram is so upset. If he knew they cheated his family out of the building, that could piss him off and make him cause problems for Ronald and Cecile with their tenants."

"But how the hell would we prove it was forged? Undoubtedly, the family raised that question when Alex died. If they couldn't prove it wasn't valid, how would we?"

"I don't know. Would you feel comfortable asking Dianne if anyone from the family looked into it?"

My phone rang, and I frowned to see the local area code.

"Are you going to answer it?"

I shook my head. "I never do when it's an unknown caller just in case it's a reporter or a crazed fan who found me somehow. But this is local. I wonder if I should, you know, since it might be something about the car. The insurance company, maybe?"

"You want me to answer it?" Dani asked.

I handed her the phone. "Sure."

"Hello," she said, and then after listening a moment, "May I ask who's calling?"

She paused for the answer, and then she looked at me as she said, "Okay, let me see if she's available."

She muted the phone and said, "It's some woman named Krista. She said Mrs. Myrtle talked to her mom and asked that she call you?"

"Oh, yes, definitely." I nodded and made hand motions for her to give me back the phone. "Hi, Krista. It's Sloane. Thank you so much for calling."

"Hi, um, yeah," Krista stammered. "I don't know why I'm calling exactly. Mrs. Myrtle told my mom you have some questions for me about the building in Cedar Creek. I'm not sure how I could help you."

"Oh, well, my business partner and I are looking to buy the building, and we just wanted to talk to the former tenants and see if you knew of any reason why we shouldn't."

"Uh, I don't know if I should say anything. Have you talked to the landlord?"

"I have, but you know how it is. People who want to sell a building aren't gonna tell you its faults, right? Did anything… *unusual*…happen while you were there?"

"You mean other than my husband having a heart attack and dying?"

I cringed and closed my eyes. This was exactly what I wanted to avoid in talking to her.

"I'm so sorry about that, and I know that must have been devastating. I would never want to cause you more pain or grief in talking about that time or thinking about it." I opened my eyes, and Dani put her hand out for the phone, but I shook my head and looked away. "I just thought perhaps you might have some insight for us. We've been leasing the building, and I have to tell you, we've seen some pretty strange things happen. Things I never would have thought could be real. I was wondering if you might have seen something like that, too."

She was silent for a moment, and I looked down at the phone to see if the call had ended.

"Krista, you still there?"

"Yeah. I don't know what to tell you. I'd love to help you, but Ronald was pretty adamant that I not talk to people about what happened. He said he'd sue me if I told anyone."

"I understand, but I promise you, Krista, I won't say a word. He will never know we talked. I just don't want to sink a bunch of money into this without knowing what I'm in for, you know? People around town are telling me the building's haunted. That it's cursed. I don't know what to believe."

Another long pause.

"Look, I don't want any trouble," Krista said. "But I also don't want anyone else to get hurt. My husband, Frank, didn't just have a heart attack for no reason." She hesitated. "He was on the ladder painting, and he'd come down because I brought in some lunch. When we walked back into that main room where the ladder was, neither of us could believe what we saw."

I quickly put the phone on speaker so Dani could hear, and I put my finger over my lips to remind her to be silent.

"Somehow," Krista continued, "somebody had scribbled the name *Alex* in the wet paint. Now, no one else was in the building, just me and Frank. So, there's no way someone else, another person, did that. We would have known. We were right there, right outside the room. I freaked out immediately. I'd always felt off in that building, like I was being watched or like there was a presence there with me. But Frank…" Her voice cracked with emotion and trailed off.

"I'm so sorry," I said. "I hate to drudge all this up for you."

"No, it's okay. It actually feels good to talk about him. No one in my family mentions him because they worry it will upset me. It's nice being able to say his name for a change." She took an audible breath and released it. "Frank was the most logical, practical guy you'd ever want to meet. He didn't believe in anything supernatural, and he'd always give me the logical explanation for whatever I thought was happening at that place. But *this…this* Frank struggled with. There wasn't a logical explanation, you know what I mean?"

"I definitely can't think of one," I said.

"He finally determined that it must have been something on the wall before. He said that somehow the fresh coat of paint didn't adhere. That maybe they'd used some substance that the paint wouldn't stick to. He painted back over it, and he said he'd ask the guy at the paint store what to do if it bled through again."

"And did it?"

"No. I went back in the front room, and then I heard Frank

scream. Something I'd never heard him do before. When I came running back in there, Frank was on the ground groaning, and to the right of where he was painting, in an area he hadn't painted at all yet, the *A* and the *L* of the word *Alex* were on the wall in fresh, white paint. I didn't get to say much to my husband after that. I ran to call an ambulance, and he only said four words to me before they took him away. He said, 'Get out of here.' It was the last thing he ever said to me. He died in the ambulance on the way to the hospital."

"I am so sorry," I said, stunned by her story.

"They told me at the hospital that he had an underlying heart condition. They said the physical exertion he'd been under trying to renovate the building was too much for him. But I know what killed my husband. It was that building and whatever's in it. I never set foot in it again, and if you're smart, you won't either."

I thanked her as best I could and said goodbye, and then I turned to look at Dani as I put the phone down. I was surprised to see her grinning.

She grabbed my hand in both of hers. "It wasn't the mob!"

"What? What wasn't the mob? What are you talking about?"

"Do you remember the morning I came into the theater and the paint was all over the floor?"

I nodded, and she continued, even more animated than before.

"When I got there that morning, the paint had hit the wall and exploded everywhere, but it was clear that someone had started drawing letters with the paint. I thought at the time it was a *V* and an *I*. I'd just gotten the call the night before about the federal charges, and I assumed someone was writing Victor's name as a message to me, as a threat. I thought they were telling me to keep quiet even though I don't know anything."

She exhaled with a loud rush of air and then she laughed.

"I was terrified, Sloane. I thought they were here, watching me. That they'd been inside my theater. This was before I had any idea about a ghost, and I thought a lot of it—the whiskey, the tools—that it must be someone screwing with me. Trying to scare me. To keep me in line. My first instinct that day was to call the cops, but then I realized while I was on the phone with the dispatcher that it might be exactly the kind of thing they were watching for, so I tried to tell her it wasn't necessary to send anyone."

"And then Seth showed up," I said.

"Yes! And the last thing on earth I want is to put him in any kind of danger. So, I tried my best to throw him off and convince him not to come back."

"I think you did a good job of that. You were pretty rough on the guy. I'd never seen you be so cold and distant."

She lay back against the sofa and ran her hands through her hair. "Oh, God. What a relief! This whole time I've been looking over my shoulder and questioning anyone who looked at me twice in a store. I've been paranoid about things being moved in my house, wondering if I left the porch light on or if someone else turned it on. Did I leave that creamer out on the counter, or did someone else? As if it wasn't enough to have a ghost throwing a wrench in my business venture, I honestly thought I had the mob breathing down my neck, too. Aargh! I feel like the weight of the world has been lifted off my shoulders."

"I can't believe you didn't tell me any of this."

"I couldn't," she said, her eyes wide and pleading. "I didn't dare put anyone else in their crosshairs, and I couldn't risk you telling Tristan and then him opening an investigation. I didn't want to draw any more attention than necessary. I just wanted to lay low and hope that once the feds questioned me, I would be in the clear and left alone."

"But don't you think we were all in the crosshairs anyway? You? Me? Steve, his crew? If you thought the mob had access to the building and to your house, then we were all in danger every time we were there. Why wouldn't you tell me that?"

Her brow creased, and she frowned. "I thought I was protecting you. I thought it would be best if I handled it without involving anyone else. I'm sorry. But the good news is, it wasn't the mob." She sat up and clapped her hands together. "I never thought I would be happy to have a ghost terrorizing me, but hey! It's not the mob. I feel like I'm just going to keep saying that over and over again. The whiskey? Not the mob. The plant knocked over on my porch? Not the mob. The black SUV? Not the mob."

"Wait, wait, whoa. What black SUV? What are you talking about?"

"About a week after the paint thing happened, I was coming out of the theater one night to go home, and a black SUV with dark tinted windows was leaving the parking lot. I tried to brush it off as someone who had found my lot to be a convenient space to pull over, but I was scared it was whoever was watching me. I didn't go back to the theater alone at night after that. But now I know, it was just some random thing. It's not the mob."

"Have you seen that same SUV since then?"

"No, I haven't. And believe me, I've been on the lookout. Wow. Okay, I feel so much better now."

I hated to burst her relief bubble, but my hands were shaking, and so was my voice.

"Dani, we have reason to believe that a black SUV ran me off the road yesterday."

Her smile disappeared, and her eyes widened. "What?"

"I was on the phone with my publicist and she says I told her that a black SUV with dark tinted windows was screwing with me."

"But this had to be like a month ago, and I haven't seen it since."

I shrugged with my right side. "Maybe it's a coincidence; I don't know. But I think I should tell Tristan."

She bit down on her bottom lip and then nodded.

"Yeah. Okay. Do it. Sloane, I am so sorry. I should have said something. Do you think it's because you helped me financially? Are they targeting you because of me?"

"I don't know, and I don't think we should jump to any conclusions, okay? We don't know that anyone is targeting me or you. It might have just been some jerk who has a thing against Ferraris, who knows? You said you haven't seen the SUV since that night. I would think if it were someone trailing you, you would have noticed. I certainly haven't noticed it, and I'm usually pretty aware of what's going on around me because of photographers."

"God, I hope you're right. If I thought even for a minute that I'd caused you to be harmed, I couldn't forgive myself. I've already worried myself sick about my family in all this. I hope I haven't endangered the best friend I've had in a really long time."

"I'm fine," I said, taking her hand in mine. "It's probably nothing, okay? But I do think we should let Tristan know."

Chapter 38

When I called Tristan, I was relieved to hear he was headed home for lunch. I'd much rather tell him about Dani's situation with Victor in person.

Holden had gotten delayed at the construction site, and Dani needed to go to the theater, so it worked out that we were alone when Tristan arrived.

"Hey," he said when he came in. "Where's my brother?"

"He had to take care of some things over at the construction site, but Dani's been here until a few minutes ago so I wasn't alone."

After a quick greeting kiss, he took my head in his hands and gently turned it to inspect the bruising at my left temple and the black circles under my eyes. He winced, and then tried to force a smile.

"You okay? Does it hurt?"

"It's not the best feeling I've ever had, but it's not the worst either. I'm fine. What did you bring for lunch?"

He set the bag on the table and took out the salad he'd brought me and the burger and fries he'd brought for himself, and then he put Holden's chicken sandwich in the fridge.

"So, what's up? What did you need to tell me?"

I took a deep breath, and exhaled it in a rush, ready to get the hard part over with.

"Dani's ex-husband was part of The Chicago Outfit, and he's in jail awaiting trial in Chicago. She thinks the mafia has someone watching her, and she's seen a black SUV hanging around the theater."

He had just shoved a French fry in his mouth, and he stopped chewing for a moment and then chewed slowly as he wiped his hands on a napkin.

"This is why you helped her?" he asked as soon as he had swallowed.

"Yeah. The government froze all her assets in connection with the case, which stopped the sale of her house and blocked her from using her savings. She would have lost everything. It was kind of a gray area on whether she could accept a loan from me with all her finances in disarray, so the attorneys advised that I should take over as owner until it all gets resolved. I wanted to tell you, and I actually was going to tell you the other night, but you were asleep in the hammock when I came outside and I didn't want to get you all riled up."

He sat in silence and stared at his food, and after a couple of minutes, I leaned forward and laid my hand on his arm.

"Say something, Deputy."

"You're telling me you knew Dani was involved with the mafia—"

"But she wasn't. Her ex-husband was. She didn't even know."

He tossed the napkin on the table and looked at me with his eyes narrowed.

"C'mon, Sloane. Don't tell me you believe that. She knew. How could she not know?"

"She didn't. He worked days. She worked nights. They were only together a couple of months. They got married after two weeks."

He smirked with a little shake of his head. "She married a guy after only two weeks?"

"It was love at first sight," I said, frustrated that I had to defend

Dani's choices rather than talk about the most important point at hand—the SUV.

"I don't know, babe," he said as he picked up another French fry and dipped it in ketchup. "I don't buy that she had no idea what the dude was doing. There's a lifestyle that goes with being part of an organized family like that. It would be really difficult not to realize what you'd gotten into."

"Yeah, well, sometimes when you're in love, you see what you want to see, and you don't see what you don't want to see."

"True," he said, popping the fry into his mouth.

"Can we skip the part where you judge her for her life choices and judge me for getting financially involved with her and discuss the possibility that someone from the Chicago mafia may have tried to kill me yesterday?"

He had taken a bite of his burger, and I waited for him to finish chewing before he responded.

"Why does Dani think she's being watched?"

"There's lot of little things that may not mean anything. They may just be coincidence. I told you about the whiskey missing."

"You said that was Hyram's ghost."

"Yeah, well, it might not be. Look, the important thing is, she saw a black SUV leaving the theater parking lot one night. Yesterday, I told Priscilla about a black SUV, and then I crashed. Don't you think they might be connected?"

He took a swig of his iced tea and looked at me with his head cocked to the side.

"Maybe. Maybe not. How long ago did she see this SUV? And did she only see it one time?"

"It was about a month ago, and yeah, just the one time."

"What else makes her think she's being watched?"

"Little stuff. A plant being knocked over on the porch. Things at the theater going missing. Just that general feeling of being followed." I watched as he took another bite of his burger. "I thought you'd be more worked up over this."

"What do you want me to say, babe? I don't even know for sure that this SUV you don't remember seeing was involved in your crash, nor do I know that it was the same SUV that Dani saw a month ago in a parking lot. Now, maybe someone's watching her; I don't know. Those kinds of things happen when you associate with crime families, which is why I'm still a little incredulous that you saw no problem linking yourself with them."

"I didn't link myself with a crime family. I made a decision to own a legitimate theater business, and my business partner just happens to have her funds frozen due to an investigation. Not because *she's* being investigated, mind you. Her attorney has assured her that all this will be cleared up as soon as it works its way through the court system."

"You realize that could take years, right?"

"Okay, so you're not even going to take this threat seriously because now you have some skewed opinion of Dani?"

"I don't have any opinion of Dani, Sloane. I don't know her well enough to have one. And it's not that I'm not taking it seriously; it's just that I haven't determined if there's a threat, yet. I have to deal with facts, babe. I have to investigate before I react."

"So, will you investigate it? Will you look into it?"

"Of course. I've already got them looking for any sign of paint transfer on your car. If we find that, I can narrow it down to a make and probably a specific model based on the paint. Then I can go from there looking for that car. Did Dani mention the make or model of the SUV she saw?"

"She didn't say, but we could ask her more about it."

"All right. I have to get back to work." He stood and gathered the remnants of his lunch and tossed them in the trash. "When's Holden back? I don't want you here alone."

"I'm fine, Tristan. I've had no dizzy spells, no nausea, nothing. I'm sore as hell and I have a raging headache, but I'm okay to be alone, I swear."

"Yeah, and what if yesterday *was* a threat? What if someone deliberately caused you to crash?"

"I thought you didn't think there was a connection."

"I told you I don't know yet, Sloane. I'm investigating. I'm gathering information. But whether it's connected to Dani or not, I'm concerned if someone actually did come after you on the road and leave the scene once you'd crashed. So, until I know what happened and why, I don't feel comfortable with you being alone, okay?"

I swallowed hard and nodded. As frustrating as it was when I thought he wasn't taking me seriously, it was sobering to realize he thought I could be in danger.

"Then take me with you and drop me off at the theater. Dani's there with Steve and his crew, and the electricians will be there all afternoon. I'm tired of being cooped up in the house, and this way, you'll know I'm with people, and I'll only be a couple of blocks from you."

He agreed, though reluctant, and when he dropped me off at the theater, he told me he might be back to ask Dani some questions.

"Questions about what?" she whispered as we stood huddled behind the concession counter for privacy. "I don't know anything."

"Just about the SUV you saw, and I don't know, maybe about the things that have happened to make you think you're followed. He just wants to rule it out, I think."

"Right. Okay. Well, I hope it's nothing. I can't stand the thought that you might have been hurt because of me."

"I'm fine, but that's all the more reason to let him look into things. If someone is watching you and following either one of us, it's best to know and do something about it, don't you think?"

She stepped out of the way so one of the painters could get past her to retrieve his paint tray.

"I've been thinking since I left your house," she said once he'd gone. "My initial thought was that Hyram has been telling us to look into Alex's will. Like, maybe he knew somehow that Ronald and Cecile scammed the family, and he was pissed. But, Sloane, what if we've gotten this all wrong? What if the ghost isn't Hyram? What if it's—"

"Alex?" I said, finishing her question as my mind caught up to hers. "I've been thinking that, too. It makes total sense that it would be Alex. We didn't even consider him since the whole town assumed this building is haunted by Hyram, but he died young, in his prime. That would be enough to make anyone angry in the afterlife."

"Yes, and this building was his livelihood just like it was Hyram's."

"Myrtle said people started talking about the building when Alex died. They assumed Hyram had cursed it and haunted it, but why would Hyram want to harm his own family member? That makes no sense. It's more likely that it has been Alex all along."

"Right?"

Dani's eyes brightened, her entire demeanor energized by the journalistic buzz she'd mentioned earlier.

"Mrs. Myrtle told you Alex was a heavy drinker," she said as she pushed herself up to sit on the counter. "Maybe that explains the fascination with my whiskey. And you felt a presence watching you from the office upstairs. Alex probably would have used that office with his motorcycle repair shop just like his uncle Hyram did before him."

I nodded as the dots continued to connect in my mind. "Bashing a can of paint against a wall and writing your name in graffiti definitely seems more like a twenty-something's act of frustration than an older man."

"Yes. This could explain why our ghost responded so poorly, too. We kept calling him Hyram. The poor guy was trying to tell us we were wrong. He wants someone to know his will was forged, and we were busy focusing on his uncle."

"So, what do we do now?"

Dani frowned. "I don't know. How would we prove the will was forged? That's not an accusation we can make lightly."

"*If* it was even forged. We're assuming that's his issue. He could just be pissed that he's dead."

"True. Dianne said the family was shocked by the will, but who knows how much Alex would have told them? Especially if he knew their opinion about his dad. I wonder if Alex had a girlfriend or a close friend at the time he died. Maybe someone who would know more about his relationship with Ronald."

I sighed with narrowed eyes. "Why do I have the feeling I'm about to have another conversation with Myrtle?"

"She likes you," Dani said. "She brought you a casserole."

The front door opened, and Tristan stepped inside.

My heart raced with one glimpse of him, and I grinned as I went to greet him with a kiss.

"Hi there," I said as he removed his hat and wrapped his arm around me.

When I'd finished with introductions for him and Dani, he said, "I've been trying to call you, and your phone's going straight to voicemail."

"It's this building," I said. "You can't get a phone signal inside here."

"It sucks," Dani said. "I need to talk to my cellular company about installing some kind of booster. It's somewhere on my list of things to do."

Tristan pulled out his phone and handed it to me.

"The news is out. Someone at the station came and told me. It's all over the internet."

"Priscilla's probably been trying to call me, too. Let me step outside and see if I can get a signal."

Tristan nodded toward Dani as he moved to the door to hold it open for me.

"Sloane tells me you saw a black SUV here not long ago. I'd like to ask you a few questions."

I left them to talk as I called Priscilla, who confirmed that she'd reached an agreement for the interview, and when she couldn't reach me, she'd decided to go ahead and leak the story.

"You'd already given me the go-ahead, and I didn't want to delay and miss the evening news cycle," she said.

"No, it's fine. I knew it was coming. I expected it." All of which was true, but I still felt like I might hyperventilate.

We talked a few minutes more about the logistics for the interview and the official statement she'd be releasing the next day, and then I went back inside.

Tristan and Dani were laughing at something, and I smiled,

happy that it hadn't been a tense questioning. I knew Dani had been nervous.

"I showed him around," Dani said. "We were just talking about our first encounters with Chelsea."

"Her mind was blown like mine was," Tristan said. "All set with Priscilla?"

I nodded and blew out a loud breath. "Yep. It's out there. The world knows we're engaged, and tomorrow it will be confirmed with an official statement."

"Congratulations," Dani said.

We said our goodbyes, and then Tristan and I headed home.

Chapter 39

"Did you get what you needed from Dani about the SUV?" I asked as he drove us home.

"Yeah."

"Do you think it's the same one I told Priscilla about?"

"Impossible to know at this point."

He had his elbow propped against the driver's window, his head leaned back against the seat rest. His eyelids seemed heavy, and the frown he wore had carved deep lines in his forehead. He looked exhausted.

"You okay, babe?" I reached across to lay my hand on his thigh.

He jerked to attention, like I'd startled him out of deep thought.

"Yeah, I'm good. I didn't sleep well last night, and it's been a hell of a day."

"Uh-oh. No nightmares, I hope. I didn't hear you during the night."

"I didn't sleep long enough to have any dreams. Just dozed a few restless minutes here and there. I went out on the porch for a while and stared at the stars." He took my hand in his and brought it to his lips. "You seemed like you were knocked out, and I figured you needed the rest. I was hoping I didn't disturb you."

"You didn't. I'm sorry I wasn't there for you. I would have gone outside with you or done something to help take your mind off things."

He grinned and cut his gaze in my direction. "You were in no shape."

"Yeah, well, I would have if I could have."

We rode a few more minutes in silence, and then I broached the subject at the forefront of my mind.

"How can you find out if someone's will was forged?"

His brow furrowed deeper. "Why? Whose will are you worried about?"

"Alex Letchworth. I think we may have had it all wrong about the ghost at the theater. I don't think it's Hyram, and I think Ronald and Cecile Fisher stole Alex's inheritance."

He looked at me, his eyes wide with surprise. "Why on earth would you think that?"

"A couple of reasons. Myrtle told me that Ronald wasn't close to his son. He wasn't involved in Alex's life until the end of it, and yet, Alex left his dad everything he had—which was evidently quite substantial given his grandparents' wealth. Dani talked to one of Hyram's cousins, who said the family was shocked by that. Ronald's wife, Cecile, has a reputation for gold-digging and forgery, so Dani and I are thinking it sounds fishy that the two of them ended up with everything."

"Okay, but if Ronald and his son had forged a relationship before Alex died, then maybe Alex made that decision on his own. What makes you think the ghost is Alex instead of Hyram?"

"We talked to one of the former tenants to ask if she noticed any paranormal activity, and she and her husband saw the name *Alex* appear on a freshly-painted wall and then again in a section of unpainted wall."

"Really?" He sat forward and crossed his forearms on the top of the steering wheel. "Damn. That's crazy."

"It makes more sense though, when you think about it. Alex has more reason to be a restless spirit than Hyram did, and we feel like with this new perspective, we're really getting somewhere. If we can prove that the will was forged, that might give Alex the peace he needs to move on."

"It also might make the theater homeless."

"What do you mean?"

"If the will is voided, then Ronald doesn't own the building, which means Dani's lease is voided."

"Oh. Crap. I didn't think of that."

"You and Dani also need to be careful who you discuss this with. You're accusing Ronald and Cecile of a vile crime. I don't think either of them would take that lightly."

"We haven't told anyone our theory except me telling you."

"Well, I wouldn't if I were you," he said as we pulled into the driveway. "It could blow back on the two of you in a big way."

"So, you're saying we should just let it go?" I stepped out into the garage and shut the door. "We shouldn't even try to find the truth?"

"I didn't say that, babe. I said the two of you need to be careful." He led us into the laundry room and turned off the alarm system.

"What would you suggest we do? How do we go about finding out if this is true without letting anyone know we think it is?"

He turned to face me with a sigh. "Babe, don't you think if the will were a forgery, someone in the family would have pursued that? You said Dani talked to a cousin. Did they investigate? Did they hire anyone to look into it?"

"Not that I know of, but that doesn't mean it didn't happen."

He came and stood in front of me, rubbing his hands up and down my arms.

"I get that you and Dani need to figure out what's upsetting your supernatural sourpuss so you can get the theater open, but I think you may be taking this a bit too far. Isn't it enough that you may very well have provoked the mafia? Do you have to go around accusing other people of crimes and make even more enemies?"

"C'mon," I said with a scowl. "I can't believe you of all people would say that. You're a law enforcement officer. Don't you want to know if a crime was committed? Don't you care if these people cheated the family out of what was rightfully theirs?"

"Of course, I care. But if the family was outraged and didn't pursue it, then it might be because there's nothing to pursue. I'm gonna go take a shower."

My phone rang as he walked down the hallway, and though I groaned to see Myrtle's number, I answered it, knowing she'd probably be able to give me information.

"I'm calling to make sure you know it wasn't me," she said after we'd exchanged greetings.

"What wasn't you?"

"The source. I saw on the news that your engagement leaked from a reputable source. It was not me."

"Oh, I know. Thank you for telling me, though."

"I noticed you had Nanette's ring on when I saw you earlier, but I didn't say anything. You realize if you're wearing that out and about, people are going to assume you're engaged."

"Yes, and it's fine. We've decided to officially announce our engagement, so it won't be a secret anymore."

"Well, hallelujah! When's the wedding?"

I feared this would become the standard reaction to our news.

"We haven't gotten that far yet. We're just enjoying the engagement right now. Speaking of relationships, do you know if Alex Letchworth was dating anyone at the time of his death?"

Myrtle paused. "I didn't know the boy well. Why do you ask?"

"I find that the more I learn about the building and its occupants, the more I want to learn. I'd love to talk to someone who knew Alex personally."

"Did Krista ever call you?"

"She did. Thank you for connecting us."

"I like to help however I can, and connecting people is my specialty. You know, my cousin Debbie is an excellent caterer. She could probably give you some ideas of beautiful locations around here for a wedding. I mean, if the two of you are planning on a local event. I know that would probably mean a lot to Rita."

"We haven't decided what we're doing yet, but I promise to let you know when we do."

We said our goodbyes, and I made my way down the hallway to the bedroom just as Tristan was stepping out of the shower.

"Myrtle called to tell me she wasn't the source that leaked our engagement."

He snickered as he rubbed his hair with the towel. "Only because she didn't get the chance to be."

"I don't know about that. She seems pretty loyal to your grand-mother. She said she wouldn't do anything to betray her."

"Maybe. I tend to believe Mrs. Myrtle is loyal to Mrs. Myrtle, but she and Nan were awful close."

He wrapped the towel around his hips and tucked it, and then he came to put his arms around my waist.

"Sorry if I was grumpy before. I'm tired, and I'm worried about you, and I'm neck-deep in a case that weighs on me day and night."

I stretched up to kiss him and wrap my arms around his neck, breathing in the scent of his lavender soap and feeling the heat and the moisture of his skin.

"It's okay. I understand. I know our theory is a stretch, and it may not come to anything, but I feel like we're on the right track with Alex and the will. I feel it in my gut, in a way I never did with anything we found with Hyram. I understand that you don't want me to seek out trouble, but I can't just ignore this possibility without knowing if something foul happened."

He smiled and released me with a kiss to grab the deodorant from the cabinet and apply it.

"It would be hard to prove that without having experts weigh in, Sloane, and you would likely need the family on board to pursue it."

"Myrtle said there was an incident with an older man in town where Cecile possibly forged some paperwork. Maybe there were other incidents too. Could you look into her background? Or Ronald's? I mean, if we establish a pattern of behavior, that might be enough to open an investigation, right?"

"I can't just randomly look into someone's background, babe. I need to have cause."

"But isn't the fact that Alex left everything to Ronald without being that close to him cause enough?"

"People do crazy stuff with their wills all the time. And again, if his family didn't fight it, they likely didn't have as big of a problem with it as you might think."

"What if it was more?"

His eyes met mine in the mirror. "What do you mean?"

"Well, there's something that's been bothering me. It's probably nothing, and you're probably going to tell me I'm overthinking and making another big leap, but hear me out. What if Ronald and Cecile had something to do with Alex's death?"

Tristan spit out the mouthwash he'd been swishing.

"Oh, I see," he said with a smirk. "Since we don't have enough cause to investigate them for forgery, you want to charge them with murder? That'll be much easier."

He rolled his eyes and chuckled.

"You don't think it's suspicious? He was only twenty-three when he died."

He scrunched his face into an expression that hinted at how crazy he found my suggestion.

"Sloane, you told me Myrtle said the kid was a heavy drinker known for not managing his insulin and food intake well. That sounds much more likely to be the cause of his death than some conspiracy by his father and stepmother to murder him and steal his inheritance. Besides, I'm sure they did an autopsy to rule out foul play at the time."

"But what if it was something that wouldn't show up?"

"What do you mean?"

"Myrtle said Alex was found in a diabetic coma and they were unable to resuscitate him. Cecile is a diabetic, too. I bumped into her at the pharmacy in Jensen, and she was raising all kinds of hell about a mistake a beginner pharmacy tech there made with her insulin syringe. Apparently, she's on some particular type of insulin for people who are insulin-resistant. She said it's five times stronger than regular insulin. What if she somehow switched hers with Alex's?"

He paused the toothbrush in his mouth and turned to look at me. Then he bent and spit.

"They would have done an autopsy on someone that young dying unexpectedly, Sloane. It would have shown up in the toxicology."

I smiled, thrilled that he was at least considering my theory and not brushing it off as nonsense.

"But would it? Would they be able to tell it was a different insulin? Or would it just show as a higher concentration of insulin in his system? Because if it only indicated he'd had too much insulin, isn't is possible they might chalk that up to him giving himself the wrong dosage? Especially if he'd been partying or wasn't fully coherent when he did it."

He rinsed his mouth and spit again, and then he dried his face on a towel.

"It's possible. I don't know what Cecile takes and if that shows up as a different insulin in the system, or just a higher level."

"I think she called it U500, or something like that. So, you agree that it seems suspicious?"

"I didn't say that." He frowned. "I said it's possible an autopsy would miss it depending on how the insulin shows up in a toxicology report."

"Can you find out? Like, can you ask somebody?"

He exhaled a loud sigh and flipped off the bathroom light as he walked into the bedroom.

"I'll call our coroner, Sandra, tomorrow and ask her what she thinks." He turned back to face me with his index finger held up. "But…that doesn't mean I'm investigating this or that I'm giving it credence, okay? If anything, I'm trying to prove you wrong, got it?"

"Got it," I said, ridiculously excited that he'd agreed. "While you're at it, could you at least take a peek at Ronald and Cecile's backgrounds? If they're lily-white, then you can prove me wrong again. And if not, and the theater's landlord has a shady past, that's important information, too, right? For my financial interests, if for no other reason."

"It would have been important information *before* you sank your finances into the place. You're stuck with him now."

"Unless we're able to prove that the building isn't rightfully his. Like you said, if the will is null and void, Ronald isn't our legal landlord."

"That's not an outcome you should be hoping for, babe. That means the building gets tied up in red tape indefinitely until they figure out who is."

Rats! I kept forgetting that part.

He came out of the closet with a pair of sweatpants on, and I walked over and traced my finger across his skin just above the low-hanging waistline, lingering at the spot beneath his navel as he quivered in response.

"Will you just look into them? Find out about the insulin in toxicology, and see what Ronald and Cecile have in their backgrounds. Please?"

He slung his arm around me and pulled me close, capturing my hand between us as he grinned.

"Are you trying to bribe me into doing your bidding by teasing me and turning me on?"

"That depends. Would it work?"

He smiled as he bent to kiss me, and I shuddered at the desire in his eyes. He walked me backward toward the bed and fell onto it with me cradled in his arms, and then he whispered against my neck, "There's only one way to find out."

Chapter 40

I slept in the next morning and woke up even more sore than the day before and cranky to boot. I'd convinced Tristan that it was safe to leave me home alone since it had been over twenty-four hours since the concussion, but he'd made me promise to keep the alarm system armed and to call him to check in often.

I dialed his number as I wandered down the hallway in search of coffee, wearing nothing but his T-shirt and a pair of lace panties.

"Hey, beautiful," he said when he answered. "You just getting up?"

"Yeah," I said with a yawn. "Thanks for setting the coffeemaker for me. How's your day going?"

"It's been interesting, for sure."

"Oh? How so?" I pulled a cup from the cabinet and lifted the pot.

"We got word this morning confirming the black paint transfer on the front right fender of your car. The whole front end had significant damage from the collision with the trees, so it wasn't detected right away, but once I told them what we were looking for, they found it."

Stunned, I paused in pouring my cup of coffee and set the pot on the counter.

"Wow. So…either I hit someone or someone hit me, and either way, they left the scene."

"Looks that way," he said, his voice somber.

"What happens now? How do we find out who it was?"

He sighed on the other end of the line. "They'll match the paint to get a specific make and model, but that could take months."

"Months? That's ridiculous!"

"There's something else I found, and it might be a coincidence, but if so, it's a strange one."

He paused, and I finished pouring the coffee as I waited for him to continue.

"After you, um, *convinced* me to look into Ronald and Cecile Fisher last night, I did some digging this morning. Ronald Fisher owns a black Cadillac Escalade."

I nearly poured the hot coffee all over myself in my efforts to set the cup back down. "Wait, what? Are you telling me that Ronald Fisher hit my car?"

"No. I did not say that, and you can't either. We have no proof of that in any way whatsoever."

"But you yourself just said that if it's a coincidence, it's a mighty strange one."

"Agreed, but Sloane, right now, I have nothing linking him to your accident."

"Black paint. And Priscilla said it was a black SUV."

"Right, but there's no concrete evidence linking him. Not until the paint analysis comes back…or I see his vehicle to determine if it has damage."

"Okay, so do that." I took a yogurt from the fridge and a spoon from the drawer.

"I intend to as soon as I locate him. Did Cecile happen to mention where they're staying when you saw her?"

I pulled back the lid on the yogurt and tossed it in the trash. "At her brother's, but she said Ronald's not with her on this trip. Do you think it was Cecile? Did Cecile Fisher run me off the road?"

"I don't know, and again, we can't just jump to conclusions here."

"Did I piss her off asking questions at the pharmacy? Christ! Who would do that? Who would make someone crash and leave the scene?"

"Calm down, okay?" He groaned. "I started not to even tell you until I knew for sure whether their vehicle was involved. I shouldn't have mentioned it. I guess maybe I hoped it would trigger something with your memory. Do you remember seeing this vehicle at all? I know you told Priscilla the windows and windshield were tinted, but don't you think you would have recognized Cecile if she was behind the wheel and you'd just seen her a little while before?"

I closed my eyes and gritted my teeth in frustration. Why couldn't I remember? Why was this crucial chunk of time still missing?

I sighed with defeat. "I don't remember anything after leaving Rachel's, but I think if I had recognized Cecile, I would have said something to Priscilla. Maybe it wasn't her. Maybe it was the mob like Dani feared, or some total jackass stranger who left me to die."

"We'll find out, babe. I've already put the word out that we're looking for a black SUV with damage on the driver's side. We're also going to canvass the neighbors up and down that stretch of road and ask if anyone remembers seeing a black SUV that day. And even though it's not likely that it's them, I'm going to find Ronald Fisher's SUV and check it out, just to be sure. I've spoken to one of my colleagues in Tennessee, and he's going to do a drive-by to see if the vehicle is there. Now that I know Cecile may be driving that vehicle in this area, I'll head over to her brother's."

"Okay," I said, tossing the half-eaten yogurt in the trash. "Keep me posted."

"I will. Stay inside, okay? Keep the alarm on, and be aware of your surroundings."

"Do you think I'm in danger?"

I couldn't help noticing that he hesitated. "No, I don't. If I did, I wouldn't have you there alone. But until we know what happened here, just take extra precautions, okay?"

267

"Yeah. I will."

He went quiet, and I stood staring out the front window, wondering if there was someone intent on doing me harm.

"Hey," I said after a moment. "Did you happen to call the coroner and ask about detecting the insulin levels?"

"Yeah, I called Sandra first thing this morning."

"And?"

He sighed. "I don't know that it's a good idea if I tell you. It's just going to put more ideas in your head. Ideas that could get you in trouble."

"Oh, c'mon. What did you find out?"

He hesitated, and then he swore under his breath with a groan. "If I tell you, you have to promise me you're not going to play judge and jury with this."

"I don't know what you mean."

"I mean that we don't know any more than we did last night. Sandra's answer doesn't tell us anything definitive."

"Would you just tell me what she said already?"

His sigh was so loud I had to pull the phone back from my ear.

"Sandra said they would need to specifically ask for insulin levels on a toxicology report; it wouldn't be done automatically with the autopsy. She wasn't the coroner at the time of Alex's death, but she seemed to think that if he was a known diabetic who'd been found in a coma, and like you said, had a reputation in the community for not managing his insulin or his alcohol and food intake consistently, the coroner probably wouldn't have looked any further for a cause of death. They would have ruled it complications from diabetes."

"I knew it. I was right!"

"Yeah, you were right in that regard, but that doesn't necessarily mean anything here, okay, Sloane? He could have died from exactly what the coroner ruled. Don't go telling Dani or anyone else that Ronald and Cecile Fisher murdered his son, okay? We don't know that. This stays between the two of us until we know more, you got it?"

"I have to tell Dani."

"No, not even Dani. You two super-sleuths are gonna get your-selves in trouble. Promise me you'll let me handle this."

"Does that mean you're going to look into it? That you'll investigate?"

"It means that I don't want you doing anything with this right now. Let me talk to Ronald and Cecile about the car first, and I'll take it from there. It's not like I can lead with asking them if they murdered his son, okay? I'll feel out the situation and try to deter-mine if maybe they're hiding something. You stay out of it for now. Promise me, Sloane."

"Okay, okay. I promise. But you're gonna keep me posted, right? You'll let me know what's going on?"

"I'll let you know what I can let you know. I gotta go. Stay inside. I love you."

"Love you, too."

We hung up and I paced the floor, unable to stop the thoughts racing through my mind.

Had Cecile tried to make me crash? Or was it a stranger?

And either way, why would someone do that?

And why, oh why, couldn't I remember what had happened?

I took a shower and dried my hair to pass the time as I waited for an update from Tristan, and Dani called just after I turned off the dryer.

"What's up?" I asked, wishing I could tell her everything Tristan had said.

"Alex had grown closer to his dad in the months before he died, and now, I'm doubting our theory that he wouldn't have named Ronald in his will."

"What? How do you know this?"

"You probably don't want to know all the specifics, but suffice to say I tracked down the girl who was dating Alex at the time of his death. Why people don't make their social media private, I will never understand, but I figured out she works at the Burger Palace in Lumberton. I went by there today and struck up a conversation with her, and she said Alex was wary of Ronald when he first came back, but that the two of them spent a great deal of time together after Alex's grandfather died. Ronald was there for Alex when he was grieving, and the two of them had gotten closer before Alex died."

"How on earth did you get this woman to tell you all that?"

"People feel comfortable talking to me. It's a skill I have that proved valuable when I was a reporter. Of course, it helped that Lumberton's Burger Palace isn't a busy place at two-thirty in the afternoon, so she was bored and willing to talk. I mentioned that I'm opening a theater in the old auto repair shop building in Cedar Creek, and the conversation blossomed from there. She said Alex always felt that he'd die young, and he talked about it all the time."

"Which might explain why a twenty-three-year-old had a will."

"Exactly."

"All right. So, if ghost Alex isn't mad about his dad having his building and he seemed to accept he'd die young before it even happened, what's he pissed about? And how do we get him to quit his shenanigans at the theater?"

"I don't know," she said with a sigh. "Maybe he didn't realize how much he wanted to live until after he died. Who knows? Hey, what are you doing right now? Are you busy?"

"Not at all."

"A lady from the Arts Alliance called and said there's a theater in Mt. Dora that's cleaning out its costume collection. I'm going up there to see if there is anything that might be good for *Midsummer Night's*. Do you want to come along?"

"Um, sure. I don't know enough about the play or the costumes to be helpful, though."

"That's okay. It's more for the company. I've got to go by the theater and get a quick how-to lesson for the new footlights, and then I'll be by to pick you up in probably, like, an hour?"

"Sounds good."

I called Tristan to tell him I was going to ride to Mt. Dora with Dani, and he said he didn't have any updates to share yet. He hadn't been able to speak to Ronald or Cecile, who he thought might have already left town en route back to Tennessee.

"Be careful," he said before we hung up. "Be aware of your surroundings."

"Always, babe."

It felt good to get out of the house, and Dani and I talked and laughed as we drove to Mr. Dora and back. We'd grabbed a late lunch while we were there, and by the time we got back to Cedar Creek, it was almost dinnertime.

Dani turned down the music as we neared the city limits.

"You want me to take you home now? Or do you want to come by the theater and see the footlights? They're pretty amazing."

"Let me call Tristan and see when he's leaving work. He could probably just swing by the theater and pick me up on his way home."

I got his voicemail and left a message that I'd be at the theater with Dani, asking him to come get me when he left work and reminding him that I wouldn't have a signal at the theater building.

The workers were in the process of packing up their things to leave for the day when we arrived, and I went into the main auditorium as Dani touched base with them and saw them out.

The footlights that lined the edge of the stage floor were beautiful. Their old-fashioned seashell shape in antique bronze gave a vintage look and feel to the stage, but the light bulbs inside were state-of-the-art, multicolor LED bulbs, thoroughly modern.

"Aren't they awesome?" Dani asked when she came back into the auditorium. "I'm so ridiculously happy with them. They may be my favorite thing we've done with renovations. Here, let me go upstairs and turn them on. I'll show you what they can do."

The replacement window for the upstairs office was a sliding one, which allowed the person in the audio-visual booth to open it and communicate easily with those in the auditorium without the need for a two-way radio or cell phone during rehearsals or any time there wasn't a performance.

Dani slid it open and called down to me. "Get up on the stage."

I climbed up and did a little curtsy at center stage, and suddenly, the entire row of footlights lit up.

I shielded my eyes with my hand and exclaimed, "Wow! That's bright."

"Check this out."

The lights muted into a soft amber, and then once I'd reacted to those, Dani went through the entire color wheel.

"Okay. I'm impressed," I said.

"Yeah, and they're connected to the overhead spotlights, so we can create almost any lighting mood or look. With the push of a single button, we can simulate morning light—"

The overhead lights and footlights shifted to a golden hue.

"Oh, pretty!" I said as I looked all around.

"Or we have a twilight setting—"

The lights morphed into a deep lavender with hints of pink and orange.

"And probably my favorite, moonlight!"

The room went almost entirely dark with the footlights glowing in a deep blue and the overhead spotlights a pale white that bathed everything in a silvery hue. It did indeed look like we were outside on a moonlit night.

"That's all I know how to do," Dani said with a laugh and a shrug. "I asked the guy to give me a couple of settings I could show off, and then when we hire someone to manage our tech, he'll come back for a full tutorial."

A knock sounded on the front door in the lobby, and I looked up toward Dani.

"Someone's here, probably Tristan. I'll get it."

I went to the front door and found myself staring through the glass at Cecile Fisher.

Chapter 41

Cecile smiled on the other side of the door, and I hesitated. Had she really run me off the road and left me there? Had she possibly killed Alex and forged a will in his name? And hadn't Tristan said she'd already left the area?

Dani came through the staircase door behind me. "Who is it?"

I turned back to face her, wishing I had explained everything Tristan told me.

"It's Cecile Fisher."

"Well, let her in." Dani walked toward me and the door. "She's my landlord," she said with a sideways glance at me. "We can't leave her standing outside."

She twisted the deadbolt to unlock it and then held the door open for Cecile.

"Hi! Sloane tells me you're Cecile Fisher. I'm Danielle Ward. I wondered if you might stop by and see the place while you were in town. I think you'll be very pleasantly surprised at all the changes."

"Hello," Cecile said as she stepped inside. She looked around, wide-eyed, which might have been due to the total transformation brought about by Dani's renovations, but the darting glances, hunched shoulders, and tight grip on her bag seemed more like she was wary and guarded.

Did she know about the building's haunted reputation? Was she concerned about being confronted by Alex's ghost?

"Obviously, this is the reception area," Dani said as she swept her arm to indicate the room. "That door there leads to the new ticket booth we've constructed on the front. Folks will get their tickets or confirm their reservations there and then come inside here. There's the concession counter, and eventually, we hope to have a bar as well."

Cecile nodded with what seemed to be an appreciative smile, and Dani led her into the main auditorium. Cecile paused at the door, and as she looked left to right and then up and down, I was certain it was trepidation in her eyes, even if she was impressed with the renovations. She took a hesitant step inside the auditorium, clutching her purse in front of her as she nodded in response to Dani's grand tour of explanations.

"What do you think?" Dani asked once she'd finished showing off her accomplishments.

"It's different, that's for sure," Cecile said. "You've done a lot of work. I'm certain my husband would be pleased with the results."

"I had thought maybe I'd send him some pictures once the place is done."

Cecile nodded. "I'm sure he'd like that."

She cast a glance in my direction, and I tried to smile. I couldn't stop wondering if the woman standing in front of me was a cold-blooded killer and if she'd been the one who'd put my life in danger.

"I'm glad you're here, Ms. Reid," Cecile said. "I wanted to talk to both of you, and this makes it easier to do that."

It was Dani's turn to look nervous, and her creased brow revealed she was worried about what Cecile might say.

"How can we help you?" Dani said, looking to me and then back to Cecile.

"Well, hopefully *I* can help *you*," Cecile said as she put her purse strap over her shoulder. She seemed to have relaxed a bit, and as she squared her shoulders and lifted her chin to speak, she looked more like the overbearing, overconfident woman I'd encountered at the pharmacy. "My husband has been quite displeased with you."

Dani's eyes widened as the shock of Cecile's statement registered, and she swallowed hard. "Why?"

"He's heard that you've called a previous tenant to discuss rumors about the building, and it's come to his attention that you've been in conversation with a member of his late son's family as well. Things like that don't sit well with Ronnie, and it's been all I can do to keep him from terminating the lease and changing the locks."

I watched Dani's reaction, her face falling as her eyes widened with shock.

"I only—I mean, what I was trying—"

Cecile held her hand up to silence Dani, and I could see that Cecile was enjoying her position of power over my friend.

"It doesn't matter why. It matters that you've done it, and Ronnie's pissed. You could have come to him directly if you had any questions, but you chose to sow seeds of rumor and innuendo behind his back."

"I never meant to—"

"I'm sure you didn't," Cecile said with a sneer, and then she turned to stare at me. "And of course, all this came at the same time as your purchase offer through the realtor—*our* realtor, mind you— so, of course, we have to assume the two of you are conspiring together against us. Ronnie never even entertained your offer, which I think was a mistake on his part."

She looked back to Dani and smiled.

"I might be able to fix this for both of you, though."

Dani and I looked at each other and back to Cecile.

"My husband can be a bit of a hard-ass," Cecile said. "He's tight with his money, and possessive of his belongings, of which this theater is one. If he's going to part with it, it will take a healthy sum of money to convince him."

She looked toward me and arched an eyebrow.

"And when I say that, Ms. Reid, I mean that the offer should be generous. It needs to give him enough of a profit to make it hard to turn down," she said, and then she turned back to Dani. "Of course, I would need to be compensated for my time and effort. For me to go to my husband on your behalf and try to convince him to change his mind, it needs to be worth my while as well."

Dani's fearful expression had turned into shocked indignation as she blinked rapidly with both eyebrows raised.

"Is this a shakedown?" Dani asked. "Are you really asking me to pay you to convince your husband not to evict me, and asking my partner to offer above market value like some kind of bribe?"

Cecile's expression didn't change. She didn't look insulted, worried, or surprised. If anything, she looked even more confident.

"I wouldn't consider it a shakedown," she said as she crossed her arms. "I would consider it a business transaction. I'm providing a service, and you would benefit from that service, so it's only fair that you would pay for it."

"Oh, and let me guess," Dani said, her hands on her hips. "You want this payment in cash, right?"

Cecile shrugged. "That would be convenient."

"Do you have any idea what kind of scrutiny I'm under right now?" Dani said, her face flushed with anger. "Even if I wanted to engage in this idiocy, which I do not, it would be impossible for me to do so."

"Oh, that's right. You had mentioned to my husband that you were having a cash flow problem that might result in delayed rental payments." Cecile turned her head and smiled at me. "But you are a wealthy woman, Ms. Reid. You stepped in and put your name all over this venture and offered to buy the building. I'm guessing you have the resources to cover what's needed for Ms. Ward in order to make things happen."

There was a glint in her eye and a glee in her voice. She was in her element, and it made me more certain than ever that Cecile Fisher was a dangerous woman who had done whatever she felt was necessary to secure what she wanted.

I no longer found it hard to believe that she could have sideswiped me and left me unconscious with my car wrapped around a tree.

"Yes, I do have plenty of resources," I said in response to her, my own chin lifted and my arms at my sides. "I'm sorry to say your husband missed his chance, though. The offer was rescinded when he replied that the building was not for sale."

Cecile didn't show any reaction, but at the sound of the front door opening, she turned toward the reception area along with Dani and me.

I gave Dani a nervous glance as she said, "I must have forgotten to deadbolt the door when we let Cecile in."

Tristan came into sight in the doorway to the reception area, and I rushed toward him, trying to communicate alarm with my eyes. He didn't give me any indication that he'd understood as he kissed me in greeting and then looked over my head toward the others.

"Dani, nice to see you again. Who's your guest?"

His tone was clipped and professional, and his demeanor was stiff. It made me think he knew exactly who she was.

He had stepped forward, and as he did so, he applied the slightest pressure with his arm around my waist, guiding me behind him.

"This is Cecile Fisher," Dani said, her arms still crossed. "She and her husband own this building, and she was just explaining our purchase options."

Cecile's sneering grin had faded momentarily when she saw Tristan in his uniform, but she recovered and widened it into an exaggerated smile full of teeth.

"Nice to meet you, Deputy…" She stared at his name badge as he filled in the blank.

"Rogers."

"My fiancé," I said, eager to see her reaction but disappointed when she didn't show any outward sign of concern. She was unflappable, I had to give her that.

"Mrs. Fisher, you're a hard lady to get in touch with," Tristan said.

There it was. It was slight, and almost imperceptible, but one eyebrow had lifted a tiny bit, and one corner of her pasted-on smile had faltered.

"Me? Why on earth were you trying to reach me?"

"I thought perhaps you could tell me where your husband is. I've been trying to locate him all day."

Another miniscule crack in her facade as her eyes narrowed a teeny bit, but if I hadn't been watching closely, I never would have noticed it.

"I would assume he's in Tennessee. Unless you know something I don't."

Tristan widened his stance and crossed his arms, a move I recognized as his interrogation mode. What did he have on Cecile? What had he learned since we'd last talked?

"When's the last time you spoke to Ronald?" Tristan asked as he took another step closer to Cecile.

She dropped her chin and squinted as she considered what he'd asked.

"A couple of days ago. Monday, maybe?"

I met Dani's eyes and wished I could shrug at the unspoken question there. I had no idea where he was headed or why, but I was confident that he did.

"And he was in Tennessee then? When you spoke to him?"

"Yes, he was," Cecile said, her tone curt.

"Was he at your house? The house the two of you share?"

A visible swallow before she answered, and then she looked down at her hands. Her demeanor was meeker when she looked back up, but the glint remained in her eyes.

"Uh, no. If you must know, we've been separated for a little while now. He left. I'm not sure where he's living."

She drew in a breath and sighed as she looked down at her hands again, twisting them together.

I didn't buy it. Nothing about Cecile conveyed a woman wringing her hands in despair after being abandoned by her husband.

Tristan must not have bought it either, because his tone wasn't any less harsh or unfeeling when he spoke.

"But you're sure he's in Tennessee?"

"Yeah, as far as I know. What is this about, Deputy?"

I was surprised it had taken her so long to wonder why Tristan was looking for Ronald. My first thought if I'd been given these questions would have been concern for my husband's safety, or perhaps fear that he was in trouble.

"Dani," Tristan said, shifting his gaze to her. "When's the last time you spoke to Ronald Fisher?"

She frowned and uncrossed her arms. "I texted him last week to confirm that I'd made the electronic transfer for the rent. He replied back with 'Thanks', which is his customary response."

"So, you had a text conversation with him last week. When's the last time you actually spoke with Ronald?"

Dani shrugged with her hands outstretched. She looked confused.

"Oh, well, I've never actually *spoken* with him. All our correspondence has been through text or email. I've called and left voice messages before, but he always texts back his response."

"Interesting," Tristan said.

He moved slightly to the right, which put his body more in front of mine, and I got the feeling it was an attempt to shield me. Cecile was still directly in my line of vision, though.

"Is that your truck outside, Mrs. Fisher?" he asked her.

Her eyes narrowed even more, and her smile had completely faded.

"No, it's my brother's. What is this all about? Am I being interrogated for some reason? Has my husband done something I should be concerned about?"

Tristan ignored her questions. "Where's your vehicle?"

She lifted her chin and glared at him as she moved her purse from one shoulder to the other.

"At my brother's house. What's with all the questions, Deputy? I demand to know what's going on."

Tristan shrugged with a smile, but it wasn't genuine. It didn't carry to his eyes.

"I'm just trying to get whatever information I can to find your husband."

Cecile ran her hand down the strap of her purse and rested it there as she shifted her weight to one leg, jutting her hip to the side.

"I've already told you I don't know where he is. I suggest you try strip clubs in Tennessee. Now, if you'll excuse me—"

She took a step forward, and Tristan lifted his hand.

"Not so fast. I have a couple more questions before you go. This vehicle at your brother's…it's a black Cadillac Escalade, right?"

Dani looked at me with wide eyes and a slack jaw.

"It's my husband's, yes," Cecile said, and for the first time since Tristan arrived, I thought she actually looked nervous.

"But you're driving it, right?" he asked. "You drove it here from Tennessee?"

"Well, yes, but it's Ronnie's."

Tristan glanced at me and then at Dani before looking back toward Cecile.

"I think that's mighty nice of him to let you drive it out of state with the two of you separated. Of course, it's still registered in Florida, right? If the two of you have been in Tennessee for the past four years, he's had plenty of time to register it in the state he's living in and get a driver's license there. But he hasn't, has he?"

"You'll need to take that up with him," Cecile said, her voice taking on an angry tone. "Now, I need to go."

Tristan took a step to the left, blocking Cecile's exit, and I instinctively went to Dani, looping my arm through hers.

"I just came from your brother's house," Tristan said. "It seems the Escalade has some damage to the left front bumper. How did that happen?"

Dani's mouth dropped open as she looked at me, and I clamped mine shut to squelch the gasp that had risen in my throat.

"I don't know," Cecile said. "Please step aside. I need to go."

Tristan didn't budge. "You don't know? Has someone else been driving the vehicle? Who? I'd very much like to speak to that person."

Cecile looked over at Dani and me, and when she turned back to Tristan, her chin began to tremble.

"I don't know what happened, okay? I don't remember. I'm a diabetic, you see. I accidentally left my insulin in a fridge in a hotel room on the way down here from Tennessee. I had to go to the pharmacy in Jensen to get more while I waited for the hotel to ship it, but my sugar levels were all over the place. I don't remember driving to my brother's, and I don't know how the damage happened."

Her face crumpled, and she looked as though she was about to cry, though there wasn't a tear in sight.

"Ah," Tristan said without a trace of sympathy or compassion in his voice. "That must have been frightening. Did you call and alert the authorities that you'd been in some kind of accident while in the throes of a health episode?"

She lifted her eyes to look at him, and the glint was still there, despite the rest of her appearing to be forlorn.

"No, I didn't. The damage to the vehicle was minor, and I assumed it was nothing more than property damage. If it had been something more serious, the authorities would have contacted me."

"Surely, you're aware that it's a crime to leave the scene of an accident in the state of Florida."

Cecile stiffened. "I told you, I wasn't aware there was an accident. Surely, *you're* aware that my medical condition can create extenuating circumstances. Now, are you going to arrest me for this? Because if not, you need to get the hell out of my way."

Tristan's hands were on his hips, and he tapped his fingers against his belt just above his weapon as he cocked his head to one side.

"I'm just trying to figure out how you could see the red paint on your front left fender where it's smashed, and not be the least bit curious who you hit. Are you saying that when you hid the Escalade in your brother's barn and covered it with a tarp, that was because you didn't know if there had been an accident? Or because you were certain there had been? You know what, Cecile? I don't believe you were impaired at all that day. I believe you knew exactly what you were doing."

"I told you I'm done answering questions, and I'm leaving."

"Fine," Tristan said. He held his arms out as though in surrender and stepped out of her way with a dramatic flourish.

Chapter 42

He waited until she'd started walking to speak again.
"Do you know what I found most interesting, Mrs. Fisher?"

She paused, but she didn't turn back to look at him.

"When I set about looking for your husband today," he continued, "no one in Tennessee has any recollection of him being at the house there. Not a single neighbor has seen him in the last four years. Not a single business owner in the small town where you reside has ever met Ronald Fisher or had the pleasure of doing business with him."

Cecile turned slowly with narrowed eyes and an eerie smile that sent shivers down my spine as I processed Tristan's words and what they likely meant.

"Ronnie doesn't get out much. I do all of the shopping, and as far as neighbors, we live on the side of a mountain. I've never met a single one of our neighbors myself, and I can't see their houses from mine. So, I don't know how they would have seen my husband from theirs."

"Your *husband*," Tristan said. "See, that's another interesting fact I found in my search. The only document of record for your union is a Jamaican marriage license on file with the Tennessee Department of Motor Vehicles, provided to them when you applied for a driver's license in your married name not long after moving to Tennessee."

"We got married in Jamaica," Cecile said, her smile widening. "Is that a crime, Deputy Rogers?"

"No, definitely not, but there's just one problem. Jamaica has no record of that marriage ever happening there."

"This conversation is over," Cecile said with a huff.

She turned to go, and Seth stepped into the doorway of the reception area, where he had likely been waiting the entire time.

"I'm afraid you're going to need to come with us, Cecile," Tristan said.

She whirled to face him, her eyes wild and her calm resolve dissipated.

"You can't prove I was driving. You don't have a single witness, and the rumor around town is your fiancée doesn't remember a thing. You might have a case against my husband, who owns the vehicle, but you have nothing on me."

I clamped my hand onto Dani's arm at the realization that Cecile had just all but confessed. Tristan had never said it was my car, but she obviously already knew. Was she right? Would Tristan not be able to do anything since I couldn't remember?

His eyes seemed filled with venom as he stared at her, and when he spoke, his voice was low and quiet. "And what if your husband was already dead at the time of the accident?"

Dani and I clung to each other's arms as the air seemed to disappear from the room. The hairs on the back of my neck stood at attention, and goose flesh rippled across my skin.

Cecile laughed, tossing her head back as a maniacal cackle escaped her lips.

"People go missing every day, Deputy Rogers. That doesn't mean they're dead. Sometimes, they decide they're done with the responsibilities of the life they've chosen, and they take off."

Tristan's steady gaze was chilling in its intensity as he replied.

"And sometimes, they're murdered."

Cecile looked over her shoulder at Seth, who took a step closer, and then she looked back at Tristan with a sneer.

"You have no body. You have no murder weapon. You have no proof that a crime ever took place."

Suddenly, the lights overhead went out, and the entire room was bathed in the soft blue-gray of the moonlight pre-set Dani had shown me earlier.

The unexpected change startled the entire room, and the already palpable tension skyrocketed. Tristan and Seth both reached for their weapons and went into a defensive stance ready to attack, Tristan moving nearer to Dani and me immediately, his eyes scanning the room.

Meanwhile, Cecile had gasped as she whirled to the left and then to the right. "Who did that? Who's there?"

Dani and I, having almost grown accustomed to such occurrences, both looked up toward the upstairs office window, and then a single, bright spotlight shone down on the floor.

I knew what he was showing us immediately, and judging by Dani's quick intake of breath next to me, so did she. I'd tripped over that very spot before Dani had hired someone to smooth out the ragged concrete that had been improperly laid when the pit of the repair shop was filled in.

Myrtle had been wrong, and so had we. Someone *had* died inside the theater building, and our ghost was neither Hyram nor Alex. It was Ronald Fisher, trying desperately to let someone know he was there.

But why had he painted Alex's name on the wall instead of his own?

Cecile stared at the spotlighted floor with her mouth agape and then she looked around the room, frantic in her search.

"Who is doing that?" she screamed. "Who's there?"

"It's Ronald," Dani whispered, and Cecile spun around to face her with terror in her eyes.

Cecile shook her head and looked at Tristan.

"Cecile, it's over," he said. "We talked to your brother, and he told us he helped you hide Ronald's body and cover it with cement. He's agreed to testify with a plea deal."

"No," Cecile shouted. "No! He wouldn't do that. You're lying. My brother has always had my back, and there is no way he would betray me."

"He didn't want to, but he feared what you might do next. He's worried about you, Cecile."

She bent over with a guttural moan and started to sob.

Seth moved closer behind her, and when Cecile saw him, she came unhinged with a screaming roar, pulling a gun from her purse as she threw the bag to the floor. She alternated leveling it at each of us as she backed up toward the spotlight.

"No," she said, her tone emphatic. "I am *not* going to jail. I deserved that money. I was promised that money. When I met Ronnie, he told me that he was about to come into a payload, and all I had to do was stick by his side. Well, I did, and the more time he spent with Alex, the less he talked about the payload. It became clear that we were never going to have control of that money if I didn't force his hand."

"You did kill Alex. I knew it," I exclaimed, unaware I'd said it out loud until everyone turned to look at me.

"It was the only way," Cecile said, her voice cracking as her eyes darted from one of us to another and then the next. "Don't you see? I knew as long as Alex was alive, Ronnie and I would never be happy. We'd never be rich. The family was surprised to see Ronnie's name on the will, but he never questioned it. He honestly thought that kid wanted him to have it. I considered adding my name, but I figured it was less suspicious to just have Ronnie's. I thought it didn't matter, because once we were married, it would be mine anyway."

She was standing beneath the spotlight by then, and her eyes had lost their focus as she rambled on, revealing her crimes and sealing her fate.

"But then that night, we were here cleaning up the place. Clearing out Alex's stuff and getting it ready to sell, and Ronnie told me it was over. That I wasn't going to Tennessee with him, and that we weren't getting married. After all I'd done, after all that waiting, I was being cut out of the reward. Well, that wouldn't do, and I told Ronnie that. I told him that I'd gotten rid of the kid for him, that I'd made sure he inherited it all. I told him that he wouldn't have any of that wealth if it hadn't been for me, and that he owed me."

Her hands shook, and her grip on the gun loosened. She stared into the darkness as tears poured down her face, and her voice cracked as she continued.

"He was furious with me. More angry than I'd ever seen him. I thought he was going to kill me." She looked to Tristan, her eyes pleading as she cried. "It was self-defense, I swear. He would have killed me if I hadn't stopped him."

A flash of movement caught my eye, and I looked away from Cecile to see a man running across the stage. She must have noticed my startled reaction, because she turned just as he jumped over the footlights and sailed through the air toward her. She let out a blood-curdling scream, and the whole thing happened so fast that he had already knocked her to the ground and kicked the gun away from her hand before I realized that he was translucent and shimmering beneath the artificial moonlight.

Chapter 43

"You all right?" Tristan asked me once they'd handcuffed Cecile and seen her safely into the back of a patrol car.

"Yeah, I'm fine. How did you know? How did you find out all that?"

He smiled as he reached to cup my cheek with his hand.

"I followed a lead from one of my favorite detectives, and she was right."

I shook my head as the entire scene with Cecile and Ronald played out again in my head.

"Some detective I am. I may have been right about Cecile, but I had no clue about Ronald. I never even considered it."

"Why would you have? You had good instincts, babe, and you refused to give up on pursuing the truth. Give yourself some credit there. I don't know that I would have ever looked into Cecile or Ronald if you hadn't pushed the issue." He took a deep breath, and his eyes darkened as he frowned. "I hate to think of what might have happened if I hadn't gotten here when I did."

"You think she meant to do Dani and me harm?"

He gave a half-shrug. "Her brother was worried that she might.

She'd promised him when he helped her hide Ronald that she'd go away and never come back. But she had become increasingly irritated with the problems the building had caused, and her hands were tied. She didn't dare sell it and risk someone demolishing it and finding Ronald. The county harassed her when it stood empty and was an eyesore, so she had to lease it even though she didn't need the income. Her skills at forgery and the ability to use digital signatures and email to conduct business had allowed her access to Ronald's finances as long as it wasn't something that required him to appear in person. Hence, the Florida license and vehicle registration. She could do online renewals but couldn't acquire new ones in Tennessee without him."

"Wow," I said, blinking slowly as I considered the depth of her ruse. "She's been impersonating him for four years, and no one even knew he was gone. Did he not have any family or friends who got worried when they didn't hear from him?"

"Evidently, one of the things he and Cecile had in common was scamming those closest to them. From what we can tell, he had no contact with any family members, and no friends who weren't appeased by the occasional email or text from Cecile posing as Ronald to check in. As far as everyone was concerned, they had moved to Tennessee, and for most who knew them, it was good riddance."

"Okay, man," Seth said as he approached. "I know you told me we might see some freaky shit and to try not to react if I saw something unusual, but what the hell was that?"

Tristan chuckled and rubbed his hand across the stubble on his chin. "I don't even know where to begin, dude. Trust me, you're probably better off not knowing."

Seth looked up at the lights. "I thought Dani was controlling the lights somehow, but what knocked Cecile flat like that? She went flying like something slammed into her, but there wasn't anything there."

"Where is Dani?" I asked, realizing I hadn't seen her since they'd taken Cecile out the front door.

I excused myself to go and look for her while Tristan tried to find a logical explanation to appease Seth, and I found her the last place I looked—the upstairs office.

"Hey, what are you doing in here?"

She gave a tired smile and hugged her arms around her waist. "Just trying to escape for a minute. It all got to be too much."

"Which part? The crazy woman wielding a gun at us? Or the dead guy we've been walking over taking over the new lights and body-slamming her?"

She rubbed both hands over her face. "All of that. And then throw in the law enforcement invasion moments later and all the flashbacks that come with that, and of course…Seth being here."

"Have you guys talked at all?"

"Not really." She frowned with a shrug. "He asked if I was okay, but then someone called him over with a question, and I disappeared up here before he could come back."

"Maybe you guys should sit down and have an actual conversation about everything that happened when you left. The tension between the two of you is off the charts, and it's obvious you've both been carrying around unresolved hurts for a long time. It might help you both to get things off your chest and forgive each other."

She stared through the window to the floor below where Seth stood talking to Tristan, and then she turned to me with a hasty smile.

"So, Ronald, huh? What the hell? Can you believe it? This is freaking crazy."

I let out a nervous chuckle that tried to be a laugh and failed. "No, I can't believe it. It's insane. Like, literally insane. She's nuts."

"She could have killed you, Sloane." Her mouth dropped open as she considered it. "Oh my God. She made you crash your car and left you there. She had to be counting on you being either seriously injured or dying. She had no way of knowing you wouldn't remember and be able to ID her."

"She could have killed us both. I don't think she showed up with a gun in her purse to negotiate money with us, and neither does

Tristan. He said her brother was worried what she might do since we'd been causing her problems."

"To think I was so outraged that she thought she could get money from us, and here the stakes were much higher. I'm so glad I didn't know. I would have been much more freaked out. I mean, I was pretty confused when Tristan first started questioning her, and then as things became clearer, I was shocked, but I also felt calm somehow. Like he had it under control. Well, until she pulled the gun."

"And then Ronald saved us."

"Yeah, I guess he did, didn't he?"

We both grew quiet as we watched the men bring in equipment to bust up the floor in search of Ronald.

Dani turned to me and cocked her head to the side. "Do you think he'll stick around? Or do you think he's at peace now?"

"I don't know," I said with a shrug. "I think he wanted us to know what she'd done, not only to him, but to Alex. If he and his son did find a way to finally forge a bond and have a relationship, and Cecile took that away from them, I'd say it would be hard to have peace about any of it. But I think it has to go a long way for the truth to be out."

"I can't believe I'm saying this, but I might be bummed if he leaves all together. It would be cool to have a theater ghost if he wasn't angry and destroying stuff, don't you think?"

"Maybe, but we don't even know that we have a theater."

Danielle's brows scrunched together, and she frowned as she said, "What do you mean?" Then her eyes widened, and her mouth formed an *O* as the realization hit.

I nodded at the conclusion she'd obviously reached.

"If the will was a forgery and Ronald's dead, then he's not our landlord, and we don't have a lease," I said.

"What do we do? Who owns the building now? Do we have any legal recourse?"

"That's a question for our lawyers," I said, covering my mouth as a yawn escaped me. The prolonged adrenaline rush of the last couple of hours had worn on me with my energy levels already sapped from the concussion. I needed sleep.

"You look exhausted," Dani said as she reached to rub her hand on the back of my arm.

"Gee, thanks," I said with a wink, and we both laughed. "I don't think Tristan will be able to leave any time soon. I know he'll want to be here when they find Ronald."

"I can drive you home," Dani offered. "Well, I mean, if we're allowed to leave."

"They already took our statements, so I can't imagine they need us. I don't really want to see the body, do you?"

She held up her hands and shook her head. "Hell, no."

We made our way downstairs and once we were officially excused, she drove me home.

She put the car in park and turned to face me with a smile.

"Sloane, I know I've said it before, but I can't thank you enough for all your help. I cannot imagine going through everything that's happened without you by my side. I am so glad you stopped by the theater that day, and no matter what happens with the building and our business venture, I hope we'll always be friends."

We hugged as much as possible with my left shoulder still hurting, and then I opened the car door to get out.

"You okay going in?" she asked. "You want me to come with you?"

"No. I'm fine. This place is locked up tight like a maximum-security prison, and I guarantee you my fiancé will be watching the alarm app to make sure I get inside safely."

"All right, if you're sure. I'll sit here until I see that you're in and have the lights on."

I waved goodbye once I'd unlocked the door and disarmed the alarm, and then I reset it to armed and walked straight down the hallway and put myself to bed. I texted Tristan that I was home and going to sleep, and the next thing I knew, the sun was streaming through the windows and the French doors.

I rolled over to look for Tristan, concerned that he hadn't come home, but he was lying on his stomach beside me.

One eye opened, and then he lifted his head off the pillow.

"You okay?" he asked.

"Yeah. What time did you get in?"

"A little after two. You were snoring—"

"I was not! I don't snore."

He grinned and moved to lie on his side, reaching for me. "You were most definitely snoring. You didn't even miss a beat when I climbed into bed next to you. You were *out*."

I snuggled into his embrace, and he kissed the top of my head as he held me.

"What time is it?" I asked as I looked up at the sunlight filling the room. "Why aren't you at work?"

"I'm going in soon. I was already awake, but I was too comfortable to get up just yet."

My phone buzzed on the nightstand, I closed my eyes, wishing it would disappear.

"Who's texting you this early?" Tristan asked as he reached to grab the phone and hand it to me.

I read the screen and groaned, tossing the phone on the bed before I buried my face in his chest.

"Who was it?"

"My mother. She's in London, and she's flying back Monday. She arranged to stop over in Orlando for a night on her way home to Houston. She wants me to meet her at the Ritz-Carlton for dinner Monday night."

"You haven't seen in her in a long while, huh?"

I shook my head. "She wants to talk me out of getting married."

He leaned back to look down at me. "Really?"

"Yes. Really. She won't be able to, but that's why she's coming to town."

"Shall I come to dinner with you and give her all the reasons I think you should get married?"

I chuckled at the thought. "No, I wouldn't subject you to that."

"I don't mind. I have to meet her eventually; why not now? We might as well get it over with and establish the ground rules."

"Ground rules?"

He nodded. "Our life is our own. She's welcome to be a part of it as long as she understands that and doesn't pressure you to conform to what she wants your life to be."

"I dread even trying to plan a wedding and including her. She's going to make it hell. Well, even more hell that it's probably already gonna be."

"It seems to me that a lot of your anxiety surrounding getting married has to do with the actual wedding." He rolled onto his back and looked at me as he stroked his thumb along my jaw. "What if we skip that part?"

"What do you mean?"

"We've been talking about going away together. What if we hop a plane to an island somewhere in the Caribbean, and while we're there, we get hitched? Just you and me, our toes in the sand, and the sun in the sky?"

A rush of excitement coursed through me, and my skin tingled with it.

"Could we do that? What about your mom? She's gonna be disappointed."

"If my mother wants a wedding that badly, she can do a vow renewal with my dad and plan whatever she wants. This is our wedding. You and me. We do it the way we want it."

"Wow." I pictured myself standing on the beach, gazing into Tristan's eyes, pledging my life and my love to him. Just the two of us. "Wait, wouldn't we need a minister or something?"

"Ministers live on islands, too, you know?"

My eyes narrowed. "Did you get this idea because of Cecile's Jamaican wedding license?"

"No. I've been thinking about it a while. When I first mentioned getting away to some tropical hut somewhere, this was in the back of my mind. But I wasn't sure you'd go for it. You know, if you needed to do something publicly for your career."

"This has nothing to do with my career. This is me and you. And I think this is a wonderful idea."

I stretched forward to kiss him, and then he rolled to the side of the bed and stood with a stretch.

"I supposed I should get dressed and get down to the station."

"Oh, yeah," I said, sitting up with the sheets wrapped around me. "Did you find the body?"

"Yeah. We did. And the gun used to kill him."

"I still can't believe how this all turned out. It's wild. This whole time, he was trying to let people know, and no one understood."

"He has you to thank."

He went into the bathroom and turned on the shower, and I lay back down and reached up to touch my fingers to my temple. It was still tender, but not as sore as the day before.

I hoped the bruising would be gone before the engagement photo shoot that Priscilla had arranged.

My thoughts drifted to the possibility of a wedding with just the two of us, and for the first time since we'd initially discussed getting married, I felt excited about the ceremony aspect of it.

I wondered how soon he'd be able to take off work for us to get away, and I worried that the dates might conflict with the run of the play.

But then I remembered that Dani and I no longer had a theater. I was still willing to purchase the building, but it was likely to be tied up in legalities and red tape for a while. All the work put in, all the construction and renovation, and all the ghost-appeasing had been for naught.

Well, maybe not for naught. After all, we had helped to catch a murderer, and we'd uncovered the true identity of the phantom in the footlights.

———

Not ready to leave Cedar Creek? Want more time with Dani? Want to know what happens between her and Seth? Get your copy of Whiskey Flight, Volume 1 *in Cedar Creek Suspense now!*

And if you love the small town of Cedar Creek, you should also check out Cedar Creek Families.

Find out more about the Cedar Creek Collection here.

I'd love for us to stay in touch! Subscribe to my newsletter to get regular updates on new releases, sales, special excerpts, and behind-the-scenes fun facts.

And if you sign up now, you can find out more about my newest series, Fallen Bloodlines. Join me on a journey into an all-new paranormal world filled with romance, humor, mystery, and suspense...along with vampires, shifters, witches, fallen angels, and much more!

You can find out more about Vampire Born, Book One in Fallen Bloodlines here!

WHISKEY FLIGHT
CEDAR CREEK SUSPENSE, VOLUME 1

Dani moved to Chicago to pursue her dreams, and one by one, she achieved them all: an exciting job, a beautiful house, and a handsome and adoring husband. But when his early morning arrest reveals that she's really married to a Mafia hitman, Dani's perfect life is shattered.

Divorced, unemployed, and almost bankrupt, Dani returned home to Cedar Creek, always looking over her shoulder in case the Mafia followed her home. But after two years have passed without incident, she's finally started to believe she can let down her guard.

Then one fateful Friday night, she wanders into a bar, intent on forgetting her problems, if only for a night. But there are two men in the bar who make that impossible. One is her high school sweetheart, the one she left behind to chase her dreams in Chicago. The other is a stranger with an ominous grin that sends chills down her spine.

As Dani's past closes in on her, she must fight for her own life and the lives of those she loves.

This first volume in the Cedar Creek Suspense series is a fast-paced, action-packed, wild ride will make you breathless! Download it now!

VAMPIRE BORN
FALLEN BLOODLINES, BOOK 1

Born of an ancient, cursed bloodline, Nick has always loathed the monster inside him, but he was never so determined to be human as when he met his true love, Aria. A deal with darkness granted Nick what he longed for most—a life as a mortal husband and father.

Aria worked hard to trust herself and others after escaping an abusive relationship. When she met Nick, his steadfast love and patience slowly convinced her that she and her young daughter could finally have their happily ever after.

Together, Nick and Aria have found peace and become their best version of themselves. But when an early morning tragedy returns Nick to his vampiric state, the future of their family is in jeopardy.

As they struggle to find a path forward and come to terms with the past, neither of them realize much darker forces are at play. Can their love withstand the trials they face? Or is their relationship doomed to end in heartache? *Find out in this non-stop series starter with an ending that will leave you desperate for more!*

www.violethowe.com

Acknowledgments

Bonnie, Sandy, Tawdra, Teresa, Lisa, and Melissa — Thanks for continuing on this journey with me and being the extra eyes and minds necessary to make magic happen. I appreciate each of you and the time and effort you give.

Jan — You cast me in my first community theater production and introduced me to an amazing world of the most wonderful people, both onstage and off. We've gone beyond friends and become family, but it all started because you believed in me, and you still do. Can't tell you how much that means!

Dan — It's probably not what you had in mind, but I hope you enjoy it anyway. Thanks for being my token male Ultra Violet and for always giving me the male point of view on how ridiculous my female characters are! Love you!

Elicia — for teal and for telling me when the story isn't good. And for oh-so-much more.

Cheryl - Thanks for answering realty and leasing questions and doing research while you waited for the scuba diver to arrive.

Michael — Thanks for your guidance, your knowledge, and your willingness to listen to my rambling questions and help me keep it real.

Sandra - Your knowledge and expertise keep my murders accurate, and I appreciate your help!

Ari - I came to you for answers, and you delivered those along with some amazing ideas that helped the story go places I never expected. I look forward to collaborating further on the next one.

Kenny - thanks for answering a random DM asking for a check on terminology. Keep instilling that love of reading in your precious girl, and let me know if you get around to reading one of mine for yourself.

About the Author

Violet Howe lives in Florida with her husband and their adorable but spoiled dogs. When she's not writing, Violet is usually watching movies, reading, or planning her next travel adventure. She believes in happily ever afters, love conquering all, humor being essential to life, and pizza being a necessity.

Newsletter
Visit www.violethowe.com to subscribe and be the first to know about Violet's new releases, giveaways, sales, and appearances.
Facebook Group
You can also find out about joining Violet's Facebook Reader Group, the Ultra Violets.

facebook.com/VioletHoweAuthor

x.com/Violet_Howe

instagram.com/VioletHowe

amazon.com/author/violethowe

bookbub.com/authors/violet-howe

tiktok.com/@violethoweauthor

Thank You

Putting together a full-length novel is quite the undertaking. So is reading one with today's hectic schedules. Thank you so much for taking the time to read this book. It makes the effort all worthwhile.

If you liked it, then please tell somebody! Tell your friends. Tell your family. Tell a co-worker. Tell the person next to you in line at the grocery store.

If you really liked it, please consider reviewing it on BookBub, Goodreads, your favorite online vendor, or any other social media site you frequent.

Also by Violet Howe

Tales Behind the Veils

Diary of a Single Wedding Planner

Diary of a Wedding Planner in Love

Diary of an Engaged Wedding Planner

Maggie

The Cedar Creek Collection

Cedar Creek Mysteries:

The Ghost in the Curve

The Glow in the Woods

The Phantom in the Footlights

Cedar Creek Families:

Building Fences

Crossing Paths

Cedar Creek Suspense:

Whiskey Flight

Bounty Flight

Fallen Bloodlines

Vampire Born

(Continued on next page)

Soul Sisters at Cedar Mountain Lodge

Christmas Sisters

Christmas Hope

Christmas Peace

Christmas Secret

Christmas Promise

Sail Away Series

Welcome Aboard

Moonlight on the Lido Deck

Visit www.violethowe.com to subscribe to Violet's monthly newsletter.

.

Made in United States
Troutdale, OR
09/18/2024

22952907R00192